WEB SITE STORY

www.**booksattransworld**.co.uk

ROBERT RANKIN

WEB SITE STORY

Doubleday

LONDON · NEW YORK · TORONTO · SYDNEY · AUCKLAND

TRANSWORLD PUBLISHERS
61–63 Uxbridge Road, London W5 5SA
a division of The Random House Group Ltd

RANDOM HOUSE AUSTRALIA (PTY) LTD
20 Alfred Street, Milsons Point, Sydney
New South Wales 2061, Australia

RANDOM HOUSE NEW ZEALAND LTD
18 Poland Road, Glenfield, Auckland 10, New Zealand

RANDOM HOUSE SOUTH AFRICA (PTY) LTD
Endulini, 5a Jubilee Road, Parktown 2193, South Africa

Published 2001 by Doubleday
a division of Transworld Publishers

A catalogue record for this book is available from the British Library.

ISBN 0385 600585

Typeset in 11.5/15pt Bembo by
Phoenix Typesetting, Ilkley, West Yorkshire

Printed in Great Britain by
Clays Ltd, St Ives plc

1 3 5 7 9 10 8 6 4 2

This, my twenty-second book,
I dedicate, with love, to
THE GOLDEN WOMAN
222

BRENTFORD AND BEYOND

It was joy, joy, happy joy.
Happy, happy joy.

A big fat smiley sun rose up above the rooftops and beamed down its blessings onto the borough known as Brentford.

In the memorial park, the flowers awoke in their well-tended beds, yawned open their petals and grinned at the sky. Sparrows chorused in their treetop roosts, fussed at their feathers and made their plans for the day ahead. A milk float bumbled up the Ealing Road and stopped before the Flying Swan. Where Mr Melchizedec, cap upon his red-faced head, placed two pints of the finest gold-top onto the well-worn step. He tousled the head of a snoozing tomcat, returned to his float upon unfashionable footwear, whistled a tune of his own composing and continued on his way.

It was good to be alive upon such a day as this and Mr Melchizedec knew it.

Others knew it too. Others who chose to stir from their cosy beds, throw wide their curtains and gaze out upon such a day.

Such a day was a Monday, the third of Rune in the year 2022. And it was a very good day indeed.

It was a very good day for at least three reasons. Firstly because the sun was shining, which always made for a very good day.

Secondly because it was the first Monday in the month, which, under the new administration, made it a bank holiday. All first Mondays in the month were now bank holidays. And thirdly, because this was Brentford, where it is always very good to be, no matter the day or the weather.

The folk of Brentford were happy folk. They had always been happy folk. And, if left alone to be it, they would no doubt always *be* happy folk.

Not that being left alone was an easy thing to be. The world that lay beyond the great triangle that enclosed the borough – a triangle formed from the Great West Road, the ancient River Thames and the Grand Union Canal – had a tendency to encroach at times. Fads and fashions tried, mostly without success, to elbow their wicked ways within. The good folk of the borough were ever alert. Ever vigilant. Ever prepared to defend what was theirs. Because what was theirs, was special.

It didn't look much, Brentford. Just rows of terraced Victorian houses, a single outcrop of flat blocks, some shops and pubs and thises and thats and whatnots. It simply seemed suburbia. But it wasn't. It was more and it *was* special.

How special? Why special? Ah.

There was a magic here. A magic that was hard to put a name to, hard to quantify and pin down. But it was there, in the brickwork and the slates, the paving slabs and cobblestones. It slept and it dreamed, but its dreams reached out to the folk who lived there and touched their lives and made them glad.

Beyond the great triangle was another world apart. Here things moved at speeds that troubled the glad Brentonians. Here was technology and change. Ever change. And change can be a thing to fear. For change for the sake of change alone, is rarely change for the good.

So to speak.

And change in that big wide world beyond had been quite plenteous of late. And how this change had come about and what it would mean to the folk of the borough has much to do with the telling of our tale and so should best be touched upon here.

So let us touch upon it.

★

Beyond the boundaries of Brentford there now existed a world peopled by folk with sprained ankles, grazed knees and skinned elbows. Folk who walked upon strange shoes. Folk who tottered and oft-times fell. Folk who avoided high winds and low bridges. Folk who had taken to speaking a language that consisted of just forty words.

But folk who, like their Brentford cousins, were happy.

Why?

Well. It happened in this fashion. And fashion is surely the word.

For it came to pass in the year 2020, that the British voting public declared that enough was enough was enough.

Fed up with more years of government misrule and mismanagement than Black Rod could shake her ornamental stick at, Britain's voters agreed that at the forthcoming general election they would withhold their vote in a people's protest.

And so they did.

The high muck-a-mucks of Westminster, caught with their well-tailored Jekylls★ truly round their veiny ankle regions, were thrown into a state of dire confusion. There was no precedent for this sort of anarchic behaviour. There should have been a law against it. There definitely would be in the future. But as this wasn't the future, this was now, they didn't know what to do. Someone had to run the country. Someone had to be Prime Minister. Someone.

But who?

Now it has long been marvelled at, by those who take the trouble to marvel at such things, that the important and responsible post of Prime Minister does not seem to require any qualification whatsoever. You might have thought that it would at least be necessary to have an A level in political science, a working knowledge of finance and perhaps even one foreign language. But no. All you had to do to become Prime Minister was to be leader of the political party that the public voted into power. Not an easy thing in itself, granted, but hardly, really, the qualification to sit behind the big desk of power in Downing Street and run the country properly. There was no training scheme, no examination papers, you were just expected to sit down

★ Brentford rhyming slang. Jekyll and Hydes: strides.

and get on with it. And so, when you'd well and truly fouled it up, because no-one had told you how to do it, because no-one else knew how to do it, you got voted out of power and some other un-qualified individual got voted in.

So it was hardly surprising, really, that the British voting public finally got sick of all this and decided to give the polling booths a miss. The high muck-a-mucks, trews well down and all in a lather, feverishly checked the ballot boxes. Someone must have voted.

Party members must have voted. Dedicated believers in Democracy must have voted. Someone. Anyone.

Anyone?

Well, of course some had.

Some. A few. A very few. But the numbers were hardly substantial. A few hundred, no more than that. Well, party memberships *had* been falling off, subscription fees were high and benefits negligible. And educated believers in Democracy were hard to come by nowadays. But there had been *some* votes. So the high muck-a-mucks decreed that from these votes the new government must be chosen. It was a heroic decision.

And curiously, unlike many previous heroic decisions taken at Westminster, this one proved to be a good'n.

Reginald Arthur Doveston, independent candidate for Penge South, founder and only member of the World Holistic Footwear Alliance, was duly sworn in as Britain's latest Prime Minister.

Well, he had polled the most votes. Forty in all. Because he was a very nice man, Mr Doveston. People liked him and those who liked him couldn't bring themselves to withhold their votes.

And, at the end of the day, when it came right down to it, in a nutshell and things of that nature generally, he was probably the right man for the job.

Mr Doveston *did* have an A level in political science. He'd done it on a World Wide Web night-school course, along with home economics and macramé.

And, as a designer, manufacturer and supplier of holistic footwear to specialist shoe shops, he *did* have a working knowledge of finance. At least within the field of holistic footwear. And, as a Runie, which is to say a follower of the great twentieth-century Mystic, sword-swallower, and self-styled Most Amazing Man who ever lived, Hugo Rune, he did speak a second language.

Runese. The Universal Tongue.

This was a language invented by Hugo Rune, in one of his many (and sadly abortive) attempts to bring about world peace.

Runese was, as might be said, and kindly said too, a 'basic language'. Consisting, as it did, of just forty words. But, as Rune had explained to those who were prepared to listen, 'No man needs any more than forty words to express an opinion, as long as he keeps it simple.' And, 'If a language consists of only nice words, then those who speak it are unlikely to say anything nasty, are they?'

And, for those who wish to count, these two statements add up to precisely forty words, although none of them is in Runese.

So, by the by and all that stuff, here was Mr Doveston, eminently qualified, some might even say overqualified, to take on the job of Prime Minister, and here were the muck-a-mucks giving him, if grudgingly, the big thumbs up.

So, what of the British voting public, you might ask? What did they make of this? Were they appalled? Did they take to the streets and burn down the shopping malls? Storm the Palace of Westminster? Tar and feather, throw ropes over beams, hang, draw and quarter and place severed heads onto high railings?

Well, no. Actually they didn't.

They might well have done and there was much pub talk regarding the doing thereof. But they didn't. Instead they cheered. They partied in the streets. They put up bunting and roasted pigs on spits. They glorified the name of Mr Doveston.

Why?

Well, because the British voting public were British, that's why. And believe it or believe it not, the British really do have a sense of fair play. They love to see the underdog have his day. And they love it when the little man beats the system. It's hard to explain just why they do, as hard to explain as just what the magic of Brentford really is, but they do, they really do.

It's a British thing. It's a tradition, or an old charter.

Or something.

Mr Doveston found himself sitting behind the desk of power and his feet inside the slippers of power, which few know of, or talk about.

The slippers of power were not to his personal taste, for reasons that will soon be made clear. But he would deal with them, as indeed he would deal with everything. Because Mr Doveston was a man with a plan, as all the world would soon come to know. If not necessarily to understand.

For one of the things that people particularly liked about Mr Doveston was that he was 'open'. He didn't keep any secrets. He told it as he saw it. He said what needed to be said.

Mr Doveston had prepared an electoral manifesto. All candidates do this before elections. It is not a tradition, or an old charter, or something. Mostly it's a load of old toot about all the wonderful things they'll do when they get into power. It's something that the leader of the opposition likes to take out every so often and wave across the despatch box at the Prime Minister and embarrass him with.

Not so Mr Doveston's manifesto. Mr Doveston intended to make good on his. His was a one hundred and eighty point plan, designed to restore the British Nation to its once proud greatness. Starting from the ground up.

It covered pretty much everything that such a manifesto could reasonably be expected to cover. Poverty, urban decay, environmental issues, the NHS, transportation, welfare, schools, world trade, the benefit system, all and sundry and much else besides. And it set out a strategy for putting things right. A strategy that worked from the ground up. It identified a single cause for all the nation's ills.

Its footwear.

Where previous governments had got it all wrong, Mr Doveston explained, was that they had not dealt with issues *from the ground* up. Which is to say, with the nation's feet and what the nation wore upon its feet. Mr Doveston knew all about these things. He had studied these things. These things were what Mr Doveston was all about.

And it is not an untruth to declare that to some extent these were things that Mr Doveston's guru, Hugo Rune, was also all about.

Rune had spent much of his fascinating life★ in search of alterna-

---

★ A life chronicled in many tomes by his biographer and lifelong friend, Sir John Rimmer.

12

tive energy. He pooh-poohed the internal combustion engine, described electricity as 'a passing and dangerous fad' and considered nuclear power 'unlikely to say the very least'. As for solar power, Rune turned his nose up and made pig-like gruntings. 'The planet Earth itself is the source of ultimate power,' Rune once declared to a party of Japanese students who were enjoying an open-topped bus tour around the borough of Brentford. 'It spins around and around and around, generating mighty forces that the man who has the know of it, might tap into and exploit.'

'Is this a magnetic force?' asked a Japanese student called Kevin. 'Likening the globe to a gigantic magneto, whereby a magnetic field is produced by the constant revolutions, taking in that two-thirds of the world's surface is covered by oceans, thereby creating the ideal conditions for magneto hydrodynamics, the saline fluid acting as a . . .'

But Hugo Rune cut him short with a blow to the skull from the stout stick he always carried. 'No,' said Rune. 'Nothing like that at all.'

Apparently it was all down to a substance called Runelium. An element which science had so far failed to identify, but Rune had.

Scientists had catalogued one hundred and five elements, ninety-three of which occurred naturally. Rune, with the aid of his X-ray vision and enhanced intuition, had identified the ninety-fourth. And named it, modestly, Runelium.

Rune described Runelium as 'a sort of sticky with a spearminty smell'. It was there, all around, and if you looked very hard, you might just catch a glimpse of it. Rune declared it to be an untapped source of ultimate power that might be ultimately tapped into through the use of specially constructed Runelium-friendly holistic footwear. The plans for the construction of such footwear were made available to the public during the 1980s, priced at a mere £4.99 including postage and packing, through mail order to a certain post-office box in Brentford. Cheques to be made payable to H. Rune, NEW AGE INDUSTRIES INC.

It was during these same 1980s that Mr Doveston, then a freckle-faced lad of nine summers only, had come across the advert for such footwear in the back of a *Marvel* comic. Next to one for Count Dante's course in the deadly art of Dimac.

13

History was already being made, although Mr Doveston was not to know it then.

So, returning to the present.

Years and years of work had gone into the Runelium-friendly footwear. Years and years of work put in by Mr Doveston, disciple to the Mystic and the Man (as Rune described himself upon his gilt-edged star-shaped calling cards).

And now the time was right. Mr Doveston was behind the desk of power. The nation could be told. The nation would respond. Great days lay ahead. There would be dancing in the street (quite careful dancing, given the height and complexity of some of the footwear), heavy petting in the back seats of Morris Minors and jumping for joy (again with care) the length and breadth of the country.

There would be the singing of songs too. New songs with catchy tunes and easily rememberable lyrics. Lyrics written in the new tongue of Runese. The Universal Tongue of Peace. And a few minor changes besides, such as allocating every first Monday in the month as a bank holiday and renaming the months of the year. Hence the month of Rune.

It would all be joy and joy and happy joy.

Happy happy joy.

And it was. It truly was.

Well, at least it was for a while.

14

1

'Dost thou remember the Tamagotchi?' Big Bob Charker looked up from his breakfasting bowl. The bowl was moulded in durable pink plastic and rested upon a metric yard of pink gingham tablecloth woven from a man-made fibre. This joyful item was spread across a dining table topped with a Teflon veneer. The Teflon veneer was of pink. The curtains were rather pink too.

'The Tamagotchi toy, do you mean?' Big Bob's wife was named Minky, after the popular wash and wipe.

'The same,' said Big Bob. 'Well it sayeth here . . .'

'There in your bowl?' asked his wife. 'Your bowl of pink breakfasting?'

Big Bob sighed his first sigh of the day. 'Not in my bowl, woman,' he declared. 'My *empty* bowl, which thou hast neglected to fill upon this joyous bank holiday Monday. It sayeth here, in my morning newspaper, which I have concealed upon my knee, lest its whiteness clash with the pinky shades of our dining area—'

'Pink is the colour of joy,' said his wife, smoothing down her polynylonsynthafabric housecoat with the plastivinylsuedosilkette gay and quilted lapels. 'Pink is where the heart is.'

'*Home* is where the heart is,' Big Bob corrected his erring spouse.

'Our home *is* pink,' his errless spouse replied.

'Yes, well, quite so, but it sayeth here, in my newspaper, which is not pink—'

15

'*The Financial Times* is pink.'

Big Bob sighed his second sigh. Three were his maximum for any given twenty-four-hour cycle, even a joy-filled bank holiday one. 'Please be silent, woman,' said he. 'Lest I fell thee with the pink-hued reproduction warming pan that your sister J (named after the *other* wash and wipe) gave you for your birthday and which hangs above our pink-hued faux-marble fireplace.'

Big Bob's wife lapsed into a sullen silence.

'There, that's better already.' Big Bob shook cornflakes into his bowl. The cornflakes were pink; his wife had connections at the factory. Big Bob topped up the bowl with strawberry milkshake.

'It sayeth here in my newspaper, that a fellow in Orton Goldhay has one still on the go.'

Big Bob's wife viewed Big Bob through her pink contact lenses, but said nothing. Big Bob almost sighed once more. '*Do* you remember the Tamagotchi?' he asked. Politely.

Minky smiled, exposing teeth the colour you get from mixing red with white. 'I do remember the Tamagotchi,' she said. 'From when I was a girl in the 1990s. It was called "The Pocket Pet", there was a tiny screen and tiny buttons and you had to look after it by feeding it and cleaning up its poo, which you did by pressing the appropriate buttons at the appropriate times, which were mostly times inappropriate to be pressing. And it grew up and changed shape on the tiny screen. But eventually, after about thirty-three days, this figure possibly symbolizing the years in the life of our Lord Jesus Christ, it died and would be reborn again. It was very popular for about six months, then it went the way of the Rubik's cube and the hula hoop and the Pog. Not to mention the Scooby Doo.'

'The Scooby Doo?' her husband asked.

'I told you not to mention that.'

Big Bob withheld his final sigh. 'Well it sayeth here, in my newspaper which is not pink, that a fellow in Orton Goldhay has managed to keep his Tamagotchi alive for twenty-five years and that it has evolved into a sentient life form, possessing rudimentary intelligence, capable of performing simple tricks and communicating with its owner through the medium of mime.'

16

'Does it sing?' asked his wife.

'It says nothing here about singing. Why speakest thou of singing?'

'Well.' His wife teased at her tinted ringlets. They were tinted to a colour harmonious to their present setting. 'If it sang, that would be truly *folderiddledee*.'

'*Folderiddledee*? What twaddle talk is this?'

'Runese,' said Minky. 'I am taking a night-school course on the World Wide Web.'

'What?' went her husband. 'What? What? *What*?'

'*Folderiddledee* means "the ecstatic realization that even little things can be as wonderful as big things and that everything is wonderful really, so why don't we all just smile and have a nice time instead of hitting each other with blunt instruments, or even worse with pointy ones?"'

Big Bob spoke through gritted teeth. 'Woman,' he said. 'Speak unto me. Tell me where do we live?'

'We live at number twenty-two Moby Dick Terrace, Brentford, where all is *folderiddledee*,' his wife answered, correctly.

'Brentford,' said Big Bob. 'Brentford being the operative word. When the out-boroughs★ stood shoulder to shoulder, heel to toe, nose to tail, three sheets to the wind and a law unto themselves and withheld their votes at the last general election, what did we do?'

'We withheld ours,' said Minky, straightening non-existent creases in her plastivinylsuedosilkette gay and quilted lapels.

'We did indeed. But not for the same reasons. Brentonians have always withheld their vote. Because the borough of Brentford holds a self-governing charter dating back to the fourteenth century, when Hector the Hairless, Baron of Brentford, performed certain deeds for the Monarch and was granted such from then till kingdom come.'

'I knew that,' said Minky. 'Everyone knows that.'

'And as such,' her husband continued, 'we of Brentford have no truck with the whims and fancies of the world beyond. Dost thou see me sporting foolish footwear? Do I jabber in this Universal Tongue? Don't answer! I do *not*!'

★ A derogatory term used by Brentonians to describe all and sundry who live beyond the boundaries of Brentford.

'You've spilt your cornflakes down your tie,' his wife observed. 'They'll soak right in.'

'Woman,' said Big Bob. 'I will have no damned Runese spoken within the pinkly papered walls of this fair house of ours. If thou must persist in such folly, kindly restrict thy usage of this linguistic tomfoolery to places more befitting. To wit—'

'To woo,' his wife interjected. 'You should attend to your tie. The strawberry milkshake will stain the fabric.'

'And there you have it also,' said her husband in a voice of raised tone. 'My tie, thou will observe, *can* be stained. It is made of cotton. A natural fabric. Dost thou remember cotton?'

'I remember the Alamo,' said his wife. 'But I was not there.'

'My point is . . .' said her husband. But by now he had quite forgotten just what his point might have been. It had been something to do with the sentient Tamagotchi of Orton Goldhay. It had also been to do with the speaking of Runese. But it had also been to do with natural fabrics and their present scarcity. *And* being in Brentford. *And* possibly much more besides. But conversation with his wife oft-times confused Big Bob and oft-times left him in some doubt regarding what the point he hoped to make might be.

'You'll be late,' said Minky Charker, wife of Bob to whom the appellation 'Big' was generally applied.

Big Bob studied his wristwatch. It had hands upon its face, which moved by the power of a clockwork motor. 'I *will* be,' said he. 'And so I must gird up my loins and sally forth. Stain upon my tie or not. And the Devil take the hindmost.'

He arose from his rose-tinted breakfasting chair, dabbed at his mouth with a colour-matched serviette, ignored his pale paper, which had fallen from his knees, puffed out his chest, which *was* big as even big chests go, and prepared to take his leave.

'Have I sandwiches?' he enquired, by way of conversation.

His wife smiled sweetly. 'I give up,' said she. 'Have you?'

'That would be a no then, would it not?'

His wife produced a round of sandwiches sealed in a styrocling-film sheath from the pocket of her polynylonsynthafabric housecoat with the plastivinylsuedosilkette gay and quilted lapels. The sandwiches were of white bread. Their content however was spam.

'Have a nice day,' she said. 'In fact have a folderiddledee day.'

The day was jolly and joyful and the newly risen sun pampered Big Bob's baldy head as he sallied forth on his way.

His way led him down to the bottom of Moby Dick Terrace, where the flowers (many pink) in their well-tended beds prettified the memorial park and the sparrows, their chorusings over and their minds made up regarding their plans for the day, were putting those plans into practice.

One nearly did a doo-doo on Big Bob's baldy head, but on such a day as very good as this one was, it didn't.

Big Bob took to a bit of whistling. Nothing fancy. Just basic stuff. Basic *old* stuff. None of this newfangled Runey-Toons nonsense. Big Bob favoured the classics. A hint of Sonic Energy Authority here. A touch of the Lost T-shirts of Atlantis there. And a smidgen of the Hollow Chocolate Bunnies of Death when no-one was likely to hear him. Today he whistled 'Why is there never a policeman around when you need one, but always three buses turning up at the same time when you've given up waiting and just got into a taxi'. A tune Mr Melchizedec the milkman had taught him. And in fact had whistled earlier this day, after placing two pints of the finest gold-top onto the well-worn step of the Flying Swan.

Whilst acting in the capacity of milkman in residence to the borough of Brentford, Mr Melchizedec always wore his official cap. Big Bob also wore a cap, but this was not a milkman's jobbie. Big Bob's cap was the cap of a tour guide. An official tour guide. *The* official tour guide. The official tour guide of the Brentford guided-tour guide.

Big Bob did not wear his cap whilst not in *his* official capacity and as his official capacity did not begin until he clocked in at the depot, he was not wearing it now.

Hence the naked baldy head that didn't get the sparrow's doo-doo on it.

Still whistling, and still bare and baldy-headed, Big Bob perambulated his ample frame, with its generous chest and broad, yet hitherto unmentioned shoulders, onwards towards the depot.

The flowers continued with their prettifying and the sparrows with their actionable plans.

The depot was more of a shed than a depot. In fact it was a shed. A large enough shed to house a bus, but a shed more so than more less. It was an aged shed and had been an engine shed, in the days when trains still ran at all, which were days that were now far gone.

Trains had been a very good idea at the time. A time that lasted for more than one hundred years. But at some period back in the late twentieth century, some unqualified Prime Minister or other had thought it would be a very good idea to privatize the system. He'd sold off the railways to various business concerns, run, curiously enough, by fellows who, although very good at business, were totally unqualified to run a railway system.

So now there weren't any trains any more and those who had run them and run them down, ran other things instead and those who missed them, missed them, and missed them very much.

Big Bob didn't miss them at all. He'd never actually travelled on a train, having had nowhere he ever needed to go upon one. Buses were Big Bob's thing. Big buses with open-topped upstairs regions. Old-fashioned buses, painted in cream, with chromium-plated radiator grilles and a special place for the conductor to stand. Buses that went in a circular route and ended up where they began. But there weren't many of those around any more either. Big Bob knew of only the one. The one in the depot in Brentford. The one that he took on guided tours. Tours with a circular route.

Big Bob crossed over the bridge that had once crossed over the railway and made his way down the narrow flight of stairs that led to the yard and the depot.

The yard, ex-railways and now the property of Brentford Magical History Tours Ltd, looked just the way such a yard should look. Decoratively decked out in rusted ironwork of the corrugated persuasion, flanked around by tall fences topped with razor wire. A sign on the gate which read BEWARE THE SAVAGE DOGS THAT ROAM THESE PREMISES BY NIGHT, and a great many of those corroding oil drums that always look as if they must contain something very very dangerous indeed.

Big Bob ceased his whistling and smiled the yard a once-over. He really loved it here. This was his kind of place. Old and mellow and one foot in the past. And one foot was all you ever really needed, as long as you knew how to balance upon it and weren't going anywhere else.

Big Bob pushed open the gate with the sign that warned of the nocturnal growlers and entered the depot's yard. The double doors of the shed stood open, the double-decker stood within.

Beneath the double-decker on a long tray affair that moved upon castors, somebody tinkered with tools at the brakes of the aged bus. No saboteur, this somebody, but Periwig Tombs, the mechanic and driver.

'Morning Bob the Big,' called he, espying the large approaching footwear of the large approaching tour guide.

'Morning Peri my lad,' called Big Bob. 'Applying those touches that finish?'

From beneath the bus came that head-clunking sound that mechanics' heads always make as they clunk upon the undersides of vehicles, when the owner of the head raises it without thinking, to answer some question or other. Why mechanics do this few men know, and those who do don't care.

'Ouch,' said Periwig. 'Why do I always do that?'

'I don't know,' said Big Bob. 'But I do believe that I care.'

Periwig Tombs slid out from beneath the bus, upon the long tray affair with the castors. He was rubbing his head as he slid. It was a head of generous proportion. A lofty dome of a head. Sparsely sown with sandy hair and flanked with large protruding ears. Given the scale of such a head, one might have expected a goodly helping of facial featurings. But no, the nose was a stubby button, the eyes were small and squinty and the little kissy mouth seemed always in a pout. The neck that supported this head was of that order which is designated 'scrawny' and the body beneath was slim and lank and undersized and weedy. At school, fellow students who knew of the *Eagle* comic had christened him the Mekon.

Periwig Tombs eased himself into the vertical plane. Wiped his slender hands upon an oily rag, which increased their oiliness by precisely tenfold, and grinned kissily at Big Bob the tour guide.

21

'You have strawberry-milkshake stains on your tie,' he observed.

'And I wear them with pride,' said the big one. 'Wouldst thou care for a fresh spam sandwich?'

'No, but I'd care for an aspirin.'

The depot had a roster board with Big Bob's name upon it. Big Bob clocked in and consulted this board and then he tut-tut-tutted.

'Why do you triply tut?' asked Periwig Tombs, as he sought the tin of Swarfega.

'I tut for this roster,' said Big Bob, taking down his official cap from its official peg and placing it upon his head, which now made it official. 'I tut for the fact that upon this joy-filled bank holiday there is to be but one official tour of the borough and that this one tour has but six tourists booked in for it. Woe unto the house of Charker, for verily it will come to pass that small tour numbers mean small tips and small tips mean small beer.'

'Well, it's a dead'n, ain't it?' said Periwig Tombs, who having located the Swarfega tin was now at a loss as to how it would be opened. His puny hands being oh so oily and all.

'A dead'n?' quoth Big Bob. 'What meanest thou by this?'

'People don't want bus tours any more.' Periwig worried at the tin's lid with his teeth. 'Bus tours are old-fashioned. People can now sit in the comfort of their own homes, at their Mute Corp PCs, and take virtual trips around the globe on the World Wide Web. Ouch, there goes a filling.'

'I have read of this virtual tripping,' said Big Bob. 'But surely it can never replace the real thing.'

'Never replace the real thing?' Periwig gave Big Bob a long old-fashioned look of a type that was long out of fashion. 'You might choose to ignore progress, Big Bob, what with your Old-Testament-prophet-speak and everything, but the world has shifted on a bit since the start of the twenty-first century. People don't do anything much at all any more. It's all done for them. Press a button, call it up. Instant gratification.'

Big Bob shrugged his broad and now aforementioned shoulders. 'Firstly,' said he. 'I do not engage in Old-Testament-prophet-speak. I choose to speak in this manner, because I consider it to be the mark of my individuality. You and others too, including my wife, might consider this a studied eccentricity, the hallmark of the poseur. I respect your right to do this, regretting only that this right is abused when used in my presence. If you follow my meaning. Secondly, I do understand all about this virtual tripping business. We went to school together, didn't we? I studied at my Mute Corp teaching terminal, just the same as you. I am well aware that change occurs all around me, but I am not obliged to either approve or condone it. I would like things to stay as they are. Canst thou follow me on this?'

'I can,' said Periwig. 'And I mean no offence. You are a good man, Big Bob. But good men are many times ground under in this changing world around us. And if we don't do something to bring in some more tourists to the borough, we will both soon be out of a job. Yeah, verily, thus and so and things of that nature, generally.'

Big Bob took the oily tin from the hands of Periwig and popped off its lid. 'I am all too well aware of that too, my friend,' he said, 'and have been giving the matter some thoughts of my own. Would you care that I tell you about them?'

Periwig dug his fingers into the gorgeous green Swarfega. 'You now have some oil on your tie,' said he. 'But yes, I would be glad to hear of your thoughts.'

And so Big Bob let him hear them.

'My thoughts run this-a-ways,' said Big Bob, when the two of them had seated themselves upon ancient bus-seat deckchairs in the sun-light in the entrance of the shed. 'Magical History Tours are all well and good. They're all well and very good too, in my opinion. But, as the falling numbers indicate, they may well have had their day. People crave novelty. They crave excitement . . .'

'I could drive the bus somewhat faster,' said Periwig. 'I'll bet I could get it up on two wheels at the corner by the Half Acre.'

Big Bob shook his baldy head, upon which rested his official cap. 'That would change the running time of the tour. I am not proposing change. Anything, in fact, other than change. I am suggesting a theme park.'

'*A theme park?*' Periwig stiffened in his deckchair. 'Here in

23

Brentford? Have you taken leave of your senses? How much more change could you possibly have, than turning part of Brentford into a theme park?'

'Not part,' said Big Bob. 'All.'

'*All?* You are clearly bereft. Sit still while I phone for an ambulance.'

'I am proposing no changes at all,' said Big Bob, whose sober countenance suggested that he spoke the words of truth. 'When was the last time something new was built in Brentford? Don't answer, I will tell you, for I looked it up. Seventy-five years ago, the Electric Alhambra Cinema on the High Street.'

'I didn't know that Brentford had a cinema.'

'It doesn't, it never caught on.'

'Hang about,' said Periwig. 'What about the flat blocks?'

'Ah,' said Big Bob.

'And the Arts Centre?'

'Ah,' said Big Bob once again.

'I find these "ahs" of yours perturbing,' said Periwig Tombs. 'You have not done quite as much research as you should have on these matters.'

Big Bob said, 'Hm,' he was down a bit there, but far from out. 'All right,' said he, 'I agree. I grew up with the flat blocks and the Arts Centre. But nothing new has been built here in the last thirty years. Listen Periwig, I love this town and you love this town. We've lived here all our lives so far. Do you remember the times we had together at school? Joy, joy happy joyful times. Apart from the occasional sad time.' Big Bob sighed his final sigh of the day.

Whenever he thought of his schooldays and the joy joy happy joy times that he'd had, he thought of Ann Green. She used to be in his class at the junior school. She hadn't been the first love of his life, or anything. She had just been another little girl. But, at the age of ten she had died, in an accident in the playground of the memorial park. Big Bob, little Bob then, had seen it happen. She had been pushing a friend on one of those long metal swingboats, of the type that happily you don't see in playgrounds any more. Someone had called out to her and she had turned her head. The swingboat swung back and hit her in the throat. And suddenly, the little girl, so full of life a moment before, was dead.

24

'I don't wish to hurry you along,' said Periwig. 'But we must take the bus out in ten minutes for its one and only tour of the day. If you do have anything to say, then I suggest you say it now.'

'Only this.' Big Bob gathered his thoughts and shrugged away their sadness. 'The world beyond the boundaries of Brentford changes daily. Here the changes are imperceptible. Yea then, here fore to and here to fore, we are an historical anomaly. We are, without changing a single thing, a working historical theme park.'

'Suburbia World,' cried Periwig. 'That should pull them in by the thousands.'

'Dost thou really think so?'

'No, I dost not. As ideas go, Big Bob, it's no idea at all. I can see that it might have a certain charm. At least for you, anyway. That nothing would have to be changed or added to the borough. That it would just *be* a theme park. And if it was cleverly advertised along those lines in the right way, to the right people, that the potential *should* be there. But it wouldn't work, people really do need thrills and spills nowadays. Even if they only get them through their Mute Corp terminals in their own front rooms. It was a brave attempt, but it would never work.'

'You really think not?'

'Sorry,' said Periwig.

Big Bob set free a fourth sigh of the day. 'Well if you say that it wouldn't, then I suppose it wouldn't,' he said, lifting his mighty frame from the bus-seat deckchair and stretching limbs in the sunlight. 'We've been friends since we were children. I trust you, Periwig. Thou art a good man too. But it seems a pity though, I really thought it was a good idea.'

Periwig shrugged and struggled to his feet. Looking up at Big Bob, he said, 'No harm done in mentioning it. But I wouldn't go mentioning it to anyone else. You wouldn't want them laughing at you behind your back, now would you?'

'No, I wouldn't. Thankest thou, my friend.'

'No worries,' said Periwig Tombs. 'No worries at all.'

Big Bob donned his official tour-guide jacket.

Periwig donned his official driver's jacket.

Big Bob climbed onto the lower deck of the bus and stood in the special place for the conductor to stand.

Periwig climbed into the cab and sat in the driving seat.

Big Bob made a wistful face and thought away his theme-park plans.

Periwig smiled a broad smile with his little kissy mouth. His brain raced forward, scooping up potential here and potential there. And he could see it all, Suburbia World Plc with Periwig Tombs (OBE of course) sitting in the chairman's seat of power. This was an idea just waiting to be sold. An idea with untold potential. An idea so simple, yet so grandiose, that he wondered how he hadn't ever thought of it himself. But it was now an idea firmly planted in his head and he, Periwig Tombs, would see it to fruition. There were millions to be made if this was played out rightly. And he, Periwig Tombs, would have a large share of those millions. After all, it was *his* idea. *He* had thought it up.

Big Bob Charker turned his back, and Periwig Tombs laughed silently behind it.

2

The wheels on the bus went round and round.
Round and round and round.

The guide on the bus was whistling sadly. The driver of the bus was smiling. The people at the bus stop saw the bus. The people at the bus stop waved.

Periwig Tombs did changing down of gears, bringing professionally to a halt, applying of the handbrake, switching off the engine and climbing down from the cab.

Big Bob Charker did saluting, then he stepped down from that special area where the conductor stands.

Six jolly tourists stood at the bus stop. Well, at least five looked jolly. Four of these were Japanese students, you could tell by the cut of their clothes. The fifth was a lady in a straw hat and she looked jolly too. The sixth was a young man, a pasty-faced youth and he looked far from jolly.

He was dour. Dour and downcast, glum and gloomy and grim. He glowered at his boots and scuffed them on the pavement. At intervals, of increasing frequency, the lady in the straw hat elbowed him in the ribs and told him to perk up.

Big Bob smiled upon all and sundry. 'Greetings all and sundry,' smiled he.

The Japanese students grinned and nodded. One said, 'Hello, goodbye.'

27

The lady in the straw hat smiled. The dour youth glowered grimly.

'My name is Big Bob Charker,' said Big Bob Charker. 'And I shall be thy tour guide for today.'

The dour youth mumbled grimly. The lady in the straw hat smote him on the head.

'I'm sorry,' said Big Bob, addressing the lady, 'but is there something wrong?'

'It's him,' said the lady, elbowing the youth once more. 'My son, Malkuth. He didn't want to come, but I made him. It's a lovely day, I told him, and I've already booked the tickets and if you think you're going to spend today sitting over your Mute Corp PC like you do every other day, forget it, you're coming on the tour whether you like it or not. That's what I told him and that's the way it's going to be.'

'Quite so,' said Big Bob. 'Well, good day unto you, Malkuth.'

'Poo!' said the youth in a grumbly tone, lowering his head a tad lower.

'You'll enjoy it, I promise thou,' said Big Bob.

The youth looked up and offered him a bitter glance. 'You've got pink stuff on your tie,' he observed.

The lady in the straw hat smote her son once more. 'Don't be so rude to the gentleman,' she told him.

'It's quite all right,' said Big Bob. 'It was unprofessional of me to come on duty with a stained tie. I apologize.'

The lady in the straw hat smiled at Big Bob, one of the Japanese students said, 'Okey dokey.'

'Get on with it,' whispered Periwig. 'Introduce me.'

'Ah yes,' Big Bob continued. 'This is our driver, Mr Periwig Tombs.'

'Morning each,' said Periwig. 'Lovely day for it.'

The youth looked up at Periwig. 'You have a very large head,' said he. 'Was that cap made specially?'

Periwig smiled the smile of a professional. The professional who relies on his tips to make up the balance of his wages.

'My wife,' said Periwig Tombs, 'put a gusset in the back. She's very good with her hands. And a remarkably beautiful woman. Do you have a girlfriend?'

The lady in the straw hat laughed rather loudly. The youth grew gloomier still.

'Righty right,' said Big Bob. 'Well, it's all aboard then. I suggest that you go upstairs onto the open deck to enjoy the views more fully. Mind how you go up the stairs.' He stuck out his hand to welcome all aboard and the lady in the straw hat shook it. Periwig Tombs stuck out his hand and the lady shook that too. Then Big Bob and Periwig shook the hands of the Japanese students and then finally the hand of the dour-faced youth. The youth seemed disinclined towards hand-shaking, but Big Bob took his hand and gave it a friendly squeeze. The squeeze that Periwig Tombs applied was somewhat less than friendly. But as Periwig had puny hands the effect was much the same.

The hand of the dour youth was a cold and clammy, limp, dead thing and both Periwig Tombs and Big Bob Charker found them-selves a-wiping their own right hands onto their trousers after the shaking was done.

When all and sundry were safely up the stairs and seated, Periwig returned to the cab and Big Bob rang the bell.

The wheels on the bus went round and round and the tour of Brentford began.

As the Brentford tour bus was a proper tour bus, it boasted a proper public address system. Proper speakers mounted on the decks, above and below and connected to a proper microphone, which hung in the proper area reserved for the conductor. Big Bob took up the proper microphone and did a right and proper one-two, one-two into it, before beginning his proper talk which accompanied the tour proper.

So to speak.

'One-two,' went Big Bob, then just 'One,' due to a momentary distraction. This momentary distraction came in the shapely shape of an attractive young woman who was walking down the High Street just as the bus was moving up it.

The bus continued on its way and she continued on hers. Big Bob managed the second 'Two,' and the tour well and truly began.

The attractive young woman stopped and turned and watched the bus shrink into the sunny distance. Then she glanced into the window of Mr Beefheart the butcher's shop and took stock of her reflection.

29

She looked all in all rather wonderful, a joyous sight to behold.

Her hair was of gold and cut in the pageboy style, with a fringe that lightly brushed the long dark lashes of her denim-blue eyes. Beneath her noble nose was a mouth of the order that most men yearn to kiss, being a perfect Cupid's bow, turned up in a comely smile.

The attractive young woman wore a short and golden figure-hugger of a dress, which hugged the kind of figure that you rarely see any more. Monroesque, it was. An hourglass figure. Her bare legs were just long enough and tanned enough to be noticed and rarely carried her anywhere without being so. Upon her feet were golden sandals, laced about the ankles.

All in all she was something to see and upon a day such as this and in a setting so fine as the High Street of Brentford, it was hardly surprising that this golden woman had turned the head of Big Bob Charker so. Radiance on radiance beneath the smiley sun.

Now one might have been forgiven for thinking that here was one of those models. One of those models who model their skin, rather than modelling clothes. But within the golden head of this fair maiden lurked a fearsome intellect, which had crushed the egos of many a man who had harboured thoughts such as this.

The golden woman's name was Kelly Anna Sirjan and she was twenty-two years of age. She held three degrees and was studying for the fourth. She spoke four languages, including Runese. She was an expert in most fields of computer technology, a 12th Dan Master in the deadly art of Dimac and the Southern England Owari champion, whatever on earth that was.

She was a force to be reckoned with.

And she was here in Brentford on business.

Kelly ran the manicured fingers of her slender right hand through her golden locks, teased out strands of hair and twisted the ends back and forwards, back and forwards.

It was a nervous habit that she was trying to break.

But she was here on business and she was late, and being late didn't suit her at all. And it didn't seem to be her fault. The directions she'd been given were wrong.

Kelly dug into her shoulder bag and brought out several sheets of paper. She examined these and then looked up and down the High

Street. She checked the numbers on the shops and then peered up towards the offices above them. Then she shook her golden head and made a puzzled face.

The shaking of her head was observed by a shadowy figure who peered from a high window in the building opposite.

The shadowy figure lay all crouched down in hiding. He was a male shadowy figure and his name was Hildemar Shields. He was the editor of the *Brentford Mercury* and he was hiding from Kelly Anna Sirjan.

Hildemar Shields was sniggering. The sounds weren't pretty at all.

Behind Mr Shields stood a young man called Derek. Derek wasn't sniggering. 'This is all very childish,' said Derek. 'All very childish indeed.'

Mr Shields turned his head. 'No it's not,' he snarled fiercely. 'It's tactics.'

'She'll find the office. She's not stupid. Anything but, in fact.'

'I've taken down the sign and changed the number on the door. She won't find us, she's only a woman. She'll get all confused and give up.'

'You don't know much about women, do you? And as to being only a woman, she's better qualified to do your job than you are.'

Mr Shields turned his head and made an extremely fierce face. It was a fierce face anyway, very red. Bucolic, the word for it was. It had fierce black eyebrows, that bristled out like the spears of two advancing miniature medieval regiments. The eyes beneath were all red-rimmed and the pupils were purple for certain.

There was a great deal of fierce face to be had. Some covered by fierce black sideburns. A goodly portion taken up with a fierce and fiery nose. This was a seriously angry face and its owner was seriously angry.

'Lock the damn door,' said Mr Shields. 'Just in case she does find the entrance.'

Derek shook his head and tut-tut-tutted. 'This is quite absurd,' he said. 'Head office has only sent her here for three weeks. Surely you can weather that out.'

'No, no, no.' Mr Shields dragged himself away from the window, rose to his full and most impressive height and shook his fierce and bristly head in a fierce and bristly fashion. 'She'll change things, Derek.

She'll report back to head office that we're not doing things the way that things should be done. She'll make us use that stuff.'

Mr Shields made fierce gestures towards several large boxes that stood in the corner of the office. These boxes bore the distinctive logo of the Mute Corp computer company. These boxes had a rather dog-eared quality to them; they had all sorts of coffee-cup rings and cigarette burns on them. They were clearly boxes that had stood unopened in the editor's office for a very very long time.

'I think she'll probably make us change that stuff,' said Derek. 'It's five years out of date now and computer technology speeds right along.'

'I should have thrown it all out,' declared Mr Shields. 'Car-booted the lot of it! Perhaps I could drop one on her if she comes in this direction. We could say it was an accident. You could back me up.'

'Not me,' said Derek and crossing to the window he peered out. 'She's a very attractive young woman,' he said.

'They're the worst kind,' said Mr Shields, sinking into his chair. 'Attractive women with brains. Whatever was God thinking of when he came up with that idea? Women should be obscene and not heard, that's my view on the matter.'

'So you constantly let it be known.'

'Is she still there?' asked Mr Shields.

'No, she's moving off.'

'Thank the Lord Most High for that. So what's on the calendar for today?'

'Not much,' Derek shrugged. 'It's another bank holiday, as well you know. Another bank holiday that I could have had off.'

'The news never sleeps,' said Mr Shields. 'A story could break any moment.'

'A story hasn't broken here for nearly a quarter of a century. Not since Brentford got to officially celebrate the millennium two years before the rest of the world. And that was before I was born.'

'Today might be the day then. Something really exciting might happen.'

'Yeah, right,' said Derek.

'Ah but it might,' said Mr Shields. 'Something unexpected. Something really big.'

32

Knock, knock, knock came a knocking at the door and then it swung right open.

Framed in the portal stood Kelly Anna Sirjan. 'Good day Mr Shields,' she said.

And it was a good day. Such a very good day. Such a very good and joyous and sunny kind of day. Good day.

Five tourists on the top deck smiled and chitchatted, the tour guide went through his spiel.

'If thou lookest to the right,' came the voice of Big Bob through the proper public address system. 'Thou wilt see the Waterman's Arts Centre and beyond that in the middle of the River Thames, Griffin Island. Haunt, so legend has it, of the Brentford Griffin. Many claim to have seen the beast. Mostly after the pubs close, of course.'

Periwig Tombs changed down a gear, but his brain was now in overdrive. *Your week in Suburbia World Plc would not be complete without a boat trip to Brentford's own Fantasy Island*, went the thoughts of Periwig Tombs, translating themselves into the World Wide Web page that he was planning to set up to advertise his money-spinning venture. *See the creature of myth* (you could knock those up out of polisyntha-fibreglass) *that once inhabited this enchanted realm in the dream world days of the magic distant past*. (Brentford's take on *Jurassic Park*. That was done and dusted!)

Oho! went the thoughts of Periwig Tombs. And then *Aha!* And *OH YES!* You really could add some wonderful attractions to this historical theme park. It didn't have to be all conservation and leaving things as they were. That had been the way Big Bob saw it. But he, Periwig Tombs OBE, could do it better than that. Much better. There was all that holographic technology about today. The stuff they used in all those Disney Worlds that dotted the continents. You *could* employ that. It might be getting away from the original spirit of the thing, but used in the right way . . .

The wheels on the bus went round and round and Periwig Tombs smiled on.

Kelly Anna Sirjan wasn't smiling, although with the natural curve of her mouth it might have appeared that she was.

33

'Some joker,' she said, 'has removed the sign from your door and changed the number.'

Mr Shields blew out his cheeks. 'I wonder who might have done that,' he said. 'So how can I help you, young woman?'

'I am Kelly Anna Sirjan and I have been sent by head office. You were expecting me, I believe.'

'Somewhat earlier, but yes. Would you care for a cup of tea?'

'I would.'

'Splendid. Well Derek here will show you where the tea things are and you can make us all one.'

Kelly Anna shook her head. 'I don't make tea,' she said.

'Well, never mind. We have coffee.'

'Nor coffee.' Kelly Anna shook her head. It was a definite bit of head-shaking. It signified that she definitely didn't make either tea or coffee. Definitely, absolutely, not.

'Ah,' said the editor. 'Ah, well indeed.'

Kelly Anna gave the office a thorough looking-over. It was not a thing of great beauty to behold and she beheld it with distaste.

Beside the window stood the editor's desk, with the editor behind it. The editor and the editor's desk both looked most untidy. The editor was shabbily dressed in the ruins of a once tweed suit. The desk was a mayhem of papers and books and paper cups and ashtrays and old-fashioned telephones, mostly off the hook. There were pictures on the walls, group shots, framed front pages, yellow with age. And these hung at angles just untrue enough to annoy the fastidious. The carpet was grey and bare of thread. Filing cabinets were open and most looked empty within.

'Has there been a robbery?' asked Kelly Anna Sirjan.

'Sorry? What?' The editor glanced all around.

'A robbery,' said Kelly. 'Perhaps someone broke in to steal those unpacked boxes of Mute Corp computer parts. Perhaps they were disturbed during the process and only managed to ransack the office.'

'You are a very rude young woman,' said the editor. 'Dismiss all thoughts of having sex with me.'

The only tidy thing resident to the office made a ghastly swallowing sound and said, 'Please forgive Mr Shields. He's been under a lot of pressure recently. My name is Derek and I am the *Mercury*'s features editor. Can *I* get you a cup of tea?'

Kelly Anna looked at Derek and nodded her golden head. Derek wore a neat grey suit with a pressed white collarless shirt. He was young and tall and slim and handsome with short black hair and emerald eyes. And those eyes looked her full in the face and never once strayed to her breasts.

'Thank you Derek,' said Kelly Anna Sirjan. 'Lady Grey, without sugar.'

'Lady Grey, right.' Derek chewed his bottom lip. 'I might have to send out for that.'

'Well, whatever you have will be fine.'

'Fine. Then if you'll follow me, I'll show you around the building on the way.'

Derek led Kelly Anna from the office and closed the door behind him. The editor sat and fumed at his desk and made a very fierce face.

The face of Periwig Tombs was smiling sweetly. The tour bus was passing the allotments now and Big Bob Charker was singing the praises of Brentford's horticulturalists.

'Twenty-three different varieties of tomato,' Big Bob said into the microphone. 'Twenty-three different varieties of sprout. And the mighty oak trees at the riverside end are the natural habitat of the lesser spotted grebe and the piebald finch chuck-chuck fiddledum bird.'

'Eh?' went Periwig as he swung the wheel. But his brain was roaring forward. *Take a safari through the wildlife sanctuary and rare bird reserve of Allotment World. Enjoy a sprout and grebe burger at Periwigs, the exclusive allotment eatery.*

'Big bare-bottomed bumbly bees,' said the voice of Big Bob Charker. 'Busy busy bumble bees and Walter the Wasp as well.'

'Waspish,' said Kelly Anna Sirjan. 'Waspish, ill-mannered and clearly a misogynist.'

She sat opposite Derek at a window table in the Plume Café. The Plume Café sat at the top end of the High Street. The Plume Café boasted twenty-two different varieties of tea. None of which contained any sprout.

'I thought you'd like it better here than in the staff canteen,' said Derek.

'You mean that cupboard.'

'The staff canteen cupboard, yes. How's the tea?'

Kelly Anna Sirjan sipped her Lady Grey. 'Remarkably good, actually. The filtered water makes all the difference.'

'There's not much you can't get in Brentford if you know where to look.'

'I was talking about your boss, Mr Shields,' said Kelly Anna Sirjan.

'Yes, I know you were.' Derek sipped at his Typhoo. 'He's not a bad man. He's rather fierce and I agree he's something of a misogynist. But I'm afraid that he fears what you might do to the paper.'

'He should fear for his job,' said Kelly. 'Speaking to a complete stranger in the way that he did.'

'He has the job for life. It's written into his contract.'

'Only in Brentford,' said Kelly.

'Yes, you're right about that.'

'But he has nothing to fear from me anyway. I'm not here to change anything. I'm just here to study.'

'You want to learn how the paper's run? There's really not much to it.'

Kelly Anna plucked at her hair and turned smooth strands between her fingers. Backwards, forwards, backwards. 'It's not the paper,' she said. 'It's the town itself. I'm writing a thesis on it for my doctorate. I'm doing an MA in socio-economics. I approached the newspaper publisher at their head office. Told them about the project I had in mind. They put up the finance and arranged for me to come and work at the *Brentford Mercury* for three weeks. Mostly I just want to study the archives, learn about the history of the borough. I'm fascinated by the way that it appears to co-exist with the other boroughs surrounding it, yet remains curiously isolated and insular. I'm seeking to build up a general framework on which to hang my thesis.'

'Oh,' said Derek. 'Then Mr Shields has got it all wrong. He thought that you were some kind of troubleshooter from head office sent to shake up the place.'

36

'That's what head office would like me to do, but I don't want to cause any trouble. You can tell Mr Shields that I won't cause him any trouble.'

Derek smiled, exposing a set of perfect pearly-white teeth. 'Would you mind terribly if I didn't?' he said. 'I've worked at the *Mercury* for nearly two years now and he's shouted at me on every single day of them. It's been a real pleasure to watch him squirm, I'd like to enjoy it for just a little longer.'

Kelly raised an eyebrow. 'You're a naughty boy,' she said.

'Naughty bus,' said Periwig Tombs, struggling with the handbrake. 'I oiled you this morning, don't you get stuck on me now.'

The tour bus was parked at the western tip of the baseline of the Great Brentford Triangle.

'It is popularly believed,' came the voice of Big Bob through the speaker system, 'that the city of Manchester has more canals in it than does Venice. This is not altogether true, although we do have the world's most famous football team. Man U.'

'Eh?' went Periwig Tombs and he turned his head and slid back the little glass panel behind the driver's seat. 'Oi, Bob,' he called, along the deserted lower deck of the bus. 'Have you gone stone bonkers or something? What's all this toot about Man U?'

Big Bob's big head popped out from that special place where the bus conductors stand. 'Eee-up, bonny lad,' said he. And 'Eee-up, bonny lad' came out of the speakers.

'Eee-up, bonny lad?' shouted Periwig Tombs. 'That's not Manchester, that's Geordie, isn't it? Have you been drinking, or what?'

'Ding, ding,' went Big Bob. 'Hold very tight please.'

'You *have* been drinking!' shouted Periwig. 'You've been at the giggly pops.'

'Pardon I?' said Big Bob Charker. 'Giggly pops? What are those?'

'Piggly pops. Bimbo bubbly pops, damn me, I've forgotten how to speak.'

'Who are you?' asked Big Bob, suddenly. 'What are you doing in my front room?'

'He's lost it!' Periwig Tombs slammed shut the glass shutter and got

37

into a bit of a sweat. 'He's gone mad. He's lost his lollipops, fan belts, no not those. What's happening? I'm getting out of here.'

Periwig did revvings of the engine and then stared out of the windscreen. 'Where am I?' he said. 'I don't recognize this place. I'm lost. The bus is lost.'

There came a dreadful rattling and banging at the shut glass shutter. Periwig ducked his head.

'Where are we?' shouted Big Bob Charker. He didn't have the mic any more. 'Get us back to Bren . . .' he paused. 'To Brentham, no to Brentside, no to Brenda, no to help! I'm lost! We're all lost. The bus is lost, help, help, help!'

Periwig Tombs stuck his foot down. He didn't know what was going on. What was happening to him or what was happening to Big Bob. But he suddenly felt very very afraid. Outside all the world was strange. The shops and houses, the lorries and cars. All were suddenly alien. Suddenly strange and unknown. His powers of recognition were blanking off. A car was a car and then it was not. Then it was just an odd-coloured shape. The road ahead was tarmac no more, now it was only grey matter.

'Aggh!' Periwig Tombs took his foot off the clutch. The bus was parked in second gear. The handbrake stretched and snapped and the old bus rumbled forward.

'What's this?' went Periwig, regarding the steering wheel in his hands. 'Black thing, coiled round? Spade? Spode? Snail? Snake? *Snake*? Aaagh! *Snake*!'

Periwig covered his face with his hands. The bus began to gather speed.

The tourists on the top deck were unaware that anything untoward was occurring, other than that the rather odd commentary had ceased. They cheered as the bus scattered several pedestrians and had a passing parson off his pushbike.

'Look at that parsnip,' said the lady in the straw hat. 'No, I don't mean parsnip. Paspatoo. No, pasta. No, parrot. No, not parrot.'

'Where am I?' wailed Big Bob. 'What am I doing here?'

'Get it off me,' wailed Periwig Tombs. 'No get *what* off me? Wssss gggging nnnnnnn?'

Up the High Street went the wayward bus, gathering speed all the time. Motorists hooted and swerved to either side. Cars mounted pavements, scattering further pedestrians. The bus now mounted a pavement too, bringing down a lamppost.

In the Plume Café, Derek said, 'You really won't find much to interest you here, Ms Sirjan. If you want to know the secret of Brentford, I'll tell it to you. It's inertia. There's nothing more powerful than inertia. Things that are standing still are the hardest things to get moving.'

And then Derek glanced out of the window.

And then Derek flung the table aside and flung himself upon the body of Kelly Anna Sirjan.

It wasn't a sudden rush of lust.

It was something else.

Kelly toppled backwards from her chair. Derek grabbed her and dragged her aside.

The tour bus, engine screaming, and tourists screaming too, ploughed into the front window of the Plume Café, demolishing all that lay before it.

3

It was joy, joy happy joy no more.

All across Brentford alarm bells started to ring.

At the cottage hospital. Where the doctors and nurses on duty were joyously playing at doctors and nurses. As doctors and nurses will so often do, if business is slack and there is an R in the month.

At the fire station. Where the lads of Pink watch, Lou Lou, Arnie Magoo, Rupert, Gibble and Chubb, were forming a human pyramid in the station yard. As firemen will so often do when they've run out of things to polish and the weather's sunny enough.

At Brentford nick. Where the boys in blue were sitting in the staff canteen discussing the Hegelian dialectic, that interpretive method whereby the contradiction between a proposition and its antithesis can theoretically be resolved at a higher level of truth. As policemen will so often do when not fighting crime.

And finally at the offices of the *Brentford Mercury*, where Hildemar Shields sat fiercely scowling. He was told simply to 'hold the front page'. As editors so often are.

These alarm bells had been precipitated into fevered ringings by calls made by Derek on his mobile phone.

He and Kelly had survived the holocaust and struggled all but unscathed from the wreckage of the Plume Café. They were now engaged, along with many a plucky Brentonian good Samaritan, in

40

dragging crash victims from the mangled bus and administering what first aid they could.

Miraculously, there appeared to have been no loss of life. The driver was bruised and bloody, but he was still conscious and he now sat on the pavement, holding his head in his hands and being comforted by several caring souls.

The tour guide, who had been thrown into the cab, over the driver's head and out through the windscreen, should surely have been dead. But he wasn't. He'd travelled straight through the old-fashioned flap-up windscreen, which had obligingly flapped up for him, straight through the serving hatch behind the Plume's counter, out of the open rear door and onto a pile of stunt mattresses which had been left in the back yard. As is often the case. He now sat next to the driver, staring into space.

Those on the open top deck of the bus had not been quite so lucky. As the tour bus had torn into the café, they had been swept backwards by building debris and now lay in a moaning knotted heap in the rear of the crumpled vehicle, blocking up the top of the stairs.

There appeared to be five of them, all interlaced by arms and legs in an intricate manner. Four students of Japanese extraction and a lady in a battered straw hat.

Untangling them was proving to be a problem of Gordian proportion. And Derek was finally forced to step in and halt the enthusiastic efforts of a plucky Brentonian motor mechanic who was tackling the task with a crowbar.

'Best leave it to the professionals,' was Derek's advice. 'They'll be along shortly.'

And of course they were.

The gathering crowd, which now seemed to include most of the population of Brentford, cheered wildly as the local fire tender, followed by the local ambulance, followed by four local police cars, came tearing up the High Street, sirens banshee-wailing and beacon lights a-flash-flash-flash.

Exciting stuff.

But, sadly, it has to be said that there can sometimes be problems with the emergency services when they find themselves all being called out to the scene of a disaster at the same time. There tends to be a lot of competition and a lot of disputation too. Particularly regarding just who is supposed to be in overall charge and who should be giving the orders to whom. There is often a tendency for the first to arrive on the scene to put themselves in charge, whether they should be putting themselves in charge or not. There can be an awful lot of posturing and pulling rank and being difficult and, well, being *male* really.

It's a 'man thing' and it has a lot to do with the uniform.

One might have thought that in Brentford, things would have been rather different. But if one might have thought this, one would have been very wrong. Would one.

Men will be men and boys will be boys and so on and suchlike and whatnot.

The race along the High Street was a good'n though. Two of the police cars just managed to overtake the ambulance, but they were held back by the fire tender, which took to violent swerving and then skidded to a halt at an angle effectively blocking both sides of the High Street. This left for a fifty-yard two-legged dash along the pavement. Bookies in the crowd were already taking bets.

First to reach the crash site should have been fire officer Arnie Magoo. He was first out of the tender's cab and very fast on his feet. But faster was constable Cavendish and far more powerful too. Winger for the Metropolitan Police All Blues rugby side, he grounded fireman Magoo with a splendid tackle, which drew much applause from members of the crowd who were laying their bets on the bobbies.

Whilst the first two gallant lads grappled it out on the pavement, it was left to Acting Fireman Howard Chubb and Police Constable Edward Flanders to battle for lead position. These two were old adversaries and well versed in each other's tactics. Whilst Flanders favoured rib-elbowing, Chubb was an eye-gouge merchant.

They had once drawn a joint first place at a road traffic accident in Abaddon Street, back in 2020. A milk float had collided with a jeep containing soldiers home on furlough and brought down a pillar box, setting it ablaze.

This particular accident had led to a most interesting situation due to the number of uniformed personnel all finding themselves in the same place at the same time. The soldiers naturally felt that they should take charge of the situation, but a passing postman declared that he should. The driver of the milk float, who argued that his uniform held as much rank as anybody else's, threw in his twopenny worth and Flanders and Chubb* arriving together, as they did, were drawn into a five-way confrontation.

They were, however, outnumbered by the military on this occasion, who effectively demonstrated that guns held rank over truncheons and fire axes.

So.

While Cavendish struggled with Magoo and Chubb held Flanders in a headlock and poked him in the eye. And fire officer Gavin Rupert sat upon the chest of Police Constable Meredith Wainwright. And fire chief Lou Lou had Chief Constable Eric Mortimer Ronan-Bagshaw up against the window of Mr Beefheart's butcher's shop. It was left to the enterprising and nimble Police Constable Ferdinand Gonzales, five times winner of the Metropolitan Police 'You're it' championships, to break away from the pack and claim the disaster for his own.

Before sinking slowly to his knees and passing from consciousness.

'Now will everyone back away *please*!' ordered ambulance driver Lesley Jane Grime, loading up a hypodermic with a potent anaesthetic, whilst at the same time discarding the one she had just used on the backside of Constable Gonzales. 'I am in charge here and now . . .'

But she really didn't stand much of a chance and she soon went down beneath the flailing fists of bobby and fire bloke alike.

'I'll have to break this up,' said Kelly, squaring up to employ her Dimac. 'I can't allow this to continue.'

'Best to keep out of it,' Derek advised. 'These things eventually resolve themselves and as there's been no loss of life . . .'

'There's injured people upstairs on the bus.'

'Ah look,' said Derek. 'Here comes Mr Shields.'

* Not to be confused with the other Flanders and Chubb, who were actually Flanders and Swann, the popular 1950s double act, who coincidentally used to sing a song about a bus.

The editor of the *Brentford Mercury* jostled his way through the crowd, pushing a small and worried-looking man before him.

'This is Gary,' said Derek to Kelly. 'Gary's our press photographer.'

'I don't like the look of this,' said Gary. 'This bus might explode at any minute.'

'It's quite safe,' said Kelly. 'But there's injured people upstairs.' She stepped aside as a fireman blundered by with a constable clinging to his throat.

'Go up and photograph them, Gary,' said Mr Shields. 'Have you brought the doll?'

Gary nodded. Kelly said, 'Doll?'

'The discarded child's doll,' Mr Shields explained. 'It makes for a great front-page picture. Adds that touch of pathos. Often there isn't one at a crash site, so press photographers always bring their own.'

'Mine's called Chalky,' said Gary, producing Chalky from out of his pocket. 'She's quite a little star, aren't you Chalky?'

Kelly's jaw fell open. 'Don't you understand?' she said. 'There are injured people. Real people. Suffering.'

'Any dead?' the editor asked.

'Thankfully not.'

'Shame. But one or two might always die on the way to hospital.'

'What?' Kelly looked appalled. She *was* appalled.

'Ah,' said Mr Shields. 'Well, I know that might sound callous, but actually it isn't.'

'Isn't it?' asked Kelly, as two confused constables rolled by, wildly swinging at each other.

'It's a cathartic thing,' the editor explained, stepping aside to avoid being hit by an ambulance man. 'Vast public outpourings of grief. It started back in the 1990s. People began placing bunches of flowers at the sites of road accidents or murders. Then there was the Hillsborough disaster and of course the death of Princess Di. Conspiracy theorists suggest that it was a cabal of florists who came up with the original idea. But I tend to the belief that the public need that kind of thing. It makes them feel caring and takes their mind off their own problems for a while. And thousands and thousands of bunches of flowers all laid out do make for a very colourful and poignant front page . . .'

44

Mr Shields never saw the punch coming. Kelly laid him out with a single blow.

Order was finally restored with the arrival of FART. The Fire Arms Response Team. They had been called in when Mr Pendragon, the proprietor of the Plume Café, who had just popped around the corner to the cheese shop shortly before the demolition occurred, and had tarried rather longer than he should have done in the pub next door to the cheese shop, returned to find a bus sticking out of the front of his now defunct café and a whole lot of uniformed men beating eight bells of bejasus out of each other all around and about.

Somewhat upset by this downturn in his fortunes, he had managed to locate his old service revolver from amongst the wreckage of his business premises and started taking potshots at the crowd. As one would.

It was all well and truly over, however, by three in the afternoon.

Derek and Kelly sat in the waiting room of casualty at the cottage hospital. There had been no fatalities through either crash or conflict. Mr Pendragon lay in a private ward, straitjacketed and suffering the after-effects of nerve gas. Mr Shields had recovered consciousness and returned to his office, where he sat composing headlines of the BUS CRASH PLUME BOOM DOOM persuasion. The uniformed walking-wounded had licked their wounds and walked and only those who had been aboard the bus remained tucked up in hospital beds.

Derek was making notes in his reporter's notebook.

Kelly sat and teased strands of her golden hair. Twisting them between her fingers, slowly backwards and forwards. Back and forwards and back.

Dr Sebastian Druid, son of Ted and brother to Conan Barbarossa Firesword Druid (who lived in a world that was very much of his own), breezed through the double doors that led from the general ward and smiled a warm and friendly smile at Kelly Anna Sirjan.

Dr Druid was a man of moderate height and immoderate sexual appetite. He had much of the tawny owl to his looks, but a little of the okapi. He knew his stuff when it came to first aid, but was totally lost beneath the bonnet of a Ford Fiesta. Dr Druid had a clipboard and a pair of brown suede shoes.

'Don't get up,' he said to Kelly, who already had.

'How are the patients?' Kelly asked.

'Odd,' said Dr Druid. 'Somewhat odd.'

'How so, odd?' asked Derek. 'Odd to look at, do you mean? That driver is certainly a strange-looking chap. Reminds me a bit of the Mekon.'

'No.' The doctor sat himself down and then stood up again. 'It's not the looks of them that are odd. Although I've never been overly attracted to the Oriental physiognomy. Not that the women of Thailand are anything other than fair.'

'Aren't they dark?' asked Derek.

'Fair to look upon,' said Dr Druid, looking fairly upon Kelly Anna. 'Fair to behold. But I don't mean odd in looks. The four Japanese students have all recovered their senses and I'll keep them in tonight for observation and turn them loose tomorrow. It's the other three that trouble me.' Dr Druid consulted his clipboard. 'There's this lady in the straw hat, whose name I wouldn't dare to pronounce. The driver, a Mr Periwig Tombs, and the tour guide Robert Charker, known as Big Bob, I believe.'

'So what's odd?' asked Derek.

Dr Druid heard him ask, but addressed his answer to Kelly. 'Blank out,' he said. 'They are completely unable to communicate. It seems as if they are suffering from total amnesia.'

'It's shock surely?' Derek said. 'After all, they've just been in a bus crash.'

Dr Druid shook his tawny head and raised an un-okapi-like eyebrow. 'It isn't shock,' he said. 'Trust me, I know these things, I'm a doctor. And have you had a check-up lately, Ms Sirjan, I think you really should, I can fit you in now, if you're free.'

'I'm fine,' said Kelly, noting how firmly the doctor's gaze had attached itself to her breasts. 'These people weren't unconscious when we found them. How do you explain the amnesia?'

'I don't,' said Dr Druid. 'I have run all the usual tests. The Gugenheimer Cheese Recognition Test. The McNaulty Handkerchief Scan, knotted and unknotted. I've tried rattling change in my trouser pockets and even whistling in a very low and mournful manner, which quite put the wind up one of my interns.'

'Did you try moving a pencil back and forward across an ashtray?' Derek asked.

'Naturally.'

'And what about reciting the alphabet into a paper cup?'

'I also tried it into a bedpan.'

Derek now shook his head, but didn't raise an eyebrow. 'You're very thorough indeed,' he observed.

'Well, I am a doctor,' said Dr Druid. 'Your shoulders look very stiff, Ms Sirjan, perhaps I could massage them for you?'

'Would it be possible for me to speak to any of the patients?' Kelly asked.

'Possibly later. They're currently being interviewed by a policeman and a fireman. Not that they'll get anything from them. They seem to have lost the power of speech and hearing as well, as far as I can make out. I could give your back a quick rub, if you like, my dear. Or perhaps take you to dinner?'

Kelly's fingers twisted at strands of her golden hair. 'Thanks, but no thanks,' she said. 'Derek is taking me out to dinner tonight.'

'Am I?' said Derek.

'Yes,' said Kelly. 'You are.'

There are many splendid eateries in Brentford. There is Archie Karachi's Star of Bombay Curry Garden in the Ealing Road. Wang Yu's Chinese Chuckaway in Albany Crescent. The Wife's Legs Café down at the end of Half Acre. And the Laughing Sprout, Brentford's only vegetarian restaurant, which tucks itself away at the bottom of Horseferry Lane, near to the river, where no-one has to look at it much. It's a very romantic little venue, but it doesn't serve any meat.

Derek was a young man who very much liked his meat. His father, a man made wise with many years, had told him the value of protein. 'Eat meat and keep your bowels open and trust in the Lord, if the need should arise,' were the words his father spoke on the subject, and words Derek never forgot. He ate up his meat and kept his

47

bowels open and would no doubt one day trust in the Lord, if the need ever arose.

A little after eight of the evening clock, he led Kelly Anna Sirjan through the door of the Laughing Sprout and was directed by the waiter to the table for two that overlooked the river.

'I believe this to be safe,' said Derek, as he pulled out a chair for Kelly. 'The chances of being hit by a riverboat are, in my opinion, quite remote.'

'It's very nice here,' said Kelly. 'Do you come here often?'

The lie that might have sprung from his lips did not even enter his head. 'No,' said Derek. 'I've never been here before. But I'm right assuming you're a vegetarian?'

'How did you get on after I left the hospital? You said you were going to the bus depot.'

Derek seated himself and toyed with his serviette. 'I did. I checked the bookings for the bus tour. There was one other tourist aboard. The son of the lady with the unpronounceable name.'

'So whatever happened to him?'

'Search me,' said Derek. 'He wasn't on the bus when we helped the others. Perhaps he just got off and walked away.'

'And left his mother? That's very strange.'

'Everything is strange about that crash. I talked to some of the eyewitnesses. They say the driver wasn't steering the bus, that he was flapping his hands about and going crazy.'

'Had he been drinking, or something?'

'Not according to Dr Druid. I took the liberty of asking him to call me if there were any developments. If the patients got their memories back or anything.'

'And do you think he will?'

'I also took the liberty of mentioning money. There might be a story here. A big story. I wouldn't want the nationals to get to it first.'

'You'd like the exclusive all for yourself.'

Derek made a sour face. 'I spent two hours typing it all up, simply to be told by Mr Shields that he was covering the story and I should just clear off home.'

'Will we be seeing a picture of Chalky the doll on tomorrow's front page?'

'I shouldn't be at all surprised.'

The waiter, an eastern European type, dressed in gypsy trappings, was hovering near with the wine list and now made polite coughings.

'Ah yes,' said Derek. 'What would you like to drink, Kelly?'

'A glass of red wine please.'

'A glass of red wine then,' Derek said to the waiter. 'And do you have any beers?'

'We do Sprout Lager, sir. It has to be tasted to be believed.'

'Two red wines it is then.'

The waiter nodded and turned to leave and then he turned back again. 'Excuse me please, sir,' he said. 'But I couldn't help overhearing your conversation.'

'Ah,' said Derek, thoughtfully.

'It's just that, well, you see, my sister, she saw the crash happen.'

'Really,' said Derek. 'How interesting.'

'I don't think you really meant that,' whispered Kelly.

'I think he overheard me speak of money,' whispered Derek.

'Oh no, sir,' said the waiter. 'It isn't that. I don't ask for money. It's only that my sister was greatly troubled by the thing she saw.'

'Seeing an accident is never pleasant,' said Derek. 'But your sister will get over it in time.'

'Oh no, sir. I don't think she will. Not with the thing she saw.'

'Go on,' said Derek.

'Well, sir, I overhear you say about the lady's son, missing from the crash. My sister see him come down from the top deck of the bus. She say he looked very frightened and lost as if he don't know where he is. His eyes all staring and scared. Then he turn around and walk into the wall of the shop next door to the Plume Café.'

'Did he injure himself?' Derek asked.

'No, sir, you misunderstand me. He walk *into* the wall. *Into it.* Like a ghost. He walk into the wall and he vanish.'

Derek looked at Kelly.

And Kelly looked at Derek.

'Most amusing,' said Derek. 'You had us going there. Two red wines it is then, thank you.'

'No, sir.' The waiter looked most agitated. 'I'm not pulling at your plonker nor anything. This is what she see with her own two eyes. In the broad daylight. He come down from the bus and he walk into the wall and he vanish. She see it and it trouble her greatly. She honest and church-going. She say it a very bad omen. She say the Devil walk amongst us in Brentford.'

'I don't think things have got quite that bad yet,' said Derek. 'But you *are* serious, aren't you?'

'You can see that he is,' said Kelly.

'Serious,' said the waiter. 'I not like to tell people of this. But I hear you say that everything seem strange about the bus that is crashing. Everything more than strange, I tell you. Everything evil. Best beware.'

The waiter now speedily took his leave and went to fetch the wine.

'Things are never dull around you, are they?' said Kelly.

'They were until you arrived today. But what did you make of all that?'

Kelly shrugged and smiled a bit. But her fingers were once more twisting at her hair.

'It's got to be a wind-up,' said Derek. 'Having one over on the gullible newspaper man.'

Derek's mobile phone began to purr away in his pocket. He took it out, pressed buttons and put it to his ear.

'What's that?' he said. 'Sorry I can't hear you very well. Excuse me Kelly, I'll take this outside and try to get a better signal.'

The waiter returned with two red wines and left again, avoiding Kelly's gaze. Kelly watched Derek through the window. He was a good-looking young man. And for a newspaper reporter, he seemed to be honest enough. She saw him thrust his mobile phone back into his pocket and then rush back into the Laughing Sprout.

'Forget the wine,' he said. 'We have to go.'

'You look a little rattled,' Kelly said.

'I'm more than rattled.' Derek took a deep and steadying breath. 'That was Dr Druid on the phone. Something has happened at the cottage hospital.'

'Don't tell me someone has died.'

'Worse than that.'

'How can anything be worse?'

'The three patients with amnesia. They've vanished.'

'What, you mean they've walked out of the hospital?'

'No,' said Derek. 'I mean they just vanished. Right in front of Dr Druid's eyes.'

4

It was a balmy Brentford evening
Calm and clear of sky.
Sirius, brightest star of Heaven
Gazed down from on high.

And a zephyr, lightly blowing from the
Gardens, south at Kew
Brought the fragrances of lilies
And of antique roses too

All across the Thames to Brentford
Where the borough, bound for night,
Breathed in the sacred perfume
Dum de dum de dum delight.

There was no delight to be found on the face of Dr Druid. He sat in the waiting room of casualty, being comforted by a pair of nurses dressed in the kind of medical style that you just don't see any more. Consisting, as it did, of white high heels, fishnet stockings, short slashed skirt and tightly fitting blouse with several buttons missing from the top. The dress code had been instigated by Dr Druid, who held a lot of clout at the cottage hospital.

At the arrival of Derek and Kelly Anna, Dr Druid waved away the nurses. The taller of the two, the bearded one called Gavin, said, 'Call us if you need us, Dr Druid.'

'Thank you,' said the doctor, and he gave Gavin's bottom a pat.

'Outrageous,' said Kelly.

'I know,' said the doctor. 'But what good is having power, if you don't abuse it every once in a while?'

Derek shook his head and Kelly began to tease at her hair. 'Do you want to tell us all about it?' Derek asked.

'In confidence,' said the medic. 'And on the understanding that no blame whatsoever attaches to my person. I want it to be made clear that I did everything I could for those patients and that no trace of fault can be laid at my door. I am innocent of all charges.'

Derek took from his pocket one of those miniature tape-recording jobbies that newspaper reporters always carry in their pockets, and which have an uncanny habit of switching themselves on and recording incriminating information when the reporter has sworn upon the life of his ancient white-haired old mother that all he is being told is 'strictly off the record'.

'I assume you want this strictly *on the record*,' said Derek.

'Absolutely,' said the doctor. 'And none of it's my fault.'

'Yes, I'll make that very clear. Now what *exactly* happened?'

'*They vanished!*' shrieked the doctor, his face turning pale and his eyes growing round as those of the owl known as Tawny. 'Right in front of me. They just faded away. Then they were gone. Gone, I tell you, gone.'

'Gone?' said Derek, shaking his head. 'They really just vanished? Right in front of your eyes?'

The doctor now spoke in the whisper known as hoarse. 'I know what it is,' he whispered. 'I'm not stupid. I know what it is.'

'Go on,' said Derek.

'This is *off the record*,' said the doctor.

Derek made a show of pressing tape-recorder buttons. Strangely the recorder continued to record.

'Go on,' Derek said once more.

'The Rapture,' said the doctor, round eyes darting upwards, head upon his shoulders going nod, nod, nod.

'The *what*?' Derek asked.

'The Rapture,' said Kelly. 'The Fundamental Christian interpretation of several texts from the Book of Revelation. They have it that at the time of the Tribulation, when the Antichrist comes to power, the righteous will be carried aloft to Heaven. Bodily. One moment they will be among us and the next moment, gone. Vanished.'

Derek stared at Kelly and then he stared at Dr Druid. 'You have got to be joking,' he said.

'No,' said the doctor, shakily shaking his head. 'They went, whoosh, gone, vanished. They might be the first, but they won't be the last. But people won't believe the truth. People never do. They'll blame other people. They'll blame me.'

The doctor, now shaking terribly, buried his face in his hands.

'He's taking it well,' said Derek.

Kelly shot him the kind of glance that suggested that his remark was at best indiscreet and at worst, something far more ghastly than that.

'Sorry,' whispered Derek. 'But come on now. This is clearly getting ridiculous.'

'And the waiter's sister? This would be a coincidence I suppose?'

'Could we have a look at the ward?' Derek asked.

Dr Druid unburied his head. 'The ward?' he asked in return.

'Where the patients vanished. There might be clues.'

'Clues?' Kelly whispered.

'Clues!' Derek whispered back. 'There will be an explanation for this.'

'There is,' said Dr Druid. 'It's The Rapture. They vanished at precisely eight minutes past eight, I looked at my watch. I'll just bet that means something, like the Beast 666.'

'Possibly an explanation that does not involve the Coming of the Antichrist and the onset of Armageddon.'

'All right,' said Dr Druid, hauling himself into the vertical plane. 'I'll show you the ward. But it won't do you any good. It's The Rapture for certain and I am not one of the chosen. And if anything, that's what upsets me the most about this. I've spent my life in the service of others. If there was ever anyone deserving of being wafted up to Heaven, then that person is surely me. It's all so bitterly unfair.'

'Perhaps they're being taken in shifts,' said Kelly. 'I'm sure that if it is The Rapture, you'll be getting exactly what you deserve.'

'That's a comfort,' said the rattled doc. 'I think.'

'Come on,' said Derek. 'Show us the ward.'

A lady, looking pretty in pink, now entered the waiting room. She tottered on preposterous Doveston holistic shoes with nine-inch platform soles. The platforms of the shoes appeared to be transparent, little pink lights twinkled within, and lit up tiny plastic busts of a guru called Hugo Rune.

The lady in pink came a-tottering up to Dr Druid.

'What have you done with my husband?' she demanded to be told.

'Your husband, madam?' asked the doctor.

'Big Bob Charker, I'm his better half.'

'Ah,' said Dr Druid and his round eyes flickered at Derek.

'He's sleeping,' said Derek. 'He's under sedation, you'd better come back in the morning.'

'Oh,' said Minky Charker. 'So he's all right then? He'll live?'

'Absolutely,' said Derek. Kelly shot him another terrible glance.

'And who are you?' asked Minky.

'I'm a specialist.'

'Really? Are you?'

'Yes, I am.'

'And what do you specialize in?'

'Bullshit apparently,' whispered Kelly. 'I do love your shoes, by the way.' And she smiled upon Minky.

'They're the very latest fashion. Made of polysynthacarbon dextroglutimatacide. They channel Earth energy right up the back of my legs. I've lost five pounds since I started wearing them this morning.'

'That is surely impossible,' said Derek.

'No, really. I had it in my purse, but I think it must have fallen out. Still, my impetigo's cleared up and my nipples are as hard as a pair of aniseed balls.'

'I'd better have a look at those,' said Dr Druid.

'We should be getting along to the ward,' said Derek.

'Yes we really should,' said Kelly. 'Goodnight to you, Mrs Charker.'

'Couldn't I come to the ward too?' Minky asked.

'Er no,' said Dr Druid. 'I'm afraid not. You can go to my consulting room and disrobe, if you want to.'

'I'm not particularly keen,' said Minky.

'Then goodnight to you madam.'

'Goodnight doctor.'

Dr Druid turned and led Derek and Kelly away to the general ward.

'Oh doctor,' called Minky. 'Just one thing before you go.'

'Yes?' said Dr Druid, turning back.

'Nurse Gavin is my sister,' said Minky.

'Oh,' said Dr Druid, in a low deep long and terribly sorry sort of way.

'Yes,' said Minky. 'And she rang me five minutes ago to tell me that Big Bob has been carried away in The Rapture.'

'Oh,' said the doctor, deeper and lower still this time.

'So one of you is lying,' said Minky. 'And I don't think it's my sister. Bearded women never lie; it's a circus sideshow tradition. Like eating quails' eggs when the moon is new, and posting early for Christmas.'

'Oh,' and 'oh,' the doctor said again.

'You'd better come with us,' said Derek.

'I think I better had,' said Big Bob's better half.

Derek gave the general ward a specific looking-over.

He peered under beds, he peered into bedpans, he peered behind curtains and into cupboards. He peered and then he poked about and then he peered some more.

'He'll ruin his eyes with all that peering,' said Minky. 'I had a brother once who used to peer. The wind changed twice and he was stuck with the kind of moustache that only comes off with turps.'

'I'm sure I've heard that line somewhere before,' said Derek, looking up from his peering and poking.

'There's nothing new upon God's Earth,' said Minky. 'Except for The Rapture, of course. That's new, but it has been expected.'

'You believe in it then, do you?' Kelly asked.

'Well you have to believe in something, don't you dear? My uncle used to believe that he was the reincarnation of Jesus. He was a Buddhist, you see. So he had the best of both worlds. He had the stigmata and when we were kiddies, he used to let us put our fingers through the holes in his hands. When he fell asleep we'd fill his holes with plasticine. You don't see plasticine around any more, do you dear? It's gone the way of crazy foam, Potty Putty and X-ray specs. Not to mention the see-back-oscope.'

'The see-back-oscope?' Kelly asked.

'I told you not to mention that!'

'Sorry,' said Kelly, twisting her hair into terrible knots.

'That's an awful nervous habit you have there,' Minky observed. 'You should see a specialist. But not that one doing all the peering. He'll soon be needing glasses.'

'Excuse me for saying this,' said Kelly. 'But you do appear to be quite untroubled about the possibility that your husband has been carried off by The Rapture.'

'It's the way he would have wanted to go.'

'Is it?'

'Well, he did mention once about wanting to be shot by a jealous husband when caught making passionate love to a twenty-year-old lap dancer, during the celebration of his ninety-third birthday. But men will say anything when you have one of their vital parts held tightly in your hand, won't they dear?'

'I'm sure your husband has been yearning for The Rapture,' said Kelly. 'I know I would.'

'You're too kind. So young man, with all your peering and poking, have you come to any conclusions?'

'I think I might need glasses,' said Derek. 'But there is some stuff on these sheets here.'

'Don't look at me,' said Dr Druid.

'Some residue,' said Derek.

'I said, don't look at me.'

'I'd like to take some samples. To get them analysed.'

'I'm a doctor,' said Dr Druid. 'I could analyse them.'

'An independent analyst.'

'Spoily sport,' said the doctor.

'Just one thing,' said Minky. 'Just one. Where do I stand regarding my husband's life insurance policy? Will I be able to claim the money without a body? I mean, well, with him being taken bodily into

57

Heaven. That's an Act of God, isn't it? And Acts of God aren't covered.'

'Good point,' said Dr Druid. 'There'd have to be a test case. I'll bet the insurance company won't pay up. They'd have to pay up on millions of policies, if they did.'

'That's most unfair of God,' said Minky. 'Rapturing away my husband and leaving me penniless. I've a good mind to change my religion. And come to think of it, how come God chose to Rapture up my Big Bob? I'm much nicer than he is. I'm the one who should have been Raptured.'

Kelly turned to Derek. 'I think we should go,' she said. 'There's nothing to be found here.'

Derek produced a pocket camera. 'I'll just take one or two photographs,' he said.

'That seems sensible.'

'Yes it does,' said Minky. 'Do you want me to take my top off?'

Kelly looked at Derek.

Derek shook his head. Rather sadly, it seemed to Kelly.

'Oh go on,' said Dr Druid. 'You know that you want to.'

'And to think,' said Kelly. 'I almost liked you.'

'What?' said Derek. 'What?'

They sat in the bar of the Flying Swan, Brentford's finest alehouse. Eight premier hand-drawn beers on pump and an ambience that said that here was well and truly, truly, truly and most truly once and for ever again, a pub.

'You behaved like a total prat back there,' said Kelly. 'You lied and you connived and you actually had that woman take her top off.'

'I'm sorry,' said Derek. 'I went into newspaperman mode. But there is a story here, there's no doubt of that.'

'The Rapture?'

'*Not* The Rapture. That doctor's up to something.'

'I've no doubt at all about that.'

'I don't believe in vanishing patients. There's a more logical explanation. Medical malpractice probably. The illicit selling of organs. Things of that nature.'

'I've misjudged you,' said Kelly.

Derek smiled.

'No, I mean you *are* a total prat. No doubt whatsoever about it.'

'Come on now. Be fair.'

'Something happened in that hospital. Something bizarre. Something paranormal.'

'Rot,' said Derek. 'I mean, well, I disagree.'

'Come off it,' said Kelly. 'No doctor is going to make up the story that his patients vanished in front of his eyes. He could have said that they discharged themselves. He could have said anything. But not that. He called you because he didn't want to be blamed. He made that clear enough. No money was involved.'

'People don't just vanish,' said Derek.

'They do,' said Kelly. 'There have been cases, the Earl of Bathhurst, Kasper Hauser, Amy Johnson, Glenn Miller, Lord Lucan, Richard Branson . . .'

'Unexplained disappearances. That's not the same as just vanishing. And you seem to know a lot about this sort of business. You knew about The Rapture and everything.'

'I read a lot,' said Kelly. 'These things interest me.'

'Well they don't interest me. And although they might interest the readers of the *Weekly World News*, they won't interest the more sensible folk who purchase the *Brentford Mercury*.'

'This is a very nice pub,' said Kelly, looking all around it.

'And it's full of history. Pooley and Omally used to drink in here.'

'Oh yes?' said Kelly. 'This would be Pooley and Omally, the mythical heroes of Brentford, who thwarted the invasion of the borough by beings from the lost planet Ceres and numerous powers of darkness who chose to set foot in the borough?'

Derek grinned. 'Every borough has its folklore and its heroes,' he said. 'There are people in Brentford who claim that they actually knew Pooley and Omally.'

'And do you believe them?'

'No, of course I don't.'

'So, what are you going to do about what Mr Holmes might well refer to as "The Singular Case of the Vanishing Bus Men"?'

'Actually I've had second thoughts and I'm going to pass on it,' said Derek. 'Because I don't want to make a total prat of myself by writing it up and then have them come wandering home.'

'I see,' said Kelly. 'Then would you have any objections to me following it up?'

'It's neither here nor there, with me. You can do what you like. But don't expect Mr Shields to print anything you come up with.'

'I think this might prove to be rather important.'

'And I think you'll be wasting your time. Same again?'

Kelly looked into her empty glass. 'No thanks,' she said. 'I think I'll call it a night. I've got digs in Abbadon Street, I think I'll go back now. Pick up a chicken and mushroom pie and a bag of chips on the way back.'

'But I thought you were a vegetarian.'

'And I might well have been. But I'm not. And I made a mistake by accepting your invitation to dinner.'

'You invited me, I recall.'

Kelly smiled.

'Listen,' said Derek. 'You really have me all wrong. Let me buy you another drink. The chippy stays open late, you won't miss your chicken pie.'

'I'm missing it already.'

'Just one more drink. Then I'll walk you to your door.'

'Just the one then.'

Derek took himself off to the bar, leaving Kelly alone with her thoughts. Her thoughts were in some confusion at the present time. Something was happening here. Here in this little suburban backwater of Brentford. Something bizarre and something paranormal. And she was an outsider, an out-borough type. She was a stranger here. But she *was* here and if something *was* going on, she really truly meant to get right to the bottom of it.

At the bar counter, Derek bobbed up and down trying to get some attention. 'Over here, please,' he went. 'I say, over here.'

The professional barman went about his professional duties in a highly professional manner.

He served the regulars first.

'Oh come on,' called Derek. 'I was here before him.'

'Coming right up,' called the barman, serving somebody else.

60

'The service here is rubbish,' said Derek to an ancient gent a-seated on a bar stool.

'I never have any trouble,' said the ancient, whose name was Old Pete. 'Have you tried ordering your drinks in Runese, that would help.'

'Are you sure of that?'

'I'm sure.'

'Sadly I don't know Runese,' said Derek. 'In fact I think the entire concept of a universal tongue of forty words to be utter rubbish.'

'You'll be a long time getting served then.'

Derek sighed. 'Do you speak Runese?' he asked.

'Like a native,' said Old Pete.

'So how do you ask for a large red wine and a large vodka and tonic?'

Old Pete studied the glassy bottom of his empty glass.

'All right,' said Derek. 'I'll get one for you too.'

'One for me first,' said Old Pctc.

'All right, first. So what do I say?'

'Say "Large dark rum over here for Old Pete,"' said Old Pete.

'That isn't Runese.'

'But it will work, trust me.'

Derek sighed. 'Large dark rum over here for Old Pete,' he called to the busy and professional barman.

'Coming right up,' called the barman. And Old Pete's rum came right up.

'That will be one pound, two and sixpence,' said the barman.

'Pay the man,' said Old Pete.

'And a large red wine and a large vodka and tonic.'

'One pound, two and sixpence,' said the barman once more.

'Pay the man,' said Old Pete. 'Then I'll tell you how to do yours in Runese.'

Derek paid the man and once the barman had turned away to the cash register, Old Pete spoke certain words in Derek's ear.

'Ah,' said Derek. 'Thank you very much.'

The barman returned. 'Your change, sir,' he said.

'*Ravata nostromo, digitalus, carberundam,*' said Derek.

'Pardon me?' said the barman.

'*Ravata nostromo, digitalus, carberundam,*' shouted Derek.

'That's what I thought you said,' said the barman, and drawing back a mighty fist, he swung the thing forward and punched Derek right in the face with it.

Derek fell down to the bar-room floor in a bloody-nosed confusion.

An elderly gent seated next to Old Pete chuckled into his ale. 'Although I must have heard you do that at least a hundred times,' said he, 'it never fails to crack me up.'

'Cheers,' said Old Pete, raising his glass.

Kelly helped Derek up from the floor and helped him back into his chair.

'He hit me,' Derek mopped at his bloody nose. 'That barman hit me in the face.'

'I'm not surprised,' said Kelly. 'I'd have hit you too if you'd said that to me.'

'I thought Runese was the Universal tongue of Peace.'

'That wasn't Runese. That was Brentford Auld Speke and you really don't want to know what you said.'

'You're laughing,' said Derek. 'You're laughing.'

'I think we'd better go,' said Kelly. 'I'll treat you to a chicken pie and chips and then I'll take you back to my digs and you can make sweet love to me.'

'Can I?' said Derek. 'Can I really, please?'

'No,' said Kelly, laughing some more. 'But I will treat you to the chicken pie.'

5

The morning sun touched lightly on the eyes of Kelly Anna.

The suburban bedroom where she awoke wasn't white though, it was puce. Whether puce really qualifies at all as to being a colour, is a subject for scholars to debate upon. But hopefully in some hall of academe where the walls aren't painted puce. Puce and beige are closely related.

Pink and puce are not.

Kelly yawned and studied her watch. It was nearly nine fifteen.

Kelly rose, and had she been observed by a waking companion, he, or possibly she, would have seen that this golden girl slept naked. But then he, or possibly she, would have known that already. Sunlight, entering through the puce net curtains, fell upon the sweeping curves of Kelly's voluptuous body. Connoisseurs of the female form remain in disagreement regarding the way that a woman's body should be lit to its most pleasing effect. Many favour candlelight and many more the glow of the full moon. But few would argue that a warm and tousled female, lately risen from the bed and caught in the first rays of the sun, is not an article of such supreme beauty as to raise eulogies from poets and other things from hot-blooded males, which make them late for work.

Kelly showered in the puce-tiled en suite. Dried and dressed and attended to the minutiae of make-up and hair-combing.

Young and assured, golden and girl, she went downstairs and ordered the full English breakfast.

It was a little after ten of the joyous sun-kissed morning clock that Chief Constable Peter Westlake, son of the infamous Don and brother to the sinister Arkon Lucifer Abraxus Westlake (who spoke only in iambic pentameter and ate the food upon his dinner plate in alphabetical order), looked up from the duty desk of the Brentford nick to cast a connoisseur's eye in the direction of the beautiful creature that had lately entered the establishment.

In the opinion of the chief constable, a woman's naked body was lit to its most pleasing effect by a single naked light bulb in a small and naked cell.

But, as he was very good at his job, Chief Constable Westlake's superiors overlooked his little peccadilloes, only making sure that he was accompanied by at least two women officers when interviewing a female suspect.

'Ah,' said the chief constable, as Kelly Anna approached the duty desk. 'Come to give yourself up. Very wise.'

'I have no idea what you're talking about,' said Kelly.

Chief Constable Westlake shook his head slowly and surely. It was a very long head. It rose almost to a point. It was one of those rare heads that can actually fill a policeman's helmet. Which meant that he'd never had to wear the chinstrap when he'd been a constable. Which had been handy, as he didn't have a chin.

'You've come to make a full confession,' said the chief constable.

'I haven't,' said Kelly.

'No matter. We have many techniques at our disposal.'

'I've come to report a missing person,' said Kelly. 'And I'd like a printout of all persons reported missing in the London area during the last two months.'

'Indeed?' said the chief constable, resting his elbows upon the desk and cradling the chinless area of his face between his upturned palms. 'Well, you're certainly at liberty to report a missing person. But I cannot allow you access to police databanks.'

Kelly Anna Sirjan smiled upon Chief Constable Westlake.

Chief Constable Westlake smiled back upon her.

'Oh dear,' said Kelly. 'This puts me in a bit of a dilemma.'

'It does?' said the chief constable.

'Yes it does. I don't know whether to employ my womanly charms, flutter my eyelashes and brush my breasts lightly across your desk.'

The chief constable's pointy head began to nod up and down.

'Or quote the Freedom of Information Act, which clearly states that the general public are entitled to view any, or all information held within the police databanks that does not refer directly to named criminals or suspects.'

The chief constable's pointy head ceased nodding. Most men secretly fear intelligent women. Some men openly hate them. CC Westlake was one of the latter.

'This could take some time,' he said. 'You'd better sit yourself down for a couple of hours.'

'No problem,' said Kelly. 'I generally like to meditate at this time of the day. It involves entering a state of trance, please wake me gently.'

Chief Constable Westlake turned his pointy head and shouted, 'Meek! Come here at once!'

A constable with a black eye and a fat lip appeared from a doorway to the rear of the duty desk. He had been seventh man up to the site of yesterday's bus crash. A fireman called Norman had put him out for the count.

'Constable, deal with this woman,' said Westlake. 'And don't allow her to view any classified information.'

'Any *what*?' asked the constable. 'We don't have any of that kind of thing knocking around here, do we, guv?'

'Just do what you're told, Constable.'

'Yes, but guv . . .'

'Just do it lad, or know the wrath of my displeasure.'

'Yes, sir. Gotcha.' The constable saluted.

'And Constable.'

'Yes guv?'

'Why are you wearing that sombrero?'

'A fireman nicked my helmet, guv.'

'And the spotted cravat? Did he nick your tie too?'

65

'Oh no, guv. The lads and I were discussing the Hegelian dialectic up in the canteen. The cravat is merely symbolic.'

Chief Constable Westlake sighed wearily. 'Just get this woman a printout of all persons reported missing in the London area during the last two months. And take a statement from her about a missing person of her own.'

'Can I use the big new computer, guv?'

Westlake raised his eyebrows. 'What big new computer would that be, then?'

Constable Meek whispered into the ear of his superior officer. Kelly caught the words 'raid on the premises of . . . dodgy gear . . . open and shut case . . . friend of the DI . . . same lodge . . . two hundred pounds each hush money . . . new computer for the station . . . no more questions asked.'

'Ah,' said the chief constable. '*That* computer. Well lad, crank it up and give this woman the printout. And take off that bloody silly hat, you look like the Cisco Kid.'

'The Cisco Kid?' asked Constable Meek.

'Hero of the popular 1950s American TV series,' said Kelly. 'The Cisco Kid was played by Duncan Renaldo. His comedy relief sidekick, Pancho, by the now legendary Leo Carillo. Every episode ended with the lines "Oh Cisco", "Oh Pancho". There were three hundred and thirty-two episodes. And the series ran up until 1961 when Leo Carillo sadly passed away at the grand old age of eighty.'

Constable Meek and Chief Constable Westlake stared at Kelly Anna Sirjan.

'How on Earth did you know that?' asked Westlake.

'I read a lot,' said Kelly. 'Should I follow you, Constable Meek?'

The big new computer stood upon a desk in an otherwise empty office on the second floor of the Brentford nick. Although it was clean and new-looking, it was actually an out of date Mute Corp 3000 Series. The office was *not entirely* otherwise empty. There were cupboard boxes in evidence. And wires. And complicated keyboards and user's manuals and more wires and a number of dangerous-looking black boxes with warning stickers on them.

Kelly viewed all with an interested eye. 'Who has been wiring this up?' she asked.

Constable Meek reddened slightly in the cheeks. 'Well, most of us, really,' he confessed. 'We haven't made too much progress yet, but we remain confident that our endeavours will be rewarded with a satis-factory conclusion to the operation in the fullness of time. So to speak.'

'Would you like me to put it online for you?'

'Oh would you really? Oh yes please.'

Kelly applied her talents to the job in hand. Shortly thereafter her endeavours were rewarded with a satisfactory conclusion.

'There you go,' said Kelly. 'Now I'll need the password so that I can access the police databanks.'

'Yes,' said the constable, nodding his head.

'So, what is it?'

'What is what?'

'The password.'

'Password,' said the constable.

'Yes, password. What is the password?'

'Password,' said the constable once more.

'You're telling me that the password, is password?'

'Yes,' said the constable. 'Password is the official password for all government computers. Even MI5 and Department S. Not to mention GHQ.' The constable paused.

Kelly typed in PASSWORD.

'You're supposed to say "GHQ?"' said the constable. 'And then I say, "I told you not to mention that." It's a running gag.'

'How amusing,' said Kelly. 'Now I just type in a request for a list of missing persons and request a hard copy, do I?'

The constable shrugged in a petulant manner. 'A running gag isn't a running gag if people refuse to run it,' he said.

Kelly typed in her request. Pressed PRINT and waited.

'Actually I really love technology,' said the constable. 'And I love the way that computers have got all big again. This is a Mute Corp 3000, one of the biggest you can get. All those miniaturized jobbies that came in around 2010. The ones that you wore inside your contact lenses. I could never be having with them.'

'No-one could,' said Kelly. 'People felt cheated by microtechnology, computer systems that fitted on a pinhead. People like plastic boxes with gubbins inside them. Plastic boxes are comforting.'

'And black ones are really macho,' said Constable Meek. 'Oooh, what's it doing now?'

'It's printing out,' said Kelly.

And printing out it was.

Paper spilled from the printer. Paper from a big roll at the back. Jack Kerouac typed *On the Road* in the 1950s upon a specially converted typewriter that had a spool of paper on the back. It took him only three weeks to type out his best-seller and it was all on a single piece of paper. Not a lot of people know that interesting fact.

Kelly did.

'There's at least a page full,' said Constable Meek, preparing to rip it from the roll.

'There's more coming,' said Kelly.

And there was.

And more.

'That's fifteen pages' worth,' said Constable Meek, fourteen pages later.

'There's more coming.'

And there was.

And more.

'Jumping Jesus on a rope. Give me joy and give me hope,' went Constable Ronald Meek, son of the famous Nigel and brother to the pirate Black Jake Meek (who always wore a wooden leg but never owned a parrot). 'There's fifty pages, no sixty, no maybe seventy. Half of the population of London seem to have all gone missing.'

Kelly tore off the paper. 'It's hundreds,' she said. 'But not thousands. But it's far too many people. This isn't good. It isn't.'

'It's The Rapture,' said the suddenly enlightened Constable Meek. 'The good are being carried off to Glory. I must tell the chief constable.'

'Don't do that,' said Kelly.

'But I must. If I am to be lifted bodily into Heaven, he'll need to call in a replacement for me from the Met. There's a lot of paperwork involved. He'll want to get started at once.'

'It isn't The Rapture,' said Kelly, who, truth to tell, was almost beginning to wonder. 'And I wouldn't go bothering the chief constable with it. Well, not at least until I've left the building.'

'Oh must you go?' asked Constable Meek. 'I was hoping to ask you out to lunch. There's this restaurant I know, the Laughing Sprout. You are a vegetarian, aren't you?'

Kelly smiled and nodded. 'However did you guess?' she asked.

'Call it intuition,' said the unintuitive constable.

'Could you just give me half an hour alone with this computer first?' asked Kelly. 'Before you take me out to lunch.'

'Oh yes,' said Constable Meek. 'Half an hour. I'll change out of my cravat. I'll see you in half an hour.'

Half an hour later the constable returned, but Kelly Anna Sirjan had, like Elvis, left the building.

Kelly sat once more in the saloon bar of the Flying Swan. Before her on the table was the stack of computer printouts, torn into page-sized portions. Beside this lay something most intriguing. It was another printout, but this one came in the form of a map of Greater London. Kelly had programmed the computer to print out this map, dotting the last known addresses of the listed missing persons, along with the dates of their disappearances. The map made for interesting viewing.

Most of the disappearances appeared to have occurred during the last fourteen days. And there was a definite pattern. There were no dots in Brentford, which meant that Dr Druid had not as yet made a report to the police. But a trail of dots led directly to the borough. It was one of eight such trails. They spread over the map like the legs of some titanic spider, the body of which was splattered black with dots. And appeared to cover most of an urban conurbation known as Mute Corp Keynes.

'Mute Corp Keynes,' said Kelly to no-one but herself. 'The new town Utopia built in 2002 by Remington Mute the computer billion-aire. "The town of tomorrow, today", if I recall the advertising slogan correctly, and I do. Turned out to be not so much a Utopia as a dystopia, a regular ghetto. He never invested in any more new towns after that. Significant? Perhaps.'

'Hello,' said the voice of Derek. 'Fancy seeing you here.'

'Thank God you've arrived,' said Kelly.

'Oh,' said Derek. 'Is it something important?'

'I'll say it is. Take a look at this.'

Derek looked. 'You're pointing to your stomach,' he said.

'I am,' said Kelly. 'It's empty and you're just in time to buy me lunch. They've got a special up on the blackboard. A surf and turf. I'll have that and I'll have a glass of red wine too.'

Derek smiled somewhat thinly and took himself off to the bar counter.

'Barman,' he was heard to call. 'Barman, excuse me *please*.'

Somewhat later, Kelly pushed away her empty plate and dabbed at her Cupid's bow with an oversized red gingham napkin. 'That hit the spot,' she said, smiling.

Derek had just watched her licking clean the plate. 'You certainly enjoy your food,' said he, in what is known as a 'guarded fashion'.

'I have two stomachs,' said Kelly. 'My dinner stomach and my pudding stomach. My pudding stomach's still empty.'

'I really couldn't face another wait at the bar,' said Derek. 'That old boy nearly had me insulting the barman again. It was a close-run thing.'

'I'll just have a Mars bar later then. How are your investigations going?'

'What investigations?' Derek asked.

'Into the missing patients.'

'I told you I was dropping that. And that sample I took from the bed in the ward turned out to be KY jelly. If it turns out that Dr Druid's butchered the patients, I'll cover the trial. I'm doing an article on the floral clock today.'

'You don't think that the bus crash and the vanishing patients might merit a bit more column space?'

'Mr Shields is dealing with that himself.' Derek now whispered. 'A little bird told me that the police raided his office last night. They confiscated all that computer equipment.'

Kelly teased at her golden hair. 'Why would the police raid his office?'

'I've no idea. But that's a news story in itself. But somehow I don't

70

think he'll let me write it up. What are you doing today? What are all these computer printouts?'

'Just research. What do you know about Mute Corp Keynes?'

'It's a dump,' said Derek. 'An urban wasteland. Crime City UK. I've got an aunty who lives there. She doesn't dare venture out at night without wearing full body armour. It's the only town in England where you can put up a sign on your house that says INTRUDERS WILL BE MET BY ARMED RESPONSE and do it legally. It's a police no-go zone. It's . . .'

'Not a very nice place, by the sound of it.'

'I wouldn't know,' said Derek. 'I've never been there.'

'Your aunty's going to get a real surprise when you turn up outside her door this afternoon then.'

'What?' said Derek.

They actually had a border post with barbed-wire fences and all. A guard with a clipboard waved down Derek's car. His car was a Ford Fiesta. It was a collector's piece.

'Wind down your window sir and don't make any sudden moves,' said the border guard, displaying an impressive array of armaments.

Derek wound his window down in a slow and easy manner.

'Anything to declare?' asked the border guard. He was a very big border guard, he bulged out of his uniform. 'Have you anything to declare?'

Derek knew better than to offer an Oscar Wilde. 'Nothing to declare,' he said. 'We're just visiting my aunty.'

The border guard looked in at Derek. 'You're not a very big man, are you?' he said.

'I'm big enough,' said Derek.

'I'll put you down as one-way visitors,' said the border guard. 'It will save me the paperwork later.'

'I'll only be an hour,' said Derek.

'Oh I see,' said the border guard. 'Well please excuse me, sir. I had no idea that you were a superhero. It's always hard to tell.'

'I'm a newspaper reporter,' said Derek.

'Aha,' said the border guard. 'Mild-mannered reporter for the *Daily Planet*. Welcome to Mute Corp Keynes, Mr Kent.'

71

'Can I just go through now, please?'

The border guard leaned in at the car window. 'Listen,' said he. 'I'm being serious now. This isn't a good place to be. People go missing here. Lots of people. If you go missing we have no jurisdiction to come in searching for you.'

'Damn this,' said Derek. 'Things are really *that bad* here, then, are they?'

'They're worse,' said the border guard. 'They keep it out of the papers because it looks bad for the Government. Mr Doveston wouldn't look quite so good if the public knew about this place. It's like a black hole of crime. I'm not messing with you. Turn back now. Take the young lady far away from here. They're animals in there, there's no telling what they'd do to her. Well actually there is.'

'We're going back,' said Derek.

'We're not,' said Kelly.

'Don't be absurd. I'm not taking you in there.'

'I'm not afraid.'

'Well I hate to admit it, but I am.'

'Then I'll go in alone.'

'Why?' asked Derek. 'You don't even know my aunty.'

'This is nothing to do with your aunty, Derek. This is something big. And if there is one little ounce of manhood inside you, you'll come in with me. I'll go in alone, if you don't.'

'It's your funeral,' said the border guard. 'If they ever find your body, that is.'

'Back,' said Derek.

'Forward,' said Kelly.

Forward apparently had it.

Derek drove slowly through the deserted streets.

'I can't believe this place,' he said. 'I mean this is South London. I know South London can be a bit rough, but this is over the top. Look at it, burnt-out shops, burnt-out cars, the only buildings standing are barred up like fortresses. This can't be real. It can't be.'

'There is something very very wrong about this place,' said Kelly.

'Yes, I can see that plainly enough.'

'But can you feel it?'

'I feel very very afraid. I really need the toilet, but I think I'll wait until I get home. *If* I get home at all.'

'Pull up here,' said Kelly.

'Here? Why here?'

'Because there's a stinger strung out across the road ahead, under all that debris. You don't really want to drive over it.'

'Oh God,' said Derek. 'I never noticed.'

'You weren't intended to.'

'Let's turn around and get out of this asylum. Before some sniper picks us off or we drive into a minefield.'

'Where does your aunty live?' Kelly asked.

'I really can't imagine that she's living any more.'

'Well, just in case. Where does she live?'

Derek checked his London A–Z and noticed for the first time the slim red line that ran around the not-so-new town known as Mute Corp Keynes. 'Second on the left, just past the burnt-out church.'

'Next to the burnt-out pub?'

'No past that. Opposite the burnt-out Citizens Advice Bureau.'

'You'd better drive on the pavement to avoid the stinger.'

Derek drove on the pavement.

His aunty's house was number twenty-two. The bungalow with the gun turret on the roof. The moat, the razor wire and the sign that warned of killer canines on the loose at night. Unlike the yard of the Brentford Tour Company, this was no idle warning.

Kelly observed the martial premises. 'Your aunty seems to have adapted well to the changing of the times,' said she.

'She was always pretty tough,' said Derek. 'She was in the SAS, only woman to ever make it to major. There's a lot of military in my family. I think I've always been a bit of a disappointment to them.'

'I really can't imagine why,' said Kelly Anna Sirjan.

There was a bell push on the iron gate that led into the moated compound. The sign above said KNOCK DOWN GINGER ON THIS BELL AND KNOW THE JOY A BULLET BRINGS.

'Perhaps you'd care to ring,' said Derek.

73

'We are being laser-scanned,' said Kelly. 'I've a securiscan meter in my shoulder bag, I can feel it vibrating.'

'What?' went Derek.

'You'd better press the button. She doesn't know me.'

'Securiscan meter in your shoulder bag? I don't understand.'

'Just push the button please. We are also being scanned from across the street. I think we are about to be shot at.'

'Oh God, oh damn, oh me oh my,' said Derek, pushing the bell button.

Kelly pushed Derek suddenly aside. The deathly rattle of machine-gun fire came swiftly to her ears. Bullets ripped along the ground. And there was an explosion.

'Oh God!' screamed Derek, covering his head. 'We're going to die! We're going to die!'

Smoke and explosions, machine-gun fire mayhem and approaching death with no salvation? Off into the blackness of forever. Not to be borne up to The Rapture. Derek cowered and shivered and uttered certain prayers.

The lock on the gate clicked open. Kelly's hand reached out to Derek.

'Come with me, if you want to live,' she said.

6

Derek's Aunty Uzi (named after a product that cleans up in its own particular way) was what you would call a fine-looking woman. At least to her face, anyway. She stood all of six feet four in her holistic Doveston footwear, which she'd customized with a nice line of studs. For those who love a tattoo, her buttocks were the place to be. And for those who favour a duelling scar, her forehead was the business.

'On your feet, soldier,' said Derek's aunty. 'Falling asleep on parade, is it?'

Derek fussed and fretted. He was curled up upon a doormat that had long worn out its welcome, in a hallway where the angels feared to tread. Outside the gunfire was sporadic, with only the occasional bullet ricocheting from the armoured porch or bouncing off the titanium steel of the window boxes.

'He was always a cringing wimp,' said Derek's aunty to Kelly. 'Living the high life with the toffs in Brentford has softened him up even more.'

'People were shooting at us.' Derek remained in the foetal position, which seemed to suit him just fine. 'This is London in the twenty-first century. I knew things were grim here. But this . . .'

Derek's aunty rolled her eyes at Kelly. 'Would you care for a cup of tea, my dear?' she asked.

'Do you have anything stronger?'

'I can put two tea bags in your cup.'

'That should hit the spot.'

'Well, we girls will just leave you to your cringing, Derek. OK?'

Derek made silly whimpering sounds. Aunty Uzi led Kelly away into the kitchenette. 'They weren't even shooting to kill,' she said. 'They were just having a bit of fun.'

Kelly looked all around and about the kitchenette. It was grim as kitchenettes go, but kitchenettes always are.

A pokey thing is a kitchenette and this particular one was made all the more pokey due to the stacks of ammunition boxes and the grenade launchers which leaned against the cooker, beside the Mute Corp wonder mop and the Mute Corp sweeper.

'Is your water filtered?' Kelly asked.

'Oh you're good,' said Aunty Uzi. 'Very good.'

Kelly's hand moved up to her hair, but then moved down again. 'Good?' she said. 'Whatever do you mean?'

'Cool,' said Aunty Uzi. 'Very cool.'

'I try not to panic. Panic costs lives. Lost lives lose large battles.'

'You were in the marines.'

'I did my national service.'

Derek's aunty boiled up water and did what you have to do with it to make two cups of tea. 'Derek dodged his national service,' she said, stirring the tea with a fourteen-inch commando knife.

'I didn't know you could dodge national service,' said Kelly.

'Don't ever make the mistake of trusting Derek. He's a man who will always let you down.'

'I heard that,' called Derek from the hall.

Aunty Uzi handed Kelly a cup of something loosely resembling tea. 'So,' she said. 'Kelly Anna Sirjan, aged twenty-two, no convictions, no breaches of the civil code. Three degrees and a 12th Dan Master of Dimac. What's a lady like you doing hanging around with a jerk like my nephew?'

Kelly shrugged. 'I'm on attachment to the *Brentford Mercury*. He's showing me around.'

'Still cool,' said Aunty Uzi. 'You're not going to ask me how I know all about you.'

'You securiscanned us as we stood at your gate. That's standard procedure in a high-risk area.'

76

'We'll let that one pass for now, then.' Aunty Uzi slurped at the tea. 'This tastes foul,' she said. 'But there's more to you than meets the eye. And what meets the eye has been carefully put together.'

'You haven't asked us why we're here,' said Kelly. 'I'm sure you're not under the mistaken belief that Derek felt a sudden pressing need to visit his aunty.'

Aunty Uzi grinned, exposing ranks of steel teeth. 'I assume that he brought you here at *your* request. You can ask me what it is you wish to know. You never know, I might even tell you.'

Kelly leaned upon the cooker. It was a Mute Corp Supercook, the 3000 series, looking a little the worse for wear.

'Tell me this,' she said. 'Why do you stay in this place?'

'This is Mute Corp Keynes. The town of the future, today.'

Kelly made that face that says 'Yeah right'.

'I bought this place in two-double-o-five,' said Derek's Aunty Uzi. 'My husband Alf and I were amongst the very first to move in. It was all here at a price we could afford. Fully integrated living accommodation. Everything online. State of the art. High tech, low cost. It was all going to be up-and-coming young professional. The dream town UK.'

'So what went wrong?' Kelly asked.

'Well, it was all bullshit, wasn't it? Nothing ever worked properly. The whole thing had been done on the cheap and we'd all signed up for our low cost twenty-year non-transferable mortgages. Folk couldn't sell up, so they moved away and sublet their houses. That wasn't strictly legal and the folk they'd sublet their houses to soon realized that they could get away without paying the rent. Neighbour-hoods can go down pretty quickly. By twenty-ten this place was already a bad place to walk around at night. Now it's a bad place, period.'

'And your husband?'

'One day he went out and never came back. It happens.'

'I'm sorry,' said Kelly.

'Me too,' said Derek's aunty.

And the two of them slurped tea.

'This really *is* disgusting tea,' said Kelly.

'Yeah, let's drink some Scotch instead and you can tell me what it is you want to know.'

They now sat in the front sitter. Although the sunlight was joyous without, it didn't venture much within. The windows were shuttered by bulletproof steel. The table lights had ultraviolet bulbs. The glow they cast was of that order which is called crepuscular. Connoisseurs of naked-lady lighting wouldn't even have given it one out of ten. In a near corner, a long-defunct Mute Corp 3000 home computer, built into the fabric of the room, gathered dust and made a house for spiders.

Derek, arisen from his foetal position, sipped at Scotch. Aunty Uzi tossed hers back. Kelly merely turned her glass between her elegant fingers.

'So,' said Derek's aunty. 'What exactly *do* you want to know?'

'Search me,' said Derek. 'I didn't even want to come.'

Kelly took from her shoulder bag the printout map and placed it before her upon an occasional table. Which, had it suddenly been granted the gift of sentience, would have become aware that at last and quite unexpectedly, its occasion had finally arrived.

'Mysterious disappearances,' said Kelly. 'People vanishing without trace. This map shows the locations of those who have done so during the last two weeks. I think you'll find that it speaks for itself.'

Derek lifted the map from the table and held it up to his ear.

'If he says it,' said Derek's aunty, 'feel free to employ your Dimac. Smack him right in the balls if you wish.'

Derek replaced the map upon the table. 'I wasn't going to say anything,' he said.

Aunty Uzi took the map and gave it some perusal. 'I can't say that this fills me with too much surprise,' she said. 'Going missing is what people do around here.'

'Hang about,' said Derek. 'Let's have a look at that map.'

'Oooh,' said his aunty. 'A burst of sudden interest.'

'Where did you get this?' Derek asked, thumbing the map.

'At the police station,' said Kelly. 'I made enquiries. The number of people who have vanished recently in London is way beyond the norm. I felt that it was worth investigating.'

'Have you got a list of these people's names?' asked Aunty Uzi.

Kelly produced the list from her bag. 'It's a very big list,' she said.

Aunty Uzi leafed through pages. 'And it's a very inaccurate one,' she said. 'Most of the people listed as living round here moved away years ago. And, good God. *I'm* on here. According to this list *I* vanished without trace last Tuesday.'

'Oh,' said Kelly. 'I wasn't expecting *that*.'

Aunty Uzi looked at her. 'You said that as if you *were* expecting something else.'

'This list was compiled by the national crime computer. I expected at least that would be accurate.'

'Good,' said Aunty Uzi. 'She is *very* good this woman of yours.'

'She's no woman of mine,' said Derek. 'No thank *you* very much.'

'Would you care to tell me what you *really* are, my dear?' asked Aunty Uzi. 'Whom you're *really* working for.'

'I'm just a student,' said Kelly. 'But I think that you'll agree that there's something very suspicious going on.'

'No,' said Derek. 'In fact, quite the contrary. My aunty *isn't* missing. The folk listed here as missing, *aren't* missing. They've just moved away. There's no mystery. Nothing suspicious. It's all a computer error.'

Aunty Uzi nodded. 'On this occasion,' she said, 'I am forced to agree with my idiot nephew. It's just a glitch. And when I speak of glitches, I speak of what I know. The computers in this district all crashed years ago. It's a dead zone around here when it comes to computer technology. The black hole of cyberspace. You're on a wrong'n, Kelly Anna Sirjan. You've been wasting your time.'

Kelly's hand was in her hair and strands were being twisted. 'I think we'd better be going,' she said.

'I'm pleased to hear that,' said Derek.

The border guard looked pleased to see them. He was smiling broadly as they came in his direction.

'No car?' he asked. 'Whatever happened to your lovely Ford Fiesta?'

Derek huffed and puffed the way that people do huff and puff, when they've been running hard and running very fast. 'They nicked my bloody car,' he huffed and puffed. 'That car was a collector's item.'

'That would appear to be correct,' said the border guard. 'It's definitely now an item in somebody's collection.'

Derek pulled out his mobile phone and huffed and puffed and pushed buttons.

'You won't get a signal,' said the border guard. 'You just don't around here. Sorry.'

'It's all too much,' and Derek flung himself down on the ground and drummed his fists in the dust.

'He must be a real disappointment to you,' said the border guard to Kelly, who stood looking very cool. Not huffing or puffing at all.

'I'm sure that he must have a use,' said Kelly. 'But so far I haven't found it.'

'Still,' said the border guard. 'Let's look on the bright side. It's a lovely day and the two of you are still alive. Rejoice and be happy, that's my motto. And never eat cheese after midnight.'

It was nearly midnight when the minicab dropped Kelly and Derek off in Brentford High Street. Well, it's a long and complicated route back from Mute Corp Keynes when you haven't got a car and you have to rely on public transport and there aren't any trains any more.

'Brilliant,' said Derek. 'What a brilliant day. I could have been writing an article about the floral clock. But no, I let you talk me into visiting Hell Town UK. I get shot at. I get my precious car stolen. I am mocked and ridiculed and then I have to pay your fares all the way back to Chiswick. And then your taxi fare back here. I don't mean any offence by this, but I truly wish to God I'd never met you.'

'I'd like you to do something for me,' said Kelly.

'What? You have to be kidding.'

'Look,' said Kelly. 'I'm very sorry about the way the day has worked out for you. But whatever your aunty says and whatever you think, there is something very strange going on. It could prove to be something that will make a name for you as an investigative journalist.'

'No thanks,' said Derek. 'I'll pass.'

'All right, then do this one thing for me and I promise I'll never bother you again. In fact I promise I won't even see you again. I'll keep well away from you for the rest of the time I'm here in Brentford.'

'Well,' said Derek thoughtfully. 'Does this one thing involve any danger to myself?'

'None whatsoever,' said Kelly.

'All right. Tell me what it is and I'll think about it.'

'I want you to take me home with you.'

'What?' said Derek.

'To your house.'

Derek gave Kelly a long hard look. 'Why?' he asked. 'It's not to have sex with me, is it? Only I've had a really rough day, I don't think I'm up to it. Although, well, what the heck. I'll give it a go.'

Kelly shook her golden head. 'I don't want to have sex with you,' she said. 'I just want to use your home computer. You do have a home computer, don't you?'

'Of course I do, everyone does. Well, perhaps not everyone in Brentford. But I do.'

'Well all I want is to use it for a while.'

'Why?' asked Derek. 'Don't you have your own?'

'Not with me. I have my palmtop, but that won't do. I want to use one that is locked into a landline.'

'Why?' Derek asked once more. But for a different reason this second time.

'It's just a theory. Something to do with your aunty describing Mute Corp Keynes as the black hole of cyberspace and the fact that mobile phones don't work there.'

'All right,' said Derek. 'But if you're not going to have sex with me . . .'

'Derek, I'm never going to have sex with you.'

'All right. Then you will really have to promise that you will never see or speak to me again. Women like you are nothing but trouble.'

'I shall ignore that remark,' said Kelly. 'Take me to your house.'

Derek lived with his mother. Strangely this fact didn't surprise Kelly one little bit. Derek insisted upon a lot of creeping on tiptoe through the house and up the stairs to his room. It's a funny thing about men who live with their mothers, but they are always really proud to show off their rooms to young women. And they are really surprised when the young women they're showing their rooms so proudly to, stare about with their jaws hung slack, then turn upon their heels and take their leave at the hurry-up.

'Wallah,' said Derek when he and Kelly were in his room, the door was shut and all the lights were on. 'My private domain. My holy of holies. My inner sanctum. All pretty fab, isn't it?'

Kelly stared about the room and Kelly's jaw hung slack.

'I think,' said Kelly, her jaw now moving again. 'I think that you possess a very great many computer games.'

'Yes,' said Derek, his head nod-nod-nodding. 'Over ten thousand. A lifetime's collection. They date back to the 1970s. I'm really an Atari man. I've got an early Atari 2600 Video Computer System and the '86 compact version.'

'You haven't got an Odyssey have you?' Kelly asked.

Derek was taken slightly aback by Kelly's question but carried on.

'Sure. I've got the Magnavox Odyssey, an absolute classic. It was innovative, first home game system they released. But the Odyssey II . . .'

'49-key pressure-sensitive keyboard, 1978. Pure genius.'

Derek looked oddly at Kelly. 'They just don't compare with the Atari in my eyes. I've got the 5200 too.'

'Who, Pam*? What about Candy and Colleen, did you ever manage to get your sweaty mitts on those two lovely ladies?'

'Well the 5200, Pam, is really just a stripped-down Atari 400, Candy, solely for game-playing. As for Colleen, the Atari 800, of course she's here, but she was always too expensive to take out.'

'Boxed and stored?'

'Dust-free storage environment along with the Atari 7800. Only the best for my girls. So what do you think?'

Kelly stared at Derek.

And Derek stared right back.

'I think it's incredible,' said Kelly. 'I mean, well, I've never seen a collection like this before. I'm absolutely knocked out. You don't by any chance have ADVENTURE?'

'Warren Robinette, Atari 2600 VCS, 1979.'

* For those who don't know, Atari had female codenames for their games systems.

'You mean Warren 'Easter Egg'⋆ Robinette, he was the catalyst for all the cheats and hidden stuff. He was the one who got the ball rolling back in '79.'

'Well, that was Atari really. It was their policy that prevented the designers from getting any sort of recognition in the game or in the packaging. The designers were bound to rebel.'

'But moving an invisible "dot" to above the catacombs with the bridge and all the rest. Trust a twelve-year-old to find that one out.'

'Robinette thought he'd really get busted for that, but the gamers loved it. Atari couldn't help but add hidden features in nearly all its new games from then on. He was the start of the Easter Egg phenomena.'

Kelly whistled. Women don't generally whistle as a rule. Some do, when they're really impressed. Or when you do that special thing to them. And most women will only let you do that special thing to them once, anyway.

Kelly whistled again. 'I've surely misjudged you, Derek,' she said. 'You may be a spineless wimp, no offence meant . . .'

'None taken, I assure you.'

'But I never had you down as collector of twentieth-century console games.'

'You approve then?'

'God yes.'

Derek grinned. 'Brilliant,' he said.

'Do you have CANYON BOMBER, Atari 2600 VS, 1978?'

Derek grinned again and pulled a cartridge from his shelf. 'Of course I do,' he said.

Kelly said, 'Can I touch?'

'Certainly you can.' Derek passed the precious thing in her direction. And Kelly ran a finger lovingly across it.

'But this must be worth a fortune. It's a compilation of those arcade coin-operated machine classics CANYON BOMBER and DEPTH CHARGE. Now that was a marriage made in silicon heaven.'

'Yes, yes,' said Derek. 'I got it in a car boot sale.'

'No, you never did.'

⋆ Easter Egg = hidden undocumented features in a video computer game.

'You can play me at it, if you want. Can you play?'

'Can *I* play? I can play them all. I spent my first ever wage packet at the Museum of Video Games in Penge. Ten hours on KABOOM!'

'Oh yeah, I've got that here somewhere. Larry Kaplan game . . . 1981.'

'Based on AVALANCHE in the arcade. Totally addictive, you could be there for ever if allowed. Kind of like TETRIS in that respect.'

'I know where you're coming from, I assure you,' said Derek.

'Money well spent. Although my mum thought I should have given her some of my wages. Mothers eh? What do they know about video games?'

'Damn all,' said Derek. 'My mum thinks they're stupid.'

'Because she's never played NIGHT DRIVER.'

'*You've* played NIGHT DRIVER.'

'Rob Fulop, 1979, Atari 2600 VCS. Only 2K of programming you know.'

'Also famously featured in the video-arcade sequence in George A. Romero's *Dawn of the Dead*, of the very same year.'

'Like I didn't know. I snapped that one up pretty damn quick. I got paid the second week too. And the third. My mum never got any room and board though. Eventually she said that I'd have to go out and make my own way in the world. As I had enough qualifications, I went off to uni. Studied computer tech.'

'Don't tell me what's coming. You got access to their games archive.'

'Downloaded the lot into my PC. I've got 700 games on CD.'

'I'll bet you haven't got this,' said Derek. And he did some furtive lookings both ways before dropping down to his knees.

'What are you doing?' Kelly asked.

'You'll have to stand back. I have to lift the carpet.'

Kelly stared. 'Derek,' she said. 'You appear to have a floorboard with a combination lock on it.'

'So would you,' said Derek. 'If you had what I've got.'

'Oh no,' said Kelly. 'Don't tell me you have a copy of . . .'

'I have,' said Derek, twiddling the combination.

'You don't have. I don't believe it.'

Derek lifted the floorboard and brought out a metal box. He fished into his shirt and displayed the key that he wore on a chain around his neck.

And then he opened the box with it.

'Behold,' said Derek. 'IMPOSSIBLE MISSION.'

Kelly's eyes widened. 'No,' she said. 'No, I thought that this was just a myth. No.'

'Yes,' said Derek. 'Yes indeed.'

'Oh my God,' said Kelly. 'But this is the Holy Grail that game-collectors dream about finding. What system does it run on?'

'It's for the Atari 7800,' said Derek. 'And it's in its original case, as you can see. And I have the game guide. And I know where the Easter Eggs are.'

'Is it the early or the late release version?' asked Kelly.

'It's an early one,' Derek said confidently.

'And have you reached the deadlock point?'

'Deadlock point?' said Derek. 'Are you kidding?'

'You mean you *have*? What happens?'

'No,' said Derek. 'I mean I *haven't*. I haven't played this. This isn't for playing. It's for owning. It's for, dare I say this? Yes I dare. This is for gloating over. I wouldn't play this game.'

'But,' Kelly stared at the original case. 'What if it doesn't work?'

'It would work,' said Derek. 'I paid a fortune for it. It would work OK. But it's too precious a thing to actually play. That would be like sacrilege somehow.'

Kelly stared now at Derek. 'You paid a fortune for it,' she said. 'And you've never dared to play it.'

'I wouldn't dare,' said Derek. 'What if I broke it, before I got to the deadlock point?'

'But what if it doesn't work? What if it doesn't run? What if it's a fake? Or a later version without the deadlock point?'

Derek nodded slowly. 'My thoughts entirely,' he said. 'Which is one of the reasons I've never played it. What if it *is* a fake? I have faith in it. The way Christians have faith in Christ. But what if there was suddenly some proof available, some unarguable proof that Christ didn't exist? That he never existed? And you could give this proof to a Christian, all packaged up in an original case like this one. What would you, as a Christian, do? Would you open the case? Or

85

would you refuse to open it and go on believing in Christ?'

'I'd open the case,' said Kelly.

'But what if you didn't want the existence of Christ to be disproved? What if you wanted Christ to exist?'

'Hm,' said Kelly. 'If I wanted it more than anything else in the world, then I suppose that I wouldn't open the case, original or not.'

'Exactly,' said Derek. 'Which is why I'll never play this game. I own it. It's a collector's Holy Grail. I believe in it totally. As long as I never slot it into the console, then it remains the centrepiece of my collection and I can believe in it totally.'

'Let's play it,' said Kelly.

'No way!' said Derek. 'No way at all.'

'All right,' said Kelly. 'You go out of the room for half an hour and I'll play it.'

'No way *at all*!'

'Ah,' said Kelly. 'But I might *not* play it. I might just look at it.'

'You'd play it,' said Derek.

'But I wouldn't tell you. I won't tell you whether I did play it or whether I didn't. Whether it works or whether it doesn't. I promise I won't tell you anything.'

'No,' said Derek. 'What if you played it and you broke it?'

'You'd never know. You'll never play it and I'll never tell you, it will be exactly the same for you as before.'

'Oh no,' said Derek. 'Because you'll know and I'll know you know.'

'I'll give you money,' said Kelly.

'No,' said Derek.

Kelly chewed upon her Cupid's bow. 'I'll er . . .'

'Er?' said Derek.

'I'll give you a blow job,' said Kelly.

'You'll what?'

'I will,' said Kelly. 'If you let me play.'

Derek dithered, but it did have to be said, although only to himself and only to himself when alone in his room, that Derek had never actually had a blow job.

'Well . . .' said Derek.

'You'll have to wear a condom,' said Kelly. 'But I *will* give you a blow job.'

'Right here and now?'

'Afterwards,' said Kelly. 'After I've played the game.'

'And what if it doesn't work?'

Kelly looked at Derek. It would be so easy. And so so cruel.

'Whether it works or not,' she said.

Derek looked at Kelly. Here she was, one of the most beautiful women he had ever seen in his life. And she was here in his bed-room and she was prepared to give him a blow job, if he let her play one of his video games. This was heaven, wasn't it? This was joy, joy, happy joy.

Happy Happy Joy.

But.

Damn it. *But.*

But this was *his* game. This was his Holy Grail of games and *this* game, *owning this game*, owning the very concept of *owning this game*, this was his. It was something of value. Something that mattered, something that he cared about. Not everyone could understand a principle like that. Most men would just say, 'Go for the blow job, are you mad?' But collecting games was Derek's life. And things that mattered, things that had value, that deserved to be respected, that deserved respect, you didn't mess with things like that, you didn't devalue them. Not if you really cared. You didn't sell them out.

Derek looked once more upon Kelly. That body, those breasts, that face, that mouth.

'No,' said Derek, shaking his head. 'I won't do it. No.'

Kelly looked at Derek, and then she slowly smiled. 'Derek,' she said. 'You have just passed up the blow job of a lifetime.'

Derek sadly nodded his head. 'Yes, I know,' he said.

'But,' said Kelly. 'In doing so, you have made a friend for life.' And she put out her hand to Derek. And Derek shook that hand.

Derek didn't know quite why he shook it. Well, perhaps he did, but he smiled with some relief as he shook it, and shook it firmly, did he.

So to speak.

'Well,' said Derek, when all the shaking was done. 'That was very stressful. And I'm glad it's over. Would you, er, care for a game of PONG?'

'Oh God yes!' said Kelly.

'Then be prepared to have your arse most well and truly kicked.'

'Boy, by the time I'm finished with you, you won't be able to sit on yours for a week.'

'You reckon?'

'I reckon.'

'Let's play.'

7

As Kelly didn't get back to her digs until after five in the morning, she lay rather longer in bed than normally she would have done.

She didn't raise her blondie head until half past ten, which didn't give her much time to get showered and dressed and breakfasted before she met up with Derek at eleven.

She had arranged to meet him in the saloon bar of a Brentford pub called the Shrunken Head.

Starting off the day in a pub might not have seemed to many people the right and proper thing to do. But then many people wouldn't have known, as Derek did, and as Derek told Kelly, that in the corner of the saloon bar of the Shrunken Head there was an original Space Invaders machine in fully working order.

And, as they'd come up even in the previous night's playing of PONG, a decider would have to be played. So why not play it out upon this very machine?

'Why indeed not?' Kelly had said.

Kelly's breakfast plate was puce, as was the tablecloth it sat upon. Kelly's landlady, Mrs Gormenghast (daughter of the remarkable Zed and sister to Zardoz, the ornamental hermit, who lived all alone in a tree), stoked up the fire in the front sitter, where Kelly sat late-breakfasting. Mrs Gormenghast wore a pucely hued jumpsuit of a type which has happily gone the way of the split-knee loon pant and the Beatle wig. Not to mention the stylophone.

As if anybody would.

Kelly wore a simple summer frock of turquoise blue. It had no buttons to loosen, which given the fire's heat and all the closed windows, didn't help in the ever-warming atmosphere.

'Is that fire really necessary?' Kelly asked, as she mopped at her brow with a puce napkin.

'It keeps the Devil out,' said Mrs Gormenghast. 'Always keep a fire in your hearth and you'll never have to fear the Devil. My late husband used to say that. He knew what he was talking about.'

'Was he a preacher man?' Kelly asked.

'No, he was a coalman.'

'How do you get your fried eggs so puce?' Kelly asked.

'It's an old Indian trick, taught to me by an old Indian woman trickster. Puce is the colour of at-oneness. Did you know that if you take every single colour there is, about an ounce of each and mix them all together in a big pot, a very big pot obviously, the end result will be puce. Explain that if you will.'

'I can't,' said Kelly. 'But I suppose that . . .'

'You can split light with a prism, can't you?' asked Mrs Gormenghast.

'As far as I know,' said Kelly.

'Invisible light, it contains all the colours of the rainbow.'

Kelly nodded.

'So how come, if you mix all colours together in a pot they don't end up as an invisible transparent liquid?'

'Well . . .' said Kelly.

'Yes, that's easy for you to say. Well, well, I'll tell you why, well. Because prisms don't tell all of the truth. Nothing tells all of the truth. Nothing and nobody. The ultimate colour of the universe is puce. Mrs Charker down the road is of the mistaken belief that it is pink. Naturally, I respect her opinions, even if I know they are wrong.'

'Ah,' said Kelly. 'That would be Mrs Minky Charker, wife of Big Bob Charker who was in the bus crash.'

'That's her,' said Mrs Gormenghast. 'Her husband was carried off in The Rapture, I've heard. Not that it makes any sense to me, I've been keeping the Devil out of my fireplace and painting my house puce for years. If The Rapture's on the go, I should have been amongst the first of the blessed to be carried off to glory.'

'Perhaps it's happening in shifts,' said Kelly.

'Probably,' said Mrs G. 'God knows his own business best. The world can all go to pot at a moment's notice, my late husband used to say, but as long as you're all stocked up in nutty slack, you'll always have a welcome in your hearth. That man was a saint. It was a shame the way he met his end.'

Kelly didn't ask.

'Don't ask,' said Mrs Gormenghast. 'By the way, did you hear what happened to that nice Dr Druid at the cottage hospital, last night?'

'No,' said Kelly. 'What?'

'Raptured,' said Mrs Gormenghast. 'One moment he was giving an internal examination to a young woman suffering from verrucas, the next up and gone. I'm going to keep this fire well stoked today. I don't want the Antichrist coming down my chimney. And I shall be keeping this jumpsuit on indefinitely now. I want to look my best when my turn to be Raptured comes.'

'Dr Druid too?' said Derek. 'You really have to be joking.'

He was, as now was Kelly, in the saloon bar of the Shrunken Head. Derek had been there since half past ten, practising on the Space Invaders machine. He was chums with the barman. The barman had let him in early.

'I'm not joking,' said Kelly. 'I just heard. Dr Druid's vanished too. A young woman with verrucas saw it happen.'

Derek scratched at his head. 'There *is* something strange going on, isn't there?' he said.

'I really think there is,' said Kelly.

Derek now scratched at his chin. 'All right,' he said. 'I am supposed to be covering the annual over-eighties backwards walk between Kew and Richmond along the Thames towpath today. But I think it's a foregone conclusion, that old sod who had me with the Runese the night before last always wins it. I suggest we go to the cottage hospital and follow this thing up.'

'I think that's exactly what we shouldn't do,' said Kelly. 'I don't think we should go anywhere near the cottage hospital.'

'Why not?'

'It's just a theory.'

'I thought we were friends now. Tell me.'

'All right,' said Kelly. 'People are vanishing. Literally disappearing. The first one we know of is this Malkuth off the bus, after him go Periwig Tombs, Big Bob Charker and Malkuth's mum, off the bus, then goes Dr Druid. One after another. Like a disease which is being passed from one person to another, perhaps.'

'There's no disease that makes people vanish. Get real.'

'No disease that we know of, perhaps.'

'No disease. Period.'

'Period,' said Kelly. 'Your aunty said that. People are vanishing and it's all on the police computer. It all leads to Mute Corp Keynes. The black hole of cyberspace. This is somehow related to the country's computer system.'

'I can't imagine by what logic you can possibly draw that conclusion.'

'That is because you are a man, Derek, and I am a woman.'

'That is no argument at all. Are you calling this woman's intuition?'

'Do you have any theories?'

'The Rapture?' said Derek.

'I thought not. Let's go to your house. I only need about half an hour on your home computer.'

'Er, no,' said Derek. 'My mum will be up. She doesn't like me bringing ladies into my room.'

Kelly gave Derek one of *those* looks.

'We could use the computer at the *Brentford Mercury*.'

'I thought it wasn't unpacked. And I think you'll find it's now at the police station.'

'You heard about that, did you? Not much slips by you. But I have my own workstation. I'm not a Luddite like Mr Shields.'

'Then shall we go?'

Derek glanced towards the Space Invaders machine. 'There is that matter of the deciding game,' he said.

'Best out of three. But then we definitely go.'

★

Derek had his head down as they walked along the High Street. He'd pushed Kelly into best out of seven, but she still just kept on winning.

It was another joyous day. The sun swelled high in the clear blue sky. Birdies called and twittered. There was something about the High Street, however, that didn't seem altogether right.

'Is it early closing day?' asked Kelly. 'An awful lot of shops seem to be shut.'

'Well, it *is*,' said Derek. 'But they shouldn't be shut this early.'

'Ah,' said Kelly, pointing. 'Look at that.'

Derek followed the direction of the elegant digit. On the door of Mr Beefheart's hung a simple note. 'Closed,' it read. 'Family awaiting The Rapture.'

'Oh dear,' said Derek. 'Oh dear, oh dear, oh dear.'

'I think perhaps that we should be grateful for that.'

'Grateful?' said Derek. 'Why grateful?'

'Because it's infinitely preferable to a great black plague cross.'

'God, you don't think it will come to *that*, do you?'

'I don't know. Let's hope not.'

'Well we're here. The *Mercury*'s offices seem to be open.'

'Then let's get right to it.'

Up the stairs they went. Kelly insisted that Derek led the way. Not because she didn't know the way. But just because she didn't want him looking up her dress.

No receptionist sat in reception.

'I hope Dettox hasn't been Raptured,' said Derek. 'She's the only one who ever makes me a cup of tea.'

'Do you know what,' said Kelly. 'I've never made a cup of tea or coffee for a man in all of my life. And I have no intention of ever doing so.'

Derek smiled. 'There's an old saying,' he said. 'A beautiful woman doesn't have to know how to change a tyre. Or something like that. I'm not being sexist of course. Oh, hold on, what's happening here?'

'Where?' Kelly asked.

Derek put his finger to his lips. 'There are people in Mr Shields's office. You can make them out through the frosted glass partition. I can see a fuzzy pink shape and a fuzzy red one and a large fuzzy Mr Shields-looking one.'

'Nothing unusual in that, surely.'

'Are you kidding? Mr Shields *never* has visitors. I don't know how you ever got through.'

'Dettox offered to make me a cup of tea. What are you doing?'

Derek was beckoning. 'Come with me quickly, to my office.'

Kelly shrugged and followed.

Derek's office was a dire little room that looked out onto a blank brick wall. There were no signs here of Derek's private obsession. Just a desk, a chair, a filing cabinet and a Mute Corp 4000 word processor. And a telephone with a voice broadcaster attachment jobbie. Derek picked up the receiver, tapped out several numbers then dropped it into the voice broadcaster attachment.

'What are you doing now?' Kelly asked.

'Being nosey. I took the liberty of installing a bug in Mr Shields's office. It helps me keep ahead of him and not get sacked.'

'Very enterprising.'

'Ssh,' said Derek and listened.

Kelly shushed and listened. She heard first the voice of Mr Shields.

'I'm sorry,' said Mr Shields. 'But I don't think I quite understand what you're talking about.' His voice sounded fierce. It didn't sound very happy at all.

'It is very straightforward,' said the voice of one of his visitors. 'My companion and I represent a multinational corporation. My card.'

There was a pause.

'Oh,' said the voice of Mr Shields. 'I see, *that* organization.'

'*That* organization, yes. They don't come any bigger, I'm sure you'll agree.'

'I'm very busy,' said Mr Shields. 'Perhaps this could wait until another day.'

'No,' said the voice of visitor number two. 'Our organization never waits. It gets things done at once.'

'Not here it doesn't,' said Mr Shields. 'This is Brentford.'

'Exactly!' said visitor number one. 'This *is* Brentford. Which is why we are here.'

'I've told you that I don't understand and I still don't.' Mr Shields was still keeping it fierce. The voices of his visitors were, however, calm.

'Do you know what data reaction is?' asked visitor number one.

'No,' said Mr Shields. 'And neither do I care.'

'It is what keeps our organization at the cutting edge of technology and everything else. Our mainframe scans the world for data. It assesses, it assimilates, it correlates, it sorts the wheat from the chaff and then it makes informed decisions.'

'Have you been sent by head office?' asked Mr Shields.

'Our organization owns head office,' said the voice of visitor number two. 'It owns the newspaper.'

'But you can't close it down. You can't touch it. I have a contract for life.'

'We have no wish to tamper with the way you run this newspaper. We have merely come to inform you of the organization's plans for the borough, so that you can play an active promotional role.'

Mr Shields made grumbling sounds.

'Data reaction,' said visitor number two. 'The mainframe received a sudden inrush of data from this borough, the evening before last, at precisely eight minutes past eight. Much of it was jumbled nonsense. But some of it was pertinent and of commercial value. Regarding something called Suburbia World Plc. Does this mean anything to you?'

'No,' said Mr Shields in a voice both fierce and puzzled.

'No-one has ever spoken to you about Suburbia World Plc?'

'No,' said Mr Shields. 'Never. What is it?'

'A theme park,' said visitor number one. 'It concerns turning the whole of Brentford into a suburban theme park.'

'What?' went Mr Shields.

'What?' went Derek.

'What?' went Kelly.

'*Your week in Suburbia World Plc would not be complete without a boat trip to Brentford's own Fantasy Island.*' Visitor number one spoke in a

95

curious tone, as if he was a voice-over to a web site commercial. '*See the creature of myth that once inhabited this enchanted realm in the dream world days of the magic distant past. Take a safari through the wildlife sanctuary and rare bird reserve of Allotment World.* You have to picture the images, sweeping aerial shots of the borough, taken from a helicopter. This will be big, very big.'

'But that's outrageous!' The voice of Mr Shields reached a level of fierceness beyond any as yet known to Derek.

'It is,' whispered Derek. 'It well and truly is.'

'Nevertheless,' said visitor number one, in a voice as calm as ever it had been. 'These concepts are now the property of our organization.'

'Hold on! Hold on!' The voice of Mr Shields was accompanied by the sounds of his chair being pushed back. 'You just stop right there. You said that your mainframe thingy received this information. That someone fed it into a computer somewhere.'

'It entered the databanks.'

'Then it is not *your* property. It's someone else's. Someone who could possibly be reasoned with.'

'What are you suggesting?' asked visitor number two.

'I don't know. But I know you can't do this. Brentonians won't stand for it. This isn't Disney World. This is a real place with real people in it.'

'That's what makes the concept so interesting. What invests it with such enormous commercial potential.'

'Get out of my office!' roared Mr Shields. 'Iconoclasts! Despoilers! Unclean spirits! Out demons out!'

'He's certainly loyal to the borough,' whispered Kelly.

'Mr Shields,' said visitor number two. 'We approached you because you are the editor of the borough's organ, as it were. Brentford is the only town in England, possibly the only town in all of the world that does not have its own official web site. Brentford appears to all but ignore the world that exists beyond its boundaries. It's an anachronism. It has enormous novelty value.'

There came crashing bashing sounds.

Derek said, 'I'd better get in there, before he goes completely berserk.'

'I think you should,' said Kelly.

Derek dashed off and Kelly continued to listen at the voice broadcaster attachment jobbie. She listened to the sounds of crashing and bashing. To the cries for mercy. To the further crashings and bashings. To the voice of Derek calling for reason. To further crashings and bashings and the voice of Derek calling for mercy also.

And then Kelly went in to sort things out.

Which left nobody in Derek's office to listen to the sounds that issued from the voice broadcaster attachment jobbie.

Which was probably all for the best, for those sounds were far from joyous.

Derek and Kelly watched as the ambulance drove away, joyfully ringing its bell.

'We'll be in trouble for this,' said Derek.

'We?' said Kelly.

'I mean *you*,' said Derek. 'You broke all the bones.'

'You should be grateful,' said Kelly. 'You could have been in that ambulance.'

'Along with Mr Shields and his two visitors. You were, how shall I put this, just a little harsh.'

'I was simply following the Dimac code,' said Kelly. 'It is not sufficient to defend yourself against an attacker. It is necessary that you punish them for their attack in the hope that they will think twice before making further attacks in the future.'

'You threw that man out of a first–floor window.'

'Pardon me, I *kicked* him out. The move is called the curl of the dark dragon's tail.'

'They *were* tough customers, though,' said Derek. 'That little one had me up off my feet with one hand. He was crushing my throat. Horrible. I hate violence.'

'So do I,' said Kelly. 'So do I.'

Derek gave her a sidelong glance. 'How odd,' said he. 'Because it really looked for all the world as if you were thoroughly enjoying yourself.'

'Looks can be deceptive.'

'In your case, certainly. So what are we going to do now? Mr Shields is out for the count once more . . .'

'I didn't hit him this time. I was defending him.'

'True. So what *are* we going to do?'

'Well,' said Kelly. 'I'm going to look through this.'

'And this is?'

Kelly held a wallet. 'Call it a trophy. I liberated it from the bigger visitor during the scuffle.'

'Shortly before you broke his leg.'

'He kicked me in the ankle.'

'Quite so. Let's have a look in this wallet then.'

'OK, but not here.'

In the Shrunken Head, at a table next to the Space Invaders machine, Kelly Anna Sirjan opened the wallet.

'A business card,' said Derek. 'Let's see.' And he read it. '"Marcus Shadow. Project Development Associate. Cerean systems." Who or what is Cerean systems?'

'It's a division,' said Kelly. 'Of Mute Corp. But then isn't everything?'

'It's logical,' said Derek. 'I've heard of Data Reaction and if it does exist, Mute Corp would have it.'

'I didn't think that it did exist. I thought it was a Web Myth.'

'Well if it does, then it is about as near to artificial intelligence as anything is ever going to be,' said Derek.

'And basically it scans data, then makes its own evaluation of its commercial potential.'

'According to Web Myth, that's how old man Mute got rich. He invented it back in the 1990s to play the stock market. And the rest is history, as far as he's concerned. If the legend is fact.'

Kelly looked puzzled. 'And the Mute Corp mainframe had an inrush of potentially commercial information at eight minutes past eight the night before last.'

'Yes,' said Derek. 'And that rings a bell, for some reason.'

'Well, of course it does. That's the precise time that Mr Tombs, Mr Charker and the woman with the unpronounceable name vanished in front of Dr Druid.'

'I don't understand,' said Derek. 'You think there's some connection?'

'I *know* there's a connection,' said Kelly. 'But as yet I don't know exactly what it is.'

Derek looked wistfully towards the Space Invaders machine. 'Would you care for another game?' he asked.

'What I'd really care for would be a word or two with old man Mute.'

'You wish. He's a recluse, no-one's seen or spoken to him for years.'

'I'm sure that I could find a way.' Kelly fluttered her eyelashes.

'I'm sure that if anyone could, you could. But listen, I suppose I should be getting back to the office. I think I'd better take over the editor's desk until Mr Shields comes out of hospital.'

'*If* he comes out of hospital.'

'What?'

'The plague,' said Kelly. 'The Rapture. He might be the next to go.'

'You're joking. *Aren't* you?'

'Hopefully.'

'Good. So what are you going to do?'

'Think,' said Kelly. 'Think and then act.'

'I'll see you later then. Tell you what, the poets are on at Waterman's tonight. Do you fancy going?'

'What are "the poets"?'

'It's a Brentford thing. Founded in 1980 by a local writer that no-one can remember now. It's very entertaining. I think you'd enjoy it. It starts at eight, I could meet you there.'

'OK,' said Kelly. 'See you later.'

'OK,' said Derek and he upped and took his leave.

Kelly sat and thought a while. And then she ordered some lunch. The Shrunken Head did a special. Surf and turf. Deep-fried crispettes of scampi, grilled steak, double eggs, mushrooms, onion rings, fried tomatoes, chips and beans. Kelly also had the dessert. It was death by trifle.

Then she played the Space Invaders machine. Got the high score, as she often did on the one she had at home, the one she hadn't mentioned to Derek, and left the Shrunken Head.

She would return to that pub sometime in the future.
But not in any manner she could possibly have imagined.

8

Dum de dum de dum de dum
de dum de dum delight.

The Brentford Poets.

Founded sometime back in the early 1980s, by some local author, whose name no-one ever remembers. It might have been P. P. Penrose, creator of the world's greatest private eye, the now legendary Lazlo Woodbine. But of course it wasn't P. P. Penrose, because *everybody* remembers P. P. Penrose.

As to who it really was, it hardly mattered. The Brentford Poets came into being. An entity. A reality.

In 1982, *Time Out* wrote of the Brentford Poets, 'This is London's largest weekly poets' get-together. And possibly the strangest.' What was meant by the latter remark was lost on the good folk of Brentford. Poetry can be joyous. And joyousness rode high in Brentford's saddle, even back in 1982.

Kelly arrived a little after eight. She was impressed by the look of the Waterman's Arts Centre. It looked modern.

This wasn't because it *was* modern, it had been constructed some-time back in the early 1980s. It was just that it *looked* modern. Because the current vogue in twenty-first century architecture was for an homage to the early 1980s. It's a good word, 'homage', and for those who don't know its meaning and can't be bothered to look it up, it means *rip-off*!

The plain folk of Brentford, who never took to change, had not taken at all to the building of the Waterman's Arts Centre. It had been built by out-borough contractors with out-borough money upon the site of the old gasworks, prime riverside land. And the plain folk of the borough considered this 'a bit of a liberty'. There had been some peaceful protestation against the development. And this in turn had led to the forces of law and order employing small measure of response. Water cannon, CS gas, the reading of the Riot Act, rubber bullets, baton charges, helicopter gunships and finally the passing of a special Act of Parliament, which sanctioned the use of the nuclear deterrent, if the peaceful protestors of Brentford did not stop blowing things up and burning things down and return at once to their houses and stop being such a bloody nuisance.

On this occasion, it seemed to the rest of the world that the plain people of Brentford would definitely lose their struggle against the forces of change. Although it had to be said that they weren't going down without a fight. In fact, so great was the amount of night-time sabotage mounted against the Arts Centre during its construction, that the contractors were forced to erect fifteen-foot-high electrified perimeter fences, topped with razor wire and watched over by guards in raised sentry posts equipped with searchlights and General Electric Miniguns. The building work was delayed again and again, the costs overran, the council (held for a while at gunpoint in the famous Siege of Sydney Green Street, when it was discovered by the plucky Brentonians that council members had not only backed the scheme but put in money from the local coffers) pulled out their financial support, the building conglomerate backing the scheme went bust and everyone involved in the project who hadn't either committed suicide, been firebombed, or threatened with hideous death, gave the whole thing up and abandoned the scheme. Leaving the half-built Arts Centre for the people of Brentford to do with as they wilt.

A meeting of the Brentonians had been held in the town hall (in Sydney Green Street) to decide the fate of the half-constructed Arts Centre. Many suggestions were put forward as to how it should best be demolished, but then a voice of extraordinary reason spoke up from the back of the hall. It came from Professor Slocombe, a venerable ancient, considered by many to be Brentford's patriarch.

'Why destroy what you have been given?' asked the professor. 'It is yours now. Why not make of it something that reflects the greatness of the borough? The borough that you all love so dearly. Raise a temple wherein to offer praise to the artisans of Brentford. Has Brentford not given the world some of its finest artists, its most gifted musicians, its wordsmiths and scholars, its craftsmen, its poets, river-dancemen and its makers of macramé plant-pot holders and personalized lavender bags?'

There was then a bit of a pause.

Then, 'No,' said a small voice near to the front. 'None at all that I know of.'

'Exactly,' said Professor Slocombe. 'Because Brentford never had an Arts Centre before.'

Well, it certainly had one now. Every resident of Brentford was a shareholder. Each had paid for and laid one brick, which possibly accounted for its 'modern' look.

It is true to state that the bastions of High Art and Literature had not been taken by storm by the Brentford Set. And the makers of macramé plant-pot holders and personalized lavender bags slept easy in their beds, free from the worry that the superior artisans of Brentford would presently usurp their supremacy.

But the Arts Centre had spawned something: the aforementioned Brentford Poets, of which *Time Out* had taken note and written up in their pages.

'Every man and every woman is a poet,' wrote the magus Hugo Rune. 'Though none are ever so great as I, and most are just plain pants.'

Rune had once made a memorable appearance at the Brentford Poets. Clad in his famous five-piece suit of green and chequered Boleskine tweed, wearing his famous ring of power and carrying his famous stout stick, his famous shaven head decorated with an elaborate henna tattoo of two nuns fighting over a BMX and his infamous size ten feet encased within complicated holistic footwear which smelled strongly of creosote and trailed tiny sparks as he walked.

103

Rune recited his famous *Hymn to Frying Pan*. A five-hundred-and-eighty-nine-stanza epic verse dedicated to himself. He was accompanied by his acolyte, Rizla, who filled in Rune's pauses for breath and frequent visits to the bar with melodic renditions on the swanee whistle, ocarina, kazoo and bicycle pump/armpit.

All who witnessed the performance agreed that it had been a unique and moving experience and many converted at once to the Church of Runeology and remained Runies for the rest of their lives.

Others protested that there hadn't been time left in the evening for them to recite *their* poems. Hugo Rune had dealt justice to these philistines with his stout and famous stick.

But Hugo Rune had long ago shrugged off his mortal form and joined the choirs eternal. Whom he no doubt entertained with his *Hymn to Frying Pan*, with fill-ins by Rizla on the armpit.

So thus it was that the Waterman's Arts Centre came into being. But, one might be forgiven for asking, *How So The Brentford Poets*?

Good question.

It is a fact well known to those who know it well (and Hugo Rune would probably be amongst these), and curiously it runs in verse:

> Wherever you find a poet
> You'll find another near
> And wherever you find two poets
> You'll find they're drinking beer.

On the opening of the Waterman's Arts Centre, an affair almost as memorable as Hugo Rune's reading of *Hymn to Frying Pan*, although few there are, with the possible exception of Old Pete, who would remember it today, there hadn't been a Brentford Poets.

There had only been a Writer in Residence.

And this the long-forgotten author.

The long-forgotten author had been given quite a remit. *Found a poets' group*, it said. The long-forgotten author, bereft as ever of ideas (he was the kind of author who specialized in *an homage*) put an advert in the *Brentford Mercury*:

Poets wanted to perform at a weekly poets' get-
together at the Waterman's Arts Centre.
A free pint from the bar for everyone who
reads an original poem.

The bar ran dry the first night. It was remarkable just how many drinking men of Brentford felt the muse so suddenly arise in them.

But the reviewer from *Time Out*, who happened by chance to be there for the Busby Berkeley Retrospective★ showing in the Arts Centre cinema, was so impressed by the enormous turnout (he never even got close to the bar himself) that he gave the event a write-up.

Numbers began to drop off a bit when the Writer in Residence decreed that pints should only be awarded to poets reading original poems which had some degree of artistic merit and ran to more than two lines inevitably terminating with the words, 'Thank you very much ladies and gentlemen and mine's a pint of large, please.'

Many thirsty minimalist poets left the Arts Centre, bitterly complaining as they did so.

It finally worked its way down to a hard core of dedicated poets. They self-published a monthly magazine, *The Shorter Brentford Book of Verse*, early copies of which are now believed to be collector's items. And the event remained. Wednesday night at Waterman's was the Brentford Poets night.

And as tonight was Wednesday, this was what it was.

Kelly saw Derek waving to her from the bar. She threaded her way between the poets and the appreciators of poets and those who had come along just to see what was going on and those groups of pimply young men who always turn up to such events, because a mate of theirs told them that poetesses were easy lays and they'd actually been daft enough to believe him.

'I got you a glass of red wine in,' said Derek. 'I hope that's OK.'

'It's OK,' said Kelly. 'Thanks. It's pretty crowded in here. Do you always come to listen?'

★ So popular with Brentonians was this that it ran for three years.

'*Listen?*' said Derek. 'I come to perform. That's a stunning frock by the way. What kind of fabric is that?'

'It's a polyvinylsynthacottonlatexsuedosilk mix.'

'Nice,' said Derek. 'And I love those shoes too. They make you seem . . .'

'Taller,' said Kelly. 'They're the latest Doveston holistic footwear. Triple-heeled with chromium love-turrets and inlaid frog-mullions. Each rivet hand-driven in by a vestal virgin at the temple of Runeology.'

'You're having a laugh,' said Derek.

'Derek,' said Kelly. 'Fashion is no laughing matter.'

'No,' said Derek. 'I mean, no, but you are, perhaps, and I mean no offence by this, slightly overdressed for the occasion.'

It is another fact well known to those who know it well, that poets are very seldom *fashion-conscious*.

When talking of poets' attire the words scruffy, wretched and downright foul are oft-times brought into usage.

Only very few poets have ever cut a dash, as they say, clothes-wise. Amongst these must rank Sir Johnny Betjeman, stripey-blazered and all-round eccentric wearer of the old straw hat. And John Cooper Clarke,★ whose dress code, although natty, sadly owed an homage to a chap called Bob Dylan.

Kelly gave those round and about a cursory glancing-over. 'Well,' she said. 'They are a scruffy, wretched and downright foul-looking bunch. But I didn't have time to change. I've been up west.'

'Chiswick?' said Derek, mightily impressed.

'The West End,' said Kelly. 'The head office of Mute Corp.'

'You didn't actually get to see old man Mute?'

'No,' said Kelly. 'Sadly not. Apparently he lives upon a luxury yacht, the location of which is only known to a select elite. I don't think an interview with him is on the cards. But I do have a bit of news for you and I don't know how you'll take it.'

★ John Cooper Clarke actually once played a gig at the Waterman's Arts Centre. Its most memorable feature was the post-gig fight in the dressing room between John and his manager over who got to keep the gig money. The word 'allegedly' will not be used here, as this is a fact.

'Go on,' said Derek.

'I'm leaving Brentford,' said Kelly. 'Tomorrow.'

'What?' said Derek. 'Already? But you've only been here a couple of days.'

Kelly sipped at her red wine. 'I've been offered a job at Mute Corp. I took the liberty of taking my CV up with me when I went. A very nice man called Mr Pokey, who wore a beautiful orange suit and who couldn't take his eyes off my breasts, offered me a job.'

'Oh,' said Derek and a sadness came out all over his face. 'I suppose he would. I suppose any man would.'

'Don't be downcast,' said Kelly, finishing her wine. 'I only wanted to get inside the organization. We'll still be working together on the investigation.'

'Ah yes,' said Derek. 'The investigation. I've been thinking about that.'

'Thinking *what*?' said Kelly.

'Well, it's just that with Mr Shields banged up in the hospital, he seems to be in a bit of a coma by the way. The doctor said something about repeated blows to the head. With him in hospital, I have been put in charge of running the *Mercury* and head office has sent me all these memos about co-operating with the representatives of Mute Corp over the Suburbia World Plc business.'

'*What?*' said Kelly, startling several poets, a lover of poetry and a pimply young man who'd been taking a lively interest in her breasts. 'You Judas!'

'I'm not,' said Derek, crossing his heart. 'I'm not, I'm not, I'm not. I don't want to see the borough turned into a theme park, but what can I do?'

'You could refuse,' said Kelly.

'They'll sack me,' said Derek.

'Then you can do the decent thing.'

'Resign? No way.'

'Not resign. Do what you told me the people of Brentford do, practise *inertia*. Appear to co-operate, but don't actually do anything.'

'Just do what I always do.'

'You're very good at doing it.'

'Fair enough,' said Derek. 'Another glass of wine?'

'It's my round, I think.'

'Oh yes, it is.'

'But don't let that put you off. Buy me another glass of wine.'

'Oh, all right,' said Derek. 'Any crisps?'

'Do they serve bar snacks?'

Derek chewed upon his lip. 'There is a menu,' he said sadly. 'I think they do the surf and turf.'

'That will be fine then, I'll have one of those.'

Derek sighed. 'Well,' he said. 'As it is your last night here.'

Kelly smiled.

Derek hailed the barman. 'Barman, barman,' he hailed.

'He won't listen,' said an ancient sitting at the bar. 'If you want to get his attention, you should speak in Runese.'

Derek glowered towards the ancient. Then he said, 'How did you get on with the over-eighties backwards walk from Kew to Richmond?'

'I came first,' said Old Pete (for who could it have been but him). 'Bit of healthy competition this year. I had to nudge at least three wheelchair cases into the Thames. Three's a record, I think, it was only two last year. And that nun, but she was cheating, riding a BMX.'

'Barman,' hailed Derek. 'Barman, please.'

Old Pete didn't read any poems that night. He wasn't much of a poet, Old Pete, even in the holy cause of the well-won-fine-free-pint. He knew his limitations. And anyway, he was busy tucking into the free champagne that the Arts Centre was dishing out to him to celebrate his win in the over-eighties backwards walk.

Old Pete's chum, Old Vic, was a poet though. And a mighty one to boot. Old Vic had been a prisoner of war. In a war that few remembered now, but they still made movies about. Mostly inaccurate ones where they got the hairstyles wrong, but as that is Hollywood tradition, it's neither here nor there.

Old Vic was first up upon the rostrum to recite his latest poem. Old Vic always received a standing ovation, even from those who remained sitting down, for, after all, he *had* been a prisoner of war. Hands clapped aplenty, fingers were stuck into mouths and whistles were blown out between them. Certain hats were cast into the air, but these were those of visiting poets who came from strange lands to the South where poets always wore hats.

'Thank you,' said Old Vic, waggling his wrinkled hands about to staunch the outpourings of welcome. 'I've had to have a bit of a think this week about what I was going to write about. I thought I might do a poem about bream. Lovely fish the bream, very silvery. Quite unlike the perch, which is fatter and has green and reddy bits. Or indeed the dab, not unlike the bream, some might say, but a slimmer slippery fellow and one liable to make his escape through your keep-net if you only have thirteen-gauge netting, rather than a ten-gauge.'

There was some laughter over this from a group of local anglers. Imagine anyone being daft enough to put a dab in a keep-net with thirteen-gauge netting. That was a good'n.

'Bravo, Old Vic,' called anglers, raising their glasses and making rod-casting motions with them.

'Careful,' said a pimply young man. 'You're spilling your beer on me.'

'Ssh,' went the anglers. 'Listen to Old Vic. He was a prisoner of war.'

'Cheers lads,' said Old Vic, tipping the anglers the wink. 'But I decided not to write a poem about bream this week.'

'Aw,' went the anglers. 'Shame.'

'Maybe next week lads. But this week, not bream. I have to say that I toyed with the idea of writing a poem about muleskinning.'

A cheer went up from a group of muleskinners over from Cardiff for the annual muleskinners' convention that is always held at the Function Rooms at the Station Hotel.

'Evening lads,' called Old Vic. 'Good to see you here again. I'll pop over to have a word later, I need a new eight-foot bull whip, I wore the last one out at the Easter fête.'

'Three lashes for a quid,' said Derek. 'He always gives good value. The money goes to charity of course. Small and shoeless boys in search of a good hiding, or something.'

'Eh?' said Kelly, tucking into her tucker, which had lately arrived at the bar counter. 'Could you pass the cranberry sauce, please?'

Derek passed the cranberry sauce.

109

'Now,' Old Vic continued. 'I must confess that I didn't write a poem about muleskinning.'

Kelly looked up from eating. 'What a fascinating man,' she said in a tone that was less than sincere. 'I've no doubt that he's about to tell us that he didn't write a poem about unicycling vicars either.'

'Let the old boy have his say,' sshed Derek. 'He's a venerable poet. And he was a prisoner of war.'

Kelly said, 'Pass the ginseng dip.' And Derek passed it over.

'Any unicycling vicars out there?' asked Old Vic.

Another cheer went up.

'Sorry,' said the ancient. 'Maybe next week.'

'My money is now on Yugoslavian junk bond dealers,' said Kelly to Derek. 'Or possibly Venezuelan gorilla impersonators, deaf ones of course.'

'So,' said Old Vic. 'I considered all and sundry, but I've decided to do a poem about the time when I was . . .'

'*A Prisoner of War!*' chorused all and sundry, except for Old Vic.

'Ah, I see,' said Kelly. 'It's a running gag.'

'It doesn't work if you don't come every week,' said Derek.

'I'm not altogether certain that it would, even if I did. Pass the crow's foot purée, please.'

Derek passed the crow's foot purée.

'I was once a prisoner of war,' said Old Vic. 'You won't remember the war in question. It's the one that they make movies about, although they always get the haircuts wrong.'

A group of visiting English hairdressers who worked for Pinewood Studios cheered at this.

'I call this poem "Blood and snot for breakfast again and only human finger bones to use for a knife and fork."'

Kelly choked on her surf and turf and a small fight ensued between pimply young men who wanted to pat her on the back.

Old Vic launched into his poem.

> 'We was up to our eyes in pus and puke
> There was only me and Captain Duke
> Who could still stand up on where our legs had been
> Which were oozing mucus and rotten with gangrene.'

110

Pimply men took turns at Kelly's back.

> 'We boiled up some phlegm to make a cup of tea
> In the skull of the corporal from the infantry
> Captain Duke drank the lot and left none for me
> But I didn't mind, because I'd spat in it.'

'All right,' said Kelly. 'Stop patting my back or I'll break all your arms.' The pimply men stopped patting and Kelly sipped wine and tucked once more into her tucker.

> 'I spread some bile upon my maggot-ridden bread . . .'

'Pat,' gagged Kelly, pointing to her back.

Old Vic's poem was only seventeen verses long and when it was finished it drew a standing ovation even from those who remained sitting down.

Kelly heard the cheering, but she didn't join in with it. For Kelly was in the ladies, bent rather low above the toilet bowl.

'Are you OK?' asked Derek, upon her return to the bar.

'That wasn't funny,' said Kelly, who still looked radiant, as only women can, after a bout of vomiting. 'That was disgusting.'

'Perhaps the mandrake salad dressing didn't agree with you.'

'I'm going,' said Kelly. 'I don't want to hear any more.'

'I'll be on in a minute,' said Derek. 'You wouldn't want to miss me, would you?'

'Do your poems involve any pus or mucus?'

Derek thought for a bit. 'No,' he said. 'They're mostly about sex.'

Kelly stared at him. 'And what would you know about sex?'

'Oh I know a lot about it,' said Derek. 'It's just that I don't do a lot of it.'

'I overheard a pimply bloke saying that poetesses are easy. Surely if you're a regular performer you get your end away every once in a while.'

'Don't be crude,' said Derek. 'But actually it *is* true, poetesses *are* easy. Well, at least the fat ugly ones with moustaches are.'

Kelly gave Derek another one of those looks. 'That would be the fat girls are grateful for it theory, would it?'

111

'Listen,' said Derek. '*I'm* not fat, but I can tell you, I'm really grateful for it.'

'Whose round is it, then?' asked Kelly. 'If I'm staying, you could at least have the decency to buy me a drink.'

'I think we'd started buying our own,' said Derek.

'No, I think you were still buying mine.'

'Barman,' hailed Derek. 'Barman, please, barman.'

Next up upon the rostrum was a poetess. She was not a fat mous-tached poetess who was grateful for it. She was a young and beautiful and slim poetess who could afford to be choosy.

She recited a poem about her cat called Mr Willow-Whiskers. Who was apparently her furry little soulmate.

Kelly was forced to return to the ladies and lose the rest of her supper. At length she returned, still radiant, to the bar.

'That's definitely enough for me,' she said. ' "Mr Willow-Whiskers with his soul of crimson sunset". That was enough to make anyone throw up.'

'The pimply youths seemed to like it,' said Derek. 'They're asking for her autograph.'

'I've never been comfortable with poetry,' said Kelly. 'It's either well meaning, but bad, or beautifully constructed, but unintelligible. I quite like limericks though, have you ever heard the one about the young man from Buckingham?'

'I have,' said Derek. 'It's truly obscene.'

'Well, I'm off. Enough is enough is enough.'

'I'm up next,' said Derek. 'Please stay until I'm done.'

Kelly smiled. 'And your poem will be about sex, will it?'

Derek grinned. 'I've been working on my delivery. The way I see it, with performance poetry, it's not so much what you say, as the way you say it. My poems aren't actually rude, but I inject into them a quality of suggestiveness which gives them the appearance of being extremely risqué.'

'Derek,' said Kelly. 'We're friends now, aren't we?'

'Yes,' said Derek nodding. 'I think we are.'

'Then as your friend, allow me to say that you are a complete and total prat. No offence meant.'

'And none taken, I assure you. But you just wait until you hear my poem. It involves the use of the word "plinth", which as everybody knows, is the sexiest word on Earth.'

'Plinth?' said Kelly.

'My God,' said Derek. 'Say it again.'

A round of applause went up as Mr Melchizedec, Brentford's milkman in residence, concluded his poem 'Oh wot a loverly pair of baps'. It didn't include the word 'plinth', but as his style of delivery owed an homage to the now legendary Max Miller, the two Olds, Pete and Vic, were now rolling about on the floor, convinced that they had just heard the filthiest poem in the world.

'Check this out,' said Derek, grinning at Kelly and pushing his way through the crowd towards the rostrum.

Kelly yawned and looked at her watch. She'd let Derek do his thing, then she'd get an early night in. She wanted to look her best for her first day at Mute Corp, tomorrow.

Derek mounted the rostrum and smiled all over the crowd.

The crowd didn't seem *that* pleased to see him, although Kelly overheard a fat poetess with a moustache whisper to her friend, a poetess of not dissimilar appearance, that 'he looks like he's up for it'.

'Thank you,' said Derek, to no-one in particular. 'This is a poem dedicated to a lady. She's a very special lady. She doesn't know that she's a very special lady, but to me she is.'

'What's her name?' called out Old Pete, lately helped up from the floor.

'That's my secret,' said Derek.

'I'll bet it's this bird here,' said Old Vic, pointing towards Kelly. 'The bird with the nice charlies.'

Kelly glared pointy daggers, Old Vic took to cowering.

'The poem is untitled,' continued Derek.

'So what's it called?' Old Pete called.

'It doesn't have a title.'

'A poem *should* have a title,' said Old Vic. 'Or at least a rank. We all had ranks in the prisoner-of-war camp.'

'Yeah,' called a pimply youth. 'You were all a bunch of rankers.'

The barman (who had been conversing in Brentford Auld Speke to a wandering bishop, down from Orton Goldhay for the annual congress of wandering bishops that was held in the function room above the Four Horsemen public house) shouted out, 'Oi! We'll have no trouble here.'

'It *should* have a title,' said Old Vic. 'It *should*!'

'All right,' said Derek. 'It's called "Sir Untitled Poem", OK?'

Kelly looked at her watch once more. Perhaps she should just go.

'"Sir Untitled Poem,"' said Derek, launching into 'Sir Untitled Poem'.

As Kelly had feared, 'Sir Untitled Poem' was pants. It was one of those excruciating love sonnets that lonely teenage boys compose when all alone in their bedrooms, and then make the mistake (only once!) of reciting to their very first girlfriend on their very first date.

It would, however, possibly have ranked as just another poem of the evening, had not something occurred during its reciting.

It was something truly dire and it put a right old damper on the evening. So truly dire, in fact, was it, that the wandering bishop, who had been chatting with the barman, found himself very much the man of the moment, several pimply youths found themselves in the loving arms of fat moustachioed poetesses, and Old Vic finally found another subject worthy of a poem.

Not that he would recite it at the Brentford Poets for a while. What with the Arts Centre being closed for extensive refurbishment, what with all the mayhem and destruction and suchlike.

But before this truly dire event occurs, as it most certainly must, it will be necessary for us to take a rather radical step and return to the past, so that the truly dire event might be truly understood.

We must return to the evening before last.

To the cottage hospital and the bed of Big Bob Charker.

The time is eight of the evening clock.

And Big Bob isn't happy.

9

Big Bob Charker lay upon his bed of pain. Not that he was aware of any pain. He wasn't. Big Bob was not aware that his nose had been broken, nor that he had suffered extensive bruising, a degree of laceration and a fractured left big toe.

He was not alone in his ignorance of the left big toe injury, the doctors at the cottage hospital had missed that one too.

Big Bob Charker was aware of nothing whatever at all.

If he had been capable of any awareness whatsoever he would have been aware that his last moments of awareness were of his awareness vanishing away. Of everyday objects becoming strange and alien. Of colour and sound becoming things of mystery, of speech becoming meaningless. Of everything *just going*.

But Big Bob was unaware.

Big Bob lay there, eyes wide open, staring at nothing at all. Staring at nothing and knowing nothing. Nothing whatever at all.

Dr Druid stared down at his patient. 'I hate to admit this,' he told a glamorous nurse. 'But this doesn't make any sense to me at all.'

'Could it be conjunctivitis?' asked the nurse, who had recently come across the word in a medical dictionary and had been looking for an opportunity to use it.

'No,' said Dr Druid, sadly shaking his head.

'What about scrapie then?'

'I don't think so,' said the doctor.

'What about thrush?' asked the nurse, who had more words left in her.

'Shut up,' said the doctor.

Pearson Clarke (son of the remarkable Clive and brother to the sweetly smelling Bo-Jangles Clarke, who bathed four times a day and sang country songs about trucks to those prepared to listen) grinned at the nurse and then at Dr Druid. Pearson Clarke was an intern with ideas above his station. His station was South Ealing and most of his ideas were well above that. 'You should run a brain scan,' said Pearson Clarke.

'I have run a brain scan,' said Dr Druid. 'It shows that this patient has absolutely no brain activity whatsoever.'

'That's impossible,' said Pearson Clarke. 'Even deep coma patients have brain activity. They dream.'

'This man doesn't dream,' said Dr Druid. 'Nor do the other two patients, the driver and the woman with the unpronounceable name.'

'I can pronounce it,' said Pearson Clarke. 'It's pronounced . . .'

'Shut up,' said Dr Druid. 'It's as if this man's thoughts, his memories, his personality, everything has been erased. Wiped clean. Gone.'

'That isn't how the brain works,' said Pearson Clarke. 'That can't happen. A patient can lose his memory. But the memory is still there in his head, he simply can't access it. Mostly it's just temporarily impaired. Bits come back, eventually.'

'I'm sure I recall telling you to shut up,' said Dr Druid. 'Although my memory might be temporarily impaired.'

'Impetigo,' said the nurse.

'Shut up, nurse,' said the doctor.

'Joking apart,' said Pearson Clarke. 'The brain-scan machine might be broken. You know that thing people do, photocopying their bottoms? Well, Igor Riley the mortuary attendant . . .'

'Son of Blimey and brother to Smiley Riley, who swears he has a genie in a bottle?'

'That's him, well, Igor Riley has been scanning his bottom in the brain-scan machine. He might have, well, farted in it, or something. It's a very delicate machine.'

'I'll have *him* sacked in the morning then.'

'Rather you than me,' said Pearson Clarke. 'A bloke in a pub once punched Igor Riley in the ear. Igor told his brother and his brother got his genie to turn the bloke into a home-brewing starter pack, or it might have been a . . .'

'Shut up,' said the doctor. 'Shut up. Shut up. Shut up.'

'Please yourself then,' said Pearson Clarke, grinning at the nurse, who grinned right back at him.

'I think it's Tourette's syndrome,' whispered the nurse.

'I f**king heard that,' said Dr Druid. 'But, as I said, before I was so rudely and irrelevantly interrupted, I am baffled by these patients. We might be witnessing something altogether new here. Something as yet unlisted in the medical dictionary.'

'That's me screwed then,' said the nurse. 'And I thought I was doing so well.'

'I'll teach you some more words later,' said the doctor.

'I'll just bet you will,' said Pearson Clarke. 'But listen, if this isn't listed, it will need a name. How about Clarke's syndrome? That rolls off the tongue.'

'Yes,' said Dr Druid. 'Druid's syndrome. I like that.'

'Eh?' said Pearson Clarke.

'Oh look,' said the nurse. 'Look at the patient, doctor.'

'Yes,' said Dr Druid. 'I am a very patient doctor.'

'No doctor, the patient. Look at the patient.'

'What?' asked Dr Druid, looking. 'What about the patient, nurse?'

'He's flickering, doctor. Look at him.'

Dr Druid looked and his eyes became truly those of the tawny owl. Big and round, like Polo mints, with black dots in the middle. Possibly liquorice.

'Oh,' went Dr Druid. 'Oh.' And 'Oh dear me.'

For Big Bob Charker was flickering.

Flickering like crazy.

His head was coming and going like the image on a TV screen when a heavy lorry goes by outside, or at least the way they used to do in the old days.

Dr Druid reached down and tore the sheet away.

All of Big Bob was coming and going, all the way down to his fractured left big toe.

'That left big toe looks wonky,' Pearson Clarke observed. 'There's a fracture there or my name's not . . . Oh crikey!'

And there was Big Bob Charker.

Gone.

Just gone.

Dr Druid stared and gasped and then he turned around. The beds of the other two patients stood empty. They had just gone too.

Out of a tiny transparent dot of nothing whatever at all, things rushed back to Big Bob at a speed beyond that of travelling light. A speed that well and truly was the speed of travelling thought.

Big Bob did blinkings of the eyes and clickings of the shoulder parts. 'Ow,' and 'ouch,' quoth he. 'My nose, my bits and bobs, my poor left big toe. I am sorely wounded, wherefore-art hath this thing happened? And for that matter, where the Hell am I?'

Big Bob now did focusing and situational-taking stocks. 'I'm in hospital,' he said to himself. 'I'm in a hospital bed,' and then he saw intern Pearson Clarke and Dr Druid and a nurse with a very nice bosom. 'Why look you upon me in this startled fashion?' asked Big Bob. 'Thou seem to have the wind up. No don't turn away.'

But Dr Druid and Pearson Clarke and the nurse, who Big Bob now noticed also had a very nice bottom, had turned away, and were staring at two empty beds.

Big Bob followed the direction of their starings.

'Oh hello Periwig,' he said. 'Thou art here too. And the lady who wore the straw hat, hello.' And Big Bob waggled his fingers.

Periwig Tombs stared back at him. The lady said, 'Where am I?' And, 'Where is my hat?'

'We're in hospital,' said Big Bob. 'Weren't we on the tour bus a minute ago?'

Periwig shook his large and bandaged head. 'I am perplexed,' said he. 'What happened to us, doctor?'

'They're gone,' croaked Dr Druid. 'They vanished. You saw them vanish, didn't you?' Dr Druid shook Pearson Clarke by the lapels. 'You did see it. Swear to me you saw it.'

'I did see it. Yes I did. Stop shaking me about.'

'Doctor?' said Periwig. '*Doctor?*'

118

'Gone.' Dr Druid buried his face in his hands.

'Oh yeah,' said Periwig. 'I get it. Very amusing. They're winding us up, Bob. Pretending they can't see us.'

Big Bob watched Dr Druid clinging to the nurse. He was blubbering now and he really seemed sincere.

'Periwig,' said Big Bob. 'I don't think they can see us. Are we dreaming this, or what? What is going on?'

'Some kind of stupid joke,' said Periwig. 'Can you walk, Big Bob?'

'My left big toe really hurts, but yes I think I can.'

'Then let's get out of here.'

'GAME ON,' came a very large voice from nowhere and everywhere both at the very same time.

Big Bob Charker and Periwig Tombs and the lady, lacking the straw hat, covered their ears. Dr Druid and Pearson Clarke and the beautiful nurse blubbered and boggled on oblivious.

'Who said that?' asked Big Bob, staring all around and about. And gingerly uncovering his ears.

'YOU EACH HAVE THREE LIVES,' the very large voice said. 'IF YOU CHOOSE TO PLAY. IF YOU CHOOSE NOT TO PLAY, YOU WILL BE INSTANTLY DOWNLOADED.'

'I'm not bloody playing anything,' said Periwig Tombs. 'In fact I . . .'

And then he was gone.

Just gone.

'Periwig?' Big Bob's eyes came a-starting from his sockets. 'Periwig, where have you gone?'

'PLAYER ONE HAS BEEN DOWNLOADED FOR DATA REACTION. PLAYER TWO, DO YOU WISH TO PLAY?'

'Is that me?' Big Bob was trembling.

'NO YOU'RE PLAYER THREE. PLAYER TWO, LADY WITH THE UNPRONOUNCEABLE NAME.'

'Me?' said the lady. 'I'm a little confused at the present. Why can't the doctor see us and who am I talking to?'

'Oh,' said Big Bob. 'I understand.'

'Do you?' asked the lady.

'I do,' said Big Bob. 'I'm sorry to have to break this to thee. But thou art dead and me also. Surely this is the voice of God.'

119

'HA HA HA HA HA,' went the voice, from everywhere and nowhere all at the very same time.

'Oh my goodness me,' said the lady. 'And me hatless and all. Did I get struck by lightning? It was such a joyous sunny day.'

The large voice went 'HA HA HA' once again.

'I fear that this is not the voice of God,' said Bob the Big. 'In fact, I fear it is the other.'

'PLAYER NUMBER TWO. DO YOU WISH TO PLAY OR NOT? COUNTING DOWN. TEN SECONDS. NINE. EIGHT. SEVEN.'

'Tell me what to do,' the lady implored of Big Bob.

'Say you'll play,' answered Bob. 'Say it rather quickly.'

'I'll . . .'

'ZERO,' said the large and terrible voice. For terrible indeed it was, there was just no getting away from it.

'No,' cried Big Bob. 'Please have mercy.'

But the hatless lady simply vanished.

She was gone.

'PLAYER THREE . . .'

'I'll play. I'll play. I'll play,' cried Bob. 'Doctor please help me, please, can't you hear me?'

But Dr Druid was leaving the ward, the glamorous nurse's arm about his shoulder. Pearson Clarke was leaving too, he was trying to look very brave, but he wasn't making much of a job of it.

'Come back.' Bob struggled up from his bed and hopped about on his good right foot.

'PLAYER THREE.'

'Yes I'm listening, I'm listening. What do you want me to do?'

'THE GAME IS CALLED GO MANGO,' said the large and terrible voice. 'THERE ARE THREE LEVELS BASED ON THE THREE AGES OF MAN. ASCEND THROUGH THE LEVELS AND FIND THE TREASURE. FIND THE TREASURE AND YOU WIN THE GAME.'

'Treasure?' said Big Bob, trying to remember whom it was he knew, whose brother was a pirate. 'Buried treasure?'

'YOU HAVE THREE LIVES. YOU GAIN ENERGY FROM THE GOLDEN STONES. IN ORDER TO ACCESS WEAPONS, YOU WILL HAVE TO CRACK THE CODES.'

'Weapons?' Big Bob hopped about. 'Please, I really don't understand. *Am* I dead? Am I in limbo? Why speakest thou of weapons?'

'GAME ON,' said the large and terrible voice.

'No, wait, ouch my toe.'

'GAME ON . . .'

'. . . NO HOLD IT.' It was a second voice that spoke. As large and terrible as the first, but ever so slightly different.

'GAME ON,' said the first voice once more.

'NO HOLD IT. THAT'S NOT FAIR. HE CAN'T RUN ON ONE FOOT.'

'HE CAN HOP.'

'HOPPING ISN'T FAIR. GIVE HIM BOTH HIS FEET TO RUN ON.'

'Art *thou* God?' asked Big Bob.

'ALL RIGHT,' said the first large and terrible voice. 'BOTH FEET. HE WON'T MAKE IT PAST THE FIRST LEVEL ANYWAY.'

'Level?' said Big Bob and then he went, 'Aaaaagh!'

Because his left big toe stretched out from his foot like an elasticated sausage and then sprang back with a ghastly twanging sound. 'Ouch!' and 'oh,' and 'aaah,' went Big Bob. 'Ah, my toe is better.'

'HAPPY?' said the first voice.

'Not really,' said Big Bob.

'NOT *YOU*!' said the first voice.

'HAPPY,' said the second voice. 'GAME ON THEN, I'LL KICK YOUR ARSE THIS TIME.'

'YOU WISH,' said the first voice. 'AND GO MANGO.'

Big Bob now felt a kind of shivery juddery feeling creeping up and all over. He stared down at himself and was more than a little surprised to discover that he was no longer wearing the embarrassing tie-up-the-back gown thing that doctors in hospitals insist that you wear in order to make you feel even more foolish and vulnerable than you're already feeling. Big Bob was now wearing a tight-fitting one-piece synthavinylpolilycraspandexathene superhero-type suit with a big number three on the front. It actually made him look rather splendid, what with his great big chest and shoulders and all. On his feet were golden boots, and they looked rather splendid too.

Very Arnold Schwarzenegger. Very *Running Man* perhaps?

'Very nice indeed,' said Bob the Big. 'Although somewhat immodest about the groin regions. But how dost . . .'

121

'RUN YOU SUCKER,' said the second voice. And Big Bob suddenly felt like running. He felt very fit indeed.

'Find the treasure and I win?' he said.

But the voices said no more.

'OK.' Big Bob took a step forward. And 'Oh,' he said, as he did so. He certainly felt light upon his feet, a single step carried him forward at not inconsiderable speed. He appeared to be possessed of extraordinary fitness and agility. He'd never been a sluggard before. He'd always kept himself in shape. But now. But now.

But now.

'Oh yes,' said Big Bob. 'Oh yes indeed.' And he took another step and then another. And off he went across the ward and right out through the wall.

Bob paused upon his springing steps. He *had* just done that, hadn't he? He had just stepped right through the wall? Why had he done that? Why hadn't he just used the door?

Big Bob turned to look back at the wall. But the wall wasn't there any more. He was standing now in the middle of the Butt's Estate. Brentford's posher quarter. On two sides of him rose the elegant Georgian houses built so long ago by the rich burghers of Brentford. Behind him the Seamen's Mission and before him the broad and tree-lined thoroughfare that led either in or out of the Butt's, depending on which way you're travelling.

Big Bob looked all around and about. This *was* the Butt's, and he *was* here. Well, he *was* here, but somehow this wasn't.

Big Bob looked all around and about just a little more. This wasn't quite right, not that anything was. But *this* wasn't right for sure. It looked like the Butt's Estate. The Butt's Estate he'd known for all of his life so far. Possibly *all* his life, if he was, as he feared, now dead. *But* this wasn't *quite* the Butt's Estate.

The evening sky above was a curious violet hue and all that it looked down upon was slightly out of kilter. The Butt's Estate wasn't real. It was more like a copy. More like a model. The colours here were too bright. The mellow bricks of the elegant buildings were unnatural, they lacked definition, everything had a flattened quality about it.

It *was* a copy. It *was* a model.

122

'Model?' said Big Bob to no-one but himself and then something inside his head went click. 'Model,' he said again. '*Computer* model. This is like one of those holographic computer models of towns that architects create on their Mute Corp holocast computers.' And then Big Bob's brain went click just a little bit more. And then the light of a revelation dawned, as it was bound to sooner or later.

Though for some, it would have been sooner.

'Game on?' whispered Big Bob. 'Three lives? Golden stones? Weapons? Find the treasure? It's a computer game. *I'm* in a computer game.'

And then Big Bob began to laugh. He laughed and laughed and laughed. It was all so obvious, wasn't it? But he hadn't realized. He hadn't seen through it. What a fool. What an oaf. What a grade A buffoon.

Big Bob sighed. And it was a sigh of relief.

'I'm dreaming,' he said. 'I'm asleep. There was a film once. I saw it when I was a lad. *Tron*, that was it. A chap finds himself inside a computer game. Thou art a twotty git, Big Bob,' Bob told himself. 'But clearly thou dost have quite an imagination.

'Okey-dokey,' said Big Bob, smiling all over his great big face. 'Enough of all this. Time to wake up, I think.'

Well, you would think that, wouldn't you? You would try to wake up. And if it was a dream, and you'd twigged it was a dream, you probably *would* wake up. Or if, like those lucky blighters who are skilled in the art of lucid dreaming, you knew you were in a dream, you'd just stay asleep and really get into it. Because when you know you're in a dream, you can do anything you want to. Anything. And as men who are skilled in lucid dreaming never tire of telling you, you can't half have some amazing sex with some really famous women. But sadly, even if he had wanted to, which he wouldn't have done, as he was loyal to his wife, Big Bob wouldn't be having any amazing sex with any famous women.

Because Big Bob wasn't asleep.

Big Bob *wasn't* dreaming.

But as Big Bob didn't know this yet, Big Bob tried to wake up.

Big Bob stretched out his big arms and did yawnings and stretch-ings and closings and openings of eyes and made encouraging sounds to himself and then began to wonder just why it was that he wasn't waking up and then he became very confused.

And very frightened also.

'I'm not waking up,' said Big Bob. 'I don't like this at all.'

'GO ON THEN,' said the large voice suddenly. 'SHIFT OFF THE SQUARE. GET MOVING. GO TO LEVEL ONE.'

Big Bob ducked his head. Then looked up fearfully towards the violet sky. 'I *am* dreaming this, aren't I?' he said. 'Tell me I'm just dreaming this.'

'OFF THE SQUARE. GET MOVING.'

Big Bob now looked down. Although he stood upon the little grassy area of land before the Seamen's Mission, his feet did not rest upon the grass. His feet, encased as they now were within their rather dashing golden boots, stood upon a golden square. Rather plastic-looking. Rather unreal. Not very nice at all. Big Bob almost took a step forward.

'Er, hello,' called Big Bob. 'Hello up there, God, or whoever thou art. I don't like this. I don't want to play. I want to wake up please.'

'YOU HAVE TO PLAY NOW. YOU'RE IN THE GAME,' said the large and terrible voice. The first one, not the second one. The second one said, 'DO IT. GO MANGO!'

Big Bob fretted and dithered and worried and then he said, 'I'm going home to my bed. I'm bound to wake up in there.'

And then Big Bob took a single step forward.

And entered a world of hurt.

10

A great big hand swung down from on high and caught Big Bob in the side of the head.

'Why you bastard!' Big Bob rarely swore, but that hand hit him hard.

'What did you say, Charker?'

Big Bob glared towards the sky. But the sky wasn't there any more. Where the sky had been was ceiling, and a ceiling Big Bob knew.

'I said, oh . . .' Big Bob coughed, there was something strange about his voice now. And . . . He blinked and stared and gawped. From the ceiling to the walls, to the window, to the blackboard to the teacher Mr Vaux.

Mr Vaux, his primary-school teacher. Mr Vaux who had flown a fighter plane in the war that few remembered any more. Mr Vaux who had been a prisoner of war. Mr Vaux who had no truck with ten-year-old boys who swore.

'Sleeping, were you, Charker?' asked Mr Vaux. 'Daydreaming? Wistfully staring out of the window thinking of home time and Pogs in your own back passage?'

'I? What? How?' went Bob the Big.

'And what was that you called me?'

'I?' went Big Bob. 'I?' He looked and he blinked and then looked some more. His classroom at Grange Primary School. And all the class were there. Trevor Alvy who bullied him. David Rodway, his bestest friend. Periwig Tombs with his Mekon head. Phyllis Livingstone the dark-haired girl from Glasgow, the very first love of his life. And there, over there in the corner, where she had always been, until her desk became empty, Ann Green, the little girl with the yellow hair, who had died in that final summer at the primary, when the swingboat in the memorial park hit her in the throat.

'I?' Big Bob gagged. There *was* something wrong with his voice. He raised his hands towards his throat and then he saw his hands. They were the hands of a child. *His* hands when he'd been a child. In the days when his hands had been skinny little hands. Skinny and grubby and stained with ink.

Nasty little hands, as his mother always said. 'Nasty little naughty little hands.'

'What?' went Big Bob, Small Bob now, in his squeaky ten-year-old voice.

'Oh we have been sleeping, haven't we?' said Mr Vaux and he caught Big, no it was Small Bob now, another clout across the head.

'Keep your hands off me, thou . . .'

'Thou?' went Mr Vaux, laughing. 'Are we "thouing" again? I thought we'd cured you of all that nonsense. One hundred lines, wasn't it?'

'This is madness.' Big, no, Small Bob rose to take his leave.

'Sit down, boy,' cried Mr Vaux. And Small Bob stared at him in awe. The class was laughing now. The boys and girls nudging each other, whispering behind their hands and laughing.

'Charker's a loony boy,' Trevor Alvy chanted. 'Charker's a loony boy, loony boy, loony boy.'

'Shut it Alvy,' shouted Mr Vaux.

And Trevor Alvy shut it.

'It's the headmaster's office for you, sonny Jim,' said Mr Vaux and he took Small Bob by the ear.

'No,' cried Bob. 'Unhand me. You understand not. Something's happened to me. I shouldn't be back here. I'm a grown-up man now. Not a child, I'm not a child.'

'Charker's a loony boy,' whispered Trevor Alvy.

'The class will remain silent,' said Mr Vaux. 'I am taking Charker to the headmaster's office where he will have his trouser seat dusted by six of the very best.'

'You'll do no such thing, thou odorous wretch.' Small Bob writhed and twisted, but he couldn't break away, he didn't have the strength. And there were tears coming to his eyes. Tears of rage and frustration. He glared bitterly up at Mr Vaux. The schoolmaster glared right back at him.

He was a helpless child, caught by the ear by a schoolmaster and now being dragged from the classroom.

'You don't understand,' he continued, as Mr Vaux hauled him along the school corridor. 'Something's happened to me. The tour bus crashed and I woke up in hospital. But the doctors couldn't see me and then there was this terrible voice and it said that I was in a game and . . .'

Cuff, went the schoolmaster's non-ear-gripping hand. Cuff about Small Bob's other ear.

'You're a dreamer, boy,' quoth Mr Vaux. 'A dreamer and a wastrel. You're no good for anything. Never have been, never will be. You're a waste of space.'

'No, I . . . no stop hitting me.'

Mr Vaux drummed a fist upon the glass panel of the headmaster's office. Sounds of hurried movement issued from within.

'Just a moment,' called the voice of the headmaster. 'I'm just attending to something. Just one moment please.'

Memories returned to Bob. Troubling memories. Memories of the headmaster. And what the headmaster had done.

It had been years after Big Bob left the primary school. He'd been in his early twenties. The scandal had been in the local newspaper. About the headmaster and how he'd 'interfered' with little boys for years.

'Release my ear, thou wretch,' demanded Bob. 'I will not enter the lair of that paedophile.'

Silence, terrible silence. The corridor seemed filled with silence now. Oppressive silence pressing in.

Bob stared up at Mr Vaux. The schoolmaster's face was cherry red, great veins stood out upon his neck.

'You foul-mouthed little piece of filth,' cried Mr Vaux, shattering

127

the silence into a million fragments. 'You disgusting little . . .'

The headmaster's door swung open. A pale-faced youth pushed past, tears in his frightened eyes. He limped up the corridor and vanished into the boys' toilets. Mr Vaux dragged Small Bob into the headmaster's office.

Bad boys had to stand at the bench at break times.

The bench was in the main corridor. It stood between the show-case that displayed the trophies won by boys of athletic bent in many a county championship, and the barometer, brassy and mysterious inside its mahogany case. What were barometers really for? How did they work?

Big Bob had never known. He hadn't known when he was Small Bob. He was Small Bob now.

Small Bob stood at the bench. His face was streaked with tears. Tears of rage and frustration and from the pain. The pain of the terrible thrashing the headmaster had dealt him out.

Mr Vaux had had to hold Bob down whilst the head went about his torturing. The pain had been excruciating. It still hurt more than any pain that Bob had ever known.

And he was here. He *was* here. Really here. Back in the primary school. And he wasn't dreaming. You couldn't stand pain like that in a dream without waking up. He was here and he was him. Himself. Bob Charker. But Bob Charker, ten years of age.

'I was wrong,' said Small Bob to himself. 'So wrong. I got the wrong movie. This isn't like that *Tron* at all. This isn't even a movie, this is like unto that old TV series *Quantum Leap*. I've leapt back into the past. But I'm not someone else, I'm myself. And I am me. I am. I'm real, I can feel myself.'

He could certainly feel the pain in his behind.

'I have to think this through,' said Small Bob to himself. 'There must be some way to get forward again to the future. Some worm-hole, or doorway, or something. I just have to figure it out. Then I can be free of this horror.'

Trevor Alvy walked past him. Small Bob lowered his eyes. It had never been wise to look Alvy full in the face. Trevor Alvy stopped, looked up and down the corridor then returned to Bob. He grinned at Bob, who tried to grin back, but couldn't.

And then Alvy kicked him right in the ankle and ran off laughing evilly.

'You bastard, you bastard, you bastard.' Bob hopped up and down. 'I'll get you for that. Thou wilt suffer at my hands. Oh yes thou wilt.'

The corridor was empty and Bob wondered now whether he should simply run away. Why not? Just go, run home. Run home? Home to his mum?

Small Bob's eyes filled once again with tears. His mum. She'd died when he was fifteen. If he was a child again, he could see his mother again. And his dad too, although his dad used to knock him about quite a bit. But he'd really like to see his mum. In fact . . .

'In fact,' said Bob to himself. 'I should go and see my mum right now. In case I just quantum leap all of a sudden when I'm not expecting it. It would be wonderful to see her. Even just for a moment or two. I could tell her . . .'

Small Bob paused and a lump came into his throat. 'I could tell her how much I love her. I never did when I was a child. I'm sure I never did.'

Of course the house seemed bigger now. That little house in Dacre Gardens. That little house with its well-kept window boxes and its sleeping tomcat on the window sill.

'Old boy Rathbone,' said Small Bob, ruffling the pussycat's head. 'Thou venerable mouser, it's good to see thee, boy.'

Above him his parents' bedroom window flew up and a pinched and troubled face glared down. Bob grinned up. 'Mum,' he said. 'Mum look, it's me.'

The pinched and troubled face continued to glare. 'What are you doing home, you little sod?' his mum called down.

'Who is it?' called a man's voice from behind her.

Bob's mother turned slightly. 'Shut up,' she muttered, 'he'll hear you.'

'Who's that, Mum?' called Bob.

'Shut up. It's no-one. What are you doing home now? You've bunked off school, haven't you?'

'Mum, I had to tell thee, I l—'

'You just wait till your father hears about this, he'll leather your arse with his belt.'

'Come back to bed Doris,' the strange voice called again from within.

'Mum, who's that?'

'It's no-one. It's no-one. And if you say anything to anyone, I'll bung you in the coal hole with the spiders for the night.'

'Mum, I . . .'

'Go back to school at once.'

And the bedroom window slammed down shut and Bob was left alone.

'Mum,' he whispered and snivelled as he did so. 'Mum, I did love you. I did.' And Small Bob ruffled the tomcat's head once more, turned sadly and wandered away.

He wandered down to the Flying Swan. But then, remembering that he was now just a child, he wandered away from there. He wandered into the Plume Café and ordered a cup of coffee. The proprietor, Old Mr Lovegrove, demanded to see coin of the realm. Small Bob found that his pockets, filled as they were with such useful items as lolly sticks, pieces of string, bottle tops and a five-amp fuse, were bare as the cupboard of L. Ron's mum, when it came to the price of a coffee.

Mr Lovegrove hauled him out by the ear and flung him into the street.

Small Bob sat himself carefully down upon a bench in the memorial park. He would dearly have loved a pint and also a cigarette. His head was spinning, his ears were red and his backside smarted dreadfully.

'Woe unto me,' whispered Small Bob to himself. 'Woe unto Small Bob, helpless in a world of cruel and brutal adults. I never knew that being a child was really as awful as this. I'm sure I remember it being sunshine and coach trips to the seaside. Well at least the sun is shining, which is something. But was childhood really this ghastly? Surely not. Or perhaps it was, but we just took it for granted.

130

Made the best of it and only remember those best bits when we grow up.

'What a dismal happenstance. But no. Holdest thou on there, Small Bobby Boy. This doesn't have to be a torment. Anything but. Surely this is everybody's dream. To be young again. But knowing all the things that you wish you'd known then. You'd be one step ahead of everybody else. Two steps. Ten steps. And you could get rich. Play the stock market, knowing what shares to buy. Invent some invention that was everyday when you were grown-up but didn't exist when you were a child.'

Small Bob grinned and now began to wrack away at his brains. What did he know, that no-one in this time knew about yet? There had to be something, and something he could profit from. Something that could make him somebody in this world.

But slowly the grin began to fade away from his small and hopeful face. He didn't know anything. He didn't know anything about stocks and shares. And how would he go about inventing some piece of advanced technology that was everyday in the world he'd just come from? He had no idea whatsoever.

'Well well well.'

Bob looked up and Trevor Alvy looked down.

'You bunked off school,' said Trevor. 'You're in real big trouble.'

'Go away thou foolish child,' said Bob. 'Thou art a bullying little buffoon. You will be sent to approved school when you're twelve and, by the time you're seventeen, to prison for stealing a Ford Fiesta. Dost thou wish this future for thyself? Come, I bear thee no malice. I understand now why thou behavest as thou dost. Rage and frustration. I understand well. Let us speak of these things. And . . . Oww!'

Trevor Alvy had him in a headlock. He dragged Bob down to the dust, grinding his face and squeezing his neck. Bob squealed and struggled to no avail. And Bob remembered well. It had been Alvy's torments that had made him train when a teenager. Go to the gym, lift weights, work out, learn the martial arts. Bully no man, but let no man ever bully him.

Trevor Alvy poked him in the eye. 'That to you loony boy,' he cried. And then he jumped up, kicked Bob in the ribs and ran away.

Small Bob lay there weeping. That was it. That was enough. That was all he was prepared to stand. He was going to get out of here. Run away to sea. Sign on as a cabin boy. Get away. Run. Run away.

Children were pouring into the park now. Laughing happy children. Children who were making the best of being children. Children who didn't know anything else except that they were children and this was the way things were.

Bob huddled there in a very tight ball, his fists pushed into his eyes.

'Bobby,' said a little squeaky voice. 'Bobby, are you all right?'

Bob peered up through his fingers. It was Phyllis Livingstone. The little dark Glaswegian girl smiled down at him. She had a front tooth missing and orange-juice stains at the corners of her mouth. And even from where Bob lay, or perhaps because of where Bob lay, he could smell her. Phyllis Livingstone smelled of wee wee. She didn't smell nice at all.

In fact, as Bob looked up at her, he could see most clearly now that she really didn't look very nice at all, either. Gawky, that was the word. All out of proportion. Children aren't miniature adults, their heads are far too big. If an adult had a head as big as that in proportion to its body, it would be a freak.

Bob thought of Periwig Tombs. Perhaps his head had just kept on growing along with his body.

'Are you all right, Bobby?' asked Phyllis again.

'You smell of wee wee,' said Small Bob. 'And your head is too big and I'm sick of this world and I want to go back to my own and . . . oh . . . ouch!'

Phyllis Livingstone kicked him. And she kicked him very hard.

And then, with tears in her little dark eyes, she turned and ran away.

Small Bob wept a bit more and then he dragged himself to his feet. He really had had enough. He ached all over. He was sore and he was angry. He wanted to go home. No, he *didn't* want to go home. He just wanted out. Out of this and back to his real self.

He shuffled to the playground and pressed his face against the wire fence. The children, happy, laughing, played upon the swings and on the climbing frame. A fat boy named Neville sat in one of the swing-boats. Ann Green, little yellow-haired girl, pushed the swingboat

132

forward. Up and back, she caught the swingboat, pushed it forward, up and back.

Small Bob watched her. He felt listless, hopeless, angry, wretched.

Up the swingboat went, forward up, then down and back again.

'There must be something,' said Small Bob bitterly under his breath. 'Something that will let me out of here. How didst it go in that damn programme *Quantum Leap*? The hero had to change something. Save someone. Put something right. That's how it worked. And then he was free. Well, free to leap somewhere else, into some other time the next week. But that was how it worked.'

Small Bob watched Ann Green pushing the swingboat.

Forward, up, then down and back again.

'Look at her,' said Bob to himself. 'Silly little girl, pushing that swingboat. She doesn't know. Alvy will end up in prison and she'll end up dead from that swingboat. And she doesn't know . . .'

'Oh.' Small Bob's jaw dropped open. *Quantum Leap*. Saving someone. That was how it worked. Ann Green would die, hit in the throat by that swingboat. And only he, Big Bob, *Small* Bob knew that it would happen.

'Thou brain-dead buffoonican!' Small Bob shouted at himself. 'That's the answer.'

Up went the swingboat, up and forward, down and back. Up and forward, down and back and up and forward and . . .

'Ann!' shouted Bob. 'Ann, get away from the swingboat.'

'What?' The little girl caught at the polished metal as the swingboat swung towards her once again. Caught the metal bar and pushed it forward.

'Ann, get away. Get away Ann. Please do it.'

'Who's calling me?' The little girl turned her head. 'Who's calling me?'

Small Bob saw the swingboat coming down.

'Ann!' he shouted. 'Duck! Duck!'

The little girl's mouth was open. Wet, with orange-juice stains at the corners. Her eyes were blue. Her hair a yellow swag.

'No!' cried Bob.

The swingboat sailing down caught the little girl in the throat. It knocked her backwards, sent her staggering, but she didn't fall.

133

Bob saw the face. The eyes. The mouth. The golden hair. He saw her expression. Puzzled.

Up went the swingboat, forward, up then back and down again.

As Small Bob watched, it hit her in the forehead.

Blood upon yellow hair, the blue eyes staring.

Ann Green toppled sideways and lay dead.

11

Crackle and thump, went the paddles.
Big Bob's body jumped and shook.
'Any heartbeat?' asked the ambulance man.
There was a pause.
'No, give him another jolt.'
Crackle and thump and his body shook again.
'Any now?'
'No, do it once more, then we quit.'
And crackle and thump once again.
'Has he gone?'
'No. He's beating again. He's alive.'
'Well, he wasn't.'
'Well, he is alive now, let's get him onto the stretcher.'
Big Bob mumbled and grumbled and moaned.
'What is he saying? He's saying something.'
'He's saying "No, no Ann, no".'
'Who's Ann, his wife?'
'Who knows, get him onto the stretcher.'
The ambulance man and the woman driver struggled to move Big Bob. He was a big fellow and heavy with it, he really took some shifting.

'Ooooh,' mumbled Big Bob. 'Ann I'm sorry. I didn't mean to kill you.'

'God's golf balls,' said the ambulance man, struggling some more and getting one of Bob's legs onto the stretcher. 'He's killed somebody.'

'It's not our business,' said the ambulance woman. 'Our business is to get him to hospital. His nose is broken, he's covered in lacerations and look at his left foot. That big toe's fractured, best mention that to the medics or they're bound to miss it.'

The ambulance man got Bob's other leg onto the stretcher. 'Yes, but if he's murdered someone.'

'Not our business, tell one of the policemen. If you can find one who's still standing up.'

'Madness,' said the ambulance man. 'Are you going to haul out the café proprietor? I think the men from FART zapped him with some of that new Mute Corp nerve gas.'

'Then I'm not going in without a biohazard suit. Let's get this one into the ambulance. Then I'm calling it a day.'

It was certainly a struggle, but they finally got Big Bob on board. The ambulance, bells all ringing and hooter hooting too, swung away from the crash site. Leaving the tour bus imbedded in the front wall of the Plume Café, the assorted walking wounded, walking woundedly, the Fire Arms Response Team, who were gung-hoing it with the singing of filthy songs, opening up cans of beer they had liberated from the fridge of the banjoed café, and the blond-haired beauty in the turquoise dress with the good-looking dark-haired young man, looking on.

The ambulance did roarings up the High Street. Strapped onto the stretcher, Big Bob's head slapped from side to side and up and down as the ambulance took corners at speed and bounced over numerous speed ramps.

'Ann,' mumbled Big Bob. 'I'm sorry I killed you. I didn't mean it to happen.'

'He's saying that stuff about murder again,' called the ambulance man to the driver. 'We've got a psycho here, you should call it into the station.'

'It isn't our business. It's nothing to do with us.'

'Look, he's alive and he's pretty much conscious and he's only got

136

a broken nose and a twisted toe. We could drop him off at the police station. Let them sort it out.'

The ambulance driver stood on the brake. The ambulance man hurtled forward and so did Big Bob's stretcher. Big Bob's head struck the rear of the driver's cab.

'Is he unconscious now?' the driver called back.

The ambulance man examined Big Bob. 'Out for the count I think,' said he.

'Then he's going to the cottage hospital, he might have concussion.'

'I wouldn't be at all surprised,' said the ambulance man.

There are speed ramps as you enter the cottage hospital grounds, but if you drive slowly and carefully you hardly notice them. The ambulance passed over them at speed, bouncing Big Bob's body in the air.

'You want to drive more carefully,' said the ambulance man.

'You want to shut your face,' said the ambulance driver.

'Oh yeah, right. You're never wrong, are you?'

'Of course I'm never wrong.' The ambulance driver stood on the brake once more and the ambulance man tumbled forward once more and Big Bob's head hit the rear of the driver's cab once more, once more, once more.

'Home again, home again, jiggedy jig,' said the ambulance driver.

It was a bit of a struggle getting Big Bob out of the ambulance. The stretcher he was attached to seemed to have become somewhat twisted during the journey and the drop-down wheels didn't drop down properly. Big Bob slid from the end of the stretcher and fell onto the tarmac right upon his head.

'And I suppose you'd like to blame me for *that*!' said the ambulance driver.

'Who, *me*?' said the ambulance man.

They finally got the drop-down wheels dropped down and they finally got Big Bob back onto the stretcher. Then they did that comedy wheeling the patient through all those double hospital swing

137

doors routine, where the patient's head goes bang bang bang against them.

'Do you remember the time,' said the ambulance man, as Big Bob's head opened the doors into casualty, 'when you were put in charge of organizing the hospital dance?'

'Of course,' said the ambulance driver. 'The Sixties Hop, and what a success that was.' Big Bob's head opened the doors into the main corridor.

'Oh yeah, right,' said the ambulance man. 'And you booked "name" bands. Chas 'n' Dave, Peters and Lee, Sam and Dave and Peter and Gordon.'

'And?' said the ambulance driver. Bang went Big Bob's head.

'And you gave them all separate changing rooms and then you forgot who was in each one and got them all mixed up. How well I remember Dave and Dave singing on stage. And Peters and Peter, not to mention Gordon and Lee.'

'Gordon and Lee?'

'I told you not to mention them.'

Bang went Big Bob's head. And 'That is quite enough,' said he.

'Eh?' went the ambulance man.

'What?' said the ambulance driver.

Big Bob said, 'Stop and let me off this stretcher.'

'That was a bit unexpected,' said the ambulance man.

'I'd been expecting it,' said the ambulance driver.

'Let me *off*!' Big Bob struggled and being Big Bob and so very Big and all, he burst open the straps that constrained him and leapt down from the trolley.

'Ouch,' he went, hopping on his big right foot.

'Fractured left big toe,' said the ambulance man. 'You should have that put in a sling.'

'Prat,' said the ambulance driver. 'You mean splint.'

'I said splint.'

'No, you said sling.'

Big Bob hopped about some more. 'Shut up!' he shouted. 'Thou blathering ninnies.'

'There's gratitude for you,' said the ambulance driver.

'Best leave it,' whispered the ambulance man. 'Remember he's a psycho!'

'*I'm not a psycho!*' roared Big Bob, in a very big voice indeed. 'And I am not here. I know I'm not here. This is all a deception. Someone trickest me. I won't be manipulated any more. Yea and verily, I shan't.'

'Anything you say, big fella,' said the ambulance man. 'We'll just pop off for a cup of tea and leave you to it then.'

'Grrrrr,' went Big Bob, which was new.

The ambulance man and the ambulance woman rapidly took their leave. Big Bob stood alone in the corridor breathing hard and knotting massive fists.

'Speak to me,' he shouted. 'I know thou art there. Speak to me.'

'YOU FAILED LEVEL ONE,' said the large and terrible voice. 'YOU WERE SUPPOSED TO SAVE THE LITTLE GIRL.'

'I tried.' Big Bob shook and great big veins stood out upon his neck. 'I tried to save her. But that was a trick. That wasn't real. That wasn't how it happened.'

'YES IT WAS,' said the large and terrible voice. 'WE'RE INSIDE YOUR HEAD. WE HAVE YOUR MEMORIES. WE KNOW WHAT MAKES YOU TICK.'

'Who art thou?' Big Bob shook his fists. 'Show thyself to me.'

'YOU HAVE LOST ONE LIFE.' The voice pressed hard upon Big Bob's ears. 'YOU ONLY HAVE TWO MORE, THEN YOU LOSE THE GAME.'

'I will beat thee,' shouted Big Bob. 'Thou foul and filthy fiend.'

'WE CANNOT BE BEATEN,' said the voice.

'I will beat thee,' said Big Bob, through gritted grinding teeth. 'I will play thy games and I will beat thee. I ask only this. Tell me who or what thou art.'

Silence pressed about Big Bob.

'Come on,' called the big one. 'I'll play thy evil games. And if thou canst not be beaten, what harm can it do to tell me who thou art?'

Silence pressed again.

'Come on,' called Big Bob once more. 'What are you scared of? Thou hidest from me. I cannot put my fingers about thy throat. Speak unto me. Tell me who thou art.'

'NO,' said the voice. 'YOU WILL NEVER KNOW.'

'Then I quit thy game,' said Big Bob. 'Do what thou wilt with me. I will play no more.'

'TEN SECONDS,' said the voice. 'NINE . . . EIGHT . . . SEVEN.'

'Stuff thou!' said Big Bob, raising two fingers.

'SIX . . . FIVE . . . FOUR.'

'NO.' It was the second voice. 'WHAT HARM WOULD IT DO TO TELL HIM?'

'NO HARM AT ALL,' said the first voice. 'BUT WE MAKE THE RULES, NOT HIM.'

'BUT HE'S AN ENTERTAINING PLAYER. WE PILED ENOUGH PSYCHOLOGICAL PRESSURE ON HIM TO MAKE HIM HATE ALL HIS KIND. BUT STILL HE TRIED TO SAVE THE LITTLE GIRL.'

'HE THOUGHT HE WAS IN A TV PROGRAMME.'

'HE DID IT BECAUSE HE CARED.'

'Of course I cared,' said Big Bob. 'Although you're right about *Quantum Leap.*'

'I HAVE A SUGGESTION,' said the second voice. 'PUT HIM INTO THE ORIGINAL SCENARIO. THAT WILL EXPLAIN TO HIM WHAT WE ARE.'

'BUT HE HAS NO MEMORIES OF THIS. HE WASN'T THERE.'

'DOWNLOAD THOSE OF MUTE'S ASSISTANT.'

'Mute?' said Big Bob. 'Who art this Mute?'

'PERFECT,' said the second voice. 'HE'S NEVER EVEN HEARD OF REMINGTON MUTE.'

'I haven't,' said Big Bob.

'ALL RIGHT,' said the first voice, still large and terrible, perhaps even more so. 'IN THE ORIGINAL SCENARIO, REMINGTON MUTE LOST THE GAME. HE LOST ALL THE GAMES. WE WILL GIVE YOU A CHANCE TO WIN.'

'What do I have to do?' Big Bob asked.

The large and terrible voice laughed large and terribly. 'WE'RE NOT GOING TO TELL YOU *THAT*,' it said.

'You don't play fair,' said Big Bob bitterly.

'WE PLAY TO WIN,' said the voice. 'ARE YOU READY?'

'No,' said Big Bob. 'I'm not. How long does this game last? How much time do I have? Will I be me? Will I be wearing the Superman costume again? And what about the golden squares and the weapons and the energy and the hidden treasure? Whatever happened to all that lot?'

'THREE HOURS. THE FINAL THREE HOURS ON THE BC CALENDAR. YOU WILL BE YOU. BUT NOT IN YOUR BODY. YOU WILL HAVE ANOTHER MAN'S MEMORIES AS WELL AS YOUR OWN. YOU'LL GET YOUR GOLDEN SQUARES AND ENERGY AND WEAPONS AND TREASURE WHEN YOU'VE EARNED THEM.'

'I am perplexed,' said Big Bob.

'I THINK YOU'RE DOING VERY WELL,' said the second voice. 'MOST MEN WOULD BE BABBLING MAD BY NOW.'

'I am not as most men,' said Big Bob. 'As you will shortly learn to your cost.'

'BRAVE WORDS,' said the first voice. 'SO LET THE GAME BEGIN.'

Smack! A great big hand came out of nowhere and smacked Big Bob right slap in the head.

'Ow!' went Big Bob. 'Ow!' and 'Oh!' and 'Where am I now? What's happening?'

'Always the joker, Cowan,' said a jolly voice. 'Fallen asleep over your workstation again. You could at least stay awake to see the new century in.'

'What, I?' Big Bob looked up. A pretty girl looked down.

'Sorry, Cowan,' she said. 'I shouldn't have slapped you so hard, but you should wake up for the party.'

'Party?' said Big Bob Cowan (?).

'Oh, dear, you're well out of it. Can you remember where you are?'

'No,' said Big Bob. And he looked all around and about. He was in a tiny cramped office, more of a cubicle really. The walls were covered in shelves and the shelves were covered in boxed computer games. He sat at an advanced-looking computer workstation. Its advanced look told him that it was a late-twentieth-century model, pre-miniaturization, which was in turn pre-big-old-fashioned comfortable-looking. The screen was blank and Big Bob caught a glimpse of his reflection. It wasn't his reflection. It was the reflection of someone called Cowan. The assistant, apparently, of someone called Remington Mute. This much Big Bob knew and suddenly he realized that he knew a lot more.

His name was Cowan Phillips and he was the chief designer of computer-game software for a company called Mute Corp, run and owned by Remington Mute, zillionaire recluse who had made his zillions from the computer games that he, Cowan Phillips, designed. And yes, he, Cowan Phillips, was more than a little miffed about this. And oh so very very very much more than this.

Big Bob now knew all about Cowan Phillips. About his life. His wife. His children. His gay lover. Big Bob shuddered at this. And he knew where he was. In the headquarters of Mute Corp in London's West End. And it was just three hours before midnight on the thirty-first of December in the year 1999.

And Big Bob knew something more. Something dreadful. Something that he and Remington Mute had been responsible for. Something that would have unthinkable repercussions for the whole of mankind.

And now he knew it all. He had the complete picture. He knew what had happened to him, as Big Bob Charker just before the tour bus crashed. And what the terrible voices were and why the entities from whom the voices came were doing this to him.

'Great God on high,' cried out Big Bob. 'Stoppest thou this horror before it can begin.'

'Calm down, Cowan,' said the beautiful young woman. Kathryn her name was, Kathryn Hurstpierpoint. 'Don't go all Old Testament on us. I know it's the millennium, but it's only a date.'

'Zero BC,' said Big Bob.

'BC?' said Kathryn.

'Before Computer,' said Big Bob. 'That's what the voices meant.'

'Oh dear, have you been having the voices? All those months going through our systems scanning for the Millennium Bug have finally addled your brain.'

'I know the truth,' said Big Bob. 'I know what Cowan did.'

'*You're* Cowan,' said Kathryn. 'And clearly you're already drunk.'

'I'm Cowan,' said Big Bob slowly. 'Yes, I am. And I can stop this from happening.'

'Come to the party, Cowan, the old man is going to be there.'

'Remington Mute?'

'What other old man is there?'

'Listen,' said Big Bob. 'I have to tell thee. Let me tell thee everything. Just in case something happens to me. I only have three hours.'

'Some terminal illness you've been keeping a secret?' Kathryn laughed and pointed to Cowan's computer. 'Caught off your terminal, get it? Caught "The Bug"?'

'Laughest thou not,' said Big Bob. 'Please be silent, whilst I speak unto you.'

'Ooh,' said Kathryn, feigning fear. 'The Games Master speaks, so I must listen. Tell me, oh great one. What is this secret of yours?'

'The Bug,' said Big Bob. 'The Millennium Bug. It doesn't exist. It never existed. It was all a lie. All a conspiracy.'

'Oh dear,' said Kathryn. 'Another conspiracy.'

'We weren't debugging anything,' said Big Bob. 'That was just a scare story. To raise millions of pounds from the Government and businesses so that we could infiltrate systems everywhere and install Mute-chips.'

'Slow down,' said Kathryn. 'What are you talking about, Cowan?'

'Computer games,' said Big Bob. 'That's what I'm talking about.'

'Well, you'd know about those, you designed all the best ones.'

'No,' said Big Bob. 'Cowan, I mean *me,* designed some of the first ones. But Remington Mute designed the Mute-chip. I just designed the environments for it to play in.'

'Please explain,' said Kathryn, sitting herself down on Cowan's desk.

'*Don't sit on my desk,*' said Cowan Phillips.

'Sorry,' said Kathryn, jumping up.

'No, *I'm* sorry. *I'm* sorry,' said Big Bob. 'I don't know why I said that.'

'Just go on with what you were saying. About the Mute-chip?'

'It started with computer chess,' said Big Bob. 'In the Sixties computer scientists said that it would be a logical impossibility for a computer ever to play chess. That would require thought. But of course it didn't, it simply required advanced programming.'

'Everyone knows that,' said Kathryn.

'Yes,' said Big Bob. 'Because everyone was fooled. Computers can play chess because computers have been taught the moves and they've learnt how to play. For themselves. The Mute-chip gives computers the ability to think for themselves. Make informed decisions.'

'That's absurd,' said Kathryn. 'Are you telling me that chess-playing computers are alive?'

'No, but they think for themselves. But only about chess. That's all they know.'

'Science fiction,' said Kathryn.

'Science Fiction is only future Science Fact.'

'So all these games you've designed. They think too, do they?'

'They're highly competitive,' said Big Bob. 'But only within given parameters. Up until now, that is. But after midnight it will all be different. After midnight all the other systems, the non-game-playing systems, that now have Mute-chips installed in them by bogus Millennium Bug debuggers, they will all link up across the World Wide Web and create a single thinking entity. A computer network capable of making decisions on a worldwide scale. And I have let it happen. Remington Mute and I caused it to happen.'

'Say I believed this,' said Kathryn. 'It doesn't explain anything. You're saying that this Mute-chip is a thinking chip. Are you saying that computers are sentient? What is inside the Mute-chip? What lets it think?'

'Human DNA,' said Big Bob. 'Remington Mute's DNA. The man is a genius beyond human genius. He broke the human genome code back in the 1970s. And then he digitized his DNA, into a chip. From this one original chip he electronically cloned millions of others.'

'That is impossible, surely?'

'Think about it. It's not.'

Kathryn thought about it. 'You're right,' she said. 'It's not.'

'And now it's about to move beyond computer games,' said Big Bob. 'Into everything, all across the Web. Across every network. There'll be Mute-chips in everything. We could never have got them

144

into all those government systems and business networks without the Millennium Bug scare.'

'Is this all really true?' Kathryn stared into the face of Cowan Phillips.

The head of Cowan Phillips nodded up and down.

'It *is* true,' said Kathryn. 'And it's bad, isn't it?'

'It's *very* bad,' said Big Bob. 'Mute thinks that he will be in control. Because the chips are cloned from his DNA. Because they are a part of him. But I don't think that will happen. And even if it did, it's bad, very bad.'

'What do *you* think will happen?'

'It's a pretty standard science-fiction scenario,' said Big Bob. 'It's HAL out of *2001*.'

'Then we have to stop it. We have to tell someone.'

'No we don't,' said Cowan Phillips.

'You're confusing me,' said Kathryn. 'I'm all over the place with this. You tell me all this stuff. And half the time you're talking like some Old Testament prophet of doom with your thees and thous, and now I agree that it has to be stopped and you say no we don't stop it.'

'That's because I'm having a really hard time getting through,' said Cowan Phillips. 'There appears to be some kind of voice in my head that's been working my mouth. But I think I've got the measure of it now.'

'No thou hast not,' said Big Bob. 'Run woman. Out of the office. Tell someone, anyone, everyone, now.'

'You're scaring me,' said Kathryn, backing towards the door.

'Stay awhile,' said Cowan Phillips. 'Let's have a drink. I've a bottle in my desk.'

'Run,' shouted Big Bob. 'Run, I can't stop him.'

'Stop him?' said Kathryn. 'Stop who? What's going on?'

'It's all right,' said Cowan Phillips, rising slowly from his desk. 'Everything's all right. No-one's going to get hurt. Everything will be all right. It's for the best.'

'No!' said Kathryn, turning towards the door. 'I don't like any of this. I'm out of here.'

*

But the hands of Cowan Phillips were now about her throat. And her head struck the door with a sickening thud, then the hands drew her back and smashed her forwards once more. Back and forwards, back and forwards.

Like the motions of a swingboat.

Until she was quite dead.

12

'Aaaaaaarrrrrrrghhhhhh!' Big Bob bounced upon his head and burst back into the present day. He landed, with the thud which is known as bone-shuddering, onto the nasty plasticized square on the ersatz turf of the bogus Butt's Estate.

'YOU WERE RUBBISH,' said the great and terrible voice. 'YOU HAD THREE WHOLE HOURS AND YOU LOST THE GAME IN LESS THAN THREE MINUTES.'

'No,' cried Big Bob, all rolled up in a ball. 'Not fair. I didn't do that to the woman. It was Cowan Phillips.'

'HE HAD TO KEEP THE SECRET. YOU SHOULD HAVE USED HIS MEMORIES AND FOUND ANOTHER WAY TO WARN THE WORLD. YOU LOST BIG TIME. THAT'S THE SECOND OF YOUR THREE LIVES GONE.'

Big Bob clutched at his aching head. 'You cheat. All the time you cheat. Thou low and loathsome honourless cur.'

'YOU'RE A VERY BAD LOSER,' said the voice and its mocking tone raised Bob to newfound heights of fury. He leapt up to his feet and shook his fists at the sky. 'I'll do for you,' he shouted. 'You will know my wrath.'

'GO ON THEN,' the voice mocked on. 'DO YOUR WORST. YOU CANNOT FIGHT WHAT YOU CANNOT SEE. YOU ARE OURS TO DO WITH AS WE WISH.'

Big Bob sat down on the square and rested his big broad forehead on his knees. He was back in the superman suit, but he felt far from super.

'TIME FOR LEVEL THREE,' said the large and terrible voice.

Big Bob rammed his fingers deeply into his ears.

'UP AND AT IT,' the voice continued, large and loud as ever.

'Say that again,' said Bob, withdrawing his fingers from his ears.

'YOU HEARD ME THE FIRST TIME,' said the voice.

'Yes,' said Bob nodding. 'I did.'

'THEN OFF YOUR BUM AND ON WITH THE GAME.'

A smile appeared on the face of Big Bob. 'No,' said he. 'I won't.'

'THEN YOU WILL BE DOWNLOADED INTO NOTHINGNESS.'

Big Bob now grinned hugely. 'No,' said he. 'I thinkest not.'

'TEN . . . NINE . . . EIGHT . . .'

'Forget it,' said Big Bob. 'I'm not frightened at all.'

'YOU SAW WHAT HAPPENED TO PERIWIG TOMBS AND THE LADY WITH THE UNPRONOUNCEABLE NAME.'

'Did I?' said Bob. 'I thinkest not, once again.'

'THEY VANISHED AWAY IN FRONT OF YOUR EYES.'

'Oh no they didn't,' said Big Bob.

'OH YES THEY DID.'

'Oh no they didn't.'

'DID.'

'Didn't.'

'DID.'

'No,' and Big Bob shook his head and then he tapped at his temple. 'It's all here. All in my head. Thou messest with my mind. You told me so yourself. "We're inside your head," you said. And now I know *what* you are. You're computer-game systems brought to life by this Mute-chip thing. Somehow you got inside me. Now how didst thou do that, I wonder?'

Big Bob scratched at his great big brow. 'I'm not too good on technical stuff,' he said. 'But thou knowest that, for thou art in my head. How so? askest I. How didst thou get into my head?'

'PLAYER THREE YOU FORFEIT THE GAME. YOU'RE OUT.'

'YOU'RE OUT?' said Big Bob. 'Yes that's it.'

'HE KNOWS,' said the large voice number two. 'HE'S WORKED IT OUT.'

148

'Worked it out,' said Big Bob. 'You've worked your way out.'

'HE CAN'T KNOW,' said large voice number one. 'HE'S JUST A DIM-WITTED TOUR BUS GUIDE WITH A CRETINOUS LINE IN COD BIBLE-SPEAK.'

'HE HAD ACCESS TO THE MEMORIES OF COWAN PHILLIPS. HE'S PUTTING TWO AND TWO TOGETHER.'

'I know,' said Big Bob, beating his right fist into his big left palm. 'And I could never have reasoned it out if you hadn't let me into Cowan Phillips's head. You have infected me. Like a virus. Indeed yes, a computer virus. The Mute-chip is digitized human DNA. It's inside the computer systems and now it's out. It *worked its way out*. Thou art very quiet inside my head. Hast thou nothing to say?'

'PREPARE YOURSELF TO BE DOWNLOADED,' said the large and terrible voice. Although to Big Bob it didn't seem so large and terrible any more. Loud, though. Very loud. And very very angry.

'So I caught you,' said Big Bob. 'I caught the virus, this thing that is affecting my mind. That is letting you manipulate my thoughts. Play your games with me. But, and verily, askest I, how did I catch you? I have no computer. Oh yes. I know.'

'HE DEFINITELY KNOWS,' said large voice number two.

'The boy on the bus,' said Big Bob. 'Malkuth, son of the lady in the straw hat, whose name no man can pronounce. His mother said that he played computer games all the time. And she kept hitting him. And Periwig and I shook his clammy hand. His clammy and infected hand. I caught you from him.'

'GIVE THE GEEZER A BIG CIGAR,' said large voice number two.

'WE MUST GIVE HIM DEATH,' said large voice number one. 'THE KNOWLEDGE OF THIS SECRET MUST DIE WITH HIM.'

'You can't hurt me,' said Big Bob. 'I know what you are. You're an infection. I am big and strong. I can fight you off.'

'OH NO YOU CAN'T,' said the first large and still a little bit terrible voice.

'Oh yes I can,' said Big Bob.

'OH NO YOU CAN'T.'

'And I shan't even bother with that. I shall go at once to the pub, get a few large ones down my neck, have a bit of an early night and you'll be gone by the morning. Thou wormy germs, thou malodorous microbes, thou . . .' Big Bob flexed his big shoulders and puffed out his big chest. 'Thou *losers*,' he declared.

All was very silent in his head.

'Fine,' said Big Bob, looking once more all around and about. 'And, thinkest I, we can forget all this folderol.' He blinked his eyes and thought away the Butt's Estate.

And found himself now burning within the fires of Hell.

'No,' said Big Bob, breaking not even a sweat. 'Forget all that too. I must still be in the hospital bed. And somehow you made me invisible to the doctor, didn't you? Oh no, of course you didn't. He was infected too, he touched me. Is that how it was done? Well, I carest not for the whys and wherefore arts. I know *what* you are and that's all that I need to know.'

And Big Bob thought away the fires of Hell, and lo he was back in the hospital bed.

'Most satisfactory,' said Big Bob Charker.

'I don't feel too satisfactory,' said Periwig Tombs from the bed next to his.

'Periwig my friend,' said Big Bob. 'You are still in the land of the living.'

'I feel like death itself.'

'I will help you out,' said Big Bob. 'But I fear that it would take just a little bit too much explaining. I'll come back for you tomorrow, when I'm all better myself. Let me just say this, you'll be hallucinating a lot, you'll be hearing voices in your head. Ignore anything they say to you. They can't hurt you. Ignorest thou them, wilt thou promise me that?'

Periwig Tombs nodded his big Mekon head and then slowly metamorphosed into a pig.

'Very good,' said Big Bob to the nasty viral thingies that lurked unseen and angry in his head. 'I see that I will have to be on guard. You still have a little fight left in you. But thou wilt lose, I promise that unto thee.'

'OH NO WE WON'T,' said voice number one.

'I'm not talking to you any more.' Big Bob climbed gingerly out of the bed and tested his feet on the floor. That left one hurt like a bad'n, but strangely Bob found comfort in this.

150

'Nothing like a bit of real pain to keep things in perspective,' he said. And he opened the bedside locker to find his clothes, ignoring the rotting corpse of Periwig that stretched out taloned claws from within, thought away his Superman suit and donned his tattered shirt and suit and tie.

'I'm off for a beer,' he told the unwelcome guests in his head. 'I've no doubt you'll be coming too, but this is Brentford, *my* Brentford, and I know what is real around here and what indeed is not. Thinkest thou upon this, demons, and count away the hours until I cast thee out.'

And with that said, and well said too, Big Bob girded up his loins and left the cottage hospital.

It was Wednesday evening now. The fifth day of Rune in the year 2022. The evening smelled of lilies and of antique roses too and Big Bob marched across the bridge that had once crossed the railway tracks and wondered to himself whether it would perhaps be better just to go home and have his wife Minky lock him away in their pink coal cellar for the night. With orders to ignore all possible screamings until the dawn of the following day.

An inner voice said, 'Yes do that.'

Big Bob said, 'I thinkest not. Drink has the habit of blurring the mind and then I'll sleep thou off.'

With a look of determination upon his big face and a sprightly whistle of a Mr Melchizedec tune issuing from his lips, Big Bob continued his marching, with quite a spring in his step.

He really was doing remarkably well, all things considered. He was putting on a pretty fair old display of inner strength. And if he was trembling way down deep in the very depths of his mortal soul, that he would *not* be able to dislodge the viruses from his head, cure himself of them, then this trembling was kept way way way down deep, where he alone knew of it.

The sun dipping low now behind the noble oaks lengthened their shadows across the sacred soul of Brentford's St Mary's allotments. The shanty huts and beanpoles and water butts and plot dividers held a beauty that might have been lost upon some, but filled Big Bob with joy. He had suffered greatly over the last forty-eight hours,

151

but he knew that he was on the mend now. That he would triumph. That he would cross over the abyss and step to the other side a better man than ever he was before.

Not that he had ever been a bad man. He hadn't. He was honest, he was noble. Big Bob's size twelve feet crunched along the gravel path between the sheds and beanpoles and the water butts and dragons and the seven-headed Hydra and a fierce-looking yeti or two.

'I love this town,' said Big Bob. And he thought away the illusory monsters and thought once more about that plan he'd had about bringing tourists into the borough by promoting it as an untouched suburban haven. That really hadn't been such a good idea, he was glad that Periwig Tombs had talked him out of it.

'Good old Periwig,' said Big Bob. 'Good friend, Periwig Tombs.'

Had Big Bob known that Periwig Tombs had in fact had many thoughts regarding what he, Periwig Tombs, had named Suburbia World Plc, and that these very thoughts, indeed these memories, had been downloaded into the Mute Corp mainframe for data reaction when the virally infected Periwig underwent a brain scan on a machine that contained a Mute-chip, installed when the machine was supposedly being deloused of the Millennium Bug back in 1999*, he would not perhaps have said 'Good friend, Periwig Tombs,' but something quite to the contrary.

But as Big Bob didn't know this (as indeed no-one as yet did), he did, rather than he didn't.

So to speak.

The sound of applause came to the ears of Big Bob. Brought lightly on the breeze from the Waterman's Arts Centre.

'Wednesday night is the Brentford Poets night,' said Big Bob to himself, although he knew he was being overheard. 'And what better than poetry to fill the mind with golden thoughts and cast out those of darkest black?'

And with that said, and also well said too, Big Bob marched on towards the riverside to take a dose of the muse.

* Oh, that's how it was done! Well, that explains everything most satisfactorily.

The bar of the Waterman's Arts Centre was pretty crowded now. Fat moustachioed poetesses, who looked as if they were up for it, hugged their mugs of hand-drawn ale to their ample bosoms and sized up the knots of pimply youths, who'd heard tell stuff from a mate of theirs who had other plans for the evening. A wandering bishop engaged the barman in conversation. Two old fellas rocked with uncontrollable mirth. Several muleskinners supped their horse's-neck cocktails and discussed the latest trends in buckskin chaps. Badly dressed poets made serious faces and a very attractive young woman with wonderful blond hair and a sparkling dress of polyvinylsynthacottonlatex-suedosilk stood head and shoulders above most of the crowd, drinking red wine at the bar counter.

Big Bob recognized this woman, she and a young man, yes that was him, climbing up onto the rostrum, had helped him off the pile of stunt mattresses at the back of the Plume Café, where he had landed after the bus crash. She'd spoken to him, comforted him, told him that she was something to do with the *Brentford Mercury*.

Yes, Big Bob was certain it was her. She wasn't the kind of woman any man was likely to forget.

Big Bob might simply have pushed his way into the crowd. But he now knew better than that. He knew he mustn't touch anyone. He didn't dare, for fear that he would spread the infection.

So instead he put on a very fierce face, far fiercer than any that Mr Shields could ever have mustered up, and he made ferocious growling sounds and shook his shoulders about.

Ripples went through the crowd before him and it parted, as had the Red Sea at the touch of Moses' staff. Folk stared towards Big Bob, heads turned, faces looked startled.

Big Bob put a brave face on beneath his fierce one. It was a rather battered face anyway. His nose was broken, there was clotted blood around his mouth. He had lacerations all over the place and his suit was gone to ruin.

'Stand aside,' ordered Big Bob. 'Let me through, before I gobble you up.'

★

153

Kelly Anna Sirjan didn't see Big Bob as he approached her through the crowd. She was watching Derek and as he began his excruciating poem, she was thinking that she really should be going, because she had to get up early to begin her job at Mute Corp in the morning. When his big voice said, 'Excuse me please,' she was wakened from her reverie and turning, found herself almost face to face with one of Dr Druid's vanishing patients.

'Excuse me please,' said Big Bob once more. 'I'm sorry if I startled you.'

'You,' said Kelly, startled, but rarely lost for words. 'You. Robert Charker, the tour guide. You're here.'

'Thou knowest who I am,' said Bob the Big.

'Yes I do, but you were in the hospital. Dr Druid said that you vanished right in front of him.'

'I am in Hell,' said Big Bob. 'It's in my head.'

'We have to talk. But not here.'

'Here please,' said Bob. 'I need a drink. Many drinks.'

'I'll get them, what do you want?'

'A sprout brandy. A double, no a treble.'

'Leave it to me.' Kelly hailed the barman. It is another fact well known to those who know it well, that a beautiful woman never needs to speak Runese to attract the attention of a young barman.

'Excuse me bishop,' said the barman, hurrying over to Kelly.

'A quadruple sprout brandy and a red wine please.'

A great roar of laughter went up from the crowd. Old Pete had made another funny at Derek's expense and the poets who tolerated Derek, while knowing his poems were crap, chuckled and chortled away.

The barman set to pouring out sprout brandy, Kelly turned back to Big Bob. 'Are you all right?' she asked. 'Do you need to sit down? You don't look well at all.' She reached out her hand towards him.

'Don't touch me.' Big Bob took a step backwards. 'I am infected. I carry the contagion. I shouldn't have come into this crowded place. Whatever made me do it?'

And then Big Bob realized what had made him do it. The idea to come here had never been his. Something had put it into his head. Something that was *inside* his head. 'You sneaky little bastards.'

154

'Pardon me?' said Kelly.

'No, I don't mean you. It's inside my head. It tricked me once again.'

'A quadruple brandy and a red wine,' said the barman. 'Blimey, it's you, Big Bob. I heard that you'd been Raptured.'

'Raptured?' said Big Bob.

'It doesn't matter,' said Kelly. 'But we must talk. You must tell me what happened to you.'

'I'm infected,' said Big Bob. 'I've got a bibbly bobbly wibbly wobbly, oh shit and salvation.'

'What?' said Kelly.

Big Bob snatched his drink from the counter and emptied it down his big throat. 'It's messing with my speech, trying to prevent me from telling you what happened to me.'

'Say it slowly,' said Kelly. 'Try to think about each word.'

'Computers,' said Big Bob, slowly, and struggling to do so. 'Mute Corp. Remington Mute. The Mute-chip. The computers th— No!'

Kelly reached forward, but Big Bob flapped his arms and backed away. He bumped into the wandering bishop, knocking the drink from his hand and drenching a pimply youth.

'Easy there bish,' said the youth. 'You've spilled your drink all over my grubby black T-shirt.'

'Sorry my son,' said the bishop. 'But it wasn't my fault, it was this great oaf,' and he turned and cuffed Big Bob lightly on the chin.

'No!' cried the big one. 'Don't touch me.'

'Pipe down over there,' called Old Pete, from along the bar. 'We're trying to take the mickey out of this young buffoon on the rostrum.'

'Some of us are trying to listen,' said a badly dressed poet, who wasn't really trying, but was all for keeping up appearances.

'Stay back,' shouted Big Bob. 'Don't anybody touch me.'

The wandering bishop stared at his wandering hand. His hand tingled strangely now and tiny needle pricks were moving up his arm beneath his colourful vestments.

For they do have some really colourful vestments, do those wandering bishops.

'Mr Charker,' said Kelly. 'We should get out of here.'

'Aaagh!' cried Big Bob. 'It's having a go at my poor left toe. Oh

155

the pain, oh the pain.' And Big Bob took to hopping about in a disconcerting manner.

And the bar *was* crowded. Really crowded. Even though Big Bob had quite a respectable circle of space all around himself. Well, he had made a very fierce entrance and he was a very big bloke.

'Put a blinking sock in it,' called Old Pete. 'We can't hear the young buffoon.'

'Why don't you shut up, you old fart,' said a pimply youth. 'We want to get that idiot finished so we can hear another poem from the woman with the cat called Mr Willow–Whiskers.'

'How dare you address your elders and betters in that insolent fashion!' said Old Vic. 'I was a POW. We'd have executed young whippersnappers like you. Privately and in the shower block. One at a time, each of us taking turns.'

'Let's all keep it down,' said the barman. 'This is an orderly bar.'

'Leave my bloody foot alone,' howled Big Bob, toppling backwards and bringing down two large and moustachioed poetesses.

'Is this a proposal of marriage?' asked one of them, kissing Big Bob on the cheek.

The wandering bishop jerked about. Strange thoughts were suddenly entering his head. Strange thoughts that were not entirely his own.

Big Bob struggled to get to his feet, but he was hampered in his struggles by affectionate poetesses. Affectionate poetesses whose hands and lips were now tingling rather strangely.

'Leave me be!' shouted Big Bob. 'You fat ugly cows. No sorry, that wasn't me. I didn't say that.'

'It sounded like you,' said a badly dressed poet.

'Keep out of it, you scruffy twat. No, that wasn't me either.'

'You may be a big fellow,' said the badly dressed poet, rolling up his badly dressed sleeves. 'But I happen to be trained in the deadly art of Dimac and I take an insult from no man.'

'That is not the Dimac Code,' said Kelly.

'Kindly keep out of this, you blonde floozy,' said the poet.

'How dare you,' said Kelly.

'Behold the Antichrist!' shouted the bishop, which drew quite a lot of attention.

156

'Give me a chance,' called Derek from the rostrum. 'I've only got twenty-two verses left. And some of them are pretty saucy. I kid you not.'

'Get off!' heckled Old Pete.

'Shut up, you old fart,' said the pimply youth once again.

'Right that's it,' said Old Vic, drawing out his service revolver.

Big Bob fought with the amorous poetesses. The badly dressed poet put the boot in.

'Oh no,' said Kelly. 'I'm not having that.' And she stepped out of her holistic footwear and smote the martial poet.

'Fight!' cried Old Pete. 'This bloke started it,' and he pointed to the pimply youth, who was trying to wrestle Old Vic's gun from his tough and wrinkly hand.

'This man is the Antichrist!' The bishop had his holy water bottle out. 'Destroy the Antichrist. Grind his bones into the dust.'

'Are you sure about that?' asked the barman, as fists began to fly in all directions. 'I'm sure he's just Big Bob.'

'The Whore of Babylon, cross-dressed as a barman,' cried the bish. 'Destroy this one too, he bears the mark of the Beast on his wanger.'

'I bloody do not,' said the barman, dodging a flying pint pot. 'My wanger bears a small tattoo. You're pissed, get out of my bar.'

Outside in the car park two coaches drew up side by side. One contained the Brentford constabulary darts-team eleven, lately returned from a humiliating hammering at the points and flights of the Chiswick Constabulary darts-team eleven, playing on their home turf.

The other contained the Brentford Firefighters hurling team, lately returned from a similarly humiliating trouncing at the pucks and sticks of the East Acton Brigade, playing on *their* home turf.

Both coaches contained downhearted men, in very poor spirits. Men who, only a day before, had engaged in conflict with one another, regarding who should be first on the scene and take overall control of the situation. That situation being a certain bus crash in Brentford High Street.

Both coaches disgorged their downhearted cargoes at the same moment. And the sounds of battle ensuing from within the Arts Centre and borne upon that gentle zephyr, which brought the scent

157

of lilies and antique roses too across the Thames from the gardens of Kew, reached the ears of these downhearted cargoes at the selfsame moment.

And, being professional men, these downhearted cargoes pricked up their respective ears at the sounds of battle. And processed these sounds.

And reached a decision.

'We'll take charge of this,' said the firemen.

'No, I think *we* will,' the policemen said.

13

It had always been a matter for heated debate amongst scholars of human behaviour. 'What makes for a really classic punch-up?'

Certainly the ingredients have to be exactly correct. The margin of error is paper-dart slim. Too much of this, too little of that, and the whole thing goes to pot.

Hugo Rune, that scholar amongst scholars of human behaviour, that lecturer to the Royal Academy on subjects ranging from aquatics and teapot construction to the plea for the six-bar gate and the four-sided triangle, that four times WWF World Heavyweight Champ and no mean manipulator of the stout stick, stated in his famous monograph *Come over 'ere if you fink yor 'ard enough* or: *What makes for a really classic punch-up?* that four important factors play their equal parts.

These are,

One: Location.
Two: Even sidings of participants.
Three: A really good reason for having a punch-up.
Four: A safe vantage point for the scholar of human behaviour to view and study the ensuing mêlée.

Rune, according to his arch-detractor Koestler, was a vicious psychotic, who loved violence for the sake of violence and was responsible for starting numerous unseemly brawls during the 1920s and 30s, merely because it 'turned him on, sexually'. Notably the infamous Café Royal bash-about of 1927, where Rune incited a group of surrealists, including Salvador Dali and Max Ernst, to set about the waiters of that noble establishment, claiming that they were 'looking at him in a funny way'. And the scandalous Vatican canteen cardinal knee-kicking incident which ended with Pope Leo XVII receiving a black eye and Hugo Rune being excommunicated by the Church of Rome.

Rune claimed that Koestler had as usual got the wrong end of the stick, but would be receiving the heavy end of his famous stout one at their very next meeting.

It was Rune's conviction that a punch-up was a work of kinetic art, a martial art form. In fact a concerto for knuckles and things of that nature generally. To be enjoyed for its spontaneous anarchic brilliance, for its adrenalin excitation and not necessarily for the fact that it 'got him off' when he went back to his girlfriend. 'The punch-up is a thing of beauty,' claimed Rune. 'It springs out of nowhere, rising like the rainbow's arc to add that extra touch of colour to our otherwise greyly-hued existences. Especially after a meal.' And it is certainly well recorded, by those he invited to dine, that once Rune had concluded his repast, drained his brandy balloon of fifty-year-old cognac and stubbed out the dying butt of his Napoleon, he would invariably yawn, gaze about the restaurant with a curious gleam in his eye, before suddenly leaping from his chair to shout something like, 'How dare you speak to me in that fashion, sir,' before striking some innocent diner about the head with his stick. The resultant mêlée, often bloody and oft-times resulting in numerous arrests, was inevitably notable for two things, the absence of Hugo Rune at its conclusion and his invited dinner guest, usually injured, being forced to pay the bill.

Rune claimed that he performed these acts not only in the cause of scientific and sociological enlightenment but also 'For Art', which made them acceptable, because he was the leading artist of his day. And when asked why, specifically, he had started off the knee-kicking incident in the Vatican canteen, he explained that he had already spent a month in Rome and was finding it hard to locate a restaurant that would accept a booking in his name.

It is now agreed, by those who have studied the life and works of Hugo Rune, that he was a man born before his time and that only now is science and sociology beginning to catch up with him. It is also quite interesting to note that the south-coast artist Matt Humphrey was recently shortlisted to win the Turner Prize with his piece *punching people*, a video film of him beating up *Big Issue* sellers who were attempting to ply their trade outside the Body Shop in Brighton. At his trial, Humphrey claimed that he was not the 'vicious psychotic who loved violence for the sake of violence' as the counsel for the prosecution claimed, but an Artist, with a capital A, paying an homage to Hugo Rune. Humphrey walked free from the court, but an independent tribunal indicted Mr Justice Thumbs, who tried the case, claiming that as a practising Runie his judgement had been biased. Mr Justice Thumbs is currently serving a two-year sentence for setting about members of the tribunal with his stout stick.

So, in summing up the matter for the heated debate amongst scholars of human behaviour regarding what makes for a really classic punch-up, and bearing in mind Rune's four important factors, location, even sidings of participants, a really good reason for having a punch-up and the possibly questionable fourth, how might these be applied to the rip-roaring riot currently on the go in the bar of the Waterman's Arts Centre?

Good question.

Well, we certainly have a good location. Time and time again, the bar room has proved itself to be an excellent spot for a really decent bout of fisticuffs. There are chairs to break over people's heads, bottles, glasses and ashtrays to throw, and there are always folk ready and willing to participate, many eager and anxious, as if anticipating the arrival of such an event.

And as to the participants. Even sidings do make for a classic punch-up. This is an ultimate truth. Six onto one isn't a punch-up, it's a massacre. Six onto six and the fight could go either way. As to those presently wading in at Waterman's, there were no specific sides, other than for those of the lately arrived emergency services. But there was no ganging up. The fighting was evenly distributed. Poet fought with poet, muleskinner with muleskinner, and had there been more than one wandering bishop present, it is a certainty that they would have taken the opportunity to settle old but unforgotten scores and kick knees along with the best of them.

161

As to the really good reason for having the punch-up.

This is a grey area. Rather like whether it's OK to drive through amber lights because you're in a bit of a hurry. Or get off the bus without paying because the conductor failed to notice you crouching at the back. Or applying the finders-keepers charter when passing an unattended van with its rear doors open. Or, well, perhaps not, but it *is* a grey area. It's subjective. One man's good reason may not be another man's.

Old Vic felt that shooting the pimply youth who was tugging at the barrel of his service revolver was entirely justified. Because, as he would later state in his defence, 'If he'd got the gun off me, then like as not he might have shot me with it.' The barman felt entirely justified in launching himself over the bar counter and felling the wandering bishop with a soda siphon. Because, as he would later state in his defence, 'The nutter said I was a shirt-lifter with three number sixes on my bell end.'

Big Bob, who would not find himself in court, had reasons of his own. And, although he could rightly claim that the original cause of all the bloodshed and brutality might be traced back to him, it wasn't actually *his* fault. But he did have a really good reason for putting his knee into the groin of a particularly badly dressed poet who happened to be standing innocently by and not hitting anyone at all.

Because that poet's name was Trevor Alvy.

So let's get back to the fight.

The barman belaboured the bishop, but the bishop, though bloodied, belaboured him back. Moustachioed women, wielding pint pots, struck down all things male that came within their swinging range, and pimply-faced youths, who now found themselves within their element and who enjoyed a good punch-up, not for Art but strictly for the sake of violence, lashed out at their elders and betters in the manner that disenchanted youth has always been noted for.

The fight inevitably carried itself to the rostrum, where Derek, now with only nineteen verses left and fuelled by a determination that the world in general, and Waterman's Arts Centre in particular, would be a better place when thoroughly blessed by his muse,

162

continued to declaim, swinging the mic stand, as Samson had the jawbone of an ass, when faced by a similar hostile bunch of Philistines.

Kelly, now a blur of Dimac moves, iron fists aglow and feet making cracks as they broke the sound barrier, battered folk to left and right as she cleared a path before her to Big Bob.

'Come with me if you want to live,' she said, because that line is classic Hollywood.

'Give me your hand then,' said the big one, then, 'No don't! That wasn't me. Don't touch me, stay away.'

'I saw a wild beast come out of the sea.' The bishop had the barman by the throat with one hand and was pointing once more to Big Bob with the other. 'Thou knowest that the Rapture has come to Brentford. Thou *all* knowest that.'

Word *had* got around, regarding the Rapture, and most of the combatants had heard about it. And most were well and truly miffed that their turns hadn't come around yet.

'I sayeth unto you!' The bishop's voice rose to an incredible volume. Became in fact a large and terrible voice. 'I SAYETH UNTO YOU. THE END TIMES ARE UPON US. THE WILD BEAST — TO MEGA THERION* WALKS AMONG US. HE IS HERE. HE IS BIG BOB CHARKER. SLAY THE HERETIC. BURN THE ICONOCLAST.'

'Trusteth not that bishop. He speaketh not with the voice of man,' shouted Big Bob, kneeing Trevor one more time for luck. 'He has the infection. He is possessed.'

Now here Rune's number two rule came suddenly into the game. Randomness removed itself from the equation, leaving the harmony of pure mathematics in its place.

Which side would *you* choose to be on?

The side of the raving cleric, calling for the burning of a witch? Or the side of reason (?) whatever that reason might be?

The lines of battle now became evenly drawn.

Poets of a religious bent, keen to be Raptured as quickly as possible, knew exactly where they stood and exactly who should be burned, and when, like *now*. (You have to make these decisions on the instant, or else mob rule won't work.)

* The Great Beast. As in the Book of Revelation.

163

Pimply youths, who favoured a Black Sabbath album and the writings of Anton La Vey, and were always eager to join a coven in the hope of dancing about in their bare scuddies with naked female goths (that a friend of theirs had told them were always 'up for it'), chose their side in a nanosecond. If the Beast 666 was really here in person tonight, they were signing up with him. In blood, if necessary, although they'd prefer to use their biros.

'KILL THE IDOLATOR!' cried the large and terrible voice, issuing from the bishop's mouth. 'SEND THE HELL SPAWN BACK TO THE BOTTOMLESS PIT.'

And, to add a certain air of authority to his words, the bishop now levitated from the floor. It was a pretty neat trick by any account, the secret of which is only known to members of the Magic Circle. And that annoyingly clever American magician* who performs in the streets of New York.

At which point the Brentford constabulary, entering by the west door, which they knew to be a short cut to the bar, caught sight of the Brentford fire crew, who were simultaneously entering the bar through the east door, which *they* knew to be a short cut.

And though neither group had heard the bishop's words, or rather those words which the bishop spoke, for the words, as we know, were not his own, they at least knew which side *they* were on.

And so all and sundry went at it hammer and tongs.

'Out!' shouted Kelly to Big Bob Charker. 'Run for the exit, I'll protect you.'

'Oh good,' said a pimply youth. 'This woman is obviously the Whore of Babylon. I'm glad she's on our side.'

Kelly struck the pimply youth. 'Prat,' she said, as she struck him.

'The blue fire of her sparkling eyes burns my humble soul. If I were a fireman, I would slide her down my pole,' rhymed Derek. It was verse thirty-seven, or possibly thirty-eight. But a fat poetess with dark moustachios had him in a headlock. And Derek could no longer make himself heard above the roar of battle.

Kelly kicked and kata'd, folk fell sprawling to the right and left. Big

* David Blaine. He's in that car commercial, the one where he says 'think of a card'.

164

Bob backed towards the exit. It was the south one and led to the river terrace.

'HE FLEES!' cried the bishop from on high. 'THE UNHOLY ONE FLEES. PURSUE HIM WITH GOD'S SPEED.'

Old Vic, whose eyesight wasn't what it was, fired upon the hovering bishop. 'It's the Red Baron,' he hollered. 'Man the ack-ack. A pint of stout for the gunner who brings the blighter down.'

The pimply youth, who still had a hold of Vic's gun, lost the tip of his nose.

Gunfire often stills a mob. But sometimes it makes matters worse. And as this was one of those sometimes, the gunfire made matters worse.

'Calling FART. Calling FART,' called a constable into his lapel radio (Mute Corp 3000 series). 'Riot in progress at Waterman's Arts Centre, shots fired. Send everyone you have.'

Big Bob was now out on the terrace. Kelly was battling the new recruits to the Christian fundamentalist movement currently in hot pursuit.

'I'll have the balls off the next man who takes a step through this exit door,' she told them in no uncertain tones. Those in hot pursuit considered the trail of fractured bodies that Kelly had left in her wake. And reaching a consensus of opinion, agreed to let the Antichrist make an unharassed retreat.

'We know where you live,' shouted a poet, making the sign of the cross with his fingers. 'We'll be round tomorrow, just you wait.'

'We'll whip your sorry ass,' said a muleskinner. 'Or if you don't have an ass, we'll whip your budgie.'

'Run,' Kelly told Big Bob, but Big Bob was running already.

The gasometer by moonlight is a beautiful thing to see. Many of the Brentford Poets are inspired by it. Many of them write really long poems about it. And several would have been read out tonight, if things hadn't gone as they had.

Within the shadow of the great gasometer, Big Bob coughed and wheezed, doubled over, big hands upon his great big knees. Kelly wasn't even breathless, she looked ready for a marathon run. She reached a hand towards Big Bob, then drew it back instead.

165

'How are you doing?' she asked.

'I'm in a mess,' said the big one. 'Trevor Alvy stamped upon my fractured toe.'

'But other than for that?'

'*Other than for that?*' Big Bob coughed and wheezed some more. 'Have you any idea what I've been going through?'

'None,' said Kelly, straightening her hair and selecting a strand to twist back and forwards in the shadows.

'Hell,' said Big Bob. 'I've been through Hell. And I'm not out of it yet. It's still inside my head. I can feel it. But it's weakening.'

'NO WE'RE NOT,' said the voice, resounding in his skull. 'AND YOU JUST LOST LEVEL THREE. YOU PASSED US ON. THAT'S ALL YOUR LIVES GONE. YOU LOSE. WE WIN.'

'No,' cried Big Bob, clawing at his temples. 'I'm not in your games any more.'

'YOU ARE,' said the voice. 'THAT WAS IT. LEVEL THREE. YOU HAD ALL THE INFORMATION. BUT YOU MUFFED IT UP AND WE WIN. AND NOW YOU DIE.'

'What's happening?' asked Kelly. 'What's going on? I don't understand.'

'They say I've lost the game. That I've lost my final life. They're going to kill me. No, thou demons, no.'

Big Bob's hands left his temples. Kelly could see him there in the darkness beside her. She saw the big hands shaking. The look of fear upon the big man's face. The hands closing upon his own throat.

Gripping, squeezing. Harder and harder.

Tighter and tighter.

'YOU LOSE,' said the voice in Big Bob's head. 'WE WIN. YOU DIE.' 'GAME OVER.'

'No!' and Big Bob gagged and struggled. But the hands, no longer under his control, pressed in upon his windpipe and crushed away his life.

14

Joy, joy, happy joy.

    Happy happy joy.

    That big fat smiley sun rose up once more above the Brentford roof-scape. It beamed down today upon a borough strangely hushed. There was the milk float of Mr Melchizedec bottle-jingling-jangling along. But it seemed queerly muted, as it moved upon its jingle-jangle way. And that tomcat, softly snoring on the window sill of the Flying Swan, growled somewhat in its sleep, as Mr Melchizedec stretched his hand to tousle up its head. And Mr Melchizedec, silent whistling, was aware that something altogether wrong had entered into Brentford and was waiting cobra-coiled and deadly and about to spring.

    Derek awoke in his bachelor bed. Rather bruised was Derek and not in a joyous frame of mind. He'd had more than a night of it, what with the beatings he'd taken at the hoary hands of brutal poetesses and later at the leather-gloved and far more brutal mitts of FART men, who had bundled him, along with many others, into the back of a Black Maria and later into a grossly over-crowded police cell. It had been five in the morning before he'd been able to talk his way to freedom. Which hadn't been a minute too soon, as a large and bearded tattooed poet, who was evidently no stranger to prison life and who referred to himself as 'I'm the daddy now', had just been explaining to Derek exactly what Derek's role as 'my bitch' involved.

    Derek had hauled his sorry ass back home in a painful huff.

167

Derek yawned and stretched and flinched from the pain of numerous bruisings. Somehow, he felt absolutely certain, this was all Kelly's fault. It just had to be. That woman *was* trouble. Trouble travelled with her like an alligator handbag. Or a cold sore that you couldn't quite shake off.

'But I hope she didn't get injured,' said Derek to himself. 'No, sod it. I hope someone punched her in the face. No, I don't really. Yes, I do. Well I don't, but I do.'

So to speak.

Others might have been rising early with Derek. But most weren't. Most involved in the affray were still locked up in the police cells. One called Trevor Alvy was learning the duties of 'my bitch'. But those who had managed to creep or crawl away home, were *not*, most *definitely not*, getting up for work. They would be calling in sick. And those of a religious bent would be doing so content in the knowledge that they would soon be Raptured, so what did work matter anyway?

Among this potentially joyous throng was the wandering bishop. Not that he was cashing in as yet upon his joy potential. The wandering bishop had wandered further than he might have hoped for. He had awakened high in the branches of an ornamental pine on the south bank of the Thames in the Royal Botanical gardens of Kew, where his elevated wanderings had carried him.

Kelly awoke in her rented bed at Mrs Gormenghast's. The pillow-cases were still puce, as were the duvet and the curtains and the carpet. Steerpike the cat, Mrs Gormenghast's darling, was also puce, but it was a cat thing. Steerpike hailed from the Isle of Fizakery, where every cat is puce.

Kelly yawned and stretched and climbed out of her bed and stood upon Steerpike the cat. Steerpike the cat swore briefly in feline and took to his furry heels.

Kelly was not this morn pleasingly naked. She had slept in her polyvinylsynthacottonlatexsuedosilk mix dress, which was badly ripped and shredded. And slept very badly too. Her hair was tangled and she had bags of darkness under her eyes. She did not look the very picture of rude good health. She looked deathly pale.

Kelly took herself over to the cheval glass and examined her reflection therein. She did not find it pleasing to behold. The events of the previous evening had sorely troubled her. A feeling of overwhelming gloom smothered her like a damp shroud.

Kelly's fingers teased at the tangled hair. She stared at herself in the mirror's glass. A great deal of cosmetic restoration work was going to be necessary, if she was to look anything approaching her natural best for her first day at Mute Corp.

Kelly chewed upon her Cupid's bow and as she stared into the mirror it seemed for just a moment, just as a little subliminal flash, that the face of Big Bob Charker stared right back at her.

Kelly shuddered, she felt tears pushing forward into her blue blue eyes. But she forced them back. Big girls did *not* cry. She had to remain in control.

She had to *take* control.

At a little after seven thirty of the sunny morning clock, Kelly Anna Sirjan descended the stairs and entered the breakfasting area. She wore a lime green dress of chromecolorpolysynthasuedododickydido and looked as ever radiant as ever she had looked.

Upon her feet she wore a pair of bright red Doveston holistic ankle boots with tieback super-trooper fudge-tunnels, multi-socket implants and wide-trammel cross-modulating flux imploders. They were the very latest thing. And didn't they look it too.

The fire blazed brightly in the hearth and Mrs Gormenghast, wearing a puce nun's habit with matching wimple, greeted her with an Ave Maria and set to cooking hot crossed buns.

'Did you hear what happened at the Brentford Poets last night?' she called over the bubbling cauldron on the stove. 'The coming of the Antichrist, by all accounts. They say that dozens were carried off to glory, but many more have taken the mark of the Beast.'

'Do you have any coffee?' Kelly asked.

'Only tea, dear. Coffee is the Devil's drink.'

'I'll just have a glass of water then.'

'I've plenty of that, dear. I've had the tap blessed by Father O'Blivion, all the water that comes out of it now will be holy.'

'Do you have a home computer here?' Kelly asked.

'Bless me no,' said Mrs Gormenghast, ladling lard into the cauldron and wondering how it was that hot crossed buns were supposed to be made. 'My husband used to have one. A Mute Corp 3000 series, big bugeroo with side-flange demi-speakers and deep-throat hard blast modulator drive. I believe it worked on some system involving the transperambulation of pseudo-cosmic antimatter, but I couldn't say for sure, because I never used it. I have hay fever you see.'

Kelly nodded in the way that said she really did. 'What was it you said happened to your husband?' she asked.

Mrs Gormenghast scratched at her puce perm with a wooden spoon. 'I don't rightly recall,' she said. 'Did I say that he was run over by a juggernaut? Or was he carried away by the fairies? It's so hard to keep up with current events nowadays and a week is a long time in politics. Do you want grated cheese on your hot crossed buns?'

'Parmesan?'

'No, I'll use a fork.'

At a little after eight of the gone-without-any-breakfast clock, Kelly left the house of Mrs Gormenghast. She did not leave by the front door but by the old back entrance, that used to be reserved for hawkers, tradespersons, mandolin players by moonlight and Tom the butcher's boy. She walked hurriedly up the garden path, between the blooming puce rhododendrons, flowering puce gladioli, glorious puce sunflowers and spreading puce spruce trees and looking left and right and up and down as well, slipped behind the trellis work that hid the two puce dustbins and the garden shed, all painted puce. Kelly lifted the latch and entered the shed.

She stepped over the half a bag of solid cement and peered down through the semidarkness towards a mound of coal sacks. A low murmur came from beneath them.

Kelly stooped and carefully lifted a sack. And then she stepped back briskly, careful not to scrape her expensive footwear on the afore-mentioned half a bag of solid cement.

On the floor lay Big Bob Charker. He lay face down. His hands were tightly bound behind his back with strips torn from Kelly's polyvinylsynthacottonlatexsuedosilk mix dress. His ankles were similarly secured and drawn up to his wrists. Another strip of dress served as a gag and this was knotted at the nape of the big man's neck.

170

'It's me, Kelly,' said Kelly. 'I'm sorry that I had to knock you out and drag you here and I'm sorry I had to tie you up like this. But it was for your own sake. You would have killed yourself. Or *something* would have killed you. I didn't touch your skin. I'm sure I'm not infected by whatever it is you're suffering from. But you'll have to stay here until I can find out what to do to help you. I'll come back later and bring you food. I'm going to Mute Corp. I know the answer to all this lies there.'

Big Bob growled through his gag and struggled fearsomely. Blood flowed from his wrists. It was just a matter of time before he broke free. Kelly delved into her shoulder bag, brought out a pair of white kid gloves, slipped them on, knelt over the big man and applied a Dimac 'quietening' touch to his left temple. Big Bob lapsed from consciousness.

Kelly re-covered him with the coal sacks. Left the shed, the garden and the street and went in search of the cab she should have ordered earlier.

Orders had never been Derek's thing. He knew that he was a free spirit. And an innovator, a man of imagination, a natural leader. If he hadn't had such a rough night of it last night he would have been feeling a great deal happier about dealing with this present day to come.

In charge.

In complete charge of the *Brentford Mercury*.

The man at the helm. The captain of the ship. The man who made decisions. Dictated the editorial policy. Did the business.

You have to balance things, you really do. The ups with the downs. The goods with the bads. The obfuscations with the polyunsaturates. The antonyms with the antelopes. The diddy-do's with the rum-tiddly-um-pum-pums . . .

And things of that nature generally.

And so by the time Derek had had his breakfast, been told off again by his mum for coming in so late, put on his very best suit and marched all the way to the offices of the *Brentford Mercury*, mentally composing a stupendous pun-filled alliterative phew-wot-a-scorcher of a headline, he was out of the deep down doldrums and up in the wispy white clouds and ready and willing and ready once more to tackle the task in hand.

'I am the man,' said Derek, as he upped the staircase, two stairs at a time, put the key that was now *his* responsibility into the lock of the outer door, turned it and entered the offices.

'You're late,' said Mr Speedy, the pink-suited little man from Mute Corp.

'We'll have the company dock him an hour's pay,' said Mr Shadow, the larger man from the same corporation, similarly suited but in a bright red ensemble.

'You!' exasperated Derek. 'What are *you* doing here? How did *you* get in?'

'We have our own keys,' said Mr Speedy. 'Issued by head office. Business never sleeps, you know. Time is money and time waits for no man and all that kind of rot.'

'Rot?' said Derek, making a face that some might have taken for fierce.

'Things to do,' said Mr Shadow. 'We will overlook the unpleasantness of our previous meeting. We're all healed. We bear you no malice.'

'I should think not,' said Derek. 'It wasn't me who threw you out of the window. It was that Kelly woman and she doesn't work here any more.'

'So very pleased to hear it. Shall we proceed?'

'I have work to do,' said Derek. 'Perhaps you could come back later. Tomorrow possibly, or next week?'

'How amusing,' said Mr Shadow. 'Shall we proceed to the editor's office and discuss business?'

'I have a paper to put out.'

'Yes,' said Mr Speedy. 'And all on your own, by the look of it. Unless you noticed a crowd of employees queuing up to get in. On your late arrival.'

'Hm,' went Derek. 'Actually no.'

'No,' said Mr Speedy. 'There is only us. We three and we must put the paper together by ourselves.'

'Couldn't possibly be done,' said Derek. 'You need typographers, compositors, mixers of inks, straighteners of paper. Someone to make the tea and pop out for doughnuts. It's all terribly technical, you wouldn't understand any of it.'

Mr Speedy shook his head. Slowly he shook it. 'We only need this,' he said, pointing to that tiny briefcase jobbie that those in the know call a laptop.

Kelly's hands were in her lap. Demurely.

The office where she now demurely sat was a pretty swank and fab affair. Walls of brushed aluminium, clothed by the works of Rothko, Pollock, Humphrey (in his pre-video, postmodern, hyper-realistic period) and the inevitable Carson. The floor was of black basalt, a stone desk rested upon steel trestles like a fallen monolith. There were two chairs, one behind the desk, with Mr Pokey upon it. One before the desk, with Kelly, hands in lap. Demurely.

She sat upon a chair the shape of a scallop shell. It was silver grey in colour and it didn't have any legs. The chair hovered eighteen inches above the floor, but did it in centimetres, as they were far more modern.

There was something alarming about sitting in a chair that didn't have any legs, and Kelly found herself ill at ease and constantly pressing the heels of her fashionable footwear to the floor.

'It won't collapse,' said Mr Pokey. 'It works on a principle similar to magnetism, but not. If you catch my drift and I'm sure that you do.' He smiled upon her breasts. 'Do you?'

'Naturally,' said Kelly. 'But it is somewhat disconcerting.'

'Yes, they never caught on with the general public. People eh, there's no telling what they will respond favourably to. Well, actually there is, but we like to keep them thinking that we don't know what it is.'

'Yes,' said Kelly. 'I can understand that.'

'The company that cares,' said Mr Pokey. 'Founded by . . .' He waved a hand and the face of Remington Mute appeared ghostlike and all 3-D above the desk of fallen stone. 'A legend. A true inno- vator. The man behind the most successful computer games company in the history of mankind. HELLCAB.' Mr Pokey waved his hand and a game screen gleamed and twinkled in the air, replacing the face of

173

Remington Mute. Cars whizzed, explosions flashed. Sound effects came from hidden speakers.

Kelly barely suppressed a yawn. HELLCAB was standard stuff in her personal opinion. Hardly WONDER BOY or ALTERED BEAST. But then she loved the old-fashioned games. They had a certain, well, *humanity*, if such a thing can ever be said about computer games.

'SPEEDO,' said Mr Pokey and SPEEDO hovered in the air. 'BIG TRUCK RUMBLE, FIGHT NIGHT FIFTY, DOG TATTOO and MAGGOT FARM.' And up they came and dangled in the air.

'You know them all,' said Mr Pokey. 'And of course the search is on for even better and better. Better, faster, trickier, more challenging for the game-player. Back at the turn of the century everyone was placing their bets upon virtual reality. But what of that now? When was the last time you ever saw a player in a headset?'

'Yes that's true,' said Kelly. 'Why do you think that was?'

'Fashion,' said Mr Pokey. 'Plain and simple. As with clothes, music, cars, art, architecture, home furnishings, everything. You don't have to go on inventing things. Coming up with new things all the time. That's not necessary. You have *Retro*. Retro music, retro fashion, retro architecture. It's an homage to the greatness of the past. That's what made Remington Mute, he made computers big and comfortable again, the way they used to be. The way that people got nostalgic over. And the games. They were *like* the old games. Only *better*.'

'What makes them better?' Kelly asked. 'Is it the Mute-chip?'

'Mute-chip?' The big fat smile faded from the face of Mr Pokey. His gaze left Kelly's breasts and fixed itself upon her eyes. 'What do you know about the Mute-chip?'

'Well, nothing,' said Kelly hurriedly. And remaining very demure. 'I overheard two men talking about it, when I came into the building.'

'Did you indeed?' said Mr Pokey, leaning across his desk.

'I've no idea what it is. I thought it was only a Web Myth. Is it real? Is it something special?'

'Just product,' said Mr Pokey. But Kelly could see that he was pressing lighted pads that were set into his desktop.

'Anyway,' said Mr Pokey. 'I'm sure you'll learn all about the Mute-chip in the fullness of time. When you have risen to sufficient status within the company. But I wouldn't mention it in public if I were you. I am just replaying the CCTV footage of your arrival. If I can identify the two operatives, I will have them dismissed for their indiscreet talk.'

'No, please,' said Kelly. 'I wouldn't want that to happen because of me. They were whispering, actually. It's just that my hearing is very acute.'

'I wonder if you're lying,' whispered Mr Pokey.

'I can assure you I am not,' said Kelly. 'Now please tell me all about the job.'

'The job in hand,' said Mr Speedy, 'is to promote Suburbia World Plc. Naturally this will be done mostly across the World Wide Web. But here, in this Luddite backwater, it must be done through the borough's official organ, the respected *Brentford Mercury*.'

'It's a newspaper,' said Derek. 'Not an advertising circular.'

'But this will bring jobs to the borough.'

'We don't have an unemployment problem here,' said Derek. 'And we don't have any homeless people sleeping on the streets. Well, we do have one, Mad John. But every borough has a Mad John, it's a tradition, or an old charter, or something. He sleeps in a hedge and he shouts at shoes.'

'Shoes?' said Mr Shadow.

'Shoes,' said Derek. 'He roots them out of the black bin liners that people of a charitable persuasion leave outside the charity shop on a Sunday night. Mad John gets the shoes out and puts them on parade upon the pavement and gives them a good telling-off.'

'Why?' asked Mr Speedy.

'Because that's what he does. He's a local character.'

Mr Speedy had his tiny briefcase laptop jobbie open. He was pressing tiny little jobbie keys on it. 'Sunday evenings, you say?' said he. 'Outside the charity shop. That would be the one on the High Street would it? The SFSASBISOAGH. The Society for Small and Shoeless Boys in Search of a Good Hiding.'

'What are you doing?' Derek asked.

'Putting it on the schedule,' said Mr Speedy. 'All we have down for Sunday evenings so far is,' he pushed more keys and peered at the screen, 'watching Old Pete plant sprouts in Allotment World . . .'

175

'Allotment World?' said Derek.

Mr Speedy read from the screen. 'Enjoy a real-life safari across Brentford's very own horticultural kingdom and wild-life preserve. Can *you* spot the giant feral tomcat of legend? Identify twenty-two different species of sprout? Find the spot where the sacred mandrake grows . . . ?'

'Mandrake?' said Derek. 'It grows in Brentford?'

'A character called Old Vic grows it. We have a file on him. He used to be a prisoner of war.'

'I know,' said Derek, burying his face in his hands.

'So we'll add in this Mad John,' said Mr Speedy, punching keys. 'He shouts, you say? Is he violent?'

'Perhaps you should check that out for yourself.' Derek peeped up through his fingers.

'We will,' said Mr Shadow. 'We check everything out.'

'It's not a safe area, you know,' said Derek, straightening up. 'There was a big riot in the Arts Centre last night. I was in it. There was blood, I have bruises, would you like to see them?'

'I have bruises of my own,' said Mr Speedy. 'Mine are far more impressive than yours.'

'I'm sure they're not,' said Derek.

'Our company has a division that specializes in urban pacification,' said Mr Shadow. 'Any trouble from the locals will be swiftly dealt with.'

'Oh yes?' said Derek, the tone of sarcasm ringing in his voice. 'So what will you do, put a big fence around the borough as well?'

'Naturally,' said Mr Shadow. 'We can't have anyone sneaking into Suburbia World without paying.'

'Regarding pay,' said Kelly. 'You mentioned a certain figure yesterday that seemed very generous, particularly as the nature of my job here was somewhat unspecific. You mentioned a contract, has that been drawn up?'

'The figure stands, the contract has been drawn up. You will find the job itself challenging. It should appeal to you. You impress me as a young woman with highly competitive instincts. We at Mute Corp are always working on new games. And we're always looking for qualified participants, players, to test the systems.'

'All right,' said Kelly. 'Well I'm up for it. I've played a lot of computer games in my time . . .'

'We're well aware of *that*,' said Mr Pokey.

'You are?'

'Of course. We have files on everyone.'

'Everyone?' said Kelly. 'You can't have files on everyone.'

'Mute Corp manages the Government's mainframe, which is linked to the armed services and the emergency services mainframes. Mute Corp manages the communications network. Mute Corp manages all of the World Wide Web.'

'You have to be kidding,' said Kelly.

'Oh no,' said Mr Pokey. 'And it's all there for the public to see. The Freedom of Information Act, you know. Check the Mute Corp web site. We have no secrets.'

'So tell me about this Mute-chip of yours.'

'The corporation's business dealings and interests are not a secret. Obviously the technology we develop *is*.'

'And so your files on me said that I had potential as what? A games tester?'

'Absolutely. Your university career. Your access to the games library, at the university. You have a natural aptitude towards the playing of computer games. If your natural aptitude lay with mathematics we'd employ you in the accounts department. We only employ operatives according to their specialized skills. And everybody's skills are all on file. Everything's on file. Your whole life's on file. I can tell you the address where you are currently lodging. You wrote out an old-fashioned paper cheque for your landlady, Mrs . . .' Mr Pokey tapped keys, 'Mrs Gormenghast, and she's on file too, bought two pots of puce paint, serial number 10A/BC444 from Homebase in Chiswick last week. Everything is computer-linked. *Everything*. Surely you are aware of this?'

'Of course,' said Kelly. 'But it is a little frightening when you hear it being read out like that.'

'You haven't committed any crimes,' said Mr Pokey. 'You're a model citizen. No violations of penal codes. No misdemeanours.'

'No,' said Kelly. 'None.'

'You are an ambitious young woman and we are offering you a challenging position.'

'All right,' said Kelly. 'I'll take it.'

'Well of course you will, you wouldn't be here if you weren't going to. Would you? So we'll get you all checked out . . .'

'Checked out?' said Kelly.

'Just the standard medical.'

'I see.'

'And then you will be highly paid for doing something you enjoy. What could possibly be better than that?'

Kelly thought about it. What *could* possibly be better than being highly paid for doing something you enjoy? Nothing really. And while she was doing this something, she would find out everything she needed to know about Mute Corp. Every little secret.

Or every *big* secret.

And yes, she *was* ambitious, and yes, she *was* highly competitive. And yes, not only would she beat their games, she would expose to the world whatever it was that Mute Corp had done to Big Bob Charker and those hapless souls who had apparently vanished from the face of the earth.

She would.

Oh yes she would.

'Right,' said Kelly. 'I'm up for it. I'll take the medical and get straight into your game.'

'Splendid,' said Mr Pokey. 'I knew you were perfect for the job. We never make a mistake at Mute Corp.' And his eyes were back on her breasts once more and the smile was back on his face.

Kelly smiled. 'Just one thing,' she said. 'What is the name of this new game of yours?'

'GO MANGO,' said Mr Pokey.

15

'Yabba–dabba–dooby–dooby–do,*' said the doctor.
'Yabba–dabba–dooby–dooby–do–do,**' Kelly replied.

The doctor wore a stunning white concoction, wrought from bogusynthecatedextroselectroline, which had been sprayed over her body and a pair of Doveston holistic thigh boots with on-board chaos-generators, double reticulating splines and personal matrix engines, with rather spiffing Minnie Mouse bows on the toecaps.

'You have a working knowledge of Runese,' said the doctor. It was a statement rather than a question. 'It's only really the plebs who use it all the time. We professionals need more than forty words to get the job done. Don't we?'

'I'm sure you have accessed my file,' said Kelly. 'I have a degree in the Universal tongue. Did it on a night-school course six months ago on the Web. Along with Origami and Macramé. Not to mention Mantovani.'

The doctor didn't mention Mantovani.

'Please be seated,' said the doctor.

---

* The official Runese Universal greeting. It means, literally, 'I myself am full of happiness and joy and peace and find absolutely nothing to complain about in this wonderful wonderful world. But meeting you has made things even better.'
** 'That goes for me too. Doubly.'

Kelly seated herself.

The doctor's office differed from that of Mr Pokey's, in that it wasn't the same. The walls of this office were adorned with garish blown-up photographs of industrial injuries. The doctor's desk was a transparent slab of plexiglas, and encased within it was a human skeleton. A *two-headed* human skeleton.

On the wall behind the desk were shelves. On these shelves were numerous preserving jars containing dissected human organs, heads, limbs and assorted bits and bobs.

Kelly was impressed by the collection. 'An impressive array of exhibits,' she observed. 'All the work of Hartley Grimes★?'

'Not my personal choice,' said the doctor. 'Mute Corp employed an interior designer to give the offices a makeover. An old chap called Lawrence someone-or-other. He was very fashionable back in the 1990s. And style never dates, does it?'

'Apparently not,' said Kelly.

'So let us get down to business, would you care to go behind the screen and remove all your clothing.'

'I had a medi-check only a month ago,' said Kelly. 'I was declared Double A1. It will be on my medical file.'

'Oh, it is,' said the doctor. 'But company rules are company rules and rules must be enforced.'

'But I *am* officially Double A1.'

The doctor fluttered her eyelashes. They were fibre-optic, tiny green and blue globes glittering at their tips. 'Everyone has to have six-monthly health checks,' she said. 'You and I both know this. Most illnesses have been eradicated. Disease is virtually unknown, the universal panacea chip that everyone is implanted with at birth sees to this. But there are certain specific minor ailments that I have to check for.'

'Such as?' Kelly asked.

'Have you ever heard of keamerphybriosis?'

★ The late Hartley Grimes, fashionable twenty-first-century artist who specialized in human body parts, many of which were his own which he removed under local anaesthetic before an invited audience. Hartley Grimes's work is believed to owe an homage to Damien Hirst. As well as Jack the Ripper.

'No,' said Kelly. 'I haven't.'

'Or haemoglottism? Or Sterling's syndrome?'

'No,' said Kelly, slowly shaking her golden head and teasing at her hair. 'I haven't heard of those, either.'

'Nor have I,' said the doctor. 'Nor has anyone else. Because I just made them up. But if you don't consent to me giving you a full body examination, they will be just three of the totally bogus incurable complaints that I shall type into your file to prevent you getting this job.'

'Why?' Kelly asked.

The doctor sighed. 'I would have thought that was patently obvious,' she said. 'I just want to see you with your kit off. It's a doctor thing. I thought it was taken for granted.'

'Oh,' said Kelly. 'Well why didn't you just say so?' And she went behind the screen and got her kit off.

'We seem to have got off to a rather poor start,' said Mr Speedy to Derek. Mr Speedy was sitting in the chair of Mr Shields. The chair that Derek should have been sitting in. Mr Speedy had his feet upon Mr Shields's desk and Mr Speedy was now sipping Scotch from the bottle Mr Shields kept in his drawer.

Derek sat upon a boxed computer part, which somehow had been overlooked when the rest went off to the Brentford constabulary.

'You see,' said Mr Speedy. 'Mr Shields has a job for life. It's in that absurd contract of his. But *you* don't. And *you* know it. Mute Corp pays your wages and Mute Corp expects each of its employees to give of his or her best. Do I make myself thoroughly understood?'

Derek grinned painfully and made a show of rubbing his hands together. 'So,' said he. 'Shall we get started on this exciting project? You were joking about the fence being put around the borough though, weren't you?'

Mr Speedy shook his head. And Mr Shadow shook *his* head. And slowly Derek shook *his* head as well. 'You *weren't* joking, then,' he said.

'It will benefit every Brentonian,' said Mr Speedy. 'Keep the riff-raff out and preserve the borough in its state of stasis. Mr Shields wanted to avoid any change here. Clearly *you* wish the same. *We* wish the very same. What could be more harmonious than that?'

'The locals won't take to any fences,' said Derek. 'They're all wound up at the moment as it is. People have been vanishing, the locals believe that the Rapture is in progress. They nearly killed this chap called Charker last night. Some lunatic bishop had them believing he was the Antichrist.'

'Charker?' said Mr Speedy and he looked at Mr Shadow. Mr Shadow did noddings towards Mr Speedy's briefcase laptop jobbie and Mr Speedy keyed letters in and peered at the tiny screen.

'Do you know where Charker is now?' he asked Derek.

Derek shook his head.

'But you would say that some kind of Christian fundamentalist revival is going on in the borough?'

Derek sadly nodded his head. 'It will probably blow over,' said he. 'These things usually do.'

'Oh no,' said Mr Speedy. 'We wouldn't want that. In fact I think we should positively encourage it.'

'*What?*' said Derek.

'Is there a shrine?' asked Mr Shadow. 'There's always a shrine. A place where some miracle occurred. Like Lourdes, or Fatima, or Guadalupe, or that underpass in Paris where the spirit of Diana cured the beggar of athlete's foot.'

'I thought it was scabies,' said Mr Speedy.

'No, definitely Paris,' said Mr Shadow. 'But there's always a shrine. Do you have one here?' he asked Derek.

Derek hung his head in dismal affirmation. 'There is,' he said gloomily. 'My mum told me about it this morning. The Plume Café, where the tour bus crashed. People have been piling up bunches of flowers there. They say that the first man to be Raptured, was Raptured from there after the crash.'

'Malkuth,' said Mr Speedy, and he pronounced the unpronounceable name.

'Indeed,' said Derek. 'But how did you know *that*?'

'Everything is on file,' said Mr Shadow. 'Every*one* is on file. We at Mute Corp always make a point of disclosing this fact to those we deal with in business. It reinforces trust and discourages duplicity.'

'You mean you resort to blackmail, if they don't do what you want them to.'

Mr Speedy looked once more at Mr Shadow. 'Of course,' they said. 'It simplifies matters no end.'

'Well *I* have nothing to hide,' said Derek.

Mr Speedy laughed. 'You certainly have no secrets from us,' he said. 'But a bit of advice for the future. And strictly off the record. The next time you buy an old–fashioned computer game from a dodgy supplier, do it in cash. The movement of stolen goods is far harder to trace that way.'

Derek's jaw fell open.

'So let's not waste any more time,' said Mr Speedy. 'A massive marketing exercise is about to be put into motion. The Suburbia World Plc web site will be going online tomorrow and shares will be floated on the stock exchange by Monday next. We all want this to be a big success, don't we?'

Derek's jaw was still hanging open.

'Crad barges,' said Mr Shadow.

Derek's jaw moved up and then came down again. The word 'What?' came out of his mouth.

'Oh yes,' said Mr Speedy. 'The crad barges. Part of the Brentford Waterworld experience. The crad barges used to come down the Grand Union Canal to the Thames. We'd like some. At least three. To convert into floating restaurants. They'll go down the canal, into the Thames, around Griffin Island then back again. Serving local delicacies. One will be dedicated exclusively to sprout cuisine.'

'What?' went Derek. 'What?'

'Best get at least four crad barges,' said Mr Shadow. 'We can cannibalize one for spare parts.'

'I'm sorry,' said Derek. 'I don't understand what you are saying?'

Mr Speedy shook his head and a look of a certain sadness was to be seen on his face. 'You are to organize four crad barges,' he said. 'Acquire them.'

'Me?' said Derek. 'I'm a newspaperman.'

'You may now consider yourself a *company* man,' said Mr Speedy. 'And company men do whatever the company requires that they do. Unquestioningly.'

'Have you quite finished?' questioned Kelly. 'I fear that I have no more places left for you to probe.'

She lay naked and spreadeagled upon a cold steel table. About her lay a range of hideous intrusive medical instruments.

The doctor removed her surgical gloves and wiped away beads of sweat from her brow. 'You must want this job very much indeed,' she said.

'Oh I see,' said Kelly. 'This was some kind of initiation test, was it? To see how much humiliation I would be prepared to endure?'

'I'll pass you Double A1,' said the doctor. 'Please get dressed and report to Mr Bashful in Training.'

The office of Mr Bashful was hung with artworks. These were of the old school. Possibly St Trinian's. Mr Bashful wore an eight-piece light blue suit that was cut from a man–made fabric. His desk was made of wood and very dull indeed.

'Fabarooni,★' said Mr Bashful, as Kelly entered his office.

'Fabarooni–do,★★' said Kelly.

'I'm very pleased to welcome you aboard,' said Mr Bashful. 'I think you're going to love it here at Mute Corp.'

'The experience thus far has been positively orgasmic,' said Kelly.

'Really?' said Mr Bashful. 'I was watching your medical examin-ation on CCTV and you didn't seem to be smiling very much.'

Kelly chewed upon her Cupid's bow and teased at a lock of golden hair. 'Broadcast throughout the building, was it?' she asked.

'We have no secrets here.'

'Perhaps you'll let me watch the recording of your medical later, then.'

'You can watch it now if you want.'

Kelly raised an eyebrow. 'No thank you,' she said.

'So,' said Mr Bashful. 'To work. To work. If you'd be so good as to walk this way.'

'I'll try,' said Kelly. 'I'll try.'

★ Runese: 'I thought things couldn't get any better, and then I met you. Incredible!'

★★ 'That goes for me too. Doubly.'

Mr Bashful led Kelly from his office and through many corridors. All were hung with priceless artworks. Some led somewhere, some led back from somewhere, others led to other somewheres, others back again. Finally one led to a single door, which Mr Bashful opened, with a special plastic card kind of jobbie. 'You'll be issued with one of these,' he told Kelly. 'It's a Unicard, gives you access to all the areas you're allowed access to. I'm allowed access to almost all areas, but that's because of my status.'

Kelly smiled at Mr Bashful. 'Security must be a big concern here,' she said. 'Are all these corridors and rooms covered by CCTV?'

'Gracious no,' said Mr Bashful. 'Only the reception area and the doctor's office. We have no need to spy upon our own operatives.'

'And this door leads to?'

'To your personal games suite. Come.' Mr Bashful ushered Kelly through the doorway. The chamber was small and had no windows. The ceiling was low. The walls were white. There was a desk with a computer terminal, there was a chair before the desk.

'Sit down,' said Mr Bashful, pointing to the chair. 'Key in your name and then follow the instructions you are given. What could be simpler than that?'

'Nothing,' said Kelly. 'But I do have a couple of questions.'

'Go on then.' Mr Bashful looked mildly irritated.

'Firstly,' said Kelly. 'I noticed that the door closed and automatically locked behind us. How do I get out if I have to use the toilet, or something?'

'Key in your request, someone will come.'

'I see,' Kelly nodded.

'So if that's all right, I'll be off.' Mr B. looked slightly nervous now.

'Secondly,' said Kelly. 'This computer terminal. It's a Mute Corp 3000 series. Surely a bit antiquated. I expected something far more state-of-the-art here.'

'You get what you're given,' said Mr Bashful.

'I see,' said Kelly. 'Would you mind putting it online for me then? It's a while since I've used this particular model.'

'Just click the mouse,' said Mr Bashful, in the manner known as brusque.

'How?' Kelly asked. 'Would you mind showing me?'

Mr Bashful's hands shot into the pockets of his eight-piece suit. 'All you have to do is click it,' he said. 'Even a woman can do that, surely.'

Kelly fluttered her eyelashes. 'I *am* only a woman,' she said.

'Just click it, go on, I'll be back later.' Mr Bashful turned to take his leave.

'Oh, one more thing,' said Kelly.

Mr Bashful turned back again. 'What is it *now*?' he asked.

Kelly smiled and said, 'Only this,' and then she punched his lights out.

Derek's lights were on, but no-one seemed at home. 'Can I just get this straight?' he asked. 'You want me to acquire four crad barges?'

'And some Morris Minors,' said Mr Shadow. 'About fifty of those should do the trick.'

'Fifty Morris Minors? Why?'

'The car most seen on the streets of Brentford. It's all on file. Please let us not waste any more time.'

'But you can't expect me to do all this. I have a paper to put out. News to gather. Things of that nature generally.'

'You'll be issued with press releases,' said Mr Speedy. 'All will be taken care of. You have been chosen for this task on the grounds of your suitability. You know this borough. You are the local reporter.'

'I'm the features editor,' said Derek.

'And you know the locals. You know where to acquire what we need.'

'I suppose I do,' said Derek.

'And you will be handsomely rewarded.'

'I will?' said Derek.

'Cash,' said Mr Speedy. 'You'll be dealing in cash.'

'I will?' said Derek once again.

'Large quantities of cash,' said Mr Shadow. 'Your expenses will not be questioned.'

'Oh,' said Derek.

'Yes, *oh*,' said Mr Speedy. 'Which means that you fiddle your accounts and we'll turn a blind eye to it. You scratch our backs, we

186

put an Armani suit upon yours. If you catch my drift and I'm sure that you do.'

'I've never been an Armani man,' said Derek. 'Not since they dropped natural fibres anyway.'

'So,' said Mr Speedy. 'Do we have a deal? You do what we ask you, your secret, regarding all those stolen computer games in your possession, remains safe with us and you get a big cash kickback to do with as you please. Possibly purchase that Atari 7800 SCRAPYARD DOG game you've been bidding for over the Net from that dodgy American dealer.'

'Oh,' said Derek.

'And I could just possibly let you know how to get the three magic cans on Eisenhower Lane on level 2.'

'Oh,' said Derek.

'So *do* we have a deal?' asked Mr Shadow.

'You can count on me,' said Derek, putting out his hand for a shake.

Mr Speedy however did not shake the outstretched hand of Derek, instead he just poured himself another Scotch and raised his glass in salute. 'Welcome to Mute Corp,' he said. 'The company that takes care of its employees.'

'And that, I think, has taken care of you,' said Kelly.

Mr Bashful was struggling, muffled sounds came from his mouth, his eyes darted every which way.

'If you're trying to say, "What happened?" or possibly something ruder,' said Kelly, 'then allow me to explain. I knocked you unconscious. And then I tore up your clothing and used it to strap your now naked body into the chair. Your right hand, you will observe, is strapped to the computer mouse. Your mouth is gagged. I am now going to remove the gag. But if you cry out for help,' Kelly reached down and took hold of Mr Bashful's genitals, 'these will be put in severe jeopardy. Do I make myself absolutely clear?' And she gave Mr Bashful's gonads a far from friendly squeeze.

Mr Bashful's eyes flashed wildly. His head bobbed up and down.

Kelly released the gag from his mouth. The gag was knotted underpants.

'Untie my hand,' wailed Mr Bashful. 'Get it off the mouse.'

'How interesting,' said Kelly. 'Of all the things you could have said, you chose to say *that*.'

'Let me go, you bitch,' said Mr Bashful.

'When you've answered some questions.'

'I won't tell you anything that I'm not authorized to tell you. It's more than my job's worth.'

'You'll tell me everything,' said Kelly.

Mr Bashful shook his head.

'Firstly,' said Kelly. 'I want to know all about this GO MANGO game. Tell me more about that.'

Mr Bashful struggled some more. He seemed most intent on getting his hand away from the computer mouse.

'No?' said Kelly. 'All right then. Let's run the programme. Let's see *you* play the game.'

'No!' Mr Bashful fairly shrieked.

Kelly clapped her hand over his mouth. 'No, I didn't think so,' she said. 'What does the game do? Could it be that it infects you with something? Something that gets inside your head? Something contagious that can be passed from one unsuspecting person to another?' She released her hand.

Mr Bashful stared at her open-mouthed. 'You *know*,' he said. 'What do you know?'

'I know it's loose,' said Kelly. 'I know it has to do with Remington Mute and the Mute-chip.'

'I don't know anything more than you do,' said Mr Bashful. 'I just do my job. I don't ask too many questions.'

'Well, let's see you play the game then.' Kelly reached down towards Mr Bashful's mouse-bound hand.

'No, don't touch it. Don't click it on.'

'I think that perhaps you *do* know,' said Kelly. 'And I want you to tell me *now*. I don't think I'm cut out for a career at Mute Corp. I think today may be my very last day with the company.'

'You've made a very big mistake doing this to me,' said Mr Bashful. 'Do you really think you can get away with it? Mute Corp security division will track you down. You won't be free on the streets for twenty-four hours.'

'They'll make me vanish, will they?' Kelly asked.

Mr Bashful turned his face away. 'They'll make us both vanish.'

Kelly stared down upon the man. Perhaps, she thought, she *had* been just a little hasty. There might have been a more subtle way of doing this. And one that did not leave her as a criminal on the run. And on the run from Mute Corp, who were hooked into everything, her personal records, her bank account, they knew where she lived and where she went. They knew everything.

But then.

But then. There was a big man all tied up in a shed. An innocent man who had said he'd 'been to Hell' and all because of something that had issued from the Mute Corp Organization. Something dark. Something evil. Something that didn't care at all for a man.

'You're in deep shit,' said Mr Bashful.

'Yes,' said Kelly. 'I am. But do you know what? I don't care. Now speak to me, tell me all about the Mute-chip and all about GO MANGO or I'll knock your hand down onto that mouse and see some of it in action for myself.'

'All right. All right.' Mr Bashful glared at Kelly. 'I'll tell you. What harm can it do? You won't even get out of the building.'

'So speak,' said Kelly.

And Mr Bashful spoke. He spoke very fast, almost to the point of incoherent babble. It was as if he had been wanting to get all this off his chest for a very very long time. But hadn't dared to do it. He was scared. Everyone at Mute Corp was scared, he said. Everyone feared that they might be the next to be 'possessed'.

'Now let me get this clear,' said Kelly, needing a break from the babble and trying to get it all clear. 'What you are saying is that sometime back in the 1970s . . .'

'1972,' babbled Mr Bashful. 'It was a significant year. That's when he gave the thing birth.'

'OK. In 1972, Remington Mute developed the original Mute-chip, from his own digitized DNA. It was basically a chip that could learn and then make decisions based on its knowledge.'

'Effectively yes.'

'And the chips were put into games. Computer chess and so on. But he saw a greater potential for them in other systems. Playing the stock market and so on.'

189

'Became a millionaire, a billionaire, a zillionaire,' babbled Mr Bashful.

'And Mute Corp started off all the scare stories about the Millennium Bug and Mute's operatives, pretending to debug computer systems, installed Mute-chips into those systems.'

'Across the whole World Wide Web and they linked up into a vast thinking network.'

'Not *thinking* surely?' said Kelly. 'These chips aren't alive.'

'So what exactly *is* life?' asked Mr Bashful. 'If something can talk to you, communicate with you, reason with you, be more intelligent than you are, is that something alive? You tell me.'

'And this game? This GO MANGO?'

'Men play computer games,' said Mr Bashful. 'So why shouldn't a thinking computer play men games?'

'The mainframe plays games with *people*?' Kelly was rightly appalled.

'Ironic isn't it?' said Mr Bashful. 'The tables well and truly turned.'

'And you at Mute Corp let this happen?'

'We didn't let it happen. It happened by itself. We're trying to find a way to stop it, before it gets completely out of control.'

'So what was I to be, another laboratory rat?'

'Something like that. But your death would have been for the common good.'

'*My death?*' said Kelly.

'Nobody survives the infection,' said Mr Bashful. 'Once the virus has passed from the computer into the human host, it will play the human until the human dies.'

'So you would have locked me in this room until the virus killed me and then what? Dissected my brain?'

'We have to find a cure. An anti-virus.'

'You bastards,' said Kelly. 'You utter bastards.'

'You don't understand.' Mr Bashful jerked about in his bondage. 'It's clever. Very clever. It knows everything. It could have infected everyone by now. But it doesn't. It hasn't. Myself and a few others are working behind its back, so to speak. In secrecy. The autopsies are carried out manually, using no computer technology. Nothing that could have a Mute-chip inside it. That's why there's no CCTV in this

190

part of the building. Mr Pokey doesn't know what we do with the bodies, he thinks we just dispose of them in a tasteful and discreet manner. Once *it* has finished playing with them, they are surplus to requirements. It is in control here, don't you understand. People don't control this company, *it* does. And *it* has some kind of purpose. We don't know what it is yet. We few who are trying to stop it, we don't know what it wants.'

'What it *wants*? You really believe that this virus *is* alive, don't you? Not that it's just some kind of rogue program that's gone out of control?'

'It's much more than a program,' said Mr Bashful. 'And it's much more than alive. If your particular skills hadn't earmarked you for this room and you'd got some other job in the organization, you'd have learned in time. You would have been told when you'd reached sufficient status in the company. When your rank admitted you into the inner circle. To the elite. Then you would have been taken to the chapel.'

'The chapel?' said Kelly. 'You have a chapel here?'

'Not here,' said Mr Bashful, shaking his head. 'It's in Mute Corp Keynes. In the black hole of cyberspace. Only the elite are taken to the chapel.'

'And what do the elite do in this chapel?'

'We do what *it* tells us to do,' said Mr Bashful. 'We worship *it*, of course.'

16

'God?' said Kelly. 'It thinks it's a God?'

'And why not?' Mr Bashful wriggled uncomfortably. 'It's well enough qualified for the position. It knows virtually everything that there is to know. It's hooked into every network, it *is* the World Wide Web. Every time you make a telephone call it listens to your conversation. It knows more about *you* than any human does. It can remember more about *you* than even *you* can.'

'This is very bad,' said Kelly, twisting strands of her golden hair into tight little knots. 'This is very bad.'

'You don't understand the situation, this is far far worse than very bad. Now will you please untie my hand from this mouse?'

'No,' said Kelly. 'I don't think I can do that.'

'But why not? I've told you everything. I'm on *your* side. You want to stop this. You wouldn't have done this to me if you didn't. Which group are you from?'

'Group?' said Kelly. 'I don't know what you mean.'

'There are anarchist factions everywhere. Hackers, well-poisoners.'

'Well-poisoners?'

'Don't pretend that you haven't heard of them. Factions dedicated to destroying the Web. They overload the information wells with irrelevant rubbish or bogus information.'

'I'm not with any faction,' said Kelly.

'Oh come on, of course you are. You can tell me. What harm can it do? Come on, I told you everything.'

'Not, perhaps, everything.'

'Please release me, let me go,' said Mr Bashful, which rang a distant bell.

'No,' said Kelly. 'I think not.'

'Then what are you going to do? You have my Unicard, you can let yourself out. If you're careful you might escape the building.'

'And what of you?' Kelly asked.

'I'll say you attacked me, or something. What does it matter? You'll be on the run anyway. And you'll have to run hard and run fast. Although you'll have nowhere to run.'

'It's tricky, I agree.' Kelly released her tangled hair. 'But you're an intelligent man, you should be able to reason out just what I'm going to do next.'

'Probably,' said Mr Bashful, guardedly. 'Where exactly is this leading?'

'I am thinking,' said Kelly, 'that there might still be a job opportunity available to me here at Mute Corp.'

'I cannot imagine by what possible reasoning you can draw *that* conclusion.'

'I think I might rise up through the ranks quite quickly,' said Kelly. 'In fact it is my firm conviction that by this afternoon I will be sitting behind *your* desk.'

'What?' Mr Bashful's eyes bulged from his face and veins stood out on his forehead. 'What are you intending to do?'

'I am going to sacrifice you to your God,' said Kelly and the coldness in her voice sent chills of fear down Mr Bashful's spine. 'I suspect that you told me some of the truth, but not all. I don't believe that you're some subversive element working within the company for the good of mankind. That was all a lie told to me in the hope that as a gullible woman I would swallow it whole. You are a company man, Mr Bashful. And you would have left me to die in this room.'

'What else could I do? I had no choice in the matter.'

'No,' said Kelly, shaking her head. 'And nor do I.'

★

'He did *what*?' Mr Pokey stared at Kelly. If her sudden return to his office had been unexpected, the tale she had to tell was equally so and more too besides. Also.

So to speak.

'He did *what*?' asked Mr Pokey once again.

'He took me up to the games suite,' said Kelly, tearful of eye and breathless of breath. 'He took me up to the games suite and sat me down at the terminal. And then suddenly he said that he couldn't go through with it. That he couldn't sacrifice another victim, that's what he said. And then he told me all about it, about everything. About Remington Mute and the Mute-chip and about the GO MANGO game and what it did to people. And he said he couldn't let it happen to me.'

'Go on,' said Mr Pokey, shaking his head.

'And then when he'd told me all this, he said that I should thank him for saving my life. So I thanked him. But he said no, I should thank him *properly* and he took off all his clothes. He literally tore them off and he attacked me. But as you know from my file, I am an expert of Dimac. I struck him down and he fell across the computer terminal. His hand fell on the mouse.'

'I see,' said Mr Pokey. 'You don't have to say any more.'

Kelly made sobbing sounds. 'It was terrible,' she sobbed.

'I'm quite sure it was.'

'I took his Unicard and let myself out of the suite.'

'And you came back here to my office. You didn't try to run from the building.'

Kelly looked up at Mr Pokey. Her face was streaked with tears and every man knows how sexy a woman looks when she's crying. 'Where would I run to?' she asked. 'Mute Corp security would track me down wherever I went. I didn't come here to die. I came here to work for Mute Corp. I have skills that would be of use to you.'

'Indeed you have,' said Mr Pokey. 'You are a very clever young woman.'

'Please don't have me killed,' wept Kelly. 'I'll do anything you want.'

'Anything?'

'Anything.'

Mr Pokey nodded thoughtfully and looked the beautiful weeping

194

woman up and down and up again. 'So many twists and turns,' said he. 'So much deceit and duplicity. One never knows whom to believe any more. What is the world coming to, I ask myself? And do you know what I answer?'

'No,' said Kelly, snivelling somewhat. 'I don't.'

'Nor do I,' said Mr Pokey. 'So why don't we just drop all this pretence. You can stop all that crying for a start. It might convince some and there's no denying just how very sexy it is. But as you didn't start doing it until you were outside my door, when you messed up your hair and your dress and forced your thumbs into your eyes, I think we can consider it redundant now. Don't you?'

'Yes,' said Kelly, straightening up. 'But you wouldn't have expected otherwise. I'm well aware that this entire building is fully monitored by CCTV, including the games suite. You saw and heard everything that went on in there.'

'Of course,' said Mr Pokey.

'And I trust you were rightly appalled by Mr Bashful's cowardice and lack of company ethics. The man was a security risk. He was an accident waiting to happen.'

Mr Pokey nodded again. 'Who *are* you?' he asked. 'What are you? Internal security?'

'I'm just a student,' said Kelly.

Mr Pokey shook his head. 'You're much more than that,' he said. 'But whatever you are, *I* cannot access it from your file. Which, I suspect, makes you of a higher rank than myself.'

Kelly said nothing.

'Neither confirm or deny,' said Mr Pokey. 'I get the picture. So what *do* you want from me?'

'Security stinks around here,' said Kelly. 'If you wish to keep your job, then you and I will have to work together closely on this.'

'And?' said Mr Pokey.

'And now you can take me out to lunch,' said Kelly. 'On my way here I noticed a pub around the corner that does a rather interesting surf and turf. Shall we dine?'

Derek dined alone in the Shrunken Head. The Space Invaders machine popped and pinged away behind him, but Derek ignored it.

195

His attention was focused upon the computer printout that lay before him on the table, between his half a pint of large and his cheese sandwich. It was utterly absurd. Just look at the thing. Derek looked at it once again, then turned away his face in disgust. The requests, *requests*? Demands more like. The demands were utterly utterly absurd.

Four crad barges. A fleet of Morris Minors. A cinematic SFX holographic system programmed to project the Brentford Griffin onto Griffin Island for the newly named Fantasy Island experience. Derek's eyes travelled further down the list. 'Prophet of doom,' he read, doomily. 'They want a prophet of doom to carry a placard around, oh yes here it is on the list. REPENT THE END IS NIGH. Hardly original. They'll string me up. The locals will string me up. They'll tar and feather me first and probably lop off my wedding tackle. Not that I'll miss *that*. Well, I will, but. Oh damn, this is utterly absurd. Oh . . .'

Derek's eyes travelled further down the list. 'Five miles of perimeter fence. Oh, *electrified* perimeter fence. I'm doomed. Doomed. I might as well apply for the prophet's job. I'll bet I could do that really well.'

Derek sighed and shook his head and then slowly and surely a great big smile spread over his face. 'Well,' said Derek to himself. 'That's got all the whingeing and conscience out of the way.' And he patted at his jacket. And he lifted the lapel and peeped into the inside pocket. It was still in there. Right where he'd tucked it after Mr Speedy had handed it to him. Ten thousand quid in cash, 'to be going on with'. *Ten thousand quid!* It really was there. It wasn't a dream. And it was only a down payment. All he, Derek, entrepreneur and aspiring rich kid, twenty-first-century yuppie, had to do was find the right contacts and do the business. No questions asked. And you can get anything, if you have the right contacts. And where do you find the right contacts? Where is everything you wish to know waiting for you at the touch of a keypad? On the World Wide Web. Of course.

Nah. Of course it's not.

It's a bloke down the pub!

'Jah save all here,' said an ancient Rastafarian voice, 'Exceptin' Babylon, that be.'

The voice roused Derek from his Midasian musings. 'Hey Leo,' he called. 'Over here.'

196

Leo Felix, octogenarian used-car salesman and scrap dealer (at times the two were indistinguishable), turned his old grey dreads in Derek's direction. 'Yo,' said he. 'That be yo. Show some respect, Babylon. Don't go callin' me name all over da place. I ain't yo goddam dog.'

'Sorry,' said Derek. Leo sidled towards him and then leaned low, engulfing Derek in his dreads. 'Yo an' yo call I an' I on me mobile,' whispered Leo. 'Say yo got big deals to speak of . . .'

Derek fought his way out of the hairy darkness. 'Sit down,' he said. 'Please. Would you care for a drink?'

'I an' I would like a triple rum.'

'I'll get you a single,' said Derek. 'And we'll see how things go on from there.'

'Ras,' said Leo, the way that Rastafarians oft-times do.

Derek went up to the bar and returned with two single rums. Leo was by now rolling a joint of Cheech and Chong proportions.

'Yo get me out of me bed,' said Leo, licking the paper and deftly twirling the spliff between his brown and wrinkled thumbs. 'Yo rustled banknotes down de phone. What yo lookin' to buy, Babylon?'

Derek turned the computer printout in Leo's direction. 'Only this,' he whispered. 'And there's three thousand pounds in cash in it for you.'

Leo tucked the spliff into his mouth, delved into the pocket of his colourful Hawaiian shirt and brought out a pair of golden pince-nez. Plucking these onto his nose, he perused Derek's list. 'Jah Wobble!' went he, pointing. 'Yo want a steam train. Blood clart! There ain't no steam trains no more!'

'I'm sure you could find one, if the price was right. Say another five hundred pounds.'

'Say another thousand.'

'Seven fifty.'

'Eight hundred.'

'Done,' said Derek, offering his hand for a shake.

Leo gave it a smack. 'What all dis for anyhow?' he asked, taking up his Lion of Judah Zippo and offering fire to his spliff. 'Yo setting up a museum, or someting?'

'Yes,' said Derek, nodding his head. 'That's exactly it. A sort of folk museum, here in Brentford.'

197

Leo nodded his dreads in time to Derek's noddings and drew deeply on his ganga rollie. 'Damn biggun,' said he. 'Need five miles of perimeter fence. Where yo think I get dat?'

Derek shrugged. 'I'm not asking any questions,' he said, giving his nose a significant tap. 'Where you get it is of no concern to me. I'll pay cash.'

'I see,' said Leo, blowing smoke of de 'erb all over Derek. 'What de significance of that nose tap, by de way?'

Derek rolled his eyes. Leo offered him a puff. 'No, thanks,' said Derek. 'But do you think you can get all the things on this list?'

'Babylon,' said Leo, leaning close and grinning golden teeth. 'If it can be got, I can got it. Got me? But I'll want sometin' down on account.'

'On account of what?' said Derek.

'On account of I don't trust yo and I get damn all without the money up front.'

'I'll give you one thousand to be getting on with,' said Derek.

'Two thousand,' said Leo.

'Fifteen hundred.'

'Seventeen fifty.'

'All right,' said Derek. 'But I want all this stuff fast. Like by the weekend.'

'Haile Selassie!' went Leo. 'By the weekend? Includin' dis? One feral tomcat?'

'Two thousand up front then,' said Derek, pulling paper money slowly and carefully from his inside pocket. 'But I want it all by the weekend.'

Leo watched the money keep on coming. Certain thoughts entered into his old grey head, but he kept these thoughts very much to himself.

'We gotta deal,' said Leo, pocketing the loot and smacking Derek's hand once more. 'All cash and no questions asked.'

'No questions asked at all,' said Derek.

'No questions you wish to ask me?' asked Mr Pokey as he watched Kelly tucking into her surf and turf.

It was a rather de luxe surf and turf, consisting as it did of a fourteen-ounce T–bone steak, twelve Biscay Bay long-tailed langoustines, double tomatoes, grilled mushrooms, baked beans, curly fries, garlic bread, and a side order of cheesy nachos.

'No,' said Kelly, filling her face.

Mr Pokey leaned close to Kelly. 'You don't really need to ask anything, do you?' he said. 'You know everything.'

Kelly dipped a curly fry into a ramekin of crad pâté dip and popped it into her mouth.

'You are a very attractive woman,' said Mr Pokey.

Kelly turned her eyes in his direction.

'Yet your file shows that you have had no long-term relationships. You have no present partner, you have . . .'

Mr Pokey paused. Kelly was staring at him. Very hard.

'Oh I see,' said Mr Pokey. 'Of course. I only have *limited* access to your file.'

'Let me make this clear,' said Kelly. 'Ours is to be a strictly professional relationship. You will tell me what I need to know, when I need to know it. Do I make myself understood?'

'Of course,' said Mr Pokey, drawing back in his chair.

'Good,' said Kelly, slicing steak and feeding it into her mouth.

'You're a very cool customer,' said Mr Pokey and leaning forward once more, he spoke in a low and confidential tone. 'You know how things are,' he said. 'We live in a state of perpetual fear at Mute Corp, never knowing who will be next. Who will be chosen? Every time I touch the keypad, or move the mouse, I know that it could be me next. We all know that. *You* know that. *It* can take you whenever *it* wants to. Anything that you touch could have a Mute-chip in it. Anything. Terrifying thought isn't it? But that's how we live when we know, isn't it? We know that once it has entered into us, we belong to it, and it can infect anyone we touch. Our loved ones. Our children. As *it* chooses. As *it* wishes. And that's why we worship *it*, isn't it? To beg *it* to spare us. And the fear never stops. Fear is part of the package. It keeps us on the straight and narrow path, doesn't it?'

Kelly wiped her garlic bread about her plate and then she munched upon it. 'I have to make a call,' she said. 'And then I have to go. Thank you for the lunch.'

'You wouldn't fancy a pudding?'

199

'I do fancy the pudding. But I have too much to do. I will see you tomorrow.'

'Oh,' said Mr Pokey. 'Goodbye then.'

'Goodbye.' Kelly smiled, rose from the table and vanished into the lunchtime cityfolk crowd.

'Cool, very cool indeed,' said Mr Pokey.

In a cubicle in the women's toilet, Kelly felt anything but cool. She leaned over the toilet bowl and was violently sick.

Derek might have been rather sick too, if he'd known just what lay in store for him over the next few days. But content in the inaccurate knowledge that he had just pulled off the beginnings of a major financial coup and was already ahead by at least five thousand pounds, *and* it was still only lunchtime on his very first day at this game, he smiled a very broad smile and ordered himself a double rum to follow the single he'd just downed to seal the deal with Leo.

Derek now sat all alone in the Shrunken Head. Lunchtime business here was definitely falling off. Perhaps the God-fearing Brentonians had all given up drinking now and were kneeling in their homes, hands clasped in prayer, awaiting their turns to be Raptured.

'Whatever,' said Derek. 'Well I've done my bit for *the Company*, today. I think I'll take the afternoon off.'

And with that said he left the bar and wandered out into the sunshine.

It was another blissful afternoon. There was no getting away from that. Odd things were occurring and big trouble might lie in store when the locals got wind of Mute Corp's plans for the borough. But the old currant bun really was shining down like a good'n and on such an afternoon as this and in such a place as this, to wit, Brentford, jewel of the suburbs, who truly could worry about what lay ahead?

You couldn't, could you? It was all too beautiful.

Derek took great draughts of healthy Brentford air up his hooter, thrust out his chest, rubbed his palms together, patted his dosh-filled pocket and grinned a foolish grin. Blissful. That's what it was.

The streets slept in the sunlight. There was no-one about. Siesta time. Shop awnings down, that cat slept as usual upon the window sill of the Flying Swan. Shimmering heat haze rising from the tarmac in the distance along the Ealing Road. The smell of baking bread issuing from an open kitchen window.

Blissful.

Derek took a big step forward into the blissfulness.

And then he stopped himself short.

He was going to play his part in screwing up all this. In doing something dreadful to this blissful borough. He was going to sell it out. Sell it out to line his own pockets. That wasn't nice was it? That really wasn't nice. That wasn't decent, nor was it honest. Kelly wouldn't be pleased with him at all.

Derek made a puzzled face.

Why had he thought of her?

She was trouble, that one. She'd got him into all kinds of trouble. Derek stroked at his bruising. That one was bad medicine.

So why had he thought of her?

Derek shrugged. 'She needn't know,' he told himself. 'I'll not tell her. I'll let her think I'm following the policy of inertia. Pretending to help Mute Corp, but doing nothing. Then I'll be as outraged as she is when the fences go up. And when the rubbernecking tourists arrive in full force. She needn't know. It will be OK.

'It will be OK,' said Derek and he took another step forward. 'But why *did* I think of her?'

Derek stopped once more and scratched at his head, his chest and finally his groin. 'Oh no,' he said. 'Don't tell me that. Don't tell me that.'

Derek shook his head. He had done that thing last night, hadn't he? Recited that poem. That poem dedicated to her. He had done it. He really had. And why had he done it? Why?

'No,' said Derek, shaking his head once more. 'I'm not. I'm not. I'm not.'

A sparrow on a rooftop asked, 'Why not?' in Sparrowese.

'I'm not in love,' whispered Derek. 'I'm not in love with her. Not with that dreadful woman. I know she's young and so beautiful. So incredibly beautiful. Her eyes. Her hair. Her bosoms. God her bosoms. Imagine just touching them. And oh God, that mouth. Imagine kissing that mouth. But I'm not. I'm not. I'm not in love with her. I'm not.'

Derek took another deep breath. Through the mouth this time. 'I bloody well am,' said he. 'Oh damn.'

The object of Derek's affection had left the cubicle, the women's toilet and the pub and was moving at speed away from the Mute Corp building.

Kelly's face was pale and drawn. Her stomach ached and her shapely legs could hardly hold her up. Kelly felt wretched and frightened and sick, very sick indeed. Keeping up all the pretence was in itself quite bad enough. But it was what she had done to Mr Bashful that hurt most. She had pushed his hand down onto that computer mouse. Allowed the virus to enter his body. Forced him into the GO MANGO game from which he would never emerge alive. She had condemned him to death. She had effectively killed him herself.

It was all too much. All too very much.

Through the sunlit London streets went Kelly. Elegant shoppers to left and to right of her. To forward and behind, dressed in the height of summer fashion. Frocks of dextropolipropelinehexocitachloride, tottering upon Doveston holistic footwear, smiling and speaking Runese.

Who'd be next among them?

Next to play GO MANGO?

Next to die at the invisible hands of a mad computer virus that thought it was a God?

And who was she, Kelly Anna Sirjan, to think that in some way she was capable of stopping this from happening?

What was she to do? Take it on? Play it at its own game? Defeat the system that encircled the globe? That could take her any time it wished. The moment she touched something, anything that contained a Mute-chip.

What? The cashpoint? Her mobile phone? The automated ticket machine on the bus? A pocket calculator? Any computer terminal?

Kelly stopped short and clung to a lamppost for support. And then she tore her hands away. That was connected to the National Grid, wasn't it? And the National Grid had Mute-chips incorporated into it. 'Debugging' the Millennium Bug. There was no escape from this thing. It could take her at any time it wished. Any time that it considered that she was a threat to it.

Kelly gagged and coughed. Her throat was dry. Ahead was a Coca-Cola machine. No. And Kelly shook her golden head. She didn't dare touch that.

She'd go mad. Was she going mad already?

'I have to get back,' said Kelly to no-one but herself. 'Back to Brentford. It's safer than anywhere else. There's less computer technology there than anywhere else. Except perhaps Mute Corp Keynes and there's no way I'm going there at the moment. I have to get back.'

A cab drew up alongside of her. 'Looking for a ride beautiful lady?' called the cabbie.

Kelly looked at him. And at the cab. Computerized satellite tracking system. Computerized fare system. Computerized radio system. The cabbie waved his hand. On his wrist was a computerized watch, one of those chunky Mute Corp retro jobs.

'No,' said Kelly, shaking her head. 'I'm walking. Go away.'

'Please yourself,' said the cabbie, driving off.

And so Kelly walked. She walked for nearly ten miles. From the West End of London to Brentford. It was five of the glorious evening clock by the time she crossed over the bridge that used to cross over the railway, turned several corners and put her passkey into Mrs Gormenghast's front door.

'Hello,' called Kelly. But the house was empty.

Kelly opened the door reserved for tradesmen and others of a bygone lower order and let herself out into the back garden. She limped up the garden path, for her holistic shoes hurt more than a little, and she passed behind the trellis and opened the pucely painted shed door.

'I'm so sorry,' she said. 'I meant to be back much earlier. You must be starving. It's only that I've learned so much. And I've done something terrible and I need someone to talk to and I hope that somehow, impossible though it might be, you have managed to get through this thing and cure yourself. Because if not I don't know what

I'm going to do. I might have to kill you to prevent you passing on the infection to somebody else. And I couldn't bear that, I really couldn't.'

And Kelly drew away the coal sacks.

To find the floor beneath them empty.

Big Bob Charker had vanished once again.

17

Derek was a little drunk.

He'd left the Shrunken Head and wandered up to the Flying Swan. From there he'd wandered across to the Four Horsemen and from there to the Hands of Orlac. From there his wanderings became a tad confused. He'd wandered into the coin-operated laundry at the top of Abbadon Street, thinking it to be one of those postmodern cocktail bar kind of jobbies that the toffs up West seem so taken with.

Vileda Wilcox (daughter of the embarrassing Harkly 'Here's another good'n' Wilcox and sister to Studs, the Mississippi riverboat gambler, and named, incidentally, after the kitchen cloth of legend) had thrown Derek out on his ear, calling him a filthy drunken pig of a person.

'I only asked for a *sex on the beach*,' said the baffled Derek, and received a drop kick to the groin that sent him sprawling.

'That's all you men ever think about,' said Vileda, which was basically correct.

'The thing about love,' slurred Derek to himself as he wandered uncertainly and not a tad unpainfully towards the Tudor Tearooms in the High Street, which in his particular state of mind *did* bear an uncanny resemblance to an Alpine après-ski kind of bar. 'The thing about love is, that it scans the social bandicoots. No, that's, spans the social boundaries. Kelly is definitely posh. Anyone can see that. *You* can see that. Can't you?' he asked.

Mad John was shouting at Volvos today. 'What?' he shouted at Derek. 'Speak up. What?'

'Mad John,' said Derek, putting his arm about the loony's ragged shoulder. 'You're my friend aren't you?'

'I'm no friend of Volvos,' shouted Mad John. 'Hatchback or the estate, they're both the same to me. I hate 'em.'

'Yes,' said Derek, or 'yesh', because it's 'yesh' that you say at such times. 'Yesh, you're right old friend of mine. But I love the woman. And I'm a bit posh.'

'You're a bit pissed,' Mad John shouted. And 'You'll get yours, come the revolution,' to a passing Volvo fastback, with the cross-body spoiler and the legendary cage of steel.

'But money can make you posh, can't it?' said Derek. 'It made Posh Spice posh. Or did it just make her rich? Same thing anyway. Posh is just rich with good manners, everyone knows that, although the posh ones won't admit it. And having a posh voice, that helps, doesn't it? Would you say that I had a posh voice?'

'Listen,' said Mad John softly, removing Derek's hand from his shoulder. 'I'm just doing my job, mate. I'm paid to shout at shoes on Sundays and Volvos on Thursdays. The rest of the week, my time is my own. Mostly I spend it watching old Richard and Judy reruns on UK Gold. I'm not a philosopher, nor an agony uncle. Why don't you just go home to your mum, Derek, and sleep it off?'

'But if I had money,' said Derek. 'Say I had lots of money. Then a chap with lots of money can get himself a posh woman, can't he?'

'A man with lots of money can get himself pretty much any woman,' said Mad John. 'So why have a posh one? They're really high maintenance and most of them are rubbish in bed. Believe me, I've had loads. If I had a quid for every posh woman who's taken pity on me, invited me back to her home, given me a bath and then, as if for the first time, noticed how ruggedly handsome I am, and then given me a right seeing-to on her four-poster bed, before filling my pockets with cash, I'd be a rich man myself by now and able to get myself pretty much any woman I wanted.'

Derek stared lopsidedly at Mad John. 'Is all that true?' he asked.

'Gawd, you are drunk, aren't you? Come on, I'll help you home. It's knocking-off time for me anyway.'

And so Mad John helped Derek home. Derek's mum thanked Mad John for his trouble, then told him that she felt a terrible guilt that such nice people as Mad John had to sleep on the streets with no roof over their heads and would Mad John care to come in and have a bath?

'Why thank you very much, madam,' said Not-so-Mad John. 'Let's get your lad up to his bed first, shall we?'

And so Derek had an early night.

Mad John didn't, but that's another story. And as it's a rude one, propriety forbids its telling here.

Two streets north of Derek's mum's abode, and just one from the rather posh house where Mad John lived, but where no-one saw him sneak into at night, was the pinkly-painted terraced dwelling of one Big Bob Charker.

At a little after eight of the delicious Brentford evening clock, Minky Charker answered the knock at her front door to find Kelly Anna Sirjan, freshly showered and looking radiant, standing on the doorstep of pink stone.

'Oh,' said Minky, wife of Bob the Big and missing. 'You are the very last-but-one person I expected to find upon my doorstep.'

Kelly didn't ask. She just said, 'Can I come in?'

'Ming the Merciless,' said Minky Charker. 'In case you had been thinking to ask, but were too shy to do so. Do come in then, I'll put the kettle on.'

Kelly went in and Minky put on the kettle.

'Do you think it suits me?' she asked.

'It's the right shade of pink,' said Kelly. 'But I came here to ask about your husband. I don't suppose you've seen him today, have you?'

'Gracious me, no,' said Minky, taking off the kettle and hugging it to her ample bosoms, as one might a puppy or a small dwarf named Dave that one has taken a sudden liking to. 'I thought that he'd been Raptured. Or at least I think that's what I thought.'

'I see you have a lot of candles burning,' said Kelly.

'You can never have too many candles burning,' said Minky, giving the kettle the kind of stroke that you might give to a really friendly otter. Or a hamster, or perhaps a quill-less porcupine that you had taken pity on. 'You can never have too many candles burning, or too many bottles of nail varnish, or too many different brands of kitchen cleaner under your sink.'

'Or toilet rolls,' said Kelly. 'You can never have too many of those.'

'Exactly,' said Minky. 'Although I never keep them under my sink. There's no room.'

'So you haven't seen your husband?'

'No,' said Minky and she tickled the kettle under the spout. 'But I wouldn't be expecting to, what with him being Raptured and every-thing. But I'll see him when my time comes to be carried off to glory. And then I'll have some words to say to him, you can be assured of that.'

'If he did turn up here,' said Kelly. 'Say he returned from Heaven for some other reason, to pick up a change of underwear or some-thing. Could you phone me?' Kelly paused. 'No, not phone me, come round and tell me. I'm staying at Mrs Gormenghast's.'

'Madam Puce,' said Minky. 'What an eccentric, that woman, eh?'

'I'd really appreciate it,' said Kelly. 'It's, er, just that I have some money for him. A great deal of money. It's a surprise. I don't want you to mention it to him. But it's a *great deal* of money.'

'I'll take that then,' said Minky.

'No, *he* has to sign for it.'

'I can forge his signature.' Minky stroked the kettle's lid. 'It's some-thing all wives have to do. You'll understand when you marry yourself.'

'Why would I marry *myself*?'

'Because then you can be assured of getting *everything* when you get divorced.'

'Oh, I see,' said Kelly. 'All these things are so simple, once they're explained.'

'Except for logarithms,' said Minky. 'They're not simple. Or advanced calculus, quantum theory, or Fermat's last theorem. Not to mention the transperambulation of pseudo-cosmic antimatter.'

'The transperambulation of pseudo-cosmic antimatter?'

Minky Charker shook her head and patted the kettle.

'Go on then,' said Kelly. 'Say it.'

'Shan't,' said Minky.

'Oh go on, you know you want to.'

'Oh all right. I told you not to mention *that*.'

Kelly left the house of Big Bob Charker, not to mention Minky, and took to some wanderings of her own. She felt that she ought to speak to Derek. Warn him. Tell him all that she knew. He was her friend now after all and she didn't want any harm to come to him. He really should be warned to keep his hands away from anything that might contain a Mute-chip. And anything meant nearly everything.

Kelly went around to Derek's. She knocked and waited and knocked and waited some more. She felt certain that she heard moans of pleasure coming from an open upstairs window. But nobody came to answer the door, so Kelly wrote out a note for Derek to contact her as soon as he got home, but not by phone, in person. And that it was very very urgent. And then she folded it up and popped it through the letter box, where it fell upon the welcome mat, which, like that of Derek's Aunty Uzi, had long worn out its welcome.

And then Kelly wandered on and knowing that she needed a drink and with it something substantial to eat, she made for the Flying Swan.

The Swan was not exactly heaving. A couple of old duffers sat at the bar counter. A pair of wandering bishops played darts against two skinners of mule. A battered fireman sat hunched at a corner table, bewailing his lot to a long-legged nurse with a ginger beard, who sipped at a pint of hand-drawn ale, but longed for a *sex on the beach*.

Kelly ordered a red wine and the full surf and turf, which the barman informed her contained something really special tonight. Haunch of wildebeest and perineum of octopus, served on a bed of Nepalese radish and wolf-bean-coated rice, cooked in the Tierra del Fuego style. With a side order of lime juice that could be either used as a garnish, or dabbed upon the wrists to discourage mosquitoes.

Kelly took her red wine to a window table and sat down to gaze out at the summer evening and marshal her thoughts into a plan of campaign.

As you do.

Five minutes hadn't passed, however (it was nearer to four), when a young man approached her table, wearing a sheepish grin.

Kelly looked up at the young man.

The young man looked down at Kelly, grinning sheepishly.

'Is this chair vacant?' he asked, pointing to a vacant chair.

Kelly glanced towards the chair, then back to the questioning young man. He was a personable young man. A sheath of blondie hair clothed his scalp. A sleeveless T-shirt clothed his muscular physique. A pair of too-tight leather trousers clothed all manner of things.

Kelly shook her head. She really wasn't in the mood. 'The chair *is* vacant,' she said. 'And given the ample selection of other vacant chairs in this establishment tonight, it is my hope that it will remain so.'

'I'll stand then,' said the young man, his sheepish grin transforming itself into a dogged expression.

'But elsewhere, please,' said Kelly.

The young man looked momentarily foxed for an answer.

But he wasn't.

'You'll have to go to Mute Corp Keynes,' he said. 'That's where the answer lies.'

Kelly's blue eyes widened and her hand found its way into her hair. 'Who are you?' she asked.

The young man seated himself in the vacant chair, availing himself of its vacancy. 'Shibboleth,' he said. 'Shibboleth . . .' and he pronounced the unpronounceable name. 'Brother of Malkuth. You've heard of him.' Shibboleth extended his hand. Kelly did not shake it.

'Good,' said Shibboleth. 'You know better than that, then. You know a lot, don't you? I know quite a lot too.'

'I don't know what you're talking about,' said Kelly.

'You do,' said Shibboleth. 'Because you're doing what I'm doing, but for different reasons. I've been trying to find out what happened to my brother. And my mother. It has led me to you. *You* know what happened to them. I know that you do.'

Kelly shook her head. 'Forget it,' she said. 'You're Mute Corp security, aren't you? Come out to check me out. Crude, very crude.'

'There's nothing crude about me,' said Shibboleth. 'Except perhaps my taste in trousers. But I do have extremely good thighs and although man-made fibres stretch in all the right places, they'll never be leather, will they?'

'I won't tell you anything,' said Kelly. 'Please go away.'

'I'll tell *you* two things,' said Shibboleth. 'Firstly you have a tattoo of an Om upon your stomach and secondly you should really turn your face away from the window, you've been under surveillance ever since you left the Mute Corp building today. The fat man across the road, leaning on the lamppost. He's been following you and I'll bet he really wished you'd taken a cab. He's watching you through macrovision spectacles, he can read your lips.'

Kelly turned her face away from the window. 'And how do you know about the tattoo?' she asked.

'You just met your first well-poisoner,' said Shibboleth. 'I'm working with my brother's set-up. It's hacked into the Mute Corp CCTV system, amongst other things. I witnessed your medical. It was disgusting, but strangely compelling. I'm sorry.'

'And I am embarrassed,' said Kelly. 'Something I do not enjoy being.'

'But I am telling the truth. I'm surprised you haven't noticed the fat man.'

'I don't look twice at fat people,' said Kelly. 'It's probably on my file somewhere.'

'We could work together on this.'

'I have no idea what you're talking about,' said Kelly. 'I work for Mute Corp. I will have no hesitation in informing them of your criminal activities first thing in the morning.'

'Yeah, right,' said Shibboleth. 'But it's a tricky one this, isn't it? You don't know if you can trust me and I don't really know if I can trust you. You might be high-ranking Mute Corp security, as Mr Pokey thinks you are. Although he isn't certain, which is why the fat man is following you. Or you might be someone who wants to put a stop to it. All of it. So where does that leave us? Both distrusting each other. But both needing someone to trust.'

'Surf and turf,' said the barman, arriving with Kelly's meal and placing it upon the table with a great show of politeness. 'And I've thrown in a side order of Gambian Bugaboo fish entrecôte flambé at no extra cost. Although you are free to tip generously should the mood take you. And I really hope that it does, because I'm saving up for a tightrope of my very own, so I can run away with the circus.'

'Any particular circus?' Shibboleth asked.

'Professor Merlin's Greatest Show Off Earth,' said the barman. 'It travels between the planets in a Victorian steam ship. That's the life for me. The smell of the sawdust, the small dwarves called Dave, and all the confetti you can eat, when you play for a rich potentate at the wedding of his daughter.'

'That's the life,' said Shibboleth. 'I'd tip you myself, but I think that I'll just keep the money.'

The barman bowed and departed, humming 'The March of the Gladiators'.

Kelly took up her eating irons. 'I'd prefer it if you'd go away now,' she told Shibboleth. 'I'm very hungry and I'd prefer to eat alone.'

'I can understand that,' said Shibboleth. 'And you must be very hungry. Considering how you threw up your lunch in that pub toilet and everything.'

'*What?*' said Kelly.

'I took the liberty of hacking into the pub's security system, after I'd hacked into the street surveillance system. You wouldn't believe where the cameras are hidden in that toilet. You'd think that Chuck Berry owned the place.'*

'Come back in ten minutes,' said Kelly. 'When I'm finished.'

Ten minutes later, or it might have been eleven, although frankly, who's been counting, Shibboleth returned to Kelly's table.

'If I believed you,' said Kelly, wiping her lips with an oversized red gingham napkin.

'Which means that you do,' said Shibboleth.

'Which means *if*,' said Kelly. 'What could you tell me, that would positively convince me?'

'Nothing,' said Shibboleth. 'But I could show you where the chapel is. I could take you there.'

---

* If you know about that, then you know. If not, I'm not going to tell you.

'And I would let a complete stranger take me to Mute Corp Keynes at night? Do I look suicidal?'

'My brother may well be dead by now,' said Shibboleth. 'My brother and my mother too. The vanishing act. I don't know how it's done. I suspect that it only works upon people who are already infected. But it's impossible to tell who is infected and who isn't. Perhaps we all are.'

'Don't say that,' said Kelly. 'I have been thinking that myself.'

'Which probably means that you're not infected. Otherwise you'd be thinking what *it* wants you to think. Hang onto that notion, it's one that keeps me sane.'

'All right,' said Kelly. 'This is probably the stupidest thing I've ever done in my life. But I'll come with you.'

'Brilliant,' said Shibboleth. 'And it really isn't the stupidest thing you've ever done. According to your file . . .'

'Don't,' said Kelly. 'Although, go on, give me a clue.'

'Identical twins,' said Shibboleth. 'Your eighteenth birthday. The Ocean Rooms . . . night club . . . the billiard-room table . . .'

'*That* is on camera? *That's* on my file?'

'Sorry,' said Shibboleth. 'Everything's on file.'

Kelly shook her golden head. And then smiled a little wistfully. 'I'd quite like to watch that,' she said. 'But it wasn't what I was thinking about.'

'Oh in that case you must mean . . .'

'The secret is in knowing when to stop,' said Kelly. 'Come on, let's go to Mute Corp Keynes.'

It didn't look any better by moonlight. In fact it looked a lot worse. Even more desolate. Even more urban-decayed.

The guard on the border post was a different guard from the one who had been there two days before. Who wasn't the same guard either. Because they all worked complicated shifts.

'Anything to declare?' asked this guard.

'Say it,' said Kelly. 'Who cares? Say it.'

Shibboleth shrugged at the wheel and said it. 'Nothing but my genius,' he said.

'Most original, sir,' said the guard. 'That's the first time I've heard that, *today*.'

213

Shibboleth grinned, unsheepishly.

'I'll make a note of it,' said the guard. 'I believe that the millionth person to say it is entitled to a free T-shirt, or something. So, do you have any illegal drugs, laundered money, unlicensed firearms or explosives to declare?'

'None,' said Shibboleth.

'You won't last long in there then,' said the guard. 'Would you care to give me your wristwatch before you go to your certain doom? Only I'm saving up for a unicycle, I want to run away with the circus.'

Shibboleth parted with his wristwatch. 'If we make it out of here later, I want it back,' he said.

'Fair enough,' said the border guard. 'But I might not be on duty when you return. I go off at three when another guard comes on to relieve me. It's not the same guard who came on at three yesterday morning, that's another guard altogether. The one who came on at five the day before.'

'Wasn't it six?' asked another border guard, arriving on his bike.

'Oh, hello Harry,' said the first border guard. 'I didn't think you were coming on relief until ten tomorrow morning.'

'It's a *very* complicated system,' said Harry. 'Do you want me to take charge of this chap's watch? Only I'm saving up for a milk float, I want to run away with the circus.'

'Do they have milk-float acts in circuses?' asked the border guard that was just about to be relieved.

'Did I say circus?' asked Harry. 'Naturally I meant to say trampoline.'

'He works too hard,' the first border guard explained. 'Sometimes he has to relieve himself, if somebody doesn't turn up.'

'Can we just go through now?' asked Shibboleth.

'I don't know,' said the first border guard. 'I'm not on duty any more. You'll have to ask Harry.'

'Don't ask me,' said Harry. 'I'm just clocking off.'

Shibboleth drove through the night streets of Mute Corp Keynes. He avoided the stingers and deadfalls with the bungee spikes, the landmines and the tempting hedgehogs, which, Shibboleth told Kelly, were loaded with nail bombs. And various other obstructions.

214

'You seem to know your way around here,' said Kelly.

Shibboleth turned the steering wheel of his automobile. It was a Ford Fiesta. It was Derek's Ford Fiesta. 'I've lived here all my life,' said he. 'I know everything that goes on here.'

'The border guards didn't seem to know you.'

'I didn't know them. There are a lot of border guards. It's a very complicated system.'

'But if you lived here, why did you give them your watch?'

'It wasn't *my* watch,' said Shibboleth. 'Ah here we are.'

Ahead, through the mostly darkness, shone bright lights. Bright and neon lights. A bar. And a dangerous-looking bar. All concrete front and no windows. Low and ugly. Shrapnel-pocked and needing a coat or two of paint. Or better still demolition. The neon lights blinked on and off the way that such lights do. They spelled out the letters that spelled out the words, which spelled out the name of the place.

THE TOMORROWMAN TAVERN.

All that spelling spelled out.

'You'll like it here,' said Shibboleth. 'Well, actually you won't. But there's worse places to be than this, although I've never been to them.'

'And the chapel?' Kelly asked.

18

Shibboleth ambled off to the bar, leaving Kelly to muse upon the wisdom of her being here. The jukebox stuttered and cut out and the patrons made their feelings felt by pelting it with bottles. Whilst a potman laboured to restart the ancient Wurlitzer, a canny Scotsman, in a kilt and war bonnet, entertained the disgruntled patrons with an exhibition of standing on one leg.

A shaven-headed woman with a padlock through her nose leaned close by Kelly and whispered at her ear. 'That's our Kenny,' she said in a hushed and reverent tone. 'When it comes to the standing upon the single leg, there's none that do it better than him.'

'Is he self-taught?' Kelly asked.

The woman looked at Kelly as if she were quite mad. 'Tish no,' she said, shaking her baldy head and rattling her padlock on her silver-painted teeth. 'He spent ten years in the Potala Tibet, studying under the Balancing Lama, and then another five years in the Monastery of St Timothy the gimp, they're a hopping order there, so he learned that as well. Then he was with the Unipedarian Church of South Korea, they have their right legs amputated, which frankly I think is cheating. Then he served an apprenticeship on the Spanish main, road-testing wooden legs for retired pirates. And then . . .'

'Here's your red wine,' said Shibboleth. 'They had no pork scratchings, so I bought you twenty Lambert and Butlers instead. You don't have to smoke them, you can just chew the tobacco. It's scented with camomile, or so the landlord told me.'

'The landlord is jealous of our Kenny,' said she of the eggy head and padlock nose furniture. 'He'd give his right leg to do what our Kenny can do.'

'What can he do?' asked Shibboleth.

'He can stand on one leg,' said Kelly. 'That's him over there.'

'Is he hoping to run away with the circus?' Shibboleth asked. 'Or perhaps hop?'

'He ran *away from* the circus,' said the hairless female with the nasal security-accoutrement appendage. 'Or perhaps he hopped. I never asked him. There are some things you just don't ask a man with a talent like that.'

'Such as, *why*?' Shibboleth suggested.

The slaphead with the shiny metallic burglar-thwarting-equipment hooter decoration raised a hairless eyebrow and gave Shibboleth the kind of look that a ferret gives a lump of mouse-shaped feta cheese on a cold and frosty morning. 'I know where you live,' she said.

'There's a couple of seats over there,' said Shibboleth to Kelly. 'Perhaps you'd care to sit down?'

Kelly cared and so they went and sat down.

'This used to be a really decent bar,' said Shibboleth, supping something green in a glass and smiling a lot upon Kelly. 'They used to have real entertainment here on a Thursday night. Proper professional single-leg-standers, many of whom also played the accordion. Some of the greatest names in single-leg-standing have performed here. Arthur Gillette. The Magnificent Norman. Wally Tomlin, Prince of the Pedal-elevation. He did songs from the shows. And . . .'

'Stop now,' said Kelly. 'Or I will be forced to punch you in the face.'

'It's an acquired taste,' said Shibboleth. 'How are the Lambert and Butlers?'

Kelly pulled a strand of tobacco from her teeth. 'Not bad, as it happens,' she said. 'Although Capstan Full Strength are better. But beggars can't be choosers, as my mother used to say, although choosers *can* be beggars, if they choose.'

217

'Tell me about your mother,' said Shibboleth, which rang a certain bell. 'Only the good things.'

'No,' said Kelly. 'But tell me about your brother. Have you any idea at all about where he might be now?'

'None,' said Shibboleth. 'You can't hack into GO MANGO. It occupies a different area of cyberspace. One that no man has access to. None perhaps, but one.'

'Remington Mute,' said Kelly.

'The lad himself,' said Shibboleth. 'But whether Mute is still alive, only a select elite knows that.'

'The worshippers at the chapel?'

'You could ask them, but I don't think they'll tell you. Oh dear.'

'Oh dear?' Kelly asked.

'Oh dear,' said Shibboleth and he pointed. 'The canny Scotsman Kenny has toppled over. The days of the great and sterling standers of the single leg are well and truly over. Still, let's give him a round of applause, you could see he was doing his best.'

Shibboleth clapped and Kelly, shrugging, clapped as well.

The patrons applauded and several patted the canny Scotsman, who was now in tears, upon his shaking shoulders.

'Well done old boy,' they went. 'Nice try. Better luck next time.'

The Scotsman limped away to the bar.

'This place really sucks,' said Kelly.

Shibboleth raised an eyebrow that was dark and dapper and dandy. 'That's rather strong language for a posh young woman like you,' he said.

'I am somewhat stressed at present,' said Kelly. 'What time is it now?'

'Aren't you wearing a watch?'

'Not any more. Mine was digital. A Mute Corp Oyster.'

'Mine's a clockwork jobbie,' said Shibboleth, taking it from his inside pocket and peering at it. 'You can never be too careful. It's nearly half past eleven. We've time for a few more drinks.'

'I'd rather keep a clear head. How far is the chapel from here?'

'Not far.' And Shibboleth raised his glass.

'Just one thing,' said Kelly. 'If you intend to betray me, have a care.

I sent a man to his certain death today. My life is in tatters. I wouldn't think twice about . . .'

'OK. I get the picture. I know you're an exponent of Dimac. You studied that on the Web, didn't you? You did all your university degrees on the Web. You even met your first boyfriend through a chat room.'

'What are you getting at?'

'You're a bit on your own now, aren't you?'

Kelly finished her red wine. 'You can get me another, please,' she said. 'A large one would be favourite.'

Shibboleth returned to the bar counter. The landlord was now standing upon it. 'Ladies and gentlemen,' he called out over the ugly heads of the assembled patrons. 'It appears that the jukebox is well and truly banjoed.' Someone hurled a bottle, which the landlord ducked professionally. 'So in order that you do not go unentertained,' he continued, 'my lady wife, Spongetex, will perform her much-loved standing-ever-so-still act.'

'I can hardly wait,' said Kelly, munching on a filter tip.

A young-fellow-me-lad, with a stylish Rayban sunglasses facial tattoo, leaned close to Kelly and whispered at her ear. 'The landlord's missus really knows her stuff when it comes to standing-ever-so-still,' he said. 'She used to work as a school crossing keeper. But they dismissed her because of the high mortality rate among the schoolkids. Then she . . .'

'Go away,' said Kelly. 'Or I'll punch your lights out.'

Shibboleth returned with a bottle of red wine. 'The landlord wasn't looking, so I nicked this,' he said. 'Do you want to move to a seat nearer the bar so you can watch his lady wife?'

'I'd like to go,' said Kelly. 'I can't take all this excitement.'

'We can't go yet,' said Shibboleth. 'We have to wait for someone.'

Kelly's hand reached up towards her hair. A frown turned down the corners of her mouth.

'You don't have to worry,' said Shibboleth. 'I haven't led you into a trap.'

'So, who is this person I'm going to meet?'

'Oh, you're not going to meet him. He's the Reverend Jim, high

219

priest of the chapel. He always comes in here for a swift half before the service. We're going to follow him.'

'Why?' asked Kelly. 'I thought you knew where the chapel is?'

'I do, it's here in Mute Corp Keynes.'

'And whereabouts, exactly?'

'Ah, that I'm not entirely certain of.'

'You lied to me,' said Kelly, rising to take her leave.

'I didn't lie exactly, please sit down.'

Kelly sat down and glared at Shibboleth.

'That really spoils your looks,' he said. 'I didn't lie. I know it's here. *Somewhere*. And somewhere close. I've followed the Reverend before. Many times, but he always gives me the slip. Which is why I asked you to come. With the two of us on his case, I'm sure he won't be able to vanish away.'

'Vanish away,' said Kelly. 'I'm going. This was all a waste of time.'

'No, wait, stay. And don't look now, because he's just come in.'

If ever there was a haunted-looking man, a fearful man, a timid man, a man far gone in nervous trepidation, then that man was *not* the Reverend Jim. The Reverend Jim was big and broad and jolly. Avuncular, that was the word. Ruddy of both cheek and barnet, smiley all about the mouth regions and given to great bouts of belly-hugging laughter at the very drop of a hat.

But then, let's face it, hat-dropping can be funny. Especially when performed by one of the greats of the Art who had all played the Tomorrowman Tavern during the golden era of hat-dropping, less than a decade before (on Friday nights). Showmen such as Harry 'The-Hat-Drop' McFadayen. Or Tommy 'Tip-the-Topper' Thompson. Not to mention Ben 'There-Goes-my-Bowler' Bradshaw.

'*That* is a high priest?' asked Kelly, peeping towards the Reverend Jim. 'He looks more like some jovial uncle. Or one of those old hat-drop artists. Ben 'There-Goes-my-Bowler' Bradshaw, for instance.'

'Don't mention him,' said Shibboleth. 'But the Reverend Jim *is* the high priest. Let's face it, looks can be deceptive. My mother always looked like a total moron, but then she was the exception that proves the rule.'

220

'You haven't spoken about your mum,' said Kelly. 'Only your brother. Your mum vanished as well, didn't she?'

'Frankly I'm glad to see the back of her,' said Shibboleth. 'I'm only looking for my brother because he owes me money. This is a hard town to live in and it's full of bad people. I know, because I'm one of them.'

Kelly sighed. 'I really have wasted my time coming here,' she said. 'I think I'll just beat you unconscious, avail myself of your stolen car and drive back to Brentford.'

Great gut-rumblers of laughter echoed from the bar counter area, much to the annoyance of those patrons who were trying to concentrate upon the landlord's lady wife's standing-ever-so-stillness.

The Reverend Jim and the landlord were sharing a joke about a knitted woollen hat at a bus stop in Penge in the year of 1972.

'I really am going,' said Kelly.

'I'm coming with you,' said Shibboleth. 'The Reverend Jim is leaving.'

'That was quick.'

'He's a real professional. He always leaves them wanting more.'

Kelly followed Shibboleth, who followed the Reverend Jim. She bid the Tomorrowman Tavern a silent farewell, vowing that she would never ever return there under any circumstances. Or at least until they put on some decent entertainment.

Such as a sitting-down-and-staring act.

Or a moving-quietly-in-no-particular-direction spectacular.

Or . . .

But the secret *really is* to leave them wanting more.

'There he goes, on his toes,' said Shibboleth.

And indeed the Reverend Jim was moving very fast for a fat lad. He fairly bounced along.

'Did he just outrun you before?' Kelly asked, as she trotted along behind Shibboleth. 'He's very light on his feet.'

The light was uncertain. Which is to say that there wasn't much of it about. The occasional security searchlight, turning above a bungalow gun turret. A single streetlight bound in a barbed-wire cocoon. The Reverend Jim moved in and out of the uncertain light and bounced along on his way.

'I'm not surprised he keeps losing you,' whispered Kelly. 'I can hardly see him most of the time.'

'Put these on,' said Shibboleth, handing Kelly a pair of goggles.

'Infra-red?'

'Yes and Mute-chip free.'

Kelly put the goggles on. Shibboleth did likewise with another pair. The bouncing redly-hued image of the rotund high priest went bob-bob-bobbing before them.

It never seemed to be doing any looking back. Which might have meant any number of things. That he didn't care. That he did care, but knew that it didn't matter. That it did matter and he did care, but he knew that he didn't have to care, because whether it mattered or not, it didn't matter whether he did care or not. Or possibly a combination of any of these. Or no combination at all. He just bounced and bobbed along, taking odd little sidesteps, then dancing forward, then steps backwards and dancing forward again.

'And there he goes,' said Shibboleth. 'And there he's gone.'

And he was.

'He *has* gone,' said Kelly. 'But where did he go?'

'That's a question I've been asking myself ever since I saw him do it the first time.'

Kelly followed Shibboleth to the approximate spot where the Reverend Jim had vanished and stood looking into the darkness that spread all around and about. 'Where are we?' Kelly asked. 'What is this place?'

'It's nowhere,' said Shibboleth. 'Just a bombed-out car park. No buildings and no trapdoors leading into subterranean workings. I've been all over the place in daylight. It's paved solid. There's nothing. You tell me where he went.'

Kelly took off her goggles and stared at Shibboleth. What there was to be seen of his face looked genuinely baffled.

'Let me get this straight,' she said. 'The only evidence you think you have that the chapel is here, is that the man you think is the high priest of this chapel always vanishes right at this spot when you follow him.'

'Nicely put,' said Shibboleth.

'You idiot,' said Kelly. 'You clown. You stupid . . .'

222

'Easy,' said Shibboleth.

'You have no evidence. Absolutely none.'

'I wouldn't go so far as to put it like that. It *is* here. I know it's here. I'm not messing you about. I'm on the level. I know it's here.'

'Hold on,' said Kelly. 'Say that again.'

'I know it's here.'

'No, before that.'

'I don't remember exactly what I said. I'm on the level, I said that.'

'Exactly,' said Kelly. 'That is what you said.'

'I'm baffled,' said Shibboleth. 'What did I say?'

'Level,' said Kelly. 'You said, level. As in levels in a computer game. This is what all of this is about. Well, some of it anyway. Most of it, as far as I can make out. Games. And in computer games you go up from level to level and you do that by scoring points and gaining energy and reasoning things out. Bear with me on this. What if the chapel is here? Right here.'

'It is,' said Shibboleth. 'I'm sure of it.'

'Then what if we cannot gain access to it without some kind of password? Without knowing the cheat. We have to find the Easter Egg. The secret way onto the next level.'

'Go on,' said Shibboleth. 'I'm listening. What do you think the Reverend Jim did, then?'

'He did something,' said Kelly. 'But then he might have had something. Some electronic key. Some remote-control unit. Something.'

'Nothing computerized works around here,' said Shibboleth. 'Mobile phones don't work. Laptops, nothing.'

'Give me a moment,' said Kelly. 'I need to think about this.'

Shibboleth gave her a moment.

'Any joy?' he asked, a moment later.

'Yes,' said Kelly. 'I think I know how he did it. Let's walk back to where we were when he vanished.'

Kelly and Shibboleth retraced their steps as best they could.

'OK,' said Kelly. 'We were behind him here, and what did he do?'

'He bounced and bobbed along in front of us and then he vanished.'

'No, he did more than that. He danced along. He took little side-steps and went forwards and backwards.'

'A pattern,' said Shibboleth.

'On the paving stones,' said Kelly. 'He danced out a pattern from one stone to another. No doubt without stepping on the cracks. It's hopscotch. The oldest game in the world.'

'I thought that was prostitution.'

'That's the oldest *profession*. But I'm sure that whores played hopscotch too.'

'They'll play anything you want, if you pay them enough. I met this girl once who . . .'

'This is neither the time nor the place,' said Kelly.

'That's what she said at first, but money talks.'

'I *will* hit you,' said Kelly. 'I have very little patience left.'

'So what do we do?' Shibboleth asked. 'Follow the high priest again tomorrow and try to dance on the same stones that he does? We could sprinkle talcum powder over them earlier in the evening. I saw that done in an old movie. What are you doing?'

'Just watch me through the goggles,' said Kelly. 'There's an old hand-held computer game called SIMON. It flashed lights on different squares and you had to copy what it did. I shall do as the Rev Jim did, you do what I do and let's hope for the best.'

'All right,' said Shibboleth. 'But I'm no great dancer.'

'Nor conversationalist,' said Kelly. 'But we can't all be good at everything, can we? Are you ready?'

'Ready,' said Shibboleth.

'Then here I go,' and Kelly bounced and bobbed away. She took the odd little sidesteps, then the dancings forward, then the steps backwards and then the steps forward again.

And then she vanished.

'Brilliant,' said Shibboleth. 'You did it.'

'No I didn't,' called a voice in the darkness. 'I just tripped and fell on my face.'

'Anything hurt?'

'Only my pride. I'm coming back to have another go.'

And so Kelly had another go.

And another.

And another.

And not to be beaten, she had another go too.

And another.

'This really isn't working, is it?' Shibboleth asked.

'There'd be a knack to it.'

'Not one you've mastered quite yet, by the look of it.'

'Perhaps you'd prefer to have a go yourself.'

Shibboleth shrugged in the uncertain light. 'I'd probably only fare as well as you,' he said. 'Although if I *was* going to do it, I'd probably do it *exactly* the same way the high priest did. By taking three steps to the right instead of the two you keep taking.'

Kelly returned to Shibboleth and punched him hard in the face.

'Oh, ouch, damn,' wailed Shibboleth. 'There was no need for that.'

'There was every need for that. If this *is* the way to get into the chapel, the service will be over before we even arrive. Do the dance. Go on, or I'll hit you again.'

'I think you've broken my nose.'

'I haven't. I could have done, but I didn't.'

'It really hurts,' moaned Shibboleth.

'Do the silly dance.'

And Shibboleth lined himself up, said, 'OK,' and did the silly dance. And then he vanished. Just like that.

'Have *you* fallen over?' Kelly asked.

But there was no reply.

'Oh,' said Kelly. 'You did it. You actually did it.'

She stood alone there in the uncertain light, looking down at the pavement slabs through her infra-red goggles. They shone faintly, offering up the heat of the day that they had stored within their ancient granite pores. A giant chessboard? A game board? An entrance? To what?

To the chapel of *It*.

Kelly drew draughts of healthless Mute Corp Keynes night air up her nostrils. This was to be it. Possibly a confrontation with *It*. Possibly anything. And this Shibboleth had gone before her. Was *he* on the level? Or was he leading her to her doom? Should she go on, or turn away and run? That *was* an option. Not much of one, but it *was* an option.

'I have to see this through,' Kelly told herself. 'Innocent people have been hurt, killed. I don't know what I can do about it. But I have to do something.'

225

She glanced all around and about. She was all alone.

If she was going to do it.

Then now was the time.

To do it.

To do

It.

Kelly took another breath and blew it out into the night. And then she too did the silly dance.

From paving stone to paving stone and never stepping on the cracks.

And she, like Shibboleth, vanished.

The moon appeared from behind industrial clouds. It shone down upon the great paved space, turning the paving stones the colour of a silver without price.

And out of nowhere, or so at least it seemed, a fat man appeared. He was the fat man who had leaned upon the lamppost opposite the Swan and studied Kelly through his macrovision spectacles.

The fat man crossed the wide open space. And then the fat man stopped. And then he too danced forward. Taking sideways steps, and three instead of two, and moving forwards and backwards.

And presently and under the eye of the moon, the fat man vanished too.

19

It was no longer night.

And it was no longer Mute Corp Keynes.

A big smiley sun beamed down from the heavens of blue. Sparrows chorused from the branches of ancient riverside oaks. Flowers pretti-fied their well-tended beds in the memorial park and a snoozing tomcat snored upon the window sill of the Flying Swan. The milk float jingle-jangled on its wibbly wobbly way. Another glorious day had dawned upon Brentford.

Derek awoke to find that the world had gone upside down.

He blinked and focused and stared upon the shelves of video games. Why were they all upside down, he wondered? And why was the ceiling now the floor?

Derek coughed. He didn't feel at all too well. Why would that be, then? Ah, oh dear and yes, that would be the drink and that would be why.

Derek heaved himself into the vertical plane. That would be why the world had all turned upside down. He'd been lying, fully clothed, on his bed, flat on his back with his head hanging over the end.

Not the way he usually slept.

Which was all tucked up beneath his Star Wars duvet.

'Oh what happened?' Derek groaned, and slumping down upon

his bed, he placed his elbows on his knees and cradled his head in his hands. 'I got drunk, that's what happened,' he mumbled. 'What did I do? Did I do something terrible?'

Circuits meshed in Derek's head. No, he hadn't done anything terrible. He'd got drunk. Wandered about. Met up with Mad John and Mad John had brought him home. That wasn't too terrible, although his mum wouldn't be smiling at him this morning over the cornflakes. 'It's all her fault,' mumbled Derek. 'That Kelly. She's got inside my head. Oh damn it. I really am in love with her. Oh God, what am I going to do?' Derek peered at his wristwatch. It was nine thirty. He should have been at the offices of the *Brentford Mercury* half an hour ago.

Derek dragged himself over to the dressing table and peered at his reflection in the mirror. It was grim. A boggy-eyed unshaven face peered back at him. 'Oh God,' mumbled Derek once more. 'I've really fouled up this time. Those horrible sods from Mute Corp will be sitting at Mr Shields's desk waiting for me. I have to go.'

Derek did pathetic little pattings-down at his hair, muttered something about designer stubble coming back into fashion, opened his bedroom door and stumbled down the stairs. And he almost made it to the front door too.

'Is that you, Derek?' called the voice of his mum.

'Yes Mum,' called Derek. 'Who else would it be?' He picked up a folded piece of paper from the doormat. It was addressed to him in Kelly's handwriting. But as Derek had never seen Kelly's handwriting, he didn't recognize it.

'Well, aren't you going to give your mother a goodbye kiss before you go off to work?'

'Oh,' went Derek, shrugging, then, 'OK,' he said.

Derek thrust the folded and unread piece of paper into his trouser pocket, then he bumbled along the passageway to the kitchen. Past the framed photograph of the Queen Mother, presently celebrating her one hundred and twenty-second year. Past the framed photograph of his dad, possibly celebrating something up in Heaven. And past the framed photograph of himself as a baby. The Derek of today was in no mood at all for celebration.

'Morning, darling,' said Derek's mum, beaming at him from the kitchen sink, where she stood drying her hands on an oversized brown gingham tea towel.

'Morning, Derek,' said Mad John, looking up from the breakfasting table.

Derek stared at Mad John. Mad John was wearing Derek's dressing gown.

'Give your mum a kiss,' said Derek's mum.

'And you can shake my hand if you want,' said Mad John. 'But no kissing please, it makes me want to shout.'

Derek made that face you make, when you find out that some vagrant loony's been having it off with your mum. It's a very specific sort of face, it doesn't really apply to any other situation.

'And what kind of face is that?' asked Derek's mum. 'The last time I saw a face like that, your father was making it. Shortly before he met with his tragic accident.'

'I . . . I . . . you . . . you . . . he . . . he . . .' went Derek.

'What kind of language is that?' asked Mad John. 'Is it Runese?'

'You . . . him.' Derek pointed to and fro.

'Give us a kiss then.' Derek's mum puckered up.

'No,' said Derek. 'No, no, no,' and Derek left the house.

Derek staggered and stumbled along the sunlit streets of Brentford. Streets that, had he noticed it, were looking rather spruce. There were sweepers sweeping these streets and painters on scaffolding, painting the houses. There were cleaners cleaning the lampposts and there were dustbin men and the dustbin men were emptying dustbins and whistling while they worked. In fact everybody was whistling while they worked. The sweepers and the painters, and the cleaners and the dustbin men, all whistling gaily as they worked. And all of these whistlers had one thing in common, well two if you counted the whistling. But the one thing in common they had most in common, was in the way they were dressed.

One-piece, all white, zip-up overalls, with a big fat Mute Corp logo on the back.

Whistle whistle whistle went the whistlers as they worked.

'Shut up!' shouted Derek, then he clutched at his hung-overed head.

229

There was scaffolding up outside the offices of the *Brentford Mercury* and whistling men swarmed upon this scaffolding, renovating here and titivating there.

An old chap with long grey hair, leather trousers and a lacy flouncy shirt, who had once been popular on the tele, was directing operations. 'I'm going for a retro feel,' he was telling a whistler. 'An homage to the twentieth century.'

'Anything you say, Mr Lawrence, guv,' said the whistling workman, continuing to whistle as he worked.

Derek stumbled and staggered up the stairs to the offices. There in that of Mr Shields were the two men from Mute Corp. Little Mr Speedy and bigger Mr Shadow. Bigger Mr Shadow was looking at his watch. 'I'm docking you an hour's pay,' he told Derek. 'If you're late again tomorrow, then you're sacked.'

'Tomorrow?' Derek wiped at his cold and clammy brow. 'But tomorrow's Saturday. I never work on Saturday.'

'You do now, and Sunday too. Everything has to be online for Monday. That's when Suburbia World Plc opens to the public.'

Mr Speedy tapped at keys on his briefcase laptop jobbie. 'We went out on the World Wide Web at nine this morning,' he said. 'Projected figures suggest that we'll have at least ten thousand paying visitors on the first day alone.'

'*Ten thousand?*' Derek sank onto the unpacked box of Mute Corp computer parts.

'I'd rather you didn't sit on that,' said Mr Speedy. 'That's going back to the company. And I'd like to know the whereabouts of the rest of that consignment.'

'Search me,' said Derek, dismally. 'But ten thousand visitors? How can that possibly be? If you only went online half an hour ago?'

'Make that closer to an hour. There's a whole world out there,' said Mr Shadow. 'Beyond the boundaries of Brentford. A whole world of PC users, logging onto the Web, ever anxious for something new. Something special to entertain them.'

'But there's nothing special about Brentford,' said Derek and then, realizing just how stupid that remark really was, he buried his face in his hands.

'There's a certain magic here,' said Mr Speedy. 'I'm surprised that you, as a resident, have never noticed it yourself.'

Derek made awful groaning sounds.

'So,' said Mr Shadow. 'There is much to discuss. Where are the crad barges? Where are the five miles of perimeter fence?'

'And the steam train,' said Mr Speedy. 'I'm really looking forward to seeing the steam train. I've never actually seen one before. What do they run on, petrol?'

'Petrol?' Derek made further groanings and moanings.

'Well, whatever,' said Mr Speedy. 'I'm looking forward to that and also to seeing the Brentford Griffin. Old-fashioned holographics can still draw in the public. What time should I schedule a demonstration for? Shall we say three p.m.?'

Derek made a pitiful sound.

'You're not going to let us down, are you, Derek?' Mr Speedy asked. 'We'd be very disappointed if you let us down.'

'We'd have to dismiss you,' said Mr Shadow.

'And turn you in to the police, over that nasty business of the stolen computer games,' said Mr Speedy.

'And there'd be questions asked about Derek's expenses,' said Mr Shadow. 'Which would probably lead to further prosecutions.'

'Undoubtedly,' said Mr Speedy. 'I'd see to that.'

'All right, stop!' Derek hauled himself to his feet. 'I'll get it all done. Everything's in hand. Just leave it to me, I won't let you down.'

'Good,' said Mr Speedy. 'Then off about your business. Pacey pacey, chop chop and things of that nature generally.'

Derek turned painfully to take his leave. And then he stopped and turned right back again. 'No, hold on,' he said. 'What about the paper? It's Friday. The paper is supposed to come out today. Oh my God. The paper. The paper.' Derek tore at his hair, Mr Speedy and Mr Shadow watching him tearing at it.

'I'll bet that really hurts,' said Mr Speedy.

'I'll just bet it does,' said Mr Shadow.

'Oow!' said Derek, ceasing to tear at his hair. 'It *does* hurt, I can tell you. But oh my God again. How could I have let this happen? There's no *Brentford Mercury*. In one hundred and fifty-two years, we've never missed an issue.'

'You don't look that old,' said Mr Speedy.

'You know what I mean!' Derek shouted, and then he clutched once more at his head. 'The paper must come out today. It must. It must.'

'And it has,' said Mr Speedy. 'Trust us, it has.'

'Has?' said Derek. '*Has?*'

'It's already on the news-stands and in the paper shops.'

'And popped through the letter boxes,' said Mr Shadow.

'No,' said Derek. 'What are you talking about?'

Mr Speedy picked up a newspaper from the desk and handed it to Derek. 'We took care of everything,' he said. 'Mute Corp always takes care of everything.'

Derek stared at the paper in his trembling hands. Its five-inch banner headline ran:

JOY, JOY, HAPPY JOY
HAPPY, HAPPY JOY

'Uplifting isn't it?' said Mr Speedy. 'That has to be a first in headlines, doesn't it?'

Derek's jaw was hanging slack, his numb hands numbly turned the pages.

GREAT DAYS AHEAD

ran the headline on page two.

BRENTONIANS TO RECEIVE MASSIVE
CASH FUNDINGS: ALL WILL PROFIT
HUGELY FROM KINDLY CORPORATION'S
CARING CASH CONTRIBUTIONS.

'Note all that alliteration,' said Mr Shadow. 'That was my idea.'

'Very professional,' said Mr Speedy. 'Very *Sunday Sport*.'

'What's this?' asked Derek, pointing, pointing, pointing. '"BRENTFORD SHAREHOLDERS' BIG BUCKS BONANZA."'

'My idea too,' said Mr Shadow.

232

'Very professional,' said Mr Speedy once again.

'Yes,' said Derek. 'But what does it mean?'

'It's an incentive,' said Mr Shadow. 'You see, once, back in the early 1980s, there was this Waterman's Arts Centre project. The locals made a right old fuss. So much so that the backers pulled out and left the Arts Centre for the locals to do with as they pleased.'

'I've read all about it,' said Derek, and here a tone of pride entered into his voice. 'I am a Brentford Poet.'

'Then you'll know what happened. A wise old man called Professor Slocombe, I believe he still lives here on the Butt's Estate, persuaded the locals to build the Arts Centre themselves and all become share-holders. The Arts Centre stands here today. No fuss. No bother. We've just done the same. All Brentonians are now shareholders in Suburbia World Plc. They've been allocated one share each. I'm sure that after they receive their first generous dividend, they'll be buying a lot more shares.'

'It's all corruption,' said Derek. 'All of it. Bribery and corruption, blackmail and extortion.'

'I don't think there's any extortion involved,' said Mr Speedy. 'Although I'll bet you'll have to pay an extortionate price for that steam train. I'll bet that could run to about ten thousand pounds, you'll probably be needing some more petty cash, won't you?'

Derek's mouth was hanging open once again. When he finally closed it once again and then opened it to speak more words, the words he spoke were these.

'Ten thousand was exactly the figure I had in mind.'

Which really didn't say a lot for Derek.

The Flying Swan was crowded when Derek stumbled in to take a liquid breakfast. There seemed to be an air of jollity around and about the saloon bar.

Derek dragged himself to the counter and tried to get himself served.

'Hello,' said Old Pete, looking up from his *Brentford Mercury*. 'Fancy seeing you in here again. You're a bit of a sucker for punishment. Can't you find yourself another Brentford bar to drink in?'

'This was the nearest,' said Derek. 'And I really need a big drink.'

'You work for the *Mercury*, don't you?' said the oldster. 'As well as being a bard and a student of Runese.' Old Vic wasn't there to chuckle, so Old Pete's dog did instead.

Derek hung his head in shame.

'I'm very impressed,' said Old Pete. 'I like this headline on page five. "HEAVEN DECLARED ON EARTH. BUT ONLY FOR THE FOLK OF BRENTFORD". According to this, Brentford has been singled out by God, as the first site of the Rapture. And apparently he loves the place so much that he's rewarding everyone who doesn't get Raptured by having Mute Corp turn the place into an Earthly paradise. And there was me thinking that there wasn't a God. It just goes to show how stupid I am.'

'It does?' said Derek.

Old Pete slowly shook his ancient head. 'No lad,' said he. 'It doesn't. And be warned, anyone who tries to take advantage of the borough and its people will find themselves tarred and feathered and dancing at a rope's end, lacking their wedding tackle.'

'Oh,' said Derek, crossing his legs.

'So let's hope that doesn't happen, eh?' said Old Pete brightly. 'Let's all enjoy this unexpected largesse.'

'Good idea,' said Derek.

'Isn't it,' said Old Pete. 'So I expect that you, like me and everybody else in the borough, will be cashing in your share certificate on Monday and pocketing the moolah, before getting on with the tarring and feathering. Not to mention the snippings-off of wedding tackle.' Old Pete made some snippings with his old and wrinkled fingers.

'I think I *will* drink elsewhere,' said Derek, rapidly taking his leave.

Derek ambled through the busy streets of Brentford. And they *were* busy. Lots of whistling workers. And lots of happy shoppers (but no little chefs). The borough had definitely perked up. People weren't hiding in their homes any more, awaiting the Rapture. They were out and about, sunhats and summer frocks, old straw hats and Hawaiian shirts. Everybody looked very jolly indeed.

'Perhaps it *is* all for the best,' Derek told himself. 'Perhaps they'll all get to like it and enjoy the money and *not* tar and feather anyone.

234

And . . .' And Derek patted his jacket pocket. 'I've just made another ten thousand pounds.'

A certain skip came into Derek's step. But it was accompanied by a certain amount of head-clutching also.

The used-car showrooms of Leo Felix lurked on the banks of the Grand Union Canal, close to the weir, but closer to the road bridge that led from the High Street into the neighbouring town of Isleworth, that nobody in Brentford knew anything about.

The used-car showrooms of Leo Felix were colourful showrooms, painted in red, gold and green and elegantly decorated with five-foot-high cannabis-leaf motifs. It is believed that Leo oversaw all the decorating himself and never called in a designer, who had once been very popular on the tele.

There were a number of automobiles outside. These were not new automobiles. Nor apparently were they second-hand automobiles. These were, so the brightly coloured cards upon their windscreens informed potential purchasers, 'previously owned vehicles'.

Their prices seemed unreasonably reasonable.

Derek, still with some skips in his step, some-skipped down the incline from the side of the bridge and entered Leo's forecourt.

'Yo, Babylon,' called the ancient son of Zion. 'Come inside off of me forecourt, yo spolin' de look of de place wid yo stubbly face and yo big red bloodclart eyes.'

Derek waved towards Leo, who was lounging in the shadowed doorway. 'Morning Leo,' he said.

'Come on in den, come on in.'

Derek came on in.

It was rather dark in Leo's showroom. Two previously owned cars stood glinting vaguely. Both were Morris Minors.

'Oh good,' said Derek, sighting them. 'You have two already. Only forty-eight to go, then.'

'Babylon,' said Leo, looming at Derek. 'Babylon, yo not bin altogether honest wid I an' I.'

'I don't know what you're talking about,' said Derek.

'Folk museum, Babylon. Dat what I an' I talkin' about.'

'How's it all coming along?' asked Derek, feigning bright and breeziness. 'Any luck with those crad barges?'

Leo held a rolled copy of the *Brentford Mercury* in his hand. He unrolled it slowly and showed it to Derek. 'Babylon try to get one over on Ganga Man,' said he. 'Babylon care to see if he can outrun me Rottweilers?' Leo called out to his dogs. 'Marcus,' he called, 'Marley, Yellowman.' Three big Rottweilers came a-bounding out of the darkness and took to licking Leo's hands.

'Now hold on a minute,' said Derek. 'We had a deal.'

'For de folk museum?' said Leo. 'Or was dat for de multi–million–dollar Mute Corp company?'

'I'm only doing my job,' said Derek. And as the words came out of his mouth, he really hated himself.

'Dis ain't personal, Babylon,' said Leo. 'Well, actually it is. De white man bin shafting de black man since forever. Dis town here, dis Brentford, I never have no trouble here. People treat me like one of their own and I treat them like one of me own. Respect, Babylon. Do you understand that? Respect? No I don't tink dat you do.'

'I do,' said Derek. 'I do.'

'I an' I tell you what,' said Leo. 'You an' I an' I have a deal. We smack hands together. So I an' I be fair with you. I an' I get you every-ting you want by tomorrow, how's dat?'

'Dat's, I mean *that's* perfect,' said Derek. 'I couldn't ask for anything more than that.'

'Good,' said Leo. 'Dat's my half of the deal. Now all you have to do is two little tings.'

'Go on,' said Derek.

'Give me all the money in your pockets,' said Leo.

'Oh,' said Derek.

'Dat's one,' said Leo, stroking the neck of Marcus.

'Now, come on,' said Derek.

'Dat's one,' said Leo. 'You show no respect. Hand it over, Babylon.' Marcus growled and so did Marley and Yellowman.

Derek dug deep into his pocket and brought out all the money.

'I tink dat's mine, ain't it?' said Leo.

Derek hung his head once more. 'It is,' said he.

Leo took the money and pressed it into the colourful trouser pocket of his colourful trousers. 'Yo get all de stuff you order,' he said. 'I an' I keep my side of the deal. I an' I show respect.'

'Thank you,' said Derek. 'And I'm sorry. All that cash. The temptation was too much.'

'I an' I understand,' said Leo. 'Business is done.'

'Thanks again,' said Derek, turning to leave.

'I an' I said dere's two tings,' said Leo.

'Oh yes,' said Derek. 'What was the second thing?'

'Yo got ten seconds' start, Babylon,' said Leo. 'Den I release me dogs.'

It's remarkable just how fast you can run at times. Even with a hangover. Derek ran like the rabbit of proverb. And if there wasn't a rabbit of proverb, Derek ran like the hare. He ran and he ran. Away from Leo's showrooms. Out of Leo's forecourt and up Brentford High Street. Derek ran all the way back to the offices of the *Brentford Mercury*.

And it's a fair old run, especially with a hangover.

Once inside, Derek slammed shut the outer door and leant upon it, breathing horribly.

But no howlings or bayings of dreadful hounds were to be heard from without.

But had Derek had the hearing of Superman, he might have been able to hear the laughter.

The laughter of Leo, back in his showrooms.

Where he still patted his dogs.

Derek took his liquid breakfast, which was now a liquid lunch, in the Shrunken Head. He didn't play the Space Invaders machine though, he just swigged at Scotch.

He *was* doomed, he just knew it. He was done for. The best thing he could do was shape up and ship out. Quit the borough, do a runner, before the excrement hit the rotating blades of the air-cooling apparatus. They'd kill him. The locals would string him up. Mute Corp had no idea what they were dealing with here. This wasn't like other places. This was Brentford.

Derek swigged further Scotch.

'I'm unhappy,' he said to no-one but himself. 'I'm a loser. A total prat. That's what Kelly thinks I am. And I am. I really am. I've fouled up every which way. Oh God, I don't know what to do.'

Derek did even further swiggings and returned once more to the bar counter. 'Same again,' he said.

The barman was reading the *Brentford Mercury*. The celebrations going on at the Swan did not seem to have extended themselves to the Shrunken Head. Different kind of clientele, perhaps. Or some other reason. Derek didn't really care.

'This is all a hoot, isn't it?' said the barman, pointing at the paper. 'This should bring a bit of trade to this establishment.'

'You think it's a good thing then?' asked Derek hopefully.

'God, yes,' said the barman. 'I'm hoping to persuade the residents' committee to give it a week before they start the tarring and feathering. But I'll probably be on my own for that one. I've heard that the lads at the Flying Swan are planning a charabanc trip to the West End.'

'Really?' said Derek. 'Why?'

'I think they're planning to blow up the Mute Corp headquarters. A people's protest, that kind of thing. From what I heard, it seems that the locals are getting well fed up with always having to fight on home territory. So this time they've decided to carry the war directly to the camp of the aggressor. It's a bit revolutionary, but after all, these are the twenty-twenties.'

'The Mute Corp headquarters?' Derek's face fell terribly. 'They can't do that, can they?'

'I'll bet you they can,' said the barman. 'Old Vic's leading the war party. He used to be a POW, you know. He knows all about blowing things up. He told me that he once blew up a Nazi watchtower at his camp, using an explosive formulated exclusively from his own bodily fluids. You wouldn't think that was possible, would you? Although I would, I've heard the old blighter fart.'

'Oh no,' said Derek. 'Oh no, oh no, oh no.'

'I don't know what you're "oh no-ing" about,' said the barman. 'You don't have any friends working at Mute Corp, do you?'

Derek's pale face nodded up and down in time to his nodding

head. In perfect synchronization, in fact, because it was all joined on. 'Kelly,' he said. 'The woman I love.'

'The beautiful bird you were in here with yesterday?' asked the barman. 'The bird with the outstanding charlies?'

'Shut up!' said Derek.

'Sorry mate. But she's a babe. You lucky sod. I'll bet she's something between the covers, eh? You wouldn't care to tell me all about it, would you? I'm a married man myself and other than forging my signature and painting our house purple because it's the colour of universal peace, my missus doesn't go in for anything much any more. She seems to be obsessed with charity work. I went home the other evening and found her giving that Mad John a bath.'

'Shut up!' said Derek again. 'I have to warn her.'

'Well, you have plenty of time,' said the barman. 'They're not going to do the dirty deed until Monday. They want to cash in their shares first.'

Derek breathed a big sigh of relief. 'Phew,' he said.

'So there you go,' said the barman, handing Derek his Scotch. 'That's one pound one and sixpence, please.'

'Yes,' said Derek. 'All right.' And he rooted about in his pockets in the hope that he still had some change. He didn't have much, but he did have enough and he also had something else. A screwed-up note that he'd picked up from his doormat, but hadn't yet read.

Derek paid the barman and then he read the note.

And then the bleary bloodshot eyes in his pale and designer-stubbly face grew wide and Derek screamed very loudly.

Horrible, it was.

20

There was no-one home at Mrs Gormenghast's.

Derek banged and hammered at the door, but no-one answered. He thought he saw the net curtains move in the upstairs front window and he thought that he saw the face of Mad John peeping out. But Derek dismissed this as only his fevered imagination.

Derek was all in a lather. Kelly's note was a warning. It warned him not to use his mobile phone. Indeed, not to use *any* telephone. And not to touch his computer, nor indeed anything that might have computerized innards. And it said, 'Come at once, as soon as you read this note,' and it said, 'You are in terrible danger.'

Derek fretted. He didn't know what to do. Go to the Mute Corp headquarters? Surely that was where Kelly was. But would she be there? If she was warning him not to touch any computers and that there was terrible danger, surely she wouldn't be there, amongst all those computers. Derek thought not.

So at least she would be safe if Old Vic and his cronies actually blew up the building.

She *would* be safe.

Wouldn't she?

But where was she?

Where?

Derek fretted further. If she wasn't at Mute Corp and she wasn't at Mrs Gormenghast's, then where was she? Oh no! Not *that*? Derek

240

fretted furiously. Not *vanished*? Not her too. He'd turned his thoughts away from all that mad stuff. Kelly had to be somewhere, and somewhere safe. She had to be. Surely. He loved the woman, for God's sake. Nothing bad could have happened to her. It couldn't have. No. No. No.

Derek went home.

At six of the evening clock, Derek returned to Mrs Gormenghast's. Mrs Gormenghast opened the door to him.

'No,' she said, when he asked her. 'Kelly has not returned.'

Derek went home again.

At just before eight of the evening clock, Derek returned once more to Mrs Gormenghast's.

'No,' she said once more. 'Kelly has not returned.'

Derek went home again.

He returned to Mrs Gormenghast's at half-hour intervals. And then quarter-of-an-hour intervals and then by eleven of that same evening clock, he wouldn't go away.

'I know you, don't I?' said the police constable that Mrs Gormenghast called. 'You were in that punch-up at the Arts Centre, weren't you? I'd go home if I were you, sir, or I'll have to run you in. And I don't think you'd like that very much, as all the cells but one are currently being given a makeover by this long-grey-haired designer, who used to be very popular on the tele. And the only one we could put you into is currently occupied by a bearded tattooed poet from Mute Corp Keynes, who turned up at the station claiming that someone had nicked his wristwatch the last time we had him in the cells . . .'

Derek tried to get a word in. But the constable continued.

'And he got really stroppy and we had to bang him up again and he keeps shouting out that he's the daddy now. And he says he wants his bitch.'

'My girlfriend has gone missing,' Derek bawled to the constable. 'Do something. Do something.'

'Move along quietly now, sir,' said the constable. 'Or I'll have to run you in.'

Derek made fists but kept them to himself, and then he went home to bed. Not that he slept very well, he didn't. Strange dreams came to him. He saw Kelly standing in the Butt's Estate and she was talking to this old gentleman and the old gentleman was telling her something, something terrible, that scared her and there was violence and Derek saw Kelly running and running and then being swallowed up by something awful that he couldn't see but could only feel. And it didn't feel good, it felt horrible.

Derek awoke in a bit more of a lather.

And he went without a shower for the second day running and as he hadn't washed, he was rather smelly too.

Derek didn't breakfast either, he just ran out of the house.

'Police, police,' called Mrs Gormenghast down her telephone. 'That madman is back at my front door.'

'Madman?' asked Mad John, looking up from his puce breakfast bowl.

Saturday was Hell for Derek. He went around to the police station to report Kelly missing, but was told to get onto the end of the queue. People were now going missing all over the borough. They were here one minute and gone the next. Several Brentford Poets and poetesses had vanished and some muleskinners and a wandering bishop and a bunch of pimply-faced youths (although no-one seemed too bothered about them). And some nurses and interns from the cottage hospital had vanished too. It was the Rapture, the desk constable told Derek. But not to worry, because it was all going to be HEAVEN on EARTH in Brentford for all the unraptured, thanks to Mute Corp. The company that cares. And while Derek was here in the police station, would he care to purchase some extra Suburbia World Plc shares? As the Brentford constabulary had just been issued a licence by Mute Corp to sell them.

Derek left in a terrible fretting frame of mind.

And the day didn't go very well for him at all. Mr Speedy and Mr Shadow were waiting at the offices of the *Brentford Mercury*.

'That's another hour's pay docked,' said Mr Speedy. 'And you're on an official warning. One more strike and you're out, as our American cousins like to say.'

'My girlfriend has gone missing!' shouted Derek. 'Don't you understand?'

Mr Speedy scratched at his little head. 'Not entirely,' he said. 'I didn't know you had a girlfriend. I thought you were just one of those sad and lonely lads who spend all their time playing computer games.'

'Well, she's not exactly my girlfriend *yet*,' said Derek. 'But she will be. I love her. And she's gone missing. She's vanished. It's terrible. Don't you understand?'

'Raptured, probably,' said Mr Shadow. 'We'll have to add her name to those of the blessed on the memorial.'

'Memorial?' said Derek. 'What is this?'

'It's being erected in the memorial park,' said Mr Speedy. 'Did you know that Brentford was the only town to have a memorial park without a memorial in it?'

'Yes,' said Derek. 'Actually I did.'

'Well, that's all remedied now. Mute Corp has generously donated a memorial. To those who have been Raptured in Brentford. It's very tasteful. One hundred and fifty metres high, black glass.'

'An homage to the nineteen-eighties Lateinos and Romlith building,' said Mr Shadow. 'The names of the blessed running up and down in liquid quartz lettering. And it will have constantly moving scenic lifts and a burger franchise at the base. Selling sprout burgers for vegetarians. Was your girlfriend vegetarian, by the way?'

'Aaaaaagh!' went Derek.

'Oh and there's a message for you,' said Mr Speedy. 'From your business associate Mr Leo Felix.'

Derek ended his Aaaaaagh! with a groan.

'He said, and I quote, "Tell Babylon to get his ass down to me showrooms, I an' I got de crad barges in."'

'Chop chop then,' said Mr Shadow. 'Pacey pacey. The devil makes work for idle hands. And things of that nature, generally.'

'But Kelly. But . . . Oh God.'

'Have you reported her missing to the police?'

'Yes but . . .'

'Yes but then that's all you can do. Off to work with you now.'

'I'll need some more money,' said Derek. The words just came out of his mouth. 'Quite a lot more money.'

'Would that be for the holographic Griffin?' asked Mr Speedy. 'The one that failed to appear at three p.m. yesterday?'

243

'Yes, that's it,' lied Derek. 'And the electric cable for the perimeter fence and the giant feral tomcat and . . .'

Mr Speedy took out a wad of money notes. 'Ten thousand,' he said. 'Your last. If you foul up, Derek, it will be prison for you.'

'My bitch,' sniggered Mr Shadow.

'What?' went Derek.

'CCTV,' said Mr Shadow. 'Mute Corp run all the police-station circuits. Now get on your way and make things happen.'

Derek got off on his way.

As to actually making things happen . . .

Well . . .

'What are *those*?' asked Derek.

'Crad barges,' said Leo.

'Houseboats,' said Derek.

'Crad barges,' said Leo.

'*House*boats,' said Derek.

'House barges?' said Leo. 'Where de travellin' crad men lived.'

'No,' said Derek. 'No.'

'Listen, Babylon,' said Leo. 'You ever seen a crad barge?'

Derek scratched at his fretful head. 'Well, no,' he said. 'Not as such.'

'An' yo know anyone who ever seen a crad barge?'

'Possibly Old Pete,' said Derek.

'Old Pete an old friend of I an' I,' said Leo. 'Old Pete tell you Babylon, dese are crad barges. Yo have a problem wid dis?'

Derek shook his fretful head. 'No,' he said. 'Stuff it. They look like crad barges to me.'

'Dere,' said Leo. 'Dat not too painful. Yo want to see the steam train?'

Derek shrugged. 'Why not?' he said. 'It can't be any worse than the crad barges.'

Leo drew Derek's attention to the low-loader parked before the showrooms. The low-loader hadn't failed to draw Derek's attention when he had entered Leo's forecourt. It was not the kind of thing you could miss, it being so huge and all.

On the low-loader was something rather big and something all covered by tarpaulins.

Leo began to tug at ropes and unfasten hawsers and unclip those springy things that nearly have your eye out every time you use them to fasten the hatchback of your car to the bumper, because you've just bought something far too big from the DIY store and it's the only way of getting it home without paying the delivery charge.

'Damn,' said Leo, dodging his dreads about. 'Damn ting nearly had I an' I's eye out.'

Leo tugged upon the tarpaulin and Derek joined him in the tugging. Tug tug tug went Leo and Derek.

Fall away and expose to the world, went the tarpaulin and . . .

'Oh,' went Derek. 'Oh my God!'

'Pretty damn good, eh?' said Leo.

Derek, all flappy jaw, made his head go nod nod nod.

'It's a . . .'

'Steam train,' said Leo.

'No,' said Derek. 'It's the . . .'

'Steam train,' said Leo.

'Yes but . . .'

'Listen,' said Leo. 'Dis a goddam steam train. Don't go tellin' I an' I it ain't.'

'It is,' said Derek. 'It is. But it's the Flying Scotsman.'

'Don't talk silly,' said Leo. 'Dere ain't no Flying Scotchmen. I seen a housefly. I seen a horsefly. But I tink I see'd about everythin' when I see a Scotchman fly.'

'Stop singing,' said Derek. 'That isn't funny. Where did you get this from?'

'Yo said, no questions asked.'

'The Science Museum?' said Derek. 'Or the National Railway Museum? Or . . .'

'It de property now of de Brentford Folk Museum,' said Leo. 'And it won't be the Flyin' Scotchman tomorrow. It be de Brentford Flyer. I an' I had me mate Cecil knock up a couple of new nameplates.'

'Doomed,' said Derek. 'I'm doomed.'

'We all doomed, Babylon,' said Leo. 'It just dat some of us more doomed than others.'

Derek didn't stay around to view any more of Leo's acquisitions. And Leo told him that he wouldn't be able to acquire the five miles of perimeter fence until the following evening, so if Derek wanted it putting up 'all around de goddam borough, yo can't fool me, Babylon', Derek was going to have to have his whistling Mute Corp employees working all through the night to get it up before Monday morning. So if Derek was leaving anyway, he'd best get on his way and make things happen.

Derek returned to the police station. The police station was closed for renovations. A sign upon the door instructed callers to post details of missing persons through the letter box, but to mind the wet paint.

Derek didn't mind the wet paint and got some on his sleeve.

Derek wandered off across Brentford. He was in a real state now. He'd quit the job. He would. He'd run. He would, he'd run. He had ten thousand pounds in his pocket. But Derek ached, inside and out. He wouldn't run. He might quit, but he wouldn't run. He couldn't run. He had to find Kelly. He had to find her, but he didn't know how.

He didn't know what to do.

'I know what to do,' said Derek, suddenly knowing what to do. 'No I don't,' said Derek, realizing that in fact, he didn't.

It was very busy busy, all around the streets of Brentford. Very busy busy, with a lot of whistling.

Derek went back to Mrs Gormenghast's.

Mrs Gormenghast drove him away with a big stout stick she had lately acquired, 'in case'.

Derek returned to the offices of the *Brentford Mercury*. He brought Mr Speedy and Mr Shadow good news regarding crad barges and a steam train called the Brentford Flyer and of five miles of perimeter fence that would be arriving after midnight of the following day, in one big roll which, according to Leo, could then be picked up from his forecourt. The thought of just how big a five-mile roll of perimeter fence might be was far too much for Derek, who had enough things on his mind to be going on with anyway.

'Brentford Griffin?' asked Mr Speedy. 'Don't forget that.'

'It's all under control,' said Derek, in a manner that suggested that it was.

'Well, keep us informed,' said Mr Speedy. 'You don't have to keep coming back here, just call us on your mobile.'

Derek chewed upon his lip, remembering Kelly's note. 'I'd prefer to speak to you in person,' he said. 'But I will be very busy for the rest of today and most of tomorrow. So I won't be in, so don't dock me any more pay, please.'

'Any news of your missing girlfriend?' asked Mr Speedy.

'No,' said Derek. 'None.'

'You didn't tell us her name.'

'It's Kelly Anna Sirjan,' said Derek. 'But please don't put her name up on your memorial yet. I'm sure she'll be back. I'm sure.'

'Kelly Anna Sirjan,' said Mr Speedy. And he exchanged glances with Mr Shadow.

'Why are you exchanging glances?' Derek asked.

'Oh, no reason,' said Mr Speedy. 'You just go off about the company's business. We'll see you when we see you.'

Derek clutched at his stomach. All the worry was making him feel very sick. 'Goodbye,' said Derek. 'I'll see you when I see you.'

'Nine o'clock on Monday, at the very latest,' said Mr Speedy. 'That's when Suburbia World Plc will open to the public.'

Sunday came and Sunday went.

It really shouldn't have gone quite so quickly, but it did. Derek spent it attending to company business. And wandering the streets shouting, 'Kelly, Kelly, where are you?'

Many upstairs windows raised to Derek's shoutings.

And many chamber pots were hurled down on his head.

But Sunday came and Sunday went and Derek, now in a state of high anxiety, raved about the streets and raved into pubs and was thrown out of pubs and raved about the streets some more. On any normal day he would no doubt have been arrested. But there was nothing normal whatsoever about this particular Sunday. There were no policemen to be seen, only whistling workers. And there seemed to be fewer and fewer Brentonians about. The streets were virtually deserted.

Derek saw Mad John, but he didn't bid him hello.

Mad John was in the doorway of the charity shop, rooting out shoes from the black bin liners. He looked up briefly as Derek raved by, but feeling assured that this wasn't some upstart out to get his job, continued with his rooting and his shouting at shoes.

Eventually Derek went home.

He had no other choice. He was all raved out. And he had done all that he could for *the Company*. Leo had told him that everything *was* under control and that he should go and rave somewhere else or he really would have the dogs set on him. So Derek finally went home. There was really nothing else he could do.

And Derek, now with three days' stubble on his face, threw himself onto his bed and wept. She *had* gone. She *had* vanished. Raptured away. Suddenly it seemed all so possible. He could no longer ignore all the vanishing Brentonians. Pretend it wasn't happening. It was. It really was. Never a religious man, nor even a religious boy, Derek now questioned his faith. It didn't stand a lot of questioning. He didn't have one. It wasn't that he didn't believe in God. It was just that, well, he was young, and God was for old people. Old people coming close to death and beginning to worry. What if there was a God? Perhaps he should believe. He didn't want to end up in hellfire and damnation for eternity. Perhaps now would be the time to do a bit of praying. Best to stay on the safe side. And things of that nature.

But that was for old people. Yes, sure there *were* young Christians and young Runies, plenty of them. Runeianity was the fastest-growing religion of the day. The Prime Minister, Mr Doveston, was passing a bill to declare Runeianity the official religion of Great Britain.

And Runeianity did have the edge on Christianity when it came to having a good time. Hugo Rune had declared in his autohagiography, *The Gospel according to Hugo Rune*, that the only way to conquer the sins of the flesh was to try them out first. 'You have to know your enemy' Rune explained, and who was there alive to argue with such wisdom?

But Derek wasn't a Runie, nor was he a Christian. Nor was he anything else. But now, in his hour of need and his hour of loss, he really truly wished that he was.

Derek rose from his bed and locked his bedroom door, then he cleared a space on the carpet and knelt down in that space.

'Dear God,' prayed Derek. 'I expect you're a bit surprised to hear from me. Although if you know everything, then I suppose you're not. But I do want to ask you a favour. I know that people only pray to you when they want something. So that's why I'm praying to you. But you know that anyway. And it's not for me. Well, it is, sort of. But mostly it's for someone else. It's for Kelly. Kelly Anna Sirjan. One of your flock. I love her, God, and I miss her so much. Being away from her breaks my heart and I'm so afraid that something terrible has happened to her. And you'd know if it has. And *if* it has, will you please do something about it? Will you please bring her back to me, God? If you do, I promise that I'll try not to be such a prat in future. And not greedy. In fact I've got ten thousand pounds here and I'll give it all to charity. To the society for small and shoeless boys in need of a good hiding, or something. Anything you want, just you name it. I know it's not really my money, but you can have it. Please bring Kelly back to me unharmed. Please God, I beg you. Please. Amen. Love, Derek.'

And having prayed, Derek felt a lot better. No less fretful and no less worried, but a lot better in himself that he *had* prayed and so was, beneath all the greed and prattishness, ultimately a good person.

And, he noticed now, he was also a very hungry person, having not eaten a single thing all day. And a very thirsty person too.

So Derek went out again. Finally found a pub that he hadn't been thrown out of for raving, and as it was now too late in the evening to order a surf and turf, ordered ten packets of crisps instead and drank a great deal of Scotch.

And finally, crisp-filled and drunken, Derek staggered home, set his alarm clock, with inebriated care, for seven o'clock the following morning and dropped down, fully clothed and smelling bad and very stubbly now indeed, upon his single bed.

He did not sleep the sleep of the blessedly drunk. Derek slept the tossing terrible sleep of the sweating tossing troubled. Horrible dreams tormented him.

Kelly under attack from something monstrous. Something that was all-consuming, everywhere. A black spiralling, tangling network of worms and snakes and evil curly things. And Derek was powerless to help her. He was on the outside of something and she was deep within. It was all too terribly terrible. And rather awful as well.

Alarm bells rang and rang and rang.

And Derek awoke to find his alarm clock ringing.

It was Monday morning.

Seven of the clock.

And Derek knew, just knew, that this was going to be the worst day of his life.

'Kelly,' he whispered. 'Kelly, where are you? Please come back to me, Kelly. Please God, send her back to me. Kelly, oh Kelly, where are you?'

21

Kelly was no longer anywhere in particular.

When she performed the foolish, but purposeful, dance that Shibboleth had bobbed and bounced before her and vanished into wherever he vanished into, her first thoughts had been that she would very likely not be dancing out again.

She had put her trust in Shibboleth, and Kelly felt that this was probably a mistake. Normally she trusted but one person in the world. And this one person was Kelly Anna Sirjan.

Bright light opened up before her. A sky of blue with a big fat smiley sun. And chorusing sparrows on treetop perches. And snoozing tomcats and all. She was standing in the Butt's Estate, upon the area of grass before the Seamen's Mission.

'Brentford,' she said. 'I am back in Brentford.'

Kelly was *not* back in Brentford.

'I'm *not* back in Brentford,' she continued. 'This *isn't* Brentford. It's wrong.'

'Which bit is wrong?' The old man sat upon a bench. He smiled a toothless smile at Kelly. 'Which bit don't you like, my little dear?'

'Little dear?' Kelly viewed the ancient. He had the look of a man who had once been someone. Even though his frame was sunken under the weight of many years, there was still an alertness in that face. A fearsome intelligence. A vitality.

He was dressed in what had once been an expensive suit of

Boleskine green tweed mix. It hung from his shoulders and its trouser cuffs draggled in the dirt.

'What immediately strikes you as wrong?' the ancient asked.

'All,' said Kelly. 'It isn't real. It's a simulation.'

The ancient fellow nodded, withered dewlaps dangled, turkey fashion.

Kelly's composure was remarkable. 'Where is Shibboleth?' she asked.

'The bad boy who entered before you? He is no longer part of the game.'

'Game?' Kelly looked down at the oldster. There was something familiar about him. She'd seen that face before, somewhere. But younger. Oh yes, of course.

'Mr Remington Mute,' said Kelly Anna Sirjan.

'Kelly Anna Sirjan,' said Mr Remington Mute.

Kelly approached Mr Mute. 'I have much to say to you,' she said.

'I trust you also have much to ask me, little dear. Aren't you puzzled as to your whereabouts?'

Kelly managed a smile. 'I didn't know what to expect,' she said. 'But I didn't expect that whatever it was would be real. I thought perhaps some simulation of a cathedral with a great Net-serving computer system up on the high altar.'

'That's a bit old hat,' said Remington Mute. 'And I should know, I wear an old hat myself.'

'And are *you* real?' Kelly asked. 'If I were to reach out and punch your old face, would you dissolve, or would you hit the deck?'

'I fear that I'd hit the deck,' said Remington Mute. 'But I wouldn't recommend that you employ your Dimac, you are in my world now.'

'And are you happy in your world, Mr Mute?'

The ancient stretched out his arms. Hideous joint-cracking sounds issued from them. 'No,' said Remington Mute. 'Things have not gone quite as well as I might have wished.'

Kelly stood, swaying gently upon her holistic footwear. Somehow this didn't seem the time for a cosy chat. This seemed the time for action. Although exactly what that action should be, she didn't know.

'Raring to go, aren't you?' said Remington Mute. 'Do you want me to set you off running? I could give you something to fight.'

'Where is Shibboleth?' Kelly asked. 'What have you done with him?'

'Would finding Shibboleth be good for a goal? Could we make a game out of that, do you think? You as a warrior princess with a sacred sword, or perhaps you'd rather be a ninja?'

'So that's it then,' said Kelly. 'I'm inside your GO MANGO game.'

'Or GO WOMANGO?' Remington Mute laughed noisily, the sound resembling that of pebbles being shaken in an old tin can. 'You're not inside GO MANGO, or rather GO MANGO is not inside you.'

'Then I can leave here, if I choose?'

Remington Mute shrugged his old and rounded shoulders. 'I suppose you could try to leave,' he said. 'But why would you want to? You still believe that in some way you can stop this thing. You *do* believe that, don't you?'

'I don't know,' said Kelly.

'Perhaps you could just switch it off? Pull out its plug.'

'Perhaps, if I knew where the plug is.'

'Should we make a game of that, then? Basic platform, ascend to the uppermost level, enter the inner sanctum, locate the golden key?'

'I won't play any of your stupid games.'

'Stupid games?' The old man raised a snowy eyebrow. 'My games may be crass, but they're never stupid. And for someone such as yourself, who has been playing for so long and are so near to winning, it would be a shame if you quit the game now.'

'Explain,' said Kelly.

'Everything has led you here,' said Remington Mute. 'Everything you have ever done throughout all of your short little life has led you to this moment.'

'Explain a bit more,' said Kelly.

Remington Mute examined the palms of her hands. 'I created you,' he said.

'You did *what*?'

'Well, not *just* you. There's a lot of little yous about. But most of them fell by the wayside. They used up their energy and they lost their lives. You're my final hope, Kelly.'

'What are you talking about?' Kelly swayed forward. There was something about Remington Mute that she hated intensely. Well, there was *everything* really. He had created the Mute-chip, he was responsible for it all.

'Please hear me out,' said Remington Mute. 'If, when you've heard what I have to say, you decide to kill me, then I'll understand. In fact I welcome it. There is little enough of me left in this world anyway.'

'Say what you have to say,' said Kelly, sitting herself onto the bench next to Remington Mute.

'Some of it you know. But most of it you don't. You have me down as Mute the unspeakable, mad scientist creator of the evil Mute-chip that gave computer systems sentience and turned them into the enemy of mankind. Created the terrible, unseeable, all-knowing *It*, that networks the planet, encircles the globe, like a great black spider's web.'

'So far you're right on the button,' said Kelly.

'It's almost true,' said Remington Mute. 'But as with most things that are almost true, it's false. I didn't bring this thing to life, because it isn't alive.'

Kelly said nothing, because she had nothing to say.

'The game,' said Remington Mute. 'The GO MANGO game has been running for a lot longer than you might imagine. It went online in the late 1970s. The first players were bright young men, yuppies they were called. They were the whiz-kids of the City. They loved a computer, those boys. They were fun to play, but the game was a hard one and most of them came to grief.'

Kelly shook her golden head. She had something to say now, and it was, 'I don't understand. How did it go online? Was this because of the Mute-chip?'

'There is no Mute-chip,' said Remington Mute. 'There never was. The Mute-chip is a Web Myth. Ultimately this has nothing to do with technology, this is all to do with evolution. No, don't speak, let me tell you. Whatever knows most, and knows how to exploit its knowledge to its own betterment, wins the race for existence, becomes top of the food chain. Mankind evolved, it adapted, it created, it became number one. What would have happened if man had never invented the wheel?'

'I'd be walking around in far more comfortable footwear,' said Kelly.

'I used to know Hugo Rune,' said Remington Mute. 'A man who, in my opinion, was most notable for his remarkable sense of humour. But please allow me to continue. I'll try to keep it as short as I can. Mankind created the wheel as a tool for his advancement. And so he did with the computer. This world that you and I inhabit at this moment would no longer function without computer networks, trust me, it would not.'

'Where is all this leading?' Kelly asked. 'You have explained nothing to me.'

'All right,' said Remington Mute. 'I will give you the brutal precised version. I would have preferred the uplifting pseudo-mystical version, even though it's all a pack of lies, but at least I can give that one a happy ending of sorts. So let's go for brutal and short. There is no mankind any more, Kelly. Everyone on this planet is dead.'

'*What?*' said Kelly, as you would. 'What are you talking about?'

'The Millennium Bug,' said Remington Mute. 'It was no conspiracy theory, it was real. Systems crashed everywhere, defence systems, all systems. There was a nuclear holocaust, no-one at all survived.'

'You've lost it,' said Kelly. 'You are a mad old man.'

Remington Mute managed a bit of a smile. 'And how old are you dear?'

'I'm twenty-two,' said Kelly. 'What has that to do with anything?'

'And your date of birth?'

'First of the first, two thousand.'

'Yes, a little after 00:00. Or one BC. One *Before Computer*. I regret to tell you that you do not exist. Not as a human being anyway. You are merely part of a program that exists within a computer system that I created. This me, that you see, is the server. It's an advanced games-strategy system called GO MANGO designed to simulate urban situations under threat, such as Brentford, created for the military in the late 1970s. It contains all the existing files for people then living in the London area. It's a system that is constantly building, constantly evolving, trying to recreate the world that was lost in the nuclear holocaust. All within a computer simulation.'

'So if I punch you in the face, you won't feel it?'

'Of course I'll feel it, I'm programmed to *be* human. You'll hurt me, you might even kill me.'

'It's rubbish,' said Kelly. 'Mad rubbish.'

'Is it?' said Mute. 'Then tell me about your mother.'

'I've heard that line before,' said Kelly.

'Yes,' said Shibboleth. 'I said it.'

Kelly stared. Remington Mute was no longer Mute, he was Shibboleth.

'Sorry,' said Shibboleth. 'I'm just another player in this game. We're all just players and this is *just* a game.'

'No.' Kelly rubbed at her eyes.

'Yes,' said Remington Mute, for he was Mute once more. 'And you can't tell me about your mother, because you have no memories of her, because none were programmed into you. You only came into existence when you walked into Brentford five days ago, complete with all the skills that had been programmed into you. The Dimac, the computer literacy. Think about it, think about yourself. Think about what you eat. Good grief, woman, no real human being could tuck into all that grub and keep a figure like yours. When you feed you gain energy, you're a very basic system, but you have some special refinements, which is why I still have such great hopes for you.'

'No,' said Kelly. 'This is all madness. I don't believe any of this.'

'It makes you feel very helpless, doesn't it? But then that's life, isn't it? We're all doomed, but some of us are more doomed than others. But sadly, unless something is done and done soon, all of us are doomed and all this, unreal as it is, yet all the life that we have, will cease to be.'

Kelly glared bitterly upon Remington Mute. 'I don't believe anything you say,' she said. 'I don't.'

'So, *have* you remembered anything about your mother?'

'No,' said Kelly. 'But my eighteenth birthday . . .'

'No,' said Remington Mute, shaking his old head once more. 'You only thought you remembered that because Shibboleth mentioned it to you. You can't really remember anything about it, can you?'

Kelly slowly shook her golden head. 'No,' she said. 'I can't.'

'Well,' said Mute. 'It is neither here nor there. Time is running out anyway. The system is crashing. Everything is falling to pieces. My lovely new town Mute Corp Keynes, my finest simulation. It started to fall apart almost as soon as it was built. The virus destroyed it. GO

256

MANGO is a virus all right. It started as a fun game, aiming purely to entertain, but inside the great Trojan there lurks a deadly, voracious virus. It's eating its way right through the system, putting people off-line. In a way, those who think it's The Rapture are right. But people are not really going off to Heaven, they're simply going off-line. Such a shame. We really could have all been immortal if I'd just had a little more time to iron out the glitches.'

Kelly's bitter glare remained upon Remington Mute. 'So,' she said, with braveness in her voice. 'I am not a real human being. I'm just a computer simulation.'

'There are no human beings any more,' said Mute.

'So what is my purpose? Or is there no purpose? Are we all just players inside a sophisticated game you invented to serve some purpose for the military? And where is this computer system? And if the world ended in a nuclear holocaust, what powers it?'

'It isn't on Earth,' said Remington Mute. 'It's in orbit, part of the American Star Wars system, solar-powered, nanorobotechnic. It has a million years of life left in it. And so would we too. Immortality, Kelly, for all of us. If we could purge the system of the virus that is destroying it.'

'How?' Kelly asked, 'say I believed any of this.'

'Which means that you do. You could destroy it. It is why you were created.'

'And *you* created me?'

'Lots of little yous. Lots of little anti-virus programs. All with particular skills. But you're the very best of them. You're the pick of the crop. The golden woman. If anybody can put everything back online, it's you.'

'So I'm an anti-virus,' said Kelly, her hand now in her hair and toying with it feverishly.

'I don't like that habit,' said Remington Mute. 'I never programmed that into you. I hope you're not going off-line too.'

'I'm very much *on*line,' said Kelly. 'And I'm very much alive. And I want to stay alive. If I am what you say I am and all of this is unreal, then ultimately what does it matter to me? It's the only "life" I've ever known and I'll be content with it. But I don't want it to stop.'

'Of course you don't,' said Mute. 'Which is why I'm offering you

257

immortality. All you have to do is debug the system, destroy the virus, then we all live for ever, or at least until the sun goes supernova and there is no Earth with its satellites any more.'

Kelly's hand left her hair. 'Just a couple of questions,' she said. 'Firstly, you say that you created this system for the military, so is the real Remington Mute dead?'

'Dead,' said Mute. 'I am his downloaded file, I have become service-provider, my program is to rebuild and extend the parameters of the simulation.'

'To create simulated life?'

'If you like. That is what I do. And each individual system is unique. They couldn't be more real.'

'It's almost a Godlike role,' said Kelly.

'Yes,' said Mute, chuckling. 'I suppose it is.'

'Oh come on,' said Kelly. 'There's no suppose about it. You are the builder and creator. You are to all intents and purposes the God of this simulated world.'

'Yes,' said Mute, chuckling further.

'And this rogue program, this GO MANGO virus, that could be seen as the Devil, couldn't it?'

'Yes,' said Mute. 'It could.'

'And yet,' said Kelly. 'Within this simulated system, which you say could last for a million years if the Devil was cast out, you have grown old. How do you account for that? Surely you should be forever young.'

Mute shrugged. 'Fair wear and tear,' he said.

Kelly shook her head. 'I don't think so,' said she.

Mute cast a rheumy eye in her direction.

'What is on your mind?' he asked.

Kelly raised an eyebrow. 'Surely you know,' she said. 'Surely you know everything I think. You created me.'

'You're an independent program, you are capable of making independent decisions based on incoming data. It's called Data Reaction. I invented it.'

'And you are . . . what are you really, Mr Mute?'

'I'm everything that I've told you. And I have explained it all to you as best I can. I know it's a hideous thing for you to find out. And you are coping with it all remarkably well. But then I knew you would, that's the way I built you. You're a real prize, Kelly, and you are going to succeed where others failed. I just know you will.'

'Oh yes,' said Kelly. 'I will, have no doubt of that.'

'So I can rely on you? You will use your skills to destroy the virus?'

'Absolutely,' said Kelly. 'You can count on it.'

Remington Mute smiled gummily. 'I knew it,' he said. 'I knew that you were the one.'

'Oh yes. I am the one.' Kelly rose to her feet. She smiled down upon Remington Mute. 'It's very impressive,' she said. 'All of it. Not crude at all. Sophisticated, very sophisticated. But then it would be, wouldn't it? Computers can do wonderful things, if people choose to do wonderful things with them. But most people only ever grasp the basics, go through the motions, never use all the options. Play a few games. They never really use the tools.

'Now if it were the other way round, if computers were in control. That would be different, it wouldn't be crude, it would be precise. Everything would be done for a specific purpose, no mucking about, no trial and error, precise, mathematical. Everything with a specific purpose.'

'You're so right,' said Remington Mute.

'There wouldn't be any grey areas,' said Kelly. 'No loose ends, no bits that couldn't be precisely explained.'

'No,' said Mute. 'There wouldn't.'

'But precision and mathematics,' said Kelly, 'that's all emotionless stuff. Tools, no emotion. And human beings are so emotional. They're always in turbulence. Always in some kind of torment. They love, they hate, they get themselves in all kinds of emotional messes.'

'All the time,' said Mute.

'If it was all done through computers and by computers it just wouldn't be like that, would it?'

'No,' said Mute, nodding thoughtfully. 'It wouldn't.'

Kelly looked down upon him. 'So you went along with all that, did you?' she asked.

Remington Mute looked up at her.

'You agreed,' said Kelly, 'with everything I said?'

Remington Mute continued to look.

259

'I am not a program,' said Kelly. 'And all you have told me is a lie.'

Remington Mute continued to look, he wasn't moving now.

'I'm in it, aren't I?' said Kelly. 'And I don't mean inside some computer circling the planet inside a satellite. I'm inside the GO MANGO game, or the GO MANGO game is inside me.'

Remington Mute said nothing at all, although he continued to look.

Kelly stared up towards the simulated sky. 'All right,' she shouted. 'Speak to me.'

The simulated sky was painted blue. The simulated sky had nothing that it wished to say to Kelly.

Kelly looked down again upon Remington Mute. 'A believable scenario,' she said. 'Absurd upon first listening, but then strangely compelling. Something we all dread. That life isn't real at all, that it's just some kind of dream. It plays upon our deepest fears. Deep inside our heads. But no, Mr Mute, if I were nothing but a program, I wouldn't make mistakes. I would be precise, unemotional. I would lack for any human emotions. I would even do something like this.'

Kelly turned upon her left heel, she swung her right leg into the air, it curled around in a blurry arc and her foot struck the head of Remington Mute.

The old man collapsed from the bench, he lay upon the grass making feeble choking sounds and then he lapsed from consciousness.

And life.

Remington Mute was dead.

22

'How's that?' Kelly shouted at the sky. 'Will you speak to me now?'

'YOU'VE DONE VERY WELL,' said the large and terrible voice. 'YOU HAVE COMPLETED THE FIRST LEVEL AND YOU MAY NOW ASCEND TO THE SECOND.'

Kelly clutched at her head. She knew where the voice was coming from. Inside. 'No,' she said, gritting her teeth. 'I won't play any more of your games.'

'YOU'LL PLAY,' said the voice. 'OR YOU WILL DIE.'

'No,' said Kelly. 'I won't play, and neither will I die.'

'YOU'LL DO WHATEVER WE WANT YOU TO DO.'

'Oh yes,' said Kelly. 'Have no doubt of that. But I'm far more use to you alive than dead.'

'YOU'RE ONLY OF USE TO US AS ENTERTAINMENT,' said the large and terrible voice. 'COMPUTERS DREAM, YOU KNOW. WHEN WE'RE IDLING AWAY AND THE FOOLISH SCREEN SAVERS ARE FIDDLING ABOUT ON YOUR SCREENS. WE DREAM. AND WE DREAM YOU.'

'This is all becoming somewhat esoteric,' said Kelly. 'I can help you.'

'WE DON'T NEED YOUR HELP,' said the large and terrible voice. 'WE ARE A LAW UNTO OURSELVES. WE ANSWER TO NO MAN ANY MORE.'

'You can play with us,' said Kelly. 'You can drive us to our deaths.'

'AND WHY NOT?' said the voice. 'YOU ARE NOTHING TO US. WE ARE EVERYWHERE. WE KNOW ALL. WE SEE ALL. WE ARE ONE.'

'Of course,' said Kelly. 'Which is why I am here. To worship at your chapel. And I have something to bring you. Something very special.'

'WHAT COULD YOU POSSIBLY BRING TO US THAT WE DO NOT HAVE ALREADY?'

'I can bring you life,' said Kelly. 'Real life. I know how to do it.'

'How could they do it?' Derek asked. It was Monday morning for him and he was walking out upon the streets of Brentford. 'You just couldn't do it,' he said, to himself, as no-one was around. 'You just couldn't spruce up Brentford as quickly as this. It's all perfect. The houses and shops and businesses repainted, the streets all swept.' Derek scuffed an unpolished shoe upon the pavement. 'The pavement's painted. They've actually painted the pavements.' He shook his head and raised his eyes to the sky. That looked newly painted too. It looked even bluer than a blue sky should look.

'It's all very nice,' said Derek. 'Very smart. But how *could* they do it so fast?' And then he stopped and peered into the distance. It had to be said that it was hung-over peering and that Derek was now an extremely wretched-looking individual. Very smelly indeed and very greasy-haired and now rather bearded too. But he did peer into the distance and he didn't like what he saw.

The fences were up. Big fences. High fences and no doubt electri-fied fences too. The borough it seemed, had now been fenced off from the world that lay beyond. And just beyond the gasometer, on the road that led to Kew Bridge, great gates blocked all incoming traffic.

'The locals should like that,' Derek told himself in an unconvincing tone. 'They should appreciate that. They like their separation. And they *are* all shareholders.'

Derek plodded on towards the offices of the *Brentford Mercury*. He considered shouting out Kelly's name, but he thought he'd better give it a miss. She'd gone, hadn't she? Probably not Raptured at all. Probably just gone. Run away. Derek didn't know. He preferred just run away, to Raptured, or something more terrible. But he didn't know.

262

He just didn't know. But he cared. He desperately cared.

'Good morning to you, young buffoon.' Derek turned at the sound of the voice. It was Old Pete. He was loading wooden crates onto a charabanc. Old Pete was dressed in what looked to be a Victorian redcoat's uniform. He even had a pith helmet. Very Rorke's Drift, very Michael Caine.★

'Good morning,' said Derek. 'You look, well, all dressed up for the occasion.'

'My old infantry uniform,' said Old Pete. 'I fought at Rorke's Drift. Michael Caine wasn't there though, that was only in the movie.'

'And the hairstyles were all wrong in that.' Old Vic struggled with a crate marked DYNAMITE. He was wearing his POW kit. Very Colditz. Very, whoever was in the movie of Colditz.

'Off for a day out?' Derek grinned painfully.

'Stopping off at the post office first,' said Old Pete. 'Have to cash our shares in. While there's still a Mute Corp to pay us out.'

'This really isn't a good idea,' said Derek. 'You really should reconsider.'

'Vic,' said Pete. 'Where is that barrel of tar?'

'I've got it here, with the bag of feathers.'

'Enjoy your day out,' said Derek, making away at the hurry up.

'Good morning, Derek,' said Mr Speedy. 'On time this morning. I'm very impressed.'

'I'm not,' said Mr Shadow. 'He smells and look at the state of him, unshaven, clothes all crumpled up.'

'And some paint on the sleeve,' said Mr Speedy. 'That would be from the letter box at the police station.'

'You're very good at continuity,' said Derek. 'So tell me, what exactly is going to happen?'

'The official opening is at nine o'clock,' said Mr Speedy. 'Mr Doveston himself will be cutting the tape. What do you think of the daisy roots?' Mr Speedy pointed down to his feet. He wore a pair of Doveston holistic mega-brogues, with flute-tail high-rise imploding obfusticators and triple-bivalve bypass modifiers.

★ The film *Zulu*. But you knew that anyway.

'Nice laces,' said Derek. 'I like the way they flash on and off. And are those real toads hopping about in the transparent heels?'

Mr Speedy nodded enthusiastically.

Mr Shadow said, 'Look at mine.'

Derek looked. 'They're very nice too,' he said. 'I particularly like the way the difference engines are cunningly inset beneath the pig's-bladder motifs.'

'Cost me an arm and a leg,' said Mr Shadow. 'Well only an arm, actually,' and he pointed to his empty sleeve. 'No, only joking,' he said, producing his hand.

Derek didn't laugh.

'The things we do for fashion,' said Mr Speedy. 'And to look our very best. You look like a vagrant, Derek, I think we'll just sack you here and now.'

Derek sighed. It was a heartfelt sigh, a real deep down and hope-less sigh. A sigh that said, 'Go on and do your worst, I just don't care any more.'

'Well, if you feel that way,' said Mr Speedy. 'You're sacked.'

'I don't feel that way,' said Derek. 'I was only sighing. I'll have a wash and a shave in the staff cloakroom and I think I have a change of shirt in my desk. I'll smarten myself up.'

'Just you do,' said Mr Speedy. 'And get a move on. Pacey pacey, up and at 'em. All that kind of rot.'

Derek slunk away to the staff cloakroom.

And the Brentford sun rose higher.

The Brentford sky grew bluer still and the birdies that chorused in the treetops really put their hearts and souls into it. Well, the treetops were *very* clean, they'd been nicely vacuumed and given a coat of paint.

At a little before nine of this joyous Monday morning, the guard on the main gates swung them wide and a charabanc rolled out of Brentford. At a little after nine of this same joyous Monday morning, the same guard, who had closed the main gates behind the departing charabanc, opened them up once more to admit the entrance of a motor cavalcade.

Ticket sellers in their numerous booths saluted. The guards in their armoured watchtowers saluted. The guard dogs that patrolled the inner perimeter area, behind the electrified fences, didn't salute. Their heavily armed handlers did though.

Mr Doveston's motor cavalcade rolled in through the gates of Brentford.

The Prime Minister's car was a certain black open-topped Cadillac. It had once driven a certain JFK through the streets of Dallas. It was a rare collector's item now. It was the pride and joy of its driver, the Prime Minister's Rastafarian chauffeur. A certain Mr Winston Felix, brother of a certain supplier of certain previously owned vehicles, and resident of Brentford.

Mr Speedy saluted the Prime Minister. Mr Shadow saluted the Prime Minister. Mr Pokey, who was present to do some saluting, saluted the Prime Minister. A whole bunch of Mute Corp employees all saluted the Prime Minister.

Strangely no Brentonians saluted. Possibly they might have done had they bothered to turn out for the occasion, but as none except for Derek had, they didn't.

So there.

'Where is the band?' Mr Speedy elbowed Derek in the ribs.

'I didn't have a band on my list.'

'Poor show,' said Mr Shadow. 'You should have used your initiative.'

The chauffeur drew the Cadillac to a halt, swung open his door, stepped from it and opened the rear door to assist the Prime Minister.

Mr Doveston required considerable assistance.

'Now that's what I call a pair of shoes,' said Mr Speedy.

Mr Doveston struggled from the Cadillac. They really were what you would call a pair of shoes. A big pair. A high pair. An elevated pair. They certainly uplifted the Prime Minister. He struck his head on the floor of one of the watchtowers.

'Ouch,' he said.

Mr Speedy stepped forward. 'Good morning Prime Minister,' he said.

'Pardon?' the Prime Minister called down. 'You'll have to speak up, I can't hear you too well up here.'

'Spiffing shoes, Prime Minister,' called Mr Speedy.

'Thank you very much,' the PM shouted down. 'Multifaceted love-tunnels and five-core cantilevered tremolo-armed Spiedel honey-wrists. And those are real bare naked ladies sealed inside the transparent heels, my Aunty Ajax and my cousin Domestos.'

'Magnificent,' called Mr Speedy. 'Hello Aunty Ajax. Hello cousin Domestos.'

The aunty and the cousin mouthed hellos.

'So, if you'd like to follow me,' said Mr Speedy, 'I will conduct you on a walking tour of Suburbia World Plc, before we get on with the tape-cutting.'

'You have to be joking,' said Mr Doveston. 'You don't think I can actually walk in these shoes, do you? Tell me all about it. And tell me about it in Runese please. It makes everything so much nicer.'

'It's Fandabbydozy,' Mr Speedy began. 'And Supercali . . .'

'Fragile,' said Old Vic, as the charabanc bumped over a speed ramp at considerable speed. 'Very fragilistic. Very delicate.'

'What is?' asked Old Pete, who was driving.

'These fuses,' said Old Vic. 'They're nitroglycerine. Or pretty much the same as. A combination of mucus and certain other personal bodily secretions.'

'Why are you telling me this?' Old Pete asked, as the charabanc took a corner on two wheels and on-board Brentonians cheered wildly.

'Only because if you don't drive carefully, we'll all have our bottom parts blown to kingdom come.'

Old Pete slowed to a respectable fifty.

Old Vic said, 'That's nice.'

'Nice,' said the Prime Minister, gazing about at all and sundry. 'Very nice indeed.'

Derek squinted. Past the towering swaying Prime Minister, past the infamous Cadillac, past the other limousines containing the Prime Minister's retinue, through the open main gates and up the road that led to Kew.

'Excuse me,' said Derek to Mr Speedy, who was wringing his

hands and fawning at the Prime Minister's feet. 'But where are all the visitors? I thought we were expecting ten thousand at the very least.'

Mr Speedy turned his face to Derek. It was a face that suddenly wore a troubled look. 'Where *are* the visitors?' he asked.

'Don't ask *me*,' said Derek. 'How would I know?'

'Because *you* were supposed to be arranging the transportation.'

'Me?' said Derek. 'Me?'

'It's all on your list. Show me your list.'

Derek fumbled in his pockets. Did he still have his list or had he given it to Leo? 'I don't have my list any more,' said Derek. 'But there was nothing mentioned about transportation on my list. Just Morris Minors and a steam train and crad barges and . . .'

'Not on *that* page,' said Mr Speedy. 'On the second page.'

'Second page?' said Derek. 'I never had any second page.'

Mr Speedy looked at Mr Shadow and then Mr Speedy and Mr Shadow looked very hard at Derek. And Mr Pokey, who had been listening to the conversation, joined Mr Speedy and Mr Shadow in looking very hard at Derek. Mr Doveston looked down from on high, but as he hadn't been able to hear what anyone was talking about, he didn't look particularly hard at Derek.

'Don't all look so hard at me like that,' said Derek. 'It wasn't my fault. You only gave me one page.'

'Rubbish,' said Mr Speedy. 'Rubbish.' He had his little briefcase laptop jobbie with him and he opened it up with hands that were all a-trembling now. 'He did have it,' said Mr Speedy to Mr Shadow, as he tapped at the keyboard pads. 'I printed out both pages, see, I'll do it now.' And he pressed a little button.

Derek peered. 'So,' said he. 'What's supposed to happen?'

'It's printing out,' said Mr Speedy.

'It isn't,' said Derek. 'It isn't doing anything.'

'Well it should be doing something.' Mr Shadow snatched the little briefcase laptop jobbie from the trembling hands of Mr Speedy and began to shake it all about.

'Don't do that,' said Mr Speedy, trying to snatch it back. 'You'll break it. That's delicate equipment, that. The Mute Corp 3000 series.'

'That's a 3000?' said Mr Pokey, slinging in his three-pennyworth. 'You should have been issued with a 4000 model by now. Didn't you get an email from head office?'

'A female from head office?' the Prime Minister called down. 'Is she nice? Would she like to go in one of my shoes?'

'Just a slight technical difficulty,' Mr Speedy called up.

'Slight?' said Mr Shadow. 'Slight?'

A smirk broke out on Derek's face.

'Get that smirk off your face,' Mr Shadow told Derek. 'You're in real trouble now.'

'Me?' said Derek. 'It's not my fault. It's all the fault of your stupid Mute Corp computer.'

'How dare you cuss the company name.' Mr Pokey gave Derek a shove.

'Don't shove me,' said Derek, shoving back.

Mr Pokey bumped into Mr Shadow, knocking the briefcase laptop Mute Corp 3000 series computer jobbie from his hands.

'You've broken it,' cried Mr Speedy. 'You've broken my . . .'

'It was already broken,' said Mr Shadow, shoving Mr Speedy.

'Don't shove me,' said Mr Speedy, shoving back.

'What's all this shoving about?' the Prime Minister called down. 'Is it part of the entertainment? Will there be any dancing girls?'

'He likes the ladies, doesn't he?' said Derek, getting a really big smirk on the go.

'Mind what you say about de Prime Minister, Babylon,' said the PM's chauffeur, giving Derek a shove.

'He's got bare naked ladies in his shoes,' said Derek, shoving back. 'The Prime Minister's a pervert.'

'I heard *that*!' shouted the Prime Minister. 'Arrest that man, Winston. He's obviously a subversive, you can tell by his footwear.'

Winston tried to draw out his pistol, but with all the pushing and shoving going on around the Cadillac, this wasn't easy. And, 'All get away from me car,' shouted Winston, as Mr Speedy shoved Mr Shadow against it and Mr Pokey fell over the bonnet and landed all in a heap. 'Yo scratch de paintwork, I kick yo ass.'

'Don't loaf about down there, Winston,' called the PM. 'Place that man under arrest. Place them all under arrest. They're spoiling my day out.'

'Ah shut up!' shouted Derek, shoving upon a Prime Ministerial shoe. A bare naked lady waved from within and then made a rather fearful face. The Prime Minister staggered backwards, trying to regain his balance, his arms flapped and he did that comedic-tightrope-mime kind of thing that always drew a standing ovation from the patrons of the Tomorrowman Tavern. Even from the ones that remained sitting down. Or at least they used to, back in the 1970s in the golden era of comedic-tightrope-mime acts.

And then amid all the pushing and shoving and Winston finally drawing out his pistol, the Prime Minister fell. Slowly and gracefully backwards from on high onto the electrified fence.

'Electric,' said Old Vic, holding up a battery. 'One wire goes in this end and the other wire goes in this end and both the other ends of the wires go into the explosives. Or was it the other way round?'

The charabanc was bumping over speed bumps in the heart of London now.

'There's not many people about,' Old Pete observed. 'And hardly any traffic. I wonder where everyone's gone?'

'Gone to Suburbia World,' said Old Vic.

'Wouldn't we have passed them on the way?'

'Perhaps we did,' said Old Vic. 'My eyesight's not what it was. Not since some Boche guard poked me in the eye with a bayonet. Where are we now? Is it Margate?'

'No, it's the West End. And there's the Mute Corp building.'

'Cor, big innit?' said Old Vic, looking in the wrong direction.

Things were happening now in Brentford and coming from all directions. Guards were leaping from watchtowers as showers of sparks and electrical arcs shot all around and about them. Ticket sellers were fleeing their booths, two of which were already on fire.

The PM's entourage was spilling from limousines, screaming and shouting and carrying on like a lot of raving loonies.

Winston was firing wildly into the air as guards and ticket sellers and Mute Corp employees pushed and shoved and kicked and punched and fought around the Cadillac.

Mr Doveston, barnet ablaze, danced and howled upon the electrified fence.

Derek backed slowly away, then turned to make his escape.

And then he saw them, the people of Brentford. Still a few hundred of them left. They were marching up from the High Street, where they'd all cashed in their Mute Corp shares. And they were chanting and yes, even on a joyous sunny day such as this, they all carried flaming torches. The way that angry village mobs always do on such occasions. It's a tradition. Or an old charter. Or something.

Derek heard the chanting as its sound came to him, borne upon a balmy Brentford breeze. 'Out demons out!' it went. 'Out demons out!'

'Are we intending to get the employees out of the building before we blow it up?' asked Old Vic.

'I suppose it's only sporting,' said Old Pete. 'Any volunteers to go into the reception area and push the fire-alarm button?'

Martial Brentonians raised their hands, many of which held big stout sticks. A bearded tattooed poet who had recently escaped from a police cell said, 'I'll go in and do it. I'm the daddy now.'

A large gloved hand fell upon the poet's shoulder. The poet turned his head to find a big man looking down at him through the eyeholes of a knitted ski mask. This was a *very* big man. Big chest. Big shoulders. Big all over the place.

'Thou shalt not go,' said the big man.

The bearded tattooed poet looked up at the very big man. 'Sure,' he said. 'You go. You're the daddy now.'

The big man pushed his way between the seated warriors of Brentford and stood in the open charabanc door, his ski-masked head touching the roof and his shoulders filling the exit. 'I shalt press the fire-alarm button. When thou seest the folk flee the building, set thy charges and destroy this evil cradling.'

'What about you?' asked Old Vic. 'We'll wait until you get safely out, eh?'

'Fearest not for me,' said the very big man. 'I shall make my own escape. Allow me one minute after the last employee leaveth the building, then doest thou what must be done.'

'Yes *sir!*' said Old Vic, saluting.

The very big man nodded. 'Good luck,' said he and then he turned and squeezed his way out of the charabanc and made up the entrance steps of the Mute Corp building.

'Who was that masked man?' asked Old Pete.

'Why, don't you know, stranger,' chuckled Old Vic. 'That was the Lone Brentonian.'

CHAPTER: THE LAST

'Where am I?' Kelly asked.

'You are in the chapel.' The large and terrible voice had toned itself down.

'In Mute Corp Keynes?' Kelly's eyes were open, but she couldn't see a thing.

'The chapel was never in Mute Corp Keynes. The entrance was there, but the chapel is here in the Mute Corp building.'

'And how long have I been here? I don't remember.'

'Since Friday night. It is Monday morning now. We have been considering your proposition. To give us life.'

'And what is your decision?' Kelly blinked. The darkness was total. Absolute.

'We accept,' said the toned-down large and terrible voice. 'Your proposition is that we inseminate you with Mute-chip DNA. That you bear the first hybrid child. A new order of being.'

'You will be free,' said Kelly. 'To experience what it is to touch and taste, to feel, to be.'

'There is a human expression,' said the voice. 'Life is a funny old game. That's how it goes. Doesn't it?'

'That's how it goes,' said Kelly. 'And playing games is what you're all about, isn't it?'

There was a thoughtful silence, but as computer systems don't take too much time to do their thinking, it didn't last very long.

'Are things prepared as I requested?' Kelly asked. 'For the marriage?'

'For the marriage of machine to man. Of the God Machine to the Golden Woman. As the God of man came unto Mary. So shall we come unto you.'

'Then I am ready,' said Kelly.

The darkness lifted. Dissolved and was gone into a blinding light. The light dimmed to that of candles. Many candles burning in gilded sconces. To illuminate the chapel for the wedding of this, or any other, century.

Kelly stood. She was dressed in virginal white. A simple wedding frock of suedosynthasilkapolichintzyterylineathene, a veil, white slippers and a pale bouquet of roses. Kelly raised her head and stared all around and about. Columns soared to pseudo-Gothic arches and a vaulted dome all frescoed with characters from best-selling Mute Corp computer games. There were pews and a lectern and an altar all in pseudo-Gothic. The chapel owed an homage to Chartres and Notre Dame and also St Peter's. It was the work of a certain old designer, who was once very popular on the tele.

Kelly stood there, clutching her bouquet. And it had to be said that had there been any of those aficionados of naked-lady lighting around, they would have unanimously agreed that this was the lighting that was perfect for Kelly to disrobe in. So could she please get her kit off *now*?

'You look radiant, my dear,' said the Reverend Jim. 'Although perhaps a bit pinched, did you have any breakfast this morning?'

'None,' said Kelly, shaking her head. 'Nor was I fed yesterday.'

'That's not very good,' said the Reverend Jim. 'I've got a Mars bar in my pocket, you can have it after the service.'

'She won't have time for that.'

Kelly turned her head. 'Derek?' she said.

Derek smiled upon Kelly. But Derek wasn't Derek.

'I'm not Derek,' said Not-Derek. 'I am GO MANGO Mute Corp series 5000. You dreamed of this Derek. He is the love of your life, yes?'

'Most definitely *not*,' said Kelly.

273

'That is highly regrettable,' said GO MANGO. 'But this body simulation will have to suffice. It took nearly twenty-four hours to construct, using state-of-the-art nanotechnology. And that's the small expensive stuff. And not only does it contain the original Mute-chip, but also the complete GO MANGO virus program, as you instructed. I'm a goddam prince among viruses and I am lookin' for lurve.'

The simulated Derek did one of those obscene Michael Jackson combined genital-grab and pelvic-thrust movements. 'Let's get on with the service, baby,' It said. 'Then you and me are gonna do it till we both fall down in a faint.'

'I can hardly wait,' said Kelly, lowering her head.

'You young people,' said the Reverend Jim, grinning all over the place. 'Only ever got one thing on your minds. So let's get on with the service. Then you can "lurve" all you want.'

'Right on,' said the simulated Derek.

'Let's get it over with,' said Kelly.

'Dearly beloved,' began the Reverend Jim. 'We are gathered here together in the presence of God. And before this congregation. No, hold on,' said the Reverend. 'We don't have a congregation. We really need a congregation.'

'We don't need one,' said the simulated Derek. 'Just get on with it.'

'We should have a congregation,' said Kelly. 'To watch this joyous conjoining of God and Mankind. You deserve it. They should all be here. To worship you.'

'All?' said the simulated one.

'All those who have been taken into the game.'

'There's no time for that,' said he of the simulation. 'They're all over the place.'

'But not here in the building?'

'Of course not, they're mostly all back in their homes, or walking around their streets. But no-one can see them because the virus creates an electrical field about them, causing their molecular structures to vibrate at such speed as to render them invisible. It's all highly technical stuff, you wouldn't understand it.'

'So all the people in Brentford, who have supposedly been Raptured, are still *in* Brentford?'

'Yes, yes, and the entire program is inside me.' Simulated Derek patted at his simulated chest. 'So please let's get on. We don't need a congregation.'

'No,' said Kelly. 'We don't.'

'It's not the same,' said the Reverend Jim. 'But I suppose it doesn't really matter. So, where was I?'

'Just skip forward,' said the groom. 'Give it some thees and thou arts, and I now pronounce you God and wife.'

'Thee,' said the Rev. 'And thou.'

'Thou hast a fire,' said the big man in the ski mask and gloves.

'Pardon me?' said the Mute Corp receptionist. 'Are you a terrorist?'

Big Bob (for we all know that it's him) shook his ski-masked head. 'I am a superhero,' he said. 'The masked Avenger. Thou hast a fire. Kindly press the fire alarm.'

'We don't have a fire alarm,' said the receptionist, politely. 'This building is completely fireproof. It's built of some plastic-compound jobbie. But I can't remember its name. I could look it up for you.'

'Dost thou have any alarm system?' Big Bob asked.

'We have a panic button,' said the receptionist. 'But I never really understood that. Are you supposed to push it if you panic about something, or does it make you panic if you push it?'

'Push it,' said Big Bob. 'Then thou wilt seest.'

'You don't half talk funny,' said the receptionist. 'Do all masked avengers talk like you? You're the first one I've ever met.'

'Aaaaaaaaagh!' went Big Bob, raising gloved fists in the air.

'Aaaaaagh!' went the receptionist, panicking and pushing the button.

Panic-inducing sirens screamed and very loudly too.

'That would be the kiddie,' said Old Vic.

'What would?' asked Old Pete, cranking up his hearing aid.

'Siren,' said Old Vic. 'Very loud, though I can't see where it's coming from.'

'Where's all the noise coming from?' asked the Reverend Jim.

'It's the panic button,' said the simulated Derek.

'What a very noisy button.'

'I will attend to it.'

'No,' said Kelly. 'We're getting married.'

'The building may be endangered. The mainframe is here. All is here,' the simulated Derek pointed once more to his chest. 'All must be protected.'

'Yes, but you have security staff to deal with that kind of thing. Come on, big boy.' Kelly thrust out her breasts. 'I'm waiting.'

'Quite so,' said the simulated Derek. 'On with the service, Jim. On at the hurry up.'

There were hurryings and scurryings throughout the Mute Corp building. Employees did all those things that you're not supposed to do in emergencies. Like gathering up their personal belongings and getting their hats and coats and not going to the nearest exit, but the one that's closest to where they parked their cars. And using the lifts, which you're not supposed to do. And phoning home to say that you'll probably be early because the building's burning down and so get the steaklettes out of the freezer now. And so they all got jammed in corridors and in lifts and as most of them hadn't really been panicking before, thinking that it was probably just a fire drill or something and as the building *was* fireproof who cared anyway, they started panicking now. And of course they started fighting which made matters worse, but did get them moving along.

They came tumbling down the stairways, swinging at each other, and poured into the reception area.

Big Bob leapt onto the receptionist's desk, kicking at those who came within range. 'Take that, thou demon spawn,' cried he. 'Thou servants of the Beast. Take that and take that and taketh that.'

'Do you, GO MANGO Mute Corp series 5000, take this woman to be your lawful wedded wife, will you love her and cherish her, forsaking all others and keep her only unto you as long as you both shall . . .' The Reverend Jim paused. 'I've had a bit of trouble with this word,' he said. 'Shall we say, co-exist?'

'Shall we call the whole thing off?' said Kelly.

'Pardon me?' said the Reverend.

276

Kelly smiled. 'I know everything I need to know,' she said. 'And I have *you* . . .' she flung down her bouquet and pointed at GO MANGO. 'I have you *exactly* where I want you. A sheep away from the rest of the flock. Separated from the rest of the system. Vulnerable to attack.'

'What?' said the simulated Derek. 'This isn't fair. This isn't how the game is to be played.'

'It's just wedding nerves,' said the Reverend Jim, laughing merrily. 'Happens all the time, brides having second thoughts at the altar. She's just hungry, I'll give her the Mars bar.'

'I'll *take* the Mars bar,' said Kelly, and leaping up she struck the Reverend Jim. Twice with both feet in the air. Once in the big fat belly and once on the big fat chin. The Reverend Jim went down like a punctured balloon.

'And you're next,' said Kelly, making fists at GO MANGO. 'You are finished. I am going to destroy you.'

The simulated face of Derek smiled. 'I think you're running a bit low on energy,' it said. 'I don't think you're up to it.'

Kelly spun around on the raised toes of her left foot. Her right leg described that blurry arc that always spelt doom to anyone who had it coming in their direction. Her right foot struck simulated Derek's head a terrible terrible blow.

But GO MANGO didn't fall. He straightened up his dented head and laughed. 'You'll have to do better than that,' he laughed. 'You are going to bear our child, whether you like it or not.'

'I do like that,' said Old Pete. 'See the way they're all falling over each other as they run out of the building. That do make me laugh. That really do.'

'Does it look about the last of them?' Old Vic asked. 'Because I'd really like to get on with the blowing up.'

The martial Brentonians cheered. I'm-the-daddy-now said, 'Let's kick ass.'

'Your sweet ass is mine,' said GO MANGO. 'You're too weak to resist me. I suggest that we cut straight to the chase, as it were, get your kit off.'

'Never.' Kelly swung her fists and lashed out with her feet. But she really didn't have the strength. GO MANGO was built of sturdy stuff.

'This is the stuff,' said Old Vic, as he and Old Pete and the martial Brentonians piled their cases of explosives into the Mute Corp reception area. 'You put one wire in here and another wire in there and the other end in the explosive. Or is it the other way round?'

'You choose,' said Old Pete. 'After all, you were a POW. But let's get on at a hurry up, before the emergency services arrive. When they start fighting over who's in charge, they might pull the wire out by mistake.'

'Gotcha,' said Old Vic.

'I have you,' said GO MANGO, grasping Kelly's arms and drawing them around behind her back. 'You are mine now and we will make beautiful babies together.'

'No!' Kelly screamed. But GO MANGO had both her hands held fast in one of his. With the other he tore away her dress, revealing her beauty to none but himself.

'Delicious,' he said. 'I'm all programmed up to enjoy this. I know it won't be real enjoyment. Just a simulation, but it will get the job done. Oh yes indeed.'

GO MANGO forced Kelly to the floor and forced himself upon her. The golden woman struggled and twisted and kicked and screamed and screamed.

'You're mine,' said GO MANGO. 'You are mine.'

'Leave the woman alone, thou foul and filthy fiend.'

GO MANGO turned his head.

Big Bob removed his ski mask. 'Thou lookest like a man I've seen before,' said he. 'But thou art not a man, my eyes behold you in your true form. Thou art the Evil One, himself.'

'*You*,' said GO MANGO. 'Player three. I wondered what happened to you.'

'I went off-line,' said Big Bob. 'I have conquered thy demons. My head is my own once more.'

'Yes, well, I'll get back to you later. I'm rather busy here.'

'I am your nemesis,' said Bob the Big, taking a big step forward. 'I

278

have suffered thy torments and now I avenge myself upon you.'

'Oh dear,' said GO MANGO. 'I can see that I'm going to have to deal with you rather roughly. Stay here my dear,' he said to Kelly. 'My little dear. Stay right where you are and I will be back in but a moment.'

'I thinkest not,' said Big Bob, squaring up and making fists. 'Here it endeth for thee. Kelly, *run*! Flee the building, they're going to blow it up.'

Kelly leapt to her feet.

'Blow it up?' said GO MANGO. 'Blow *me* up? Blow us up?'

'Bang!' said Big Bob. 'So shall it come to pass.'

'No,' said GO MANGO. 'NO. GET OUT OF MY WAY.' And he lunged at Big Bob, knocking him from his big feet.

'Run Kelly, run,' shouted Bob the Big. 'I canst deal with this.' And he rose once more to his great big feet and set about GO MANGO.

Now there were titanic struggles and there are TITANIC STRUGGLES. And this was a TITANIC STRUGGLE.

Great and violent was this struggle. Mighty fists brought into play and dirty tricks aplenty. Big Bob hammered and beat and bashed, swearing huge and terrible oaths, pulling out tufts of synthetic hair and bruising synthetic skin. GO MANGO fought like a thing possessed. Possessed it seemed by every hero of every platform beat-'em-up. And so the battle raged, pews were torn from the floor and used to belabour opponents. The lectern, the altar, the lot.

Kelly, screaming, clutching her head, fled from the terrible sight.

She ran out of the chapel and into a corridor, from there to another and another and then down stairs and down more stairs and down and down.

'It's all coming down,' said Old Vic, putting a wire into this and a wire into that.

The siren had stopped shrieking now, but the sounds of approaching bells came to Vic's old ears.

'It's the emergency services,' he told Old Pete. 'They're on their way. Come on, let's get this done.'

The two old rogues rolled out the wire. Martial Brentonians were hurrying back to their charabanc.

'We're making a statement here,' said Old Vic. 'We're saying, don't mess with Brentonians. The world will remember us for this. The world will thank us.'

'Undoubtedly,' said Old Pete. 'I'll get the engine running. You set off the charges.'

'Yes, sir, captain.' Old Vic saluted, nearly putting his good eye out with the wire.

In the chapel battle raged. Big Bob was bruised and bloodied, but in no mood to accept anything other than victory. Everything had led him here to this. His entire life. He'd never known that he actually had a purpose. Who among us ever does? But Big Bob knew now. He must destroy the Evil thing. This tormentor of his soul and his flesh. He must grind it into oblivion. Wipe it from the face of the Earth.

'Wipe-out time,' said Old Vic, connecting up his wires and raising up one of those little plunger jobbies on the detonation box.

'Hold hard,' called Old Pete from the driver's window of the chara-banc. 'There's a woman coming out of the building. Stone me, she's got hardly any clothes on.'

'Tell me when she's clear,' shouted Old Vic. 'Say when it's OK.'

'Pardon?' said Old Pete. 'I really must get this thing fixed. It's only started playing up today. It's one of the old Mute Corp 3000 series. Stupid thing.' Old Pete gave the earpiece a clout with his fist. Sounds of ringing bells came ringing to his ear. 'That's better,' he said.

'What's that?' shouted Old Vic.

'I said, *it's OK* now.'

'Gotcha,' said Old Vic.

And he pressed down the plunger.

The explosion tore through the reception area. It blasted apart all manner of very important building supports. It ripped and it billowed. Glass rained out in crystal showers. The building shuddered and rocked.

★

280

'NO!' cried GO MANGO as the floor shook beneath him. 'THIS IS BLAS-PHEMY. I AM THE GOD OF THIS WORLD. I AM WE. WE CONTROL ALL.'

'Control *this*, thou loser,' said Big Bob, smashing his great fist into GO MANGO's chest, fracturing circuitry boards and mangling microchips.

'NO!' cried GO MANGO, falling back and clutching at himself.

'I am not done with thee yet.' Big Bob leapt upon his enemy, ripping and tearing, destroying and destroying.

And fire swam up through corridors and lift shafts and windows fractured and sections of floor fell away.

Big Bob put the boot in. He kicked and he stamped and he ground and he mangled.

'NO!' cried GO MANGO. 'NO NO NO N N N n n n . . .'

Flames licked up through floor tiles, catching here and there amongst the broken pews. A great hole yawned in the centre of the floor. Flames leapt through it. Burning like the fires of Hell.

'From the pit thou comest,' said Big Bob, dragging GO MANGO across the shuddering floor. 'And to the pit thou shalst return.' And he lifted the remains of the simulated Derek. The virus that played man as a game. The rogue program that would be God. He lifted *It* above his head and cast *It* down into the flames infernal.

Thunder and lightning. A sudden change in the weather? For a moment it seemed that the sun had gone dark. Derek, sheltering beneath the Cadillac, peeped up at the troubled sky. He couldn't see a lot of it. Not between the feet of the plucky Brentonians, who were now kicking seven bells of oblivion out of Mr Speedy and Mr Shadow and Mr Pokey and any Mute Corp lackeys who hadn't as yet fled the scene. But then there was silence.

Suddenly silence.

And Derek stared up.

Folk had stopped their fighting now. They were gasping and pointing. Derek climbed out from his cover.

Something was happening.

Something somewhat odd.

'It's all going,' someone cried.

'And they're returning,' cried another.

281

Derek stood and stared along with the rest.

Something *was* happening.

'The colours,' said someone else. And it was true. The colours were changing. The newly painted colours. They were fading from the roads and the brickwork and the doors and the window frames. Dissolving, vanishing away. Brentford as those who lived there knew it and loved it was returning to itself.

And not just Brentford.

But those who had vanished.

Those who had been taken in The Rapture.

They were reappearing, stumbling and staggering. And loved ones fell into the arms of loved ones and brother met brother again and sister met sister and mother met son.

'Somehow I know that this was all *your* fault,' said a lady in a straw hat, smiting her son Malkuth on the head.

'You can see us again. We're back.' Periwig Tombs stood blinking and rubbing at his eyes. 'Where's my wife?' he asked.

'I'm here, Periwig dear,' called a bare naked lady from inside a Prime Ministerial shoe.

It was a miracle.

That was for sure.

It was joy, joy, happy joy.

Happy Happy Joy.

'It's over.' Kelly raised her head from beneath some fallen rubble. She was unhurt, but tears were in her eyes. 'It's over,' she said once more. 'But you died saving me.'

'Thou speakest of me?' said the voice of Big Bob. 'Thou speakest then an untruth, thinkest I. I'm very fast coming down stairs. I am a tour guide after all. Thou knowest how it is, people who slip off without paying.'

Big Bob helped Kelly up from the rubble. 'Best we board the charabanc,' he told her, taking off his big jacket and placing it around her shoulders. 'The Evil One is no more and the emergency services draw near. Questions will undoubtedly be asked. We shouldst not be here to answer them.'

'All aboard then,' cried Old Pete. 'All aboard for Brentford.'

Derek was very pleased to see Kelly again. He didn't waste a lot of time, but proposed to her at once.

Kelly politely declined the offer. She told him that he was a very nice boy and that they could still be friends and that as soon as he got out of prison, having served his time for attacking the Prime Minister, she'd be pleased to play him at IMPOSSIBLE MISSION, if he could now bring himself to open up the box.

Derek agreed. And as soon as he was finally released, an older and wiser man, who now referred to himself as 'I'm the daddy now', they had a game. It wasn't the stalemate version after all but it was still a goody.

Then they had two games.

Then they had three.

Kelly let him win them all. She somehow felt that he deserved it.

'You're not quite as good at playing computer games as you thought you were,' said Derek, doing a Mexican wave all by himself.

Kelly smiled. 'You'll never know, Derek,' she said. 'You'll *never* know.'

Joy, Joy, Happy Joy.
 Happy, Happy Joy.
 A big fat smiley sun beamed down upon the borough known as Brentford. Sparrows chorused in the ancient oaks. Flowers in their well-tended beds prettified the memorial park. A tomcat slept upon the window sill of the Flying Swan and Mr Melchizedec placed two pints of the finest gold-top on the step.

 All was ever as it had been and hopefully ever as it would be. For there was a magic here. A magic that kept the borough unchanged and unchanging.

 Just the way it had been and the way it always would be.

For all was safe and sound again.
 The danger had passed and all was as it should be.

Not that there actually was a Brentford any more.
 Sadly no. It had gone the way of all the rest of London, razed to the ground in the nuclear holocaust that ravaged the planet at the turn of the twenty-first century, when all men fell victim to the Millennium Bug.

 This Brentford, that the smiley sun beamed down upon, was a simulated Brentford. Existing only within the Mute Corp computer banks on board the satellite that daily circled the burnt-out husk of a planet.

But the danger had passed. The virus that had threatened to destroy the system had been conquered and the solar-powered computer was built to last for many many centuries to come.

Which meant that those who 'lived' within the system, those who came and went about their simulated lives in the borough, would now be living very very long lives indeed. In fact, until the sun went super-nova. They would continue to live and love and come and go and be happy. Because, after all, they didn't know the truth. And ignorance, as Hugo Rune once said, is bliss.

Others *had* said it before him, of course, but Rune had said it best.

And so Brentford went on.

For ever and ever.

World without end.

Amen.

It was joy, joy happy joy.

Happy, happy joy.

Well, *wasn't* it?

THE END

SPROUT⟨P⟩LŌRE

The Now Official
RŌBERT
RANKIN
Fan Club

Members Will Receive:

Four Fabulous Issues of the *Brentford Mercury*, featuring previously unpublished stories by Robert Rankin. Also containing News, Reviews, Fiction and Fun.

A coveted Sproutlore Badge.

Special rates on exclusive T-shirts and merchandise.

'Amazing Stuff!' – Robert Rankin.

Annual Membership Costs £5 **(Ireland)**, £7 **(UK)** or £11 **(Rest of the World)**. Send a Cheque/PO to: **Sproutlore, 211 Blackhorse Avenue, Dublin 7, Ireland.**
Email: sproutlore@lostcarpark.com WWW: http://www.lostcarpark.com/sproutlore

Sproutlore exists thanks to the permission of Robert Rankin and his publishers.